DINNER WITH LISA

R. L. PRENDERGAST

Dekko Publishing

For information about special discounts for bulk purchases for sales promotions, fundraising, or educational use, please contact Dekko Publishing at sales@dekkopublishing.com.

Dekko Publishing can bring R. L. Prendergast to your live event. For more information or to book an event contact Dekko Publishing at authorevents@dekkopublishing.com.

Published in Canada by Dekko Publishing, Edmonton, Alberta, Canada.

Library and Archives Canada Cataloguing in Publication

Prendergast, R. L., 1970-
Dinner with Lisa / R. L. Prendergast.

ISBN 978-0-9784548-2-1

I. Title.
PS8631.R45D56 2011   C813'.6   C2011-903586-3

www.RLPrendergast.com

Art by Ausilia J. Corso
Edited by Marion Hoffmann

Also by R. L. Prendergast

The Impact of a Single Event

For Kathleen and Clark—
The best parents anyone could have asked for.

CHAPTER 1

MAY 1933

The engine chuffed and the wheels clacked as the train powered its way through Ontario. Over glacier-scraped bedrock it passed, through forests of dark green pine and budding oak trees toward the plains of Manitoba, Saskatchewan and Alberta, where years of unrelenting sun and suffocating dust had baked the once fertile earth dry and hard.

Inside the third carriage back from the engine, on seats set up like bus benches, men, women and children huddled together. Joseph Gaston, a widower, and his four children occupied two of those seats. They were travelling to—what? He didn't quite know. He stood with six-month-old Clare in his arms. As he gazed out the window into the darkness, his reflection stared back at him.

Joseph was nearly forty. His hair, a dull light brown with the odd wisp of grey above the ears, was combed back from a prominent forehead. His eyes were the blue-green of the ocean on a sunny day. Laughter lines curved around them when he smiled, but this was something he did almost never of late.

Joseph looked at his sons. Nolan, eleven, and Cole, seven, sat together on one bench. After the better part of a day on the train, they were bored. Now and then they gave each other a punch or a kick, usually because of some minor slight such as crossing the imaginary line that separated each half of the seat. Sarah, Joseph's four-year-old daughter, shared the bench behind the boys with the family's three suitcases. She'd been suffering from motion sickness since their departure and held a tin bowl on her lap. As he reached over to brush her long, blonde curls gently from her half-closed eyes, Joseph wished he could do something for her. Had Helen been alive, she would have known instinctively how to make Sarah feel better; Joseph had always relied on her in such matters.

The train shuddered as if a chill had run down its spine. The movement caused the little girl to drop the bowl just as she retched again; yellow-brown fluid ran down the front of her dress. Joseph, his nose filled with the acrid smell of vomit, wondered if he'd be able to find fresh clothing for Sarah. Handing the baby to Nolan with instructions to rock her, Joseph knelt down in the narrow aisle and opened the suitcase holding their clothes. Of the three bags, one contained the family's clothing. The other two held bedclothes, cutlery, a few basic household items and keepsakes: photos, locks of the children's hair, letters from Helen written while they'd been courting, Nolan's toddler handprints and other reminders of the past. It took him a while to sort through the contents, but eventually he found a pair of Coles' overalls—they would do for now.

He looked up when Nolan suddenly exclaimed, "Dad!"

"What?" Joseph felt drained as he pulled the overalls from the suitcase.

"The baby isn't moving!" Nolan sounded alarmed.

Clare had been crying all day; for the first time she was silent. "She's sleeping," Joseph said, his attention still on Sarah.

Nolan's brown eyes were wide with panic. "But, Dad, she's not breathing!"

The words brought Joseph instantly back to his feet. Bending over the baby, he studied her closely. Nolan was right. Clare showed no sign of life. Quickly Joseph put his face to Clare's nose and mouth, and waited—prayed—for her to exhale. Nothing. Were her lips blue or was he imagining it? He wasn't sure. "Christ!" he muttered, as he grabbed the limp infant from Nolan's arms and shook her gently.

"Did she swallow something?" he barked at his son, startling nearby passengers.

"No," Nolan said tensely, as he watched his father part the baby's lips and investigate her mouth with his fingers.

Joseph balled up Cole's overalls and placed them under Clare's shoulders, arching her head back and opening her windpipe. In an effort to force air into her lungs, he drew her arms up and over her head. When that didn't work he flipped her onto her belly, turned her head to the side, placed her hands beneath her chin, and lifted her elbows to expand her lungs. All this took less than a minute.

Joseph had never been so frightened. He had done everything he'd been taught in the army, but Clare still didn't respond. Oblivious to the silence in the car and the distress of those around him, he began to strike Clare's back. Again and again he struck, each time a little harder. By now the baby's small hands and feet were grey.

"Help! Someone please help!" he screamed, looking around pleadingly. "My baby's not breathing!"

The other passengers were frozen with shock. No one moved.

Guided by instinct, Joseph put his lips to Clare's mouth and sent his own breath into her. All at once, as if by some miracle, the little chest expanded then settled. He breathed into her mouth again. Suddenly Clare coughed. Her eyes opened and she let out a wail like a newborn's cry. In moments, her colour turned from sickly grey to pale pink.

"Thank God!" exclaimed a woman across the aisle, but Joseph barely heard her. With the crisis over, he could only think of the tragedy that might have been. He was trembling violently as he sat down, holding Clare close to him. A ball of emotion rose in his throat and tears formed in his eyes. Lowering his head, he swallowed hard in an effort to control his feelings. It took him a minute to realize that Cole and Sarah were crying. He reached out to them and they scrambled onto his lap, making space for themselves beside the baby. Only Nolan sat alone, his breathing jerky. Clare, recovered from her trauma, fell asleep in Joseph's arms. Momentarily he thought Clare had stopped breathing again, but before he had to take action her nostrils flared, and he gave a sigh of relief.

A few people now offered their help. Joseph declined politely. *Where were you a few minutes ago?* he wanted to ask them, but didn't. The combination of adrenaline and fatigue made him feel unsteady and nauseous. As he waited for his energy to return he looked at the passengers around him.

The car was crowded. The day was passing and it was growing dark. Before long, conversation ebbed as people began to settle themselves for the night. From their dress, their deportment and their general look of hunger, Joseph sensed the other passengers were also attempting to escape from destitution to something better. Like him, they were all victims of a system that had gone terribly wrong. The catastrophe was said to have started with the stock market crash in 1929. Opinions as to who was to blame were rampant. Unscrupulous moneylenders. Avaricious company presidents. Incompetent political leaders. Whatever the reason, the world's economy had disintegrated, resulting in global devastation. Trade between nations had dwindled. Heavy industry had come to a standstill. Construction had halted. Crop prices had fallen by half, and then half again. Soon, farms had been foreclosed and unemployed men evicted from their homes.

Now, nearly four years later, the situation had grown even worse. The strength that had enabled people to endure hardship in the early years, was wearing out. People could be badly housed, poorly clad and undernourished for only so long. At this point, the Depression was no longer confined to the economy; it affected the morale of all those who could no longer afford the basics of staying alive. The dollars in the pockets of working folk became tattered and greasy as their owners counted and recounted them, praying there would be enough for a family to survive another day. Those who worked were often at the mercy of mean-spirited men who exploited them for cheap labour. They earned only enough to buy a loaf of bread and cook a thin soup—not enough to keep a man on his feet, let alone feed other mouths.

Despite all these privations, the passengers in Joseph's car were the "lucky" ones; not everyone could afford a train ticket to a new life. Many rode on the roofs of the trains or in the empty boxcars, or even on the truss rods beneath the boxcars. Carrying their worldly possessions in bindles—bundles of clothes tied to the ends of sticks—some two million men and thousands of women illegally rode the trains that crisscrossed the North American continent.

It was dangerous as well as difficult to catch a free ride. For one thing, railroad companies did whatever they could to prevent people from riding without paying. Special police protected railroad property from the hoboes who were blamed for damaging freight inside the boxcars and for ripping up the wooden floorboards for firewood. These railway police—bulls, as they were often called—brutally beat anyone caught trying to ride a train without a ticket. The hoboes learned ways to dodge them. Hiding either behind nearby buildings or further down the tracks, hoboes waited for a train to move and then ran alongside it. Then came the most dangerous part: a person had to either jump into an open boxcar or grab hold of a ladder in order to climb to the roof. If a man missed his footing or failed to achieve a good grip, he could stumble and end up under the train. Each year, thousands lost body parts in unsuccessful attempts to get free rides. Many hundreds more lost their lives.

Yet although the practice was dangerous, some trains had more men riding above the carriages than inside them. For the first time, now that talk inside the carriage had ceased, Joseph became aware of sounds overhead. It was a few moments before he understood that people were riding the roof of the train.

It was time to get the children to bed. When he had changed Sarah into Cole's overalls, he put Sarah and Cole on the two benches and covered them with thin blankets. He used his ragged jacket to cover Nolan, who lay on the floor below Cole. There was no room for luggage beneath the seats, so he wedged the three suitcases into the space in front of Sarah. Standing in the aisle with Clare in his arms once more, he listened to the steady breathing of his children and wondered whether he would have to endure the rest of the journey on his feet.

Clare whimpered once and moved to make herself more comfortable. As Joseph looked down at her, a memory came to him: a cold December night just before Christmas, when the thermometer had dipped to 42 below. Clare had been born that night in a one-room rented farmhouse where layers of old newspapers glued to the walls formed the dwelling's only insulation. Although Joseph had spent most of the previous night chopping wood to keep the stove burning, the doctor he'd called to help with the birth had remarked on the frigidity of the room. But Joseph had had more to worry about that night than the doctor's possible chilblains: Clare's birth was premature. The doctor had warned she might not survive even a day. And Helen was bleeding badly. Fortunately, a sensible neighbour who had come to help had lined an old shoebox with cotton batting and she placed Clare inside it, near the open oven door, letting Joseph attend to his dying wife. Upon seeing his tiny baby sister the next morning, Cole had exclaimed, "What do you got there, Dad? A rat?"

All my children are so different, Joseph mused, as he watched them sleep. Nolan was healthy, sturdy and as fair as his father. Olive-skinned Cole, with his mother's dark brown hair, was not quite as robust as his older brother. Sarah was prone to illness. And then there was little Clare, who seemed to have no strength at all. It was as if Helen had given the best of herself to their first-born and less to each successive child, until she had nothing left for herself.

Clare had defied the odds twice: the first time at birth, when she had survived despite the doctor's predictions and the second time today, when she had stopped breathing and given her father such a horrible fright. What if Clare were to stop breathing again? What if it were to happen while Joseph slept? Though he had been a father for some years, without his wife Joseph felt like a boy playing at being a parent. The responsibility of caring for tiny, helpless Clare in addition to his other children, weighed on him. It was as if his skin had been peeled away, leaving his nerves and flesh raw and exposed. Joseph thought: *a week on this train—I'll never make it.*

Putting Clare down beside Sarah, Joseph opened the window above his sleeping family. A blast of wind gusted in, carrying icy air from nearby Georgian Bay. At the rear end of the carriage a man standing watch over his own family looked up and frowned disapprovingly at Joseph, but Joseph didn't notice him. In a frenzy of unreasoning despair, he seized one of their suitcases and hurled it out of the window. A second case followed. The watching passenger, troubled by Joseph's behavior and fearing what he might do next, hurried toward him. If Joseph intended to throw out the baby, he had to be stopped. But Joseph had no such intention. He closed the window as quickly as he'd opened it. The other man paused in mid-step. When Joseph showed no further signs of madness the man returned to his seat, from where he could keep an eye on his fellow passenger.

After making certain that Clare was secure in her place beside Sarah, Joseph settled himself on the floor and rested his back against the remaining suitcase. Lost in weariness, hunger and loneliness, he allowed himself to close his eyes at last. As the train chugged westward on its way toward a new home and an uncertain future, he was filled with a terrible need for hope.

CHAPTER 2

Addison Philibuster was impressed by the Canadian government's offer to deed 160 acres of the newly opened western lands to any adventurous settler. There were terms, of course; anyone who applied for the land had to pay an administration fee of ten dollars and had to cultivate a minimum of forty acres and build a permanent residence within three years. These terms did not deter the young man. The west was one of the last unpopulated places in North America, and Addison Philibuster considered the proposition the greatest deal on earth.

The idea of providing cheap land in western Canada was a defensive measure implemented by the leadership of a young and growing country. The Canadian government's aims were to protect its sovereignty over the large and sparsely populated territory purchased from the Hudson's Bay Company in 1869 and to prevent American settlers from moving into the prairies and potentially annexing the land to the United States.

When 25-year-old Addison arrived at his spread in the late summer of 1872 he was pleasantly surprised at first. The land that was soon to be his comprised a generous portion of prairie grassland interspersed with clusters of spruce and poplar. No need to slash and burn endless undergrowth or pull out stumps in order to cultivate the minimum 40 acres. Furthermore, the swift Elk River—called the Waskasoo Seepee by the local aboriginal population—ran right beside his parcel of land.

Addison Philibuster eventually satisfied the minimum requirements for his 160 acres, but the project had been more difficult than he'd initially anticipated. His first home had been a soddy, a house built from pieces of the thickly rooted prairie sod, cut into rectangles and laid one above another like bricks. Until such time as he could build a wood house, the temporary structure had provided some protection from the scorching heat of summer and the brutal cold of winter. In the meantime, as Addison colourfully put it, the soddy was "wet as an otter's pocket and dirty as your backside."

Addison had almost starved, that first winter on his land. Instead of asking the other settlers for help—which would have been freely given, for everyone understood the need to work together—he managed by turning to underhanded ways. One stormy winter night he stole his neighbours' only milking cow, correctly guessing that the blowing snow and howling winds would cover his tracks. Knowing the owners would go looking for the valuable animal, and to hide the evidence of his skullduggery, he brought the cow into his small soddy. He combined the cow's turds with stinkweed and burned the mixture for heat while he lived off the animal's milk.

When winter broke and the weather was mild enough to travel, Addison stole four horses, rode them two days to Fort Edmonton, the nearest Hudson's Bay fur-trading post, and sold three of them. He spent much of his profits on a week of debauchery with any woman he could buy and used the rest to purchase necessities such as sugar and flour, as well as a few non-essentials such as alcohol, molasses, red ink and tobacco. On his return, he concocted a brew that he passed off as whisky and sold illegally to the unsuspecting people of the Cree, Blackfoot and Stoney tribes.

Although Addison was able to conceal much of his dishonesty, it became known that he had a wild temper. A neighbour claimed to have witnessed an incident between Addison and a cow. Addison had been trying to brand a newly born calf when its mother had butted him and knocked him to the ground. According to the witness, Addison had picked himself up, walked into the bush, emerged with a branch the size of a train axel, and beat the offending cow to death. The man didn't know that an enraged Addison had then ridden to Fort Edmonton and spent a day with a whore. When he returned to find the calf still mewling over its fallen mother he used the same branch to kill it, then rode back to the whore.

While Addison Philibuster prospered by stealing and selling his vile liquor, most of the early settlers struggled to survive. Land that had at first produced good gardens and crops, as well as being fertile grasslands for grazing cattle, dried up after drought plagued the area for several summers in a row. Although the pioneering families had earned their 160 acres through hard work and strength of character, it was as if the natural elements had conspired to defeat them. Farmers wanting to return east to the familiar homes they'd left a decade earlier, made heartbreaking decisions to pull up stakes and abandon their hard-earned homesteads. Travelling back across the thousand miles of arid prairies was so expensive that desperate farmers resorted to selling their land, livestock and farm implements at a fraction of their value.

At the same time, in an effort to open up the west even further, the Canadian government sponsored construction of a railway that would connect the country from the Atlantic Ocean to the Pacific. The proposed railroad was to run just north of, and parallel to, the border between Canada and the United States, through the newly constructed Fort Calgary. Built to house a detachment of the North West Mounted Police that would safeguard the area and protect it from American whisky traders, the fort was located only 90 miles south of Addison's property.

Addison calculated that the land half way between the two major settlements in the area—Fort Edmonton to the north and now Fort Calgary to the south—would become a strategic location. In addition, the Elk River, which had allowed easy transportation of the aboriginal hunters' fur pelts to the Hudson's Bay Company trading stations, and from there to markets in Europe, had few viable crossing points. By good fortune, Addison had discovered a rare shallow point near his land that would make a convenient crossing place for both people and animals: a settlement might even develop at that spot. He was shrewd enough to understand that if he owned the surrounding land he could sell it to the merchants and farmers who would congregate there. It was even possible the settlement might be named in honour of its founder. With all this in mind, Addison began to exploit desperate farmers and buy up their land with his ill-gotten liquor money.

Addison's dreaming and scheming came to fruition when the railroad finally reached Fort Calgary in 1883. Indeed, the land he had purchased from desperate families wanting to leave the Canadian west had become a valuable asset due to its situation between the two major outposts. Now Addison was able to stake out lots and sell them for between $75 and $200 each. He used the proceeds of the sales to build himself a mansion on the best piece of land in the newly christened hamlet of Philibuster.

Addison Philibuster did not let making money and creating a village in his name change him. For years he continued to cheat and swindle anyone who could not or would not defend himself. In June of 1897 he sold some riverside property to a man who wanted to start a ferry operation. The buyer had been led to believe that his purchase included the land on both sides of the river. Only when he tried to register his claim with the village office did he learn that Addison had sold him just the property on the south bank of the proposed ferry crossing, and that someone else already owned the land on the north side.

Seeking satisfaction, the furious man tried to confront Addison outside his mansion, but Addison beat him soundly. Then, as was his custom after an altercation, Addison Philibuster headed directly to the local bordello, unaware that the cheated buyer was following him. When Addison, now in fairer mood, exited the premises, the man he had swindled shot and killed him. The man's triumph was short-lived, however; he was convicted of murder and executed.

More than 35 years after Addison Philibuster's death, people in the area still remembered him. Had he been alive they would have crossed the street to avoid him, but the years had blurred their memories. Now they spoke of his gumption for taking the risk of tackling the wilderness of the west, and of his foresight at recognizing how the Canadian Pacific Railroad and the Canadian government's migration policies would open up this part of the country to Europeans.

In time, Philibuster fulfilled its early promise. It became an area that produced excellent wheat crops, with good grazing for vast cattle ranches. By that point, memories of Addison, the dishonest exploiter, had evolved into a legend about a man of remarkable courage and prescience. In 1901 the town's official population had been 598; by the end of 1928 it was over 15,000. But by 1930 things had come full circle again, with the return of drought on the heels of more general economic chaos.

When Joseph and his children arrived in Philibuster in May of 1933, the town's rapidly deteriorating economy had already decreased its population to less than 10,000. And the situation was growing steadily worse.

"Next stop—Philibuster!" hollered the conductor on entering Joseph's carriage. Joseph touched the letter in his pocket for the umpteenth time. It was still there. Why wouldn't it be? He changed Clare's diaper, combed Sarah's hair and told the boys to tuck in their shirts. It was important that his brother and sister-in-law gain a favourable first impression of his children.

The train began to slow down as it approached the station. It was still moving when Joseph spotted shabby-looking men flinging themselves off the carriage roof and darting away like frightened rabbits. These, he knew, were the fugitives and hoboes who needed to disembark before they got into trouble.

With a shriek of brakes, the train came to a stop. At the same moment, a dozen policemen materialized—apparently out of nowhere—and began to dart between the carriages in chase of the hoboes. Seconds later, twenty railway bulls emerged from behind nearby grain elevators and buildings to block and corral the men trying to escape. The hoboes were terrified. Some managed to elude the net closing in on them. Others ran directly into the bulls and their billy clubs.

A woman sitting behind Joseph gasped with horror. Another shrieked. Alerted to the skirmish, passengers leaned over in their seats and craned their necks to see the mêlée. Frightened by the violence and determined to avoid the fray, parents grabbed children and belongings and scrambled off the other side of the train. After all, this was not their fight. A middle-aged man bent over Nolan and Cole to get a better look. "*Gott im Himmel!*" he exclaimed. Joseph turned and saw the question in his eyes: *I am disgusted—but what are we to do?*

Trapped by the net of cops, and with no means of escape, several hoboes ran back to the train—and more waiting police. Below Joseph's window a young officer swung his truncheon at a hobo's head. The helpless man tried to fend off the blow with his bindle. The cop swung again, knocking the bindle from the hobo's hands. The man cowered in terror, but the swinging truncheon caught and broke the arm that shielded his head. As he writhed on the ground in visible agony, the cop readied his weapon for another blow.

Seeing the wildness in the cop's face, Joseph understood that the viciousness would end only with the man's death. Thrusting the baby into Nolan's arms with a quick "Hold her!" he ran to the nearest exit and leaped to the ground. Managing to deflect the cop's arm as he was about to strike the hobo's head again, Joseph yelled, "Enough! Enough!"

The cop gave a harsh exclamation. Wrenching free of Joseph's grip, he swung around to make certain there was only one attacker. Then he turned on Joseph. Joseph sidestepped and was about to tackle him. At that moment his head was jerked violently backwards and a club was clamped beneath his chin, as if to stop his breath. Instinctively, Joseph grabbed at the club with both hands and struggled to pull free from it, but the person holding it was too strong for him. As the club tightened against Joseph's throat, the young cop punched him in the stomach, knocking the wind out of him. His legs buckled. Had the cop not held him up by the throat, he would have fallen.

"What the hell are you doing?" a menacing voice growled.

Then came a second punch in the stomach. Unable to breathe with the club still at his throat, Joseph's vision blurred and he felt consciousness slip away from him.

"Daddy!" screamed Cole, appearing suddenly in front of him.

The chokehold eased slightly. Joseph took a few heaving breaths and tried to hold on to a returning awareness.

"Name!" snarled a strident voice.

"Joseph ... Joseph Gaston," he managed to whisper.

"What the hell were you doing?"

"He was ... going ... to kill him," Joseph gasped, nodding in the direction of the young cop and the injured hobo. He tried to move, but the truncheon tightened on his throat again.

"Address?"

With the club restricting his airway, Joseph could only grunt.

"Let my dad go!" Cole screamed, frightened for his father.

The club eased slightly. "Where do you live?"

"Here. We're ... moving here."

Joseph was forced to his knees. Lifting his head, he found himself looking into a pair of icy blue eyes. The insignia on the man's uniform indicated his rank: Chief of Police. Thick black eyebrows, an overly large nose, ramrod bearing and the sinews standing out on his neck reminded Joseph of a throwback to an earlier age. The Chief of Police was clearly a dangerous man.

"You're moving to Philibuster?" The question was directed at Cole.

"Yes, sir."

"And the address?"

Cole's mouth turned down and his chin quivered.

"I asked you your address, boy!"

"We're going to live with my Uncle Henri and Aunt Tilda," Cole whispered. Then he ran to his father and buried his head against Joseph's chest.

The police chief's expression changed from fury to annoyance. He took a long look at Joseph, as if committing his face to memory. "Interfere again and I'll throw you in jail!" he threatened, poking Joseph in the chest with the end of his club. "I'll be watching you. Now beat it!"

By the time Joseph got to his feet, the Chief of Police had already turned his attention to the scuffles all around them. Joseph wondered what would happen to the poor man on the ground. He had stopped the young cop from beating the hobo to death, but now there was nothing more he could do for him.

He picked up his son and carried him into the train. Sitting down beside Sarah and holding a shaken Cole on his lap, Joseph rubbed his bruised throat. From where he sat, he saw the Chief of Police order his men to take the hoboes to jail. The cop who had attacked the hobo forced his victim to his feet and hustled him away.

Joseph waited until the police were gone before he moved. After checking that he still had his precious letter of employment on him, he picked up the baby and the remaining suitcase, told Nolan to hold Sarah's hand, and led his children off the train.

Joseph made certain they all kept together as they joined the crowd escaping the unseasonably hot sun for the cover of the train station. The hum of voices in the building was unnaturally subdued as husbands greeted wives, parents hugged children, and friends and acquaintances shook hands. The violence had unsettled the arriving passengers as well as those who had come to welcome them.

Clutching his family to him, Joseph spent a minute or two looking around him, nose wrinkled in distaste at the acrid odor of sweat in the crush of overheated bodies. The place was packed with unfamiliar faces; nowhere did he see his brother and sister-in-law. Realizing it would be impossible to spot them in the crowd, he guided his children toward the exit, past posters exhorting people to "Do Your Duty! Grab the Gopher!"

A mixture of conveyances thronged the parking lot—horse-drawn wagons, taxis and trucks. There were also the ubiquitous Bennett Buggies, vehicles pulled by two-horse teams because their owners could no longer afford gasoline, and named after Richard Bennett, prime minister of Canada since the beginning of the economic malaise. Here, too, were policemen, escorting their ragged, handcuffed victims toward the courthouse and its basement jail. The sight reminded Joseph of the menacing Chief of Police. He had to force his thoughts elsewhere and concentrate on finding his brother.

Where was Henri? In his last letter to his brother, Joseph had mentioned his expected day of arrival in Philibuster: the 17th of May—today. Had Henri received the letter? If not, the family was in for a long wait at the station, because Joseph had lost the note with his brother's address on it when he'd hurled their cases out of the train. Now, when it was too late to do anything about it, he wondered why he had yielded to that frantic moment of despair.

Joseph and Henri did not know each other well. Joseph had been eight when his mother had died and his father had abandoned him and his two younger sisters. After deserting them, his father had moved back to his hometown of La Tuque, Quebec, and started a second family. The first of those children was a boy named Henri Philippe. When their father died, Henri, now in his teens, had decided to leave home and explore the country. In the course of his travels he had sought out his much older half-brother. By that time Joseph was married to Helen, and working for a steel company in Hamilton, Ontario. Henri lived with Joseph and Helen for six months, learning English and working as a labourer at the same steel mill where Joseph worked. A year before Nolan's birth, Henri's wanderlust and his growing confidence in his English skills had lured him back onto the road. The brothers had stayed in touch rather sporadically, by way of letters, but Henri had never returned to Hamilton to visit his family. Indeed, they might not have met again had Henri not sent Joseph the advertisement of a job with the Philibuster Dairy.

Joseph sighed with relief when he suddenly spotted a large man at the edge of the crowd. "I think I see your uncle," he said. He began to make his way through the throng of people and conveyances with Clare in his arms, the other children following him like baby ducks.

Henri, deep in what looked like a whispered conspiratorial conversation, did not see his brother approach. It was the other man who spotted Joseph and pointed him out to Henri.

Henri spun around. "Joseph!" he exclaimed, throwing his arms around his brother and nearly suffocating Clare. "And 'deese must be duh little ones." Henri had never lost the strong accent of his mother tongue.

The children looked up in awe at their uncle, who was half a head taller than their father. Brown eyes looked back at them from beneath slicked-back dark hair, receding at the sides. His tiny moustache, as thin as if it had been pencilled in above his lips, was almost inappropriately delicate on a person of such immense stature.

"Please' to meet you," Henri said, treating the children to a curtsy.

Sarah giggled. "Daddy, he curtsied. Girls curtsy."

"You're right," said their uncle's friend, with a chuckle. "Girls curtsy, and boys bow. Unless, of course, the curtsier is The Great Henri, and then the rules don't apply."

So Henri's nickname had followed him to Philibuster. Joseph smiled for the first time since leaving Ontario.

"Dis cad who calls 'imself my buddy is Raven Mullens," Henri said, introducing his friend.

Raven was of average height, with wavy grey hair, crooked teeth, wide-spaced eyes and white eyebrows. His smile was so sincere that Joseph felt the man was truly happy to see him. Raven endeared himself to Joseph immediately.

"Pleasure to meet you. I won't hold it against you that your brother is The Great Henri. Everyone has a cross to bear," he said, grasping Joseph's hand.

"Pleasure's mine," Joseph said.

"Why are you called The Great Henri?" Cole asked.

Raven laughed. "A joke, son. It's like calling a tall man 'shorty' or a fat man 'skinny.'"

"Pay no attention to dis jealous guy. I am named Duh Great Henri because I can do duh work of ten men," said their uncle, as he hoisted Cole effortlessly onto his broad shoulders.

In spite of Henri's marked accent, Joseph noticed that his brother's English had improved a lot since the time they had spent together a dozen years ago.

"How was your journey?" Raven enquired.

"Dad got into a fight," Nolan said, excitedly.

"Joseph?" Henri looked at his brother alertly.

"With a policeman!" Cole added.

As briefly as he could, Joseph explained what happened, whereupon Raven looked gravely toward the hoboes who were being led away in handcuffs. "I'm sorry you had to see the ugly side of Philibuster so soon. Our exalted mayor ordered the round-up. Claims the communists are trying to stir up something in town and will do their best to incite the vagrants. There've been a few demonstrations lately and he's worried things will get worse."

It was the same everywhere, thought Joseph. Some considered the demonstrators unruly troublemakers; others spoke of them as "the forgotten." These unemployed men, many of them single, wanted only to work for a living wage, so they gathered and protested, but to no avail.

Raven shook his head in disgust. "Westmoreland's a fool."

Westmoreland? It was a man by that name who'd offered Joseph the job at the Philibuster Dairy. His signature was on the letter in Joseph's pocket. Joseph asked Raven if it was the same man.

Raven nodded. "Yes, one and the same. Mayor and majority

owner of the Philibuster Dairy. The Great Henri told me you were going to be working for him. I don't like to put you off, but I think I should warn you—Westmoreland is a mean devil. Deep down mean. Watch out for him."

"There's the man who hurt Daddy." Cole pointed to the Chief of Police.

"Chief Grumpy," Henri said.

"Chief Grumpy?" echoed Joseph.

"Montgomery Quentin," Raven told him. "Another not-very-nice man."

In some dismay, Joseph wondered what kind of place he'd moved to. His future boss was apparently a man to be avoided, and he'd just had a run-in with the head of the police department, sarcastically nicknamed Chief Grumpy.

Raven extended a hand and made to leave. "Sorry if we've alarmed you, Joseph. We didn't mean to. Welcome to Philibuster. And good day to you all." With a quick parting glance at Henri, he said briefly, "We'll talk again."

Joseph was about to ask his brother about Westmoreland when they were joined by a pretty woman with a petite figure, fine features and pale skin. Her attire—immaculate lilac dress, white gloves and a white purse—suggested a person who valued propriety. Henri's wife, he guessed.

"Aha, my Tilly! Meet my bro'der, Joseph Gaston." Henri made the introduction as formally as if Joseph had been a royal personage.

Joseph took Tilda's small hands in his. "It's a great pleasure to meet you at last. Thank you for all you've done." He knew Tilda had been the one who had found a place for him and the kids to live. She had purchased some furniture with the money he had sent and had offered to look after the children when he was working.

"Thanks are not necessary. After all, we're family." Tilda's slight drawl was warm and pleasant. She hugged the children, inquired about their journey and asked if she could hold Clare.

She was visibly shocked when Nolan mentioned the altercation between his father and the Chief of Police, whom Cole already spoke of as Chief Grumpy. An awkward silence followed.

"Well, that's unfortunate," Tilda said then, as she cradled Clare protectively in her arms. "Now, let's get the baby out of the heat."

Henri said, expansively, "If the sun, she is too bright—I shall push 'er away!" Then, with Cole still on his shoulders, he scooped up Sarah with one hand and seized the suitcase with the other.

"Where is duh rest of your luggage, Joseph?" he asked.

"Coming later," Joseph lied, and wondered whether moving to Philibuster had been a mistake.

CHAPTER 3

The Great Henri bounced along merrily, carrying Sarah in his arms and Cole on his shoulders. He was like a playful child, Joseph thought in amazement, talking and laughing happily as he pointed out landmarks he thought important. The most trustworthy mechanics—as if Joseph could afford a car!—"Duh Samson Bro'ders Garage." The best places for "duh pie and duh ice cream." "Duh Farmers Bank." "Duh drug store." "Duh newspaper office."

As they walked through the streets, Joseph noticed pasted to the exterior walls of various businesses more of the gopher posters he had seen at the station. His brother explained that gophers were a threat to the farmers of the western wheat-growing provinces. Ground squirrels, as they were properly called, ate newly planted seeds, chewed on young green stems and devoured mature heads of grain. Along with drought and grasshoppers, gophers were a farmer's nightmare.

Local and provincial governments had created a program to eliminate the gopher population. A gopher tail turned in to an approved government agent was worth a reward of five cents—more, in badly infested areas. At a time when a single dollar was a lot of money, it was hoped the offer would be incentive enough to cull the gophers and to curtail the damage they inflicted. The previous year, more than 600,000 gopher tails had been turned in by school children and adults, close to one gopher for every person in the province. On hearing this, Nolan declared he'd catch 20 gophers every morning and spend his profits at the cinema every afternoon.

Henri was uncharacteristically silent as they reached the Buffalo Hotel, with its beer parlour that took up half the ground floor. Like similar establishments in Alberta, and indeed in most of Canada, the windows were covered so that the sight of liquor consumption would not offend passersby. The temperance movement had not succeeded in preventing all public drinking, but those who preached abstinence had managed to spread the idea that drinking was immoral. Joseph doubted that his brother had given up drinking—although it was true a woman could make her husband give up just about anything but breathing. It was more likely that Henri had refrained from pointing out the place in deference to Tilda and the children.

"And dis is 'oogaboom's," he said, as they walked by a corner grocery store. The words elicited a disapproving glance from Tilda, as if the very mention of the store were offensive. Joseph wondered what his sister-in-law had against the place, but thought it better not to ask.

It seemed to him, as they walked further, that apart from a newly built theatre and an Eaton's department store, Philibuster looked no better than the dilapidated towns and cities in Ontario. Here and there, seeing the debris of wooden buildings devastated by fire, he could guess what had occurred. Some poor devil, just trying to earn a living with a café or clothing store, had found business increasingly sluggish. Before long, the man was months behind on his bank loan and unable to feed his family. Who could blame him, then, for torching a business no longer worth a hoot in hell? The insurance money would pay off his loan and enable him to start again.

21

Henri's letters had given the impression that Philibuster's streets were paved with the proverbial gold. No wonder Joseph had expected concrete sidewalks, colourful awnings, bright neon signs, and men and women dressed as gaily as in the twenties, before the onset of the bad years. The reality was depressing: peeling signs, empty buildings and skinny, unkempt, hollow-eyed vagrants walking the streets in search of a meal. Everywhere Joseph looked he saw a film of dirt covering sidewalks, awnings and lampposts, as if some giant caretaker had neglected to take a feather duster to the town. The air was dry and smelled of dirt. Joseph could feel the grit in his mouth.

Leaving the downtown area, they came to a well-treed residential neighbourhood. The people who lived there didn't have much, but they took care of what little they did have. Paint was peeling off some of the houses and some of the sidings had been replaced with odd-shaped boards, but the lawns were trimmed, the trees pruned and the odd flower was blooming.

"Our castle," Henri said, as they reached a small, single-storey white house surrounded by a high fence from which the paint was also peeling.

Joseph was just opening the gate for Tilda, when what looked like a giant wolf came running around the corner of the house. "Christ!" he exclaimed and shut the gate quickly.

The wolf barked as it thrust its front paws onto the gate. Sarah screamed in fright. The baby awoke and began to cry. Nolan and Cole stepped behind Joseph, as if for protection.

"For heaven's sake, Henri, control the dog!" Tilda said crossly.

"Jasper. *Couche!*" Henri ordered, whereupon the wolf lay down instantly.

"Look what that monster has done. I thought you'd tied it up," Tilda scolded, as she rocked the baby and tried to comfort her.

"Jasper. *Attends,*" Henri said and opened the gate. The huge dog remained obediently prone. A rope led from its collar to a wooden stake that must have been yanked from the ground.

Squatting beside the dog and petting him, Henri looked at the children. "It is okay, my lovelies. Jasper will not 'arm one 'air of your 'ead."

Although at first glance the animal indeed resembled a wolf, it was a Siberian husky—crossed with a horse, Henri joked. Jasper was the biggest dog Joseph and his children had ever seen. The boys, fascinated by the dog's unusual eyes—one azure, the other light brown—laughed when the sickle-shaped tail thumped the ground with happiness. No longer frightened, they began to stroke Jasper. After a few minutes Sarah stroked him too, giggling as she buried her face in the dog's deep fur.

While Henri and the children played with Jasper, Tilda, who was still carrying Clare, led Joseph into the house. Joseph felt a pang of envy as he looked around the clean, bright home, much of it painted in a cheerful yellow. If only he could provide such a home for his family. At least, he thought, it would be pleasant for the children here, cared for by Tilda when he was away working.

Sitting down with his sister-in-law in a pretty nook next to the kitchen, Joseph was conscious of an uncomfortable silence. For some reason, he felt out of place as he waited for her to say something. He was sure Tilda would offer her condolences. "I'm so sorry about Helen," she would say, as so many others had done back home. He dreaded the words and the memories they evoked.

Invariably, certain questions would follow. "How are you doing?" And then, "How are the children?" Joseph always said he was fine, even though he was not. He was terribly lonely, and he found raising the children on his own to be overwhelming.

He also understood that people expected him to give up the kids—the girls, at least—to one of his sisters or some other female relative. They felt he was not doing right by the children in keeping them all with him. But despite the disapproval, Joseph was adamant that his family would not be separated. Helen would not have wanted it.

He knew his children better than anyone else did, and he'd seen how losing their mother had changed them. Nolan had become more daring than ever, climbing the highest trees and jumping off roofs. Until Helen's death, Cole had seemed perfectly content playing on his own: now he would not be parted from his brother. Sarah, his darling little girl, had become sad and clingy. Only Clare, who had never known her mother's love, was unchanged.

Tilda broke the silence with an unusual question. "What are you feeding Clare?"

Joseph hid his surprise. "Condensed milk."

Tilda nodded, her eyes never leaving the baby in her arms.

"Would you like me to take her?" Joseph asked.

Tilda smiled and held the baby closer. "No, thanks. I can manage."

Joseph was marvelling at how comfortable Clare seemed in Tilda's arms when his brother bounded into the house. "So, Joseph, when do you start work?"

Joseph pulled Westmoreland's letter from his pocket. "I'm to report tomorrow." He turned to Tilda: "If that's okay with you, of course?"

"Oh, yes, I'm all ready for the darlings," she answered sweetly.

"In that case, I should make you look presentable," said Henri.

As Tilda began to prepare dinner, Henri took Joseph to the back yard and set him up on a kitchen stool. The children played with Jasper as their uncle cut their father's hair.

"I do dis on duh side for extra money," Henri explained, as he started to trim Joseph's sideburns. "But I won't do shaves. People complain I don't do a good job. Dey t'ink I don't sharpen my razor enough. *Me*!" He gave an incredulous laugh. Then he told Joseph that he took pride in knowing his way around metal. He worked primarily as a saw filer; a man highly skilled in metal work, whose main job it was to set and sharpen teeth at the lumber mill. "It's duh grit in de air dat makes trouble for duh razor," he explained. "It gets into duh skin and dulls my blade before I finish duh first stroke. Even when I sharpen after every customer, it is no good. So I geeve it up."

As he shaped Joseph's hair, Henri spoke enthusiastically of all they would do together now that Joseph was in Philibuster: Sunday picnics and trips to the lake in the summer, tobogganing and skating in the winter. Joseph was glad his brother was so thrilled with the family's arrival, but he could not share his enthusiasm. Since Helen's death, he had been unable to rid himself of the belief—irrational though it was—that an ominous force meant him harm and wanted to see him broken and destroyed. Joseph had never considered himself superstitious, but recently, almost as a way of averting evil, he had decided to ignore the pleasant things in life. He would keep his head down and focus on what mattered: work and feeding his children.

When he could get in a few words of his own, Joseph asked his brother about Winfield Westmoreland. After what Raven had said at the train station, he was a bit nervous about his new employer. Henri told Joseph as much as he knew, most of which he'd gathered from newspapers.

Westmoreland had spent part of his childhood in Philibuster, leaving the town as a teenager to seek his fortune in Toronto. There he had worked as a labourer for a construction company, learning all he could about erecting buildings before starting his own company. When the Great War had started five years later, Westmoreland had already created a name for himself. After spending the war as an ambulance driver in France, he'd returned to Toronto where his construction firm continued to flourish. In 1926 he moved back to Philibuster to look after his ailing mother. Once there, he had become involved with the business elite and was elected to the city council on his first attempt. In the next election he had run for mayor and won.

Henri had never met Westmoreland, but had heard he was a little aloof and sometimes unfriendly. Yet who could blame him? Westmoreland had his businesses to manage and the city to run, not to mention the sacrifices he made for his mother. Instead of cavorting with the princes of industry in Toronto, Montreal or even New York, he continued to live in Philibuster.

Philibuster's residents did not seem to mind Westmoreland's standoffishness; they were grateful to have such a successful man running their town. He performed his mayoral duties efficiently, if not always with geniality. He had, in fact, recently been re-elected to a second mayoral term, handily beating the other candidate, William "Raven" Mullens. Hearing this, Joseph figured that Raven was probably sore at losing to his rival. Moreover, Raven had been fired from his job as the city's chief engineer when Westmoreland was a councilman. Since Raven had personal reasons for disliking Westmoreland, Henri advised Joseph to keep an open mind about his new employer. And indeed, having heard the facts, Joseph was already feeling more confident.

Before long Tilda called everyone to dinner. The meal was the best Joseph and the children had eaten in many months: cold chicken, potato salad, coleslaw, pickles and preserved blueberries for dessert. Only little Clare declined to take anything, pushing away her bottle of milk, though both Joseph and Tilda tried to feed her.

The hot afternoon had merged into a warm evening by the time Joseph stood up to go. Tilda gave him a few provisions: a jar of sugar-and-milk for Clare, and some of the meal's leftovers for the rest of the family. "There's no ice in your cold closet, but the milk will keep until you have a chance to buy some," she told Joseph. "Henri will show you the way. We'll see you all tomorrow."

Joseph tried to conceal his anxiety as they walked a block and a half to a three-storey rooming house. They had stayed in places like this before. Rooming houses were often owned by out-of-work people trying desperately not to lose their homes. In order to make the mortgage payments, an owner would move his family into the biggest room of a house and rent out the rest. Some people turned their homes into boarding houses, where a renter could get a meal or two. Others did not want to bother with providing meals and simply rented out rooms. But what seemed like a good idea to homeowners needing extra money sometimes led to their undoing. An inexperienced landlord might not realize that the increased cost of heat and light for a house full of people could exceed the rent collected. Transients often caused damage. And getting rent money out of people who were unable to pay even for food could prove extremely difficult.

As Joseph followed his brother up the grimy stairs to the second floor of the building he wrinkled his nose at the familiar smell of cooked cabbage. In rooming houses across North America, families ate what was cheapest. If the man of the house had a job, his wife could feed her family stew or macaroni and cheese. If money was exceptionally tight, a family might have to survive on mashed potatoes or boiled cabbage.

Even in good situations, boarding house accommodation entailed risk. Rooms were poorly lit, paint peeled off walls, mould grew in corners and dead mice rotted in poorly covered water barrels. Sometimes there was no privacy: a curtain on a wire might be all that separated neighbours from one another. Moreover, in a house full of strangers, a prospective renter knew nothing about the other occupants; they could be deranged women or sinister men who were overly fond of children. All these thoughts passed through Joseph's mind as he reluctantly put the key in the lock and opened the door.

To his astonishment, the room was quite decent. Tilda, it seemed, had made something of a silk purse out of what had been, essentially, a sow's ear. On one side of the room stood a pram for the baby and a double bed, already made up with clean bed linens, for the three older kids. Joseph would sleep on the floor. On the other side was a converted kitchen with a table and four mismatched chairs, a hotplate for cooking and a sink with a hand pump. There was also a cold closet—an icebox incorporated into the kitchen shelving. A Quebec Heater to keep the room warm stood by the window. The old stove was missing both the foot-rail and the finial top—removed, no doubt, for their nickel plating, which had probably fetched a few dollars for some starving family.

Joseph wondered what all these furnishings had cost. After selling everything he owned back home, he had wired the proceeds to Tilda with a request to do the best she could. Either Tilda was a world-class haggler—Joseph's money could not have bought all he saw in the room—or she had spent some of her own funds. Hell, she'd even made a curtain for the window. He would have to talk to her about it. For now, he was simply relieved that the place was livable.

The children were excited. "Daddy," Cole shouted, "are we going to live here?"

"Yes," answered his father, wishing he could match his children's enthusiasm for new things.

"Dare is a shared privy at duh end of duh 'all," Henri told them, whereupon Nolan and Cole ran down the hall to inspect it, their feet banging loudly on the bare floor.

The door next to theirs opened and two children with almond-shaped eyes and coal-black hair peeked out into the hallway. From behind the door, someone said a few words in an unfamiliar language. Immediately, the children drew back and the door closed.

Before leaving them, Henri gave Joseph directions to the Philibuster Dairy. Then he enfolded his brother in a great hug and said, "I'm so glad you and duh children 'ave arrived!" Joseph gratefully reciprocated the gesture.

As the kids exuberantly investigated their new home, Joseph unpacked their only suitcase. He was happy to find, tucked in amongst the clothes, an old dictionary, its brown leather cover deeply scarred and slightly water damaged.

Having been forced to leave school in grade six, Joseph had often dreamed of completing his schooling and even attending university. Unfortunately, circumstances had made this impossible. Certain he would be laughed at by people who would not consider him smart enough for such lofty ambitions, he had never told anyone of his aspirations. He had even kept his dreams hidden from Helen. But his wife, who had known him better than he'd realized, had surprised him soon after their marriage by giving him a dictionary for his birthday. "Because I know you want to better yourself," she'd said. When he understood that she believed in him, he had come close to tears.

Joseph had made a habit of studying his dictionary for a while every night. No matter how tired he was after working twelve-hour—or longer—shifts in the stifling heat of the steel mill's blast furnaces, he would learn a new word. Sometimes he spent hours researching the definition of a particular word, while Helen sat beside him reading or knitting, always silent and supportive. Even after the children were born, Joseph and Helen had tried their best to continue their nightly ritual. For Joseph, the ritual meant much more than a way of staying connected with the woman he loved; he kept hoping that his constant efforts to improve himself would eventually lead to a better life for his family. But he had not opened the dictionary since Helen's death.

Sighing as he put down the book, Joseph told the children it was "time to hit the kip." Sarah fell asleep immediately. The two boys were still too excited to sleep. They had to be reminded to keep it down and stop talking a number of times before they finally closed their eyes.

Tired though Joseph was, he could not yet relax. It was time to feed Clare the mixture of sugar-and-milk Tilda had prepared. Certain the baby would be hungry, he was concerned when she refused to open her mouth. Clare had taken in so little during the journey, and Joseph had hoped the return to stable surroundings would bring back her appetite.

"Do you want to sleep?" he whispered, and put her down in the pram. But far from sleeping, the baby grew restless and began to cry. Within minutes she was sobbing so urgently that Joseph picked her up, put her over his shoulder and patted her back gently. Every twenty minutes or so he tried to feed her, but she rejected him every time. Back in her pram, she cried until Joseph picked her up again and paced the room; four strides one way, four the other, until well after midnight.

Eventually, the cause of Clare's distress became apparent: painful gas filled her little belly, making it hard as a rock. Now, at least, Joseph knew what to do. Putting Clare on his lap facing away from him, he worked her little legs in a cycling movement. A series of loud burps finally gave both baby and father relief.

It was after two in the morning before Joseph was finally able to put a sleeping Clare in her pram. He was exhausted by the time he turned off the light and stretched out on the hard wood floor with his coat pillowed beneath his head. He wondered whether he would get any sleep at all before it was time for him to start his first day at work.

CHAPTER 4

Fearing he would sleep through the alarm, Joseph placed the clock in a tin pie plate where its ring would be extra loud. When it went off at 5:00 AM, he jumped up and slapped his hand over the bell, as startled as if he'd been stabbed with a hot fork. Before doing anything else, he checked his pocket for his letter of employment. Reassured to find it, he got the children up and dressed, and fed them Tilda's leftovers.

Henri had already left for work by the time a bleary-eyed Joseph reached the house. Joseph left instructions with Tilda: he would arrange for the boys to start school as soon as possible, but until then they were free to explore the neighbourhood as long as they stayed together; Sarah would not eat porridge, but enjoyed toast; Clare usually napped at 9:00 in the morning and then again at 2:00 in the afternoon, and Tilda would know Clare wanted to sleep when the baby pulled on her ears.

Tilda acknowledged the instructions good-naturedly and told Joseph not to worry—she knew all about little girls, she had been one herself. She could handle boys, too. After all, she joked, she had married The Great Henri.

Sarah began to wail when she realized Joseph was leaving. Her father gave her a hug. "Your aunty will look after you today, honey."

"I don't want her! I want you!"

Joseph held the child tightly. "It's okay, it's okay," he whispered repeatedly into her ear. When her crying ceased after a few minutes he tried to leave again, but again Sarah sobbed. This time Tilda was able to distract the child with a pretty spoon, and after a "Try not to kill each other," to the boys, Joseph snuck out the back door.

As he hurried to the Philibuster Dairy, he found himself looking forward to an occupation that came with a salary. His recent experiences had taught him that physical work, no matter how hard, did not compare with looking after young children. Caring for oneself was one thing; having other human beings depend on you entirely for their survival was quite another. A day fully occupied with feedings, changing and washing diapers, and tending to sick children was far more tiring than heaving a shovel or pounding nails.

The front doors of the Philibuster Dairy were still locked when Joseph arrived. From his pocket he drew out his precious letter and a strip of newspaper. He had read them both so often that he knew the words by heart, but he read them again anyway. "Help Wanted, Male." The Great Henri had cut the ad from employment section of *The Philibuster Post* and mailed it to Joseph some time back. The body of the ad read: "Experienced man of good character wanted to run dairy farm and milk route. Regular job for decent man. Must be good horseman. State wages in first letter." The ad ended with an address to which applicants could write.

Next, Joseph glanced at the letter, its envelope stamped in an Alberta post office. "We are pleased to offer you the position of Route Operator for the Philibuster Dairy. Report for work on May 18." He remembered how the weight of the world seemed to have lifted from his shoulders as he read those words. It had been so long—sometimes it felt like forever—since he'd had steady work. All the years of sweat and toil he had endured in the steel mill, four years before the war and another ten afterward, seemed like a nightmare now, with nothing to show for it.

Joseph had worked with blast furnaces, immense barrel-shaped structures in which raw ore and limestone were subjected to heat fiery enough to melt rock and turn iron ore into molten pig iron and slag. Seven days a week, twelve hours a day, Joseph had worn cotton gloves and leather shin guards, surrounded by rows of blast furnaces cooking the raw ore at over 1000 degrees Fahrenheit. When sweat dripped from his sweltering body, it sizzled on the floor like drops of water in a hot, oiled frying pan. So intense was the heat from the rows of blast furnaces that he drank two pails of water daily without quenching his thirst.

Not only had working at the blast furnaces been backbreaking, it had also been extremely dangerous. The molten iron and slag, handled properly, would pour down open channels. If mishandled, however, the liquid iron caused horrendous accidents, singeing clothing and cooking skin. Joseph had once seen a man beside him at the blast furnace burn to death when he failed to lower a stopper in time. As a result, liquid iron poured out of the blast furnace, struck the edge of the channel and erupted in the man's face. The desperate man had died screaming in anguish. It was commonly joked by the other workers that a person seeking employment at a steel mill should wait outside the mill until a man was carried out—because that was the right moment to apply.

Joseph had dreamed of buying a dairy farm even before he'd married Helen. To that end, in an effort to save money he had spent 14 years toiling in unbearable noise and heat. By the year

1928, Joseph and Helen understood they could not wait any longer. Though they didn't have as much money as they'd have liked to have for their down payment, especially with interest rates so high at the time, they realized that Joseph had been fortunate to escape working in the steel mill without major injury, thus far; best not to continue pushing their luck. They used every penny of their savings to purchase a farm near Strabane, Ontario, about 20 miles southwest of Toronto.

The farm had been a dream come true for Joseph and Helen. They had started with 12 Jersey cows, a few pigs and chickens, enough fertile land to grow whatever they needed and a healthy place to raise their growing family. Unfortunately, they had purchased the farm when optimism in the world economy was at its strongest and prices for land and buildings were at their height. By 1931 milk prices, along with the prices for every other commodity, were the lowest they'd been in 30 years. The Gastons could no longer earn enough to pay their mortgage and the bank had foreclosed on their farm.

Joseph, Helen and their three children—Clare was not yet born—had moved back to Hamilton, where Joseph found work on a tractor assembly line. The job lasted six months then Joseph was laid off. His next job, building office furniture, lasted only three months before his employers went bankrupt. By 1932 times were even tougher and Joseph had to go further afield in search of work. Companies everywhere were cutting employees or shutting their doors for lack of business. Joseph took a position as a travelling salesman, though he knew the position would be short-lived— which it was. Things became so desperate that he eventually took a badly paid job as a log driver on the French River, a few hundred miles north of his home in Hamilton. Apart from the poor pay, working conditions were abominable. Swarms of black flies were so thick in the area that there were times when Joseph could barely see, and with every breath he choked on the flies he inhaled. But work was work and he stuck it out as long as he could. When even that job ended in his employer's bankruptcy, there was nothing more to be had.

Joseph was pulled from his thoughts when a distinguished-looking man approached the front doors of the dairy. Of Joseph's height, about five-foot-eleven, he trod a fine line between being well fed and pudgy. He was clean-shaven, pale-skinned and had narrow lips and small eyes. His clothing was expensive: a perfectly pressed, three-piece navy suit, a matching blue fedora, a blue tie with white polka-dots, and a white handkerchief in his upper welt pocket.

Joseph stood up immediately and walked toward him. "Morning," he said with a friendly smile.

The man gave Joseph only a careless glance. Then, without a word of acknowledgment, he unlocked the door of the dairy and went inside.

Joseph was dismayed. *Do I look that desperate?* he wondered, as he looked down at his own clothing. His shirt, jacket and pants were clean, although the cuffs were frayed and the shirt was not quite white any longer. Did the other man assume he was looking for a handout?

Minutes later a middle-aged woman emerged from the building. She, at least, returned Joseph's greeting. "Are you here to see someone?" she asked.

"Why, yes, ma'am, Mr. Westmoreland. My name is Joseph Gaston."

"I see," she said non-committally. "Well, you may as well come in and sit down."

As Joseph followed her into a tastefully appointed reception area, he tried to remain calm. On the walls, a series of photos showed the dairy's development from the ground breaking ceremony to the laying of the foundations to the putting up of the walls. The last photos showed the ribbon-cutting ceremony which had occurred just 18 months earlier. Below that picture were listed the names of the attendees, one being the Canadian prime minister, R. B. Bennett. Next to him stood the president of the dairy, Mr. Winfield Westmoreland—the man who had snubbed Joseph a few minutes earlier. A bad feeling came over Joseph.

By now the staff had begun walking through the door in ones and twos. Wanting to make a good impression, Joseph smiled at them all. He waited for almost an hour before the secretary appeared again and informed him that Mr. Westmoreland was ready to see him.

Joseph was ushered down a hallway and into a lavish office with a terrazzo floor, panelled ceiling and polished oak furniture. Behind a large desk sat Winfield Westmoreland. He made no attempt to extend his hand in greeting when Joseph was introduced. Nor did he invite him to sit.

"What do you want?" Westmoreland asked gruffly. If he recognized Joseph from their brief contact an hour earlier, he did not show it.

Joseph stepped forward and held out the letter of employment. "I'm here for the job you offered me."

Westmoreland took the letter and skimmed it briefly. "Humph," he said.

Joseph smiled and waited nervously.

"You were supposed to start work today," the man said.

"Yes," Joseph agreed.

"But you didn't. I had to get someone else to fill the position."

Joseph's heart raced. *This could not be happening!* "But, sir, I'm reporting for work now. Today. As you requested."

Westmoreland frowned at him. "I needed you to start milking this morning. To do so, you should have reported to me yesterday."

"But the letter … that's not what it said. It said to report today."

"Obviously, you misunderstood our correspondence. Unfortunately, there is nothing I can do about it."

Then, before Joseph's disbelieving eyes, Westmoreland deliberately tore the letter in two.

Joseph was close to tears as he stared at the man behind the desk. For weeks the letter had kept him going. The prospect of a job had represented clothes for the children, shelter from the elements and food—above all else, food. All of it now gone.

"But you offered me the job!" Joseph blurted out, staring at the ripped letter in Westmoreland's hands.

"By not showing up in time for work, you've forfeited it."

"But ... we moved across the country to get here ..."

"Not my problem," Westmoreland said coldly. He called to his secretary. "Mrs. Brown, please show Mister ... Mister ... the gentleman out."

Moments later, Joseph found himself once more on the front steps of the dairy. Stunned, he staggered aimlessly down the dirt road and back toward town.

CHAPTER 5

Joseph stared at the ground as he walked, puffs of dirt rising with each footfall. His mind was a blur of misery and confusion. What had just happened? It was impossible that he could have misunderstood the letter. Its meaning could not have been clearer. He had been asked to start work today! Nowhere had it been suggested that he should report a day earlier. There had to be a mistake, and Joseph wanted to know what it was.

Angrily, he turned around and walked back to the dairy. He requested the secretary to get an appointment for him with Westmoreland. When she was reluctant to do as he asked, he told her there had been a mistake, and that only Westmoreland could help him get to the bottom of it. The secretary left her desk; she was not gone long. Frostily, with no pretence at her former politeness, she made it clear that Westmoreland would not see Joseph; he was not to disturb the great man again. When Joseph left the dairy a second time he was outraged.

So much had been riding on this job. The train tickets alone had used up most of his fast-dwindling savings. He had nothing of value left to sell. His belongings at the rooming house were worth four or five bucks, at most. How was he going to feed the kids? And why did these terrible things keep happening to him?

As he strode back to town, he tried to shrug off his feelings of anger and self-pity. He didn't have the money to get his family back to Ontario—not that there was work for him there either— but he had to do *something*. Rummaging through a few garbage cans in search of newspapers with Help Wanted ads, he found what looked like a complete copy of the *Philibuster Post*. Glancing at the front page before leafing through the paper for the section he wanted, a picture leaped up at him: Winfield Westmoreland.

The accompanying story related Mr. Westmoreland's promise to take a salary cut if he were re-elected mayor. Now, in his second term, he had, in fact, already taken a voluntary ten percent roll-back. "The city is in deficit," he was quoted as saying, "and everyone, including me, must tighten their fiscal belts." The article went on to mention that, without fanfare of any sort, Winfield Westmoreland and a number of other city council members had personally arranged for a 60-ton train car to be filled with flour, cereal and potatoes to be shipped to Weyburn, Saskatchewan.

"It is well known that the district of Weyburn may be the hardest hit of any area in Canada these last four years. When the Post *learned of this generous gift, we spoke to one of the donors, prominent business-man and our mayor, Winfield Westmoreland. He said, 'I believe we all owe it to our fellow men to serve them as best we can. I also believe we should treat each and every person with whom we come into contact with dignity and kindness, especially when they are in their great-est need.' This newspaper would like to thank the very humble Mr. Westmoreland for his generous and brotherly project, which will reflect greatly on our fair city."*

Joseph felt like spitting on Westmoreland's picture and throw-ing the paper in the trash, but he restrained himself and turned to the Help Wanted section. The only job he saw advertised was for an experienced machinist, for which he was unqualified. Frustrated at the lack of opportunity—here, just as back home—he refolded the paper, put it beside the refuse container for the next person, and started walking the streets in search of a job.

When Joseph got to Tilda's late that afternoon, he expected the house to be in a shambles with the boys out of control, Clare screaming with gas pains and Sarah in tears. Instead, he found the boys building a castle out of playing cards at the kitchen table, Clare napping soundly in a bassinet in the guest bedroom—"She ate well today," Tilda told him—and Sarah playing house in the living room. "Can I go play outside now, Daddy?" she asked, when Joseph hugged her and put her on his lap.

In some perverse way, Joseph would have been happier to find the house less serene. Not that he wanted things to go badly for Tilda, who was doing so much to help him, but after losing the dairy job and having spent a fruitless day spent searching for work, he badly wanted to feel needed.

His brother came through the back door with Jasper moments later. "'Allo, Joseph," he said as he kicked off his shoes and kissed Tilda's cheek. "'ow was your first day?"

"Not good," Joseph said with a wince, and explained.

"Well," Henri's tone was offhand, "I am certain in time you will find somet'ing."

Expecting his brother to be outraged at Westmoreland's treatment of him, Joseph was surprised by Henri's cavalier attitude. But had he been able to read his brother's mind, he would have understood.

Although they had spent no time together as children, Henri had never lost a younger sibling's awe of his much older brother. The six months they'd spent together when he was sixteen and Joseph twenty-eight had left an indelible impression on Henri. By this time he had already acquired his moniker, The Great Henri, because even as a young boy he'd been able to cut down trees faster than a grown man. So when he came to live with Helen and Joseph, Joseph hadn't had any problems finding the strong youngster a job at the steel factory. He worked in the stockyard, filling skips with rocks of iron ore. Sometimes he would have the satisfaction of bringing the ore to the blast furnace where Joseph worked, marvelling at his brother's skill with the molten pig iron.

In the evenings, when they sat around the fire, Joseph and Helen helped the lad with his English. They took turns pointing to different objects, which Henri had to name in English. As his vocabulary improved, they encouraged him to combine words in sentences. Every day the youngster became more confident in his ability to speak English, and every day he grew fonder of his brother and sister-in-law.

Until his arrival in Ontario, Henri had known only the mountains and forests surrounding his hometown in Quebec. Though he was happy with his brother and Helen, the time he spent with them had opened his mind to a larger world and he wanted to see more of it. When the moment came to part, Joseph and Helen presented the young man with a French-English dictionary, and all three shed some tears.

And so Henri resumed his journey across the continent. With the money he'd earned at the steel mill, he made his way to Lake Winnipeg where he looked for work as a fisherman. He had no fishing experience, but his great size, amiability and faith in himself made up for that lack. He was soon working on a barge, catching pickerel, perch, pike and lake sturgeon.

Bored after a season of fishing, he left the Lake and meandered south into Minnesota, where he talked himself into a position as a hunting guide, only to be fired when he proved himself a poor guide—good with a rifle but lacking knowledge of the area. The penniless boy spent two cold winter months living off little more than carrots stolen from farmers. He wrote to his brother and told him of his situation. He did not ask for money or help, he simply wanted to share the tale of his journeys. In time, he received a letter from Joseph, together with enough money to feed himself for a month.

Henri also managed to get himself into other bad situations. He would arrive in a town, take a liking to a street, a building, or, more likely, a girl, and inquire about work. Each time he laid claim to experience he did not have. He built coffins in Minot, North Dakota. He was a cashier in a grocery store in Sidney, Montana. He broke horses at a ranch south of Regina, Saskatchewan and cut hair in Brooks, Alberta. Finally, he ended up in a logging camp in northern British Columbia, where he remained for a while before making his way to Philibuster and making a home there. Whenever Joseph sensed his younger brother was in trouble, he would send him a few dollars. Henri never forgot Joseph's kindness.

When Henri learned of Helen's death and Joseph's intention to raise his four children alone, his belief that his brother was a saint was strengthened. A man who could take sole responsibility for a young family was capable of doing anything. So when Joseph told him he'd lost the dairy job, Henri knew, just knew, that his brother's bad luck could only be temporary. Such a good man would not be denied his due. In time, Joseph would find work and prosper.

"Dinner will be ready soon," Tilda announced.

"In that case we'll be off," Joseph said.

Tilda looked surprised. "You're not eating with us?"

"Thanks, but we can't impose—you've done so much for us already today."

"That's silly," Tilda said from the stove, where she was stirring the gravy. "Everything is ready and there's plenty for everyone. You might as well sit."

Joseph reluctantly accepted the invitation. The children washed their hands and everyone sat around the table. During dinner, Tilda gave Joseph a few recommendations, such as a good place for second-hand household goods, the names of stores carrying inexpensive children's clothes and the best times to buy low-priced groceries.

The children spoke about their day. Sarah had helped her aunt cook, clean and feed the baby. The boys had explored the neighbourhood. They had met the iceman who had given them each a piece of his wares.

And, Cole said, they had found some bottles in a back alley. "Traded them in at Hoogaboom's and got licorice. And, Daddy!" Cole's eyes widened with excitement. "You should see the lady there. She wears pants!"

Tilda's eyebrows came together in a frown. "You children shouldn't be going to Hoogaboom's."

Remembering Tilda's reaction to Hoogaboom's the previous day, Joseph wondered again what was wrong with the store. Just then Tilda screamed and Jasper barked, startling them all. Through the window, Joseph saw a skinny man peering in at them.

"Goodness!" Tilda exclaimed, Hoogaboom's forgotten as she put a hand to her chest. "Scared the daylights out of me, that did. Henri, quieten that beast. What's he doing inside anyway?"

The man at the window smiled and waved. Jasper went on barking.

"Henri!" Tilda demanded.

Her husband silenced the dog before going to the door. He returned to the kitchen accompanied by the stranger, introduced him as Ethan, and invited him to sit at the table.

Tilda was silent as Henri told the young man to fill his plate. Ethan needed no urging. The look in his eyes as he regarded the food told a tale of desperate hunger.

When he had swallowed a few bites he smiled at the others. "Right decent of you folks to ask me in. Right decent. Haven't had a proper meal since Hector was a pup." He speared a piece of chicken with his fork, then looked up again. "Right good food you got here. Mighty good. Came in today. Headed for the rally in Vancouver. Hopped off before the bulls could get me."

Ethan was very young, eighteen at most. His hair stood up on one side of his head, like a child's after an afternoon nap. His clothes were in reasonable repair; somewhat dishevelled, yet without patches or obvious holes. He was, Joseph figured, an inexperienced young kid on the road, an "Angellina." A farm boy, perhaps, who had left home because his family could no longer afford to support him and he didn't want to burden them.

If Ethan's clothing was one indication of his innocence, his constant banter was another. He talked too much. He used hobo terms too freely. He spoke of "bone polishers"—mean dogs—who chased him as he "padded the hoof"—travelled on foot—across the prairies, looking for a place where a "bo"—a hobo—could get a meal. In contrast, men who'd been on the road for a long time said little and bragged less about where they had been. They were tired, hungry and generally ashamed of what had become of them. Joseph, like so many others who had come of age earlier in the century, believed that every man should be able to make something of himself. This belief originated partly with the Horatio Alger rags-to-riches stories they had read as children. Growing up with such expectations had made the Depression even more difficult for the unemployed. In their minds, people who were unsuccessful were either lazy or stupid, and they did not want to think of themselves in those terms.

"Looked all over the main drag. Couldn't find a soupy anywhere," Ethan said. "Yep. Don't nobody want a bo hanging around."

"Dis is true, dare is no soup kitchen in Philibuster," Henri said, "but you might try duh Sunshine Society on 56 Street." His friend Raven Mullens was, among other things, the president of an organization that helped feed the destitute.

Joseph knew Ethan was right. A man without a job was not welcome anywhere, nor did anyone make it easy for a person to get on his feet. Sure, some of the larger cities might give you a $1.25 room ticket so you had somewhere to sleep for a few nights. There might even be a soup kitchen where you could eat twice a day for a couple of days before you were forced to move on. But that was it. Without a job, you were a liability anywhere.

Although political parties at the federal level had made promises to help the unemployed, the responsibility for housing, feeding and clothing the jobless fell mainly on the shoulders of civic committees and private charities such as the Salvation Army or local emergency relief associations. When federal government funds were available—although there wasn't much being doled out by the Bennett government—individual municipalities administered the money. Each town made its own decisions about how to maintain a subsistence level of existence for the impoverished men, women and children who lived there.

Typically, members of the tax-paying public constituted the civic relief committees. These committees determined who received relief and how much assistance they could obtain. Those who qualified did not receive cash. Concerned that public funds would be misused by men spending their relief money on alcohol or gambling, municipalities used a system by which privately owned businesses would accept relief vouchers for rent, food and heating fuel. No money was available for "luxuries" such as toothpaste, needles, thread, wool, light bulbs or toilet paper. As for the things that made life more bearable and were a way of keeping up one's spirits—a movie or an ice cream cone—these were not even considered.

Men who qualified for relief—almost always family men—were put to work performing "public works." The theory was that such work gave people the chance to feel useful, a principle Joseph understood. In practice, however, the work programs became what the *Chicago Tribune* termed "boondoggles." For political reasons, useful activities such as building houses for the homeless, paving roads and improving water treatment facilities were avoided. Too often, men found themselves picking dandelions or raking leaves: doing busywork, in other words. In any event, the ins and outs of the public works system were purely academic for men like Joseph and Ethan, as a person had to live in a town or a city for a year and a day to become eligible for $11 a month for rent and $15 a month for food. The reason for this policy was obvious: the homeless should not be allowed to bankrupt a place.

So Joseph could identify with the young man when he said, "Haven't eaten in a few days and was sure I'd be putting another notch in my belt. Started knocking on doors, I did. As I said, no one wants to help a bo. Wanted nothing to do with me, until you folks. Right Christian of you, right Christian."

Ethan's chatter went on in this fashion all through dinner. He talked constantly between bites, perhaps because in Tilda's comfortable kitchen he felt safe for the first time in who knew how long. Only near the end of the meal did his torrent of words slow to a trickle, and he showed signs of leaving. Joseph gave the boy credit; he knew better than to overstay his welcome.

"Well, you folks been right decent, right decent. Hope I can repay you some day," he said at the door. He shook hands with Henri and Joseph, bowed to Tilda and waved to the kids. Joseph thought he saw his brother sneak a dollar into Ethan's hand.

"Poor boy," Tilda said when Ethan had gone. "I don't mind feeding a starving man. The problem is, if you feed one, they tell their friends and pretty soon they're all at your door. Henri caught one of them putting a chalk mark on our front gate the other day, to let others know we're a soft touch. We usually leave Jasper outside. There's not a man alive interested in opening the gate when that beast is loose."

From where Joseph sat he was able to see Ethan walk toward the street. Listening to the young man talk, he had wondered how Ethan could be so cheerful. But as Ethan walked away, evidently thinking himself unobserved, the young man's shoulders drooped and his posture suggested a certain vulnerability. A lonely boy, for a boy was all he was—homesick, moneyless, defenceless. Where would he spend the night? Leaning against a tree somewhere?

Under a railway bridge? Certainly not in the entryway of a store, where he would be hounded or arrested. Joseph's eyes went to Nolan, probably no more than seven years younger than Ethan, and he was filled with a sudden and overwhelming sadness.

CHAPTER 6

At home that evening, Joseph kept thinking about Ethan. He looked down at his sleeping children, his heart aching at the thought that any of them might have similar experiences one day. He could not imagine Nolan and Cole, his beautiful boys—mischievous Nolan, gentle Cole—being cold, hungry and frightened. The thought made him feel ill.

He knelt down beside the children. Nolan had flung his arm over his face and was muttering something in his sleep. Sarah was smiling. Cole stirred, rolled over and began to snore softly. In her pram, Clare slept quietly. Very lightly, so as not to waken them, Joseph stroked each head in turn.

With the children asleep, he sat down with his dictionary. He did not want to think about the loss of his job, or his lack of money and prospects. If he allowed himself to dwell on his disappointments, he would tie his mind in knots and never get to sleep. Opening the old dictionary, he began to leaf through it for an interesting new word. His eyes paused at "abandon." Despite his resolve not to focus on his situation, the word led him to think about his childhood.

Three days after the death of Joseph's mother, his Aunt Jackie had stopped by the house to check on the family. To her horror, she discovered her brother-in-law gone and eight-year-old Joseph feeding his younger sisters pickles and raw potatoes he had found in the pantry. Joseph's father had abandoned his children. Jackie and her husband Peter brought Joseph and his sisters to live with them and their own three young children—sickly youngsters aged one, two and three, who were in constant need of attention. With so many children in the small house—Joseph's sisters were five and three—the boy was largely overlooked.

In contrast to Joseph's father, who had been somewhat of a tyrant, his mother had been a loving woman. She had heaped abundant praise on her first-born, who had responded to her attentions by being obedient and helpful. After her death he'd felt compelled to gain his aunt and uncle's approval by continuing his excellent behaviour. He did his chores quickly, earned A's in school and was obedient. But he was frustrated when his good conduct garnered no notice, let alone praise, from his relatives. Eventually he began to act out, in an effort he only now recognized, to get the attention he craved.

Joseph's tricks were relatively harmless, at first: a dash of pepper in his uncle's drinking water or salt swapped for sugar in his aunt's baking. The pranks got him whippings, but at least his existence was acknowledged. Soon he was getting into fights at school. He stopped doing his chores and he began to talk back to his uncle and aunt, all of which certainly got him more attention, though not the gentle kind that he craved.

When his minor offences began to be ignored he came up with new ways to get into trouble. One hot summer night he sprinkled powdered milk over his aunt and uncle's double bed: it stuck to their sweaty bodies while they were sleeping, and they woke up in a gooey mess. Uncle Peter used a switch to punish the offence, cutting Joseph's hands and the backs of his legs.

That Hallowe'en, Joseph filled neighbourhood mailboxes with manure. It wasn't the most heinous of Hallowe'en pranks, but for Uncle Peter, who had fed and sheltered the "ungrateful little hellion" for more than a year, it was the last straw. Joseph was separated from his sisters and passed on to another aunt and uncle.

The next relatives were little different from the previous ones. They, too, had children of their own, and took Joseph into their home only because they considered it their duty as good Christians to do so. Joseph's behaviour, as should have been expected, did not improve.

A year later he was forced to move again. This time he was sent to his Uncle David, a bachelor who used Joseph as slave labour. Without waiting for the boy to misbehave, at school or home, his uncle hit him, called him stupid, and told him his father had abandoned him because he was worthless. "He's like a colt," he informed anyone who would listen. "He has to be broken before he'll be of any use." The merest misdemeanour, even if it was unintentional, was punished harshly with beatings and days without food or shelter.

Eight months after Joseph began living with his uncle, David came home drunk one night and passed out in the kitchen. Joseph tried to rouse him. When he was unsuccessful, he tied two splints made from wood and strips of cloth to one of his uncle's legs, from hip to ankle, immobilizing him. Next morning Joseph told the unhappy man that he had broken his leg jumping over a ditch on his drunken way home, and that the doctor had ordered complete bed rest for at least a week. He solemnly assured his uncle that he would take care of him and keep the farm running in the meantime.

Superficially, at least, the boy appeared to be keeping his word, preparing his uncle's meals and going to the barn to do his chores. Initially mistrustful of Joseph, and watching him as closely as he could, David eventually came to the happy realization that he had trained Joseph so well that it was safe for him to relax during his nephew's absences from the house.

When his week of convalescence ended, David went to the kitchen expecting breakfast. Finding none, and getting no response when he shouted for his nephew, he hobbled to the barn. There he gazed about him in horror. Stalls had been destroyed. The horses and cattle were gone. Chicken feathers and blood were everywhere.

Managing, somehow, to reach town, he found the doctor who had supposedly splinted his leg. Upon learning the truth, David tore off the splint and went in search of his nephew. After making a few inquiries he found Joseph at the hotel, living off the money he'd made from selling his uncle's animals. Joseph's punishment was a terrible beating with a knotted rope, so severe that he was unable to walk, stand or touch his face for a few days.

When he had recovered somewhat, and knew his uncle was out searching for his remaining horses and cattle, Joseph struggled to his feet. Weak from hunger and thirst, he knew he had to get away. He understood that after what he had done, none of his relatives would take him back. If he wanted to survive, he needed to fend for himself. So he raided a neighbour's garden, gorging himself on fresh peas, then stumbled off in search of work.

He found a job topping beets at a local farm. His task was to pull out the beets and lop off the tops with a very sharp knife. A few times he also cut chunks from his fingers. Instead of complaining, he tore strips from his shirt, bound his wounds and kept going down the rows.

At the end of the summer Joseph returned to school. He spent a few weeks hiding in the barn of a school chum, Ben. When Ben's parents found out about Joseph, they took pity on him and took him into their home. The boy helped Ben and his father milk cows, care for calves, fix fences, dig ditches and do whatever else was necessary. He joined the family at mealtimes and shared a room with Ben. He was happy for the first time since his mother's death.

His happiness lasted until the evening he overheard Ben's parents discussing their finances. The family was apparently having a hard time paying their bills. Although Joseph was reluctant to leave the people who had been so kind to him, he was determined not to be a burden to them. Without letting them know what he'd overheard, he packed his few possessions and left for the nearest big city, Hamilton, Ontario.

He'd never been in a town of more than a few hundred people. Now he was walking the streets with 70,000 other souls. Hamilton was huge, and bustled with activity. At first Joseph was confused and overwhelmed. Wherever he looked he saw unfamiliar things: electric streetlights glowing in the night, eight-storey buildings and castle-like houses, trams moving without horses pulling them. He also saw many rows of men digging trenches and filling the channels with large iron pipes. The city was in the midst of a growth spurt and was spending a lot of money to upgrade and improve its sanitation system.

Joseph knew his way around a shovel. He was convinced he could dig ditches. Plucking up his courage, he asked one of the diggers to point out the foreman. The man's answer was incomprehensible, so Joseph asked a second man, who, in broken English, pointed out the foreman to him.

"So, you're lookin' for work," said the obviously Irish foreman, his words running together in a Celtic lilt.

"Can you use another man?" Joseph asked.

The Irishman grinned. "Sure, 'an I can. D'yah know one?"

Joseph heard a few chuckles, but didn't realize he was being teased. "Me," he said, as a few men within earshot leaned on their shovels, wiping the sweat from their foreheads as they watched the eleven-year-old ask for a job.

The foreman decided to have some fun with Joseph. "Don't mind working with Dagos, lad?"

Joseph had no idea who or what Dagos were. He did know he was hungry and would do just about anything to feed himself. "No, sir," he replied.

"Well, then, boyo. Pick up that shovel and go on with yeh to the end of the line."

Joseph did as ordered and began digging away at the hard earth. To the amazement of the other men, he kept up with them almost shovel for shovel. The work was tough, but he understood what was at stake. The foreman kept an eye on him, wondering when the boy would drop from exhaustion. By the end of the day, he was so impressed with Joseph's capacity for hard work that he asked him to come back again the next day. Exhausted, Joseph fell asleep in a nearby doorway that night. A policeman woke him around midnight and told him to go home. Too tired to be frightened, Joseph found another doorway and sank back into sleep.

The next day he worked hard again, only stopping when he mistakenly thought he heard the foreman call him, "Hey, Joe." He was to learn that the other labourers all spoke Italian, and that the foreman, like other English-speaking Canadians, referred to these immigrants collectively as "Dagos" and individually as "Joe."

Joseph listened to the men as they worked. In a few days he had absorbed several basic Italian words—*per favore, grazie, buon giorno*—and used them when he spoke to his co-workers. Impressed with the English kid's friendliness, they were friendly in return. When they learned he had nowhere to sleep they brought him to a rooming house on Barton Street, where many Italian immigrants lived. Plaster fell from the ceiling and there were more men than beds, but the place was tidy and had a sense of community that made Joseph feel comfortable.

As foreigners in a country where anyone not of British descent was deemed second-class, most Italian men could only find jobs in the most strenuous and poorest paying work situations. The men Joseph roomed and worked with were either single men who had come to Canada to earn money to send back home to Italy, or married men who were saving their money in order to send for their families. Living in cramped quarters where the rent was low made it possible for them to do so. Their only extravagance, for the most part, was a keg of beer on a Saturday night. And, as if to give the shabby place some sense of warmth and personality, they pasted pictures on the walls above their beds—drawings, postcards from home or photographs cut from newspapers and magazines.

Joseph, who had never set foot in a museum or an art gallery, loved to look at the pictures. No matter that they were tattered or fly-specked or showed signs of wear, he looked at them often, moved by a beauty he had not known existed. The picture he returned to again and again was the portrait of a woman with long dark hair and a half-smile. Her face bore an expression which he could not give a word to until years later, when he found it in his dictionary. The word was "enigmatic." Who was the woman, he asked. One of the older men enlightened him. The picture, he told Joseph, was very famous. It hung in a gallery in France, but the man who had painted it was an Italian named Leonardo da Vinci. Italians called the woman *La Gioconda*. Her English name was Mona Lisa.

In later years, when Joseph talked of the time he had spent living amongst the Italians, he was often asked about things people knew only from rumours and newspapers, about dirt and depravity, quarrels and fatal knife fights. But Joseph experienced nothing of the sort. Inevitably there were disagreements, unavoidable when 23 men shared too few beds, but he never saw or heard anything worse than some raised voices and insults. He could attest to the fact that the Italians had behaved no worse than the English Canadians he had met.

In fact, what Joseph remembered most vividly was how badly the Italians were treated. The trenches dug by Joseph and his co-workers often ran beside the tramlines. English-speaking shift-workers rode the trams to and from work. With shift changes occurring at various times of the day, the trams were often crowded. In summer, contemptuous passengers would spit their tobacco juice through the open windows, aiming at the Italian labourers only a few feet away. Usually they would miss their intended targets, but once in a while a filthy gob landed on a pant-leg or shirt-sleeve, whereupon the men on the trams would hoot, whistle, laugh and shout at the Italians, telling them to go back to their own country. In turn, the unfortunate recipient of the gob would shake his fist and yell back at the cowards on the tram. Afterward, as he cleaned off the mess, he would wonder whether he was crazy to think of bringing his wife and children to a country where they would experience such indignities.

Joseph had spent quite some time working in the trenches

when he learned of better paying positions being offered by some of the new steel mills that provided the manufacturing sector with raw material. He found a job at a steel mill and worked there until the start of the Great War in 1914.

Absorbed in his memories, Joseph did not hear the gentle tap at his door. It was only when the sound was repeated that he noticed it, and even then he was not certain where it came from. The walls of the house were so thin that the sound could have come from anywhere in the building. As it was, he was glad of the distraction and opened the door.

A man with short black hair stood there, his eyes lowered politely. His neighbour, Joseph knew, though they had never met face to face, and the father of the children who had peered into the hallway the day Joseph and his family had moved into the house.

"Good evening, sir," said the man. His accent, surprisingly, was British.

The man's name was Tom Wah. Still keeping his eyes down, he apologized profusely for disturbing Joseph's evening. He lived next door, he said. He and his wife ran a wet wash service. If Joseph wanted things laundered, he could leave them in a basket outside the Wahs' door in the morning and they would be returned the following day. Joseph had used such services occasionally in the past. Though he could take care of the children's clothing himself, towels and sheets would be hard to wash in the sink. He sensed Tom Wah and his wife would be happy to dry the washing as well, but that would cost more, and it would be easy enough for Joseph to hang everything on the clothesline in the back yard.

After thanking the man for stopping by, and saying that he might well use his services, Joseph held out his hand. "Pleasure to meet you."

As Tom Wah lifted his head and made eye contact for the first time, Joseph saw a look of surprise in his face. Then, ignoring the extended hand, Tom bowed and walked away quickly.

The small incident brought back to mind the Italian immigrants Joseph had gotten to know so well. Tough as conditions had been for them, he was aware that no one was lower in the social hierarchy of North America than the Chinese. It was depressing to think that a man needed to walk with his eyes down and head lowered in order to avoid confrontation and survive.

CHAPTER 7

Shortly after arriving in Philibuster, Joseph's days took on a certain routine. Clare woke up every night crying between 1:00 and 2:00 AM. Sometimes she would drink a little milk then go back to sleep. Other times she'd wake and remain inconsolable for an hour or two, and her father would stay awake with her. By 6:00 the other three children would be up. A weary Joseph would feed them breakfast, going without eating himself in order to stretch the family's food money, and then take them to Henri and Tilda.

After saying goodbye to the boys he would extricate himself from a tearful Sarah. The remainder of the morning was spent trudging from one business to another, knocking on doors and enquiring about work. Most people were not interested in talking with him, but on the odd occasion when he did have a chance to communicate with a potential employer, he did his best to promote himself, stretching his work experience beyond his true skills.

After many hours of unsuccessful job searching, a hungry Joseph usually returned to Tilda's home. Turning down her offer of a meal with the lie that he had already eaten, he would turn instead to the Help Wanted section of the day's *Philibuster Post*. Rarely did he see advertisements for men. And when he did see a position, for an experienced electric welder or mushroom grower, for instance, he was not qualified to apply.

After studying the few ads, Joseph would scan the rest of the paper, looking for any possible hint of work. He could not help noticing how often the *Philibuster Post* trumpeted the successes of Mayor Westmoreland and the city council. One day the council voted to improve the sewer system, with the work to begin immediately. Another day it confirmed construction permits for new warehouses at the southwest end of town. Other enterprises were mentioned too, a packing plant and a brickyard relocating to Philibuster. Thinking that the various projects would need labourers, Joseph tried to find out more about them from Raven Mullens.

But Raven, manager of the Great West Sawmill, the potential source of lumber for the reported ventures, dismissed the articles as fabrication rather than truth. According to him, Westmoreland and his cronies were in the habit of faking these stories to make it appear they were performing their civic duties.

"Hell, you ever hear of bread and circuses?" Raven asked. "Two thousand years ago Roman politicians tried to win the votes of the poor by giving them cheap food and entertainment as a way of diverting them from more pressing problems. Westmoreland and those other bastards in office are doing the same thing, except that they aren't even giving out bread."

Discouraged by his lack of success, Joseph took to peeking between the slats of the wooden sidewalks, hoping to find dropped change. So desperate was he that whenever he saw the dump wagon go by, heaped high with cinders, garbage and street refuse, he wondered if he might find something in the pile that he could sell to a scrap dealer for a few cents. The afternoon usually ended when Joseph, tired and famished, stopped at Jackson's Grocery Store to pick up a few essentials for the family's dinner. Since his culinary abilities were limited—he fed the kids a steady diet of sandwiches or mashed potatoes with corned beef—it never took him long to decide on his purchases.

He usually passed Hoogaboom's store on his way to Jackson's. It still seemed odd to him that whenever the boys mentioned Hoogaboom's in Tilda's presence, she would sniff, as if at a bad odour, make a face, and tell the boys to stay away from "that place."

Fearing she might get into one of her snits—for Tilda tended to get prickly when she was upset—Joseph refrained from asking her why she objected to the store.

One Sunday afternoon while he was weeding Tilda's back garden—one of the many chores he did to repay her for looking after the children—he finally broached the subject with Henri. His brother was relaxing on the porch, and for once Joseph and Henri were alone.

Henri gave Joseph a long look. "Tilly does not like Beth," he said.

"Who's Beth?"

"Duh owner of 'oogaboom's."

"Why doesn't she like her?"

"Jealous!" Henri said, with a hint of satisfied amusement in his voice.

Seeing Joseph's curiosity, he began to explain. After leaving the logging camp in northern British Columbia in the spring of 1928, Henri had returned to Alberta, longing for the flat lands and big sky he fondly remembered. In Philibuster, he had become acquainted with Raven Mullens, who had found him a job at the sawmill.

About this time he also began to patronize Hoogaboom's, then owned and run by a stern man named Ambroos Hoogaboom and his pretty wife, Beth. Months after Henri arrived in the town, Ambroos was walking across the Elk River when melting ice broke beneath his weight and he drowned. Attracted to Beth, Henri had tried to woo her for a while, but she was not interested in him. Then he met Tilda, fell in love and married her. Not long after their wedding, he made the great mistake of telling his new wife about his recent crush on Beth.

Henri had not known at the time that Tilda's dislike of Beth was founded on a jealousy that went beyond her husband's erstwhile desire for another woman. As a pretty and rather proper young girl, Tilda had been much sought after by the men of

Philibuster. Her dance card had always been the first to be filled—at least, until Beth moved to town. She was a few years older than Tilda, and taller, with a strangely captivating appearance. Beth began to attract the men who had once wooed the younger girl. Beth didn't know about Tilda, but Tilda was very much aware of Beth, especially when a handsome older man named Ambroos Hoogaboom—on whom Tilda happened to have set her own eyes—married Beth.

But Beth's conquest of Ambrose Hoogaboom was not the only reason for Tilda's dislike of her. Tilda was unable to bear children. Beth had two healthy girls, and the initial dislike turned to hatred.

Henri's story sparked such curiosity in Joseph that he became like a child who'd been warned to keep away from matches, yet was unable to stop himself from playing with them. He had to meet Beth.

On the afternoon Joseph decided to visit Hoogaboom's, he noticed the birds chattering loudly and fluttering about nervously, as if they sensed something unusual was about to happen. Although it had been nearly 90 degrees at midday, the temperature had dropped significantly in just four hours. Joseph thought the drastic change in temperature odd, but was so grateful for the break from the oppressive heat that he didn't think to question it.

As he approached Hoogaboom's, the first thing he noticed was a church pew, a sturdy old thing made of poplar. Joseph recognized it immediately as a liar's bench. Every town had at least one, a place where men congregated and told stories—mostly exaggerated—of things they'd seen and done. Six men were sitting there now, conversing amicably together.

To the left of the bench, beneath a white awning that read "Hoogaboom's Grocery Store," was a single large window and a door. In the window were displays of canned goods piled into pyramids and the ubiquitous poster: "Do Your Duty! Get the Gopher!" As Joseph entered the store he heard a bell above the door, and a radio.

"… and, Dr. T. E. Shaw of the London School of Economics added, this world crisis would be brought to a swift conclusion if the world's leaders had the courage to say to their countries, 'We have lived beyond our means too long, and must have the boldness to pursue such actions as might prove painful in the short term but will be to everyone's benefit in the long.'"

The radio was perched on a shelf by the back wall. A few men at the rear of the store listened quietly as the announcer continued.

"In Chicago, the Boy Scouts of America National Council endorsed development of a scouting program for older boys, designed to give new avenues of adventure and appeal to those youths unable to find employment. Dr. James E. West, Chief Scout Executive, stressed the need of a program for youths forced out of school because of economic conditions at a time when jobs are at a low ebb."

The listening men shook their heads sadly.

"In local news, charges of unlawful assembly were dropped against 46 city relief recipients for their part in the uprising in the south side potato patch last week. Initially accused of being communist agitators, the Court found a lack of evidence in the case against the accused. And that is your news of the moment."

When the bulletin ended and music took over, the men entered into an animated discussion over whether the relief recipients had been let off too easily. After all, nobody wanted "their" kind of trouble in this part of the country, and "the sooner we get rid of the communist rabble-rousers, the better off the country will be."

Joseph only half-listened to the chatter as he walked around the store. On one side, canned goods were stacked on wooden shelves, everything from tins of peas, corn and grapefruit to molasses, coffee, corned beef and salmon. On the bottom shelf sat baskets of produce—apples, carrots, potatoes, cabbages, onions, lettuce, rhubarb and more. Meat was in a glass cabinet on the other side of the store, minced beef, boiling beef, loin lamb chops and bacon. Dairy products and soda pop occupied yet another cabinet. Bread and baked goods were on the counter.

Checking prices as he went along—milk, nine cents a quart; bread, a nickel a loaf; round steak, ten cents a pound—Joseph thought Hoogaboom's prices were as good as or better than the prices at Jackson's. He grabbed two cans of Hereford corned beef and a loaf of day-old bread, filled a sack with potatoes, and walked to the rear of the store.

He was standing by the cash register, waiting for someone to attend to him, when one of the men by the radio shouted, "Beth! Customer!" An attractive woman with flawless skin, hazel eyes and dark hair pulled back in a bun appeared from the storage room. Joseph remembered Cole's comment that Mrs. Hoogaboom wore pants and men's shoes, and he saw that she did. He had the feeling he'd seen her before.

"If you old buzzards would stop hanging around my store I'd hear customers come in," she said. The comment was made teasingly, and the men grinned in response.

She smiled pleasantly at Joseph. "What can I do for you?"

Joseph felt awkward, as he tended to do around women. Unable to meet her eyes, he indicated his purchases and said, "Just these, please."

Mrs. Hoogaboom was weighing the potatoes when the bell rang, the door flung open, and one of the fellows from the liar's bench burst into the store.

"It's coming!" he screamed.

In a flash, Beth and the men by the radio ran to the window and stared west down the street.

"Great Caesar's Ghost!" Beth exclaimed.

Joining the nervous crowd at the window, Joseph wondered whether the day of reckoning had arrived. "What is it?" he asked urgently, as Beth and the men exchanged brief glances of surprise.

"A Black Blizzard," Beth whispered in awe. "A bad one."

The words struck a chord in Joseph: he had read about Black Blizzards. For thousands of years the natural grasses of the plains had kept the topsoil in place, even during times of drought. When settlers moved into the North American west and cleared the land to plant wheat, they had plowed the native grasses under. Years of intense plowing combined with an acute lack of rain or snow had robbed all the moisture from the soil. When the dry soil was hoisted aloft and blown by strong winds, immense dust storms—Black Blizzards—were the result.

Black Blizzard. Joseph heard that the dust from such a blizzard could cover the interior of a house even when all the doors and windows were tightly closed: the fine particles would leave streaks of dirt on floors, coat dishes in cupboards with light powder, and penetrate any food not sealed in Mason jars. He remembered other, more terrifying, details. Static electricity given off during a particularly bad Black Blizzard could be enough to light up a large city. Storms of sand and soil could create such high drifts that roads had to be closed, trains couldn't pass and cattle strayed over fences. A person driving a vehicle had to turn off the ignition to keep the dust from smothering the engine. Most frightening of all, a person out in the open had to find immediate shelter, because dust pneumonia, caused when the dirt was inhaled, could permanently impair even the strong, and kill the young.

Until today, Joseph had taken descriptions of Black Blizzards to be exaggerated. Now, for the first time, he realized the terrible dangers of the dust storm. He could see it coming in from the west, a wall of black, thousands of feet high. To Joseph it looked as though a massive, unbroken wave was moving toward him.

Unnerved by the wall of blackness, he raced to Tilda's, glancing backward every few steps to check whether the dark mass was about to engulf him. Reaching the house, he burst through the front door. Tilda and Sarah were stringing beads in the living room.

"Where's Clare?" Joseph shouted, as he dropped his groceries on the floor.

Tilda clapped a hand over her mouth. "Oh, my, Joseph! You scared me! Clare's napping."

"And the boys?" It was nearly four o'clock. The boys would be out of school by now.

Catching the fear in his voice, Tilda jumped to her feet. "What is it?"

"A Black Blizzard," Joseph told her tersely.

Tilda ran to the window. She saw the approaching storm from between the houses across the street. Alarmed, she glanced at the clock over the mantle. "They dawdle after school."

"I'm going to look for them," Joseph yelled, running to the door.

"Hurry!" Tilda shouted after him.

Joseph was in a panic as he ran along the route he guessed Nolan and Cole would take home. Would he find the boys in time? They knew nothing about Black Blizzards. Unless the kids were safe inside somewhere by the time the storm hit, their lungs could fill with dirt and they could be killed.

CHAPTER 8

The ominous black wall rolled steadily toward Joseph. If at first he had thought the Black Blizzard looked like a giant wave, now it was like an advancing mountain range, crushing everything in its path. The blizzard was moving so rapidly that Joseph figured he had no more than five or six minutes in which to find Nolan and Cole before the storm engulfed them.

As he ran to the school, yelling his children's names, he was vaguely aware of people darting frantically into churches, stores and homes. Finding the school playground deserted, Joseph ran to the rooming house, but the boys were not there. Where could they be? Their friends must surely have warned them of a Black Blizzard's dangers. If only he could trust in Nolan's common sense.

But his older son had become such a risk taker that he didn't always behave rationally. Joseph could only go on running along the streets, frenziedly calling the boys' names.

The world grew dark as the growing blackness blotted out the sun. Joseph felt the electricity in the air. The hair on his forearms stood on end. He saw a man run toward a car and grab the door handle, only to be hurled to the ground. As the man got up unsteadily and staggered away his hair was smoking.

Suddenly, miraculously, Joseph spotted the boys. They were standing side by side on the Cree Creek traffic bridge, watching the incoming storm. Joseph ran toward them, screaming to make himself heard above the ferocious wind.

"Daddy! Look!" Cole yelled excitedly, pointing down the ravine.

"Let's go!" Joseph screamed. "Now!" He seized their hands.

"But, Dad ..." Nolan protested.

"Now!"

Sparks flew off the telephone wires. Church bells clanged in warning. It was too late to get home; the storm would be on them in seconds. Quickly, Joseph dragged the boys off the bridge and pushed them into a niche below it, shielding them with his body. Moments later an unearthly howl filled his ears and the storm rolled over them. It was dark as midnight.

After enduring several minutes of buffeting winds and stinging dirt, Joseph realized the storm could last for hours, even days: he had no way of knowing. They had to find proper shelter. He pulled out his handkerchief, tore it into three pieces, gave a piece to each boy, and ordered them to cover their eyes, mouths and noses. Unsure whether they could hear him above the howling winds, he pushed their hands tightly against their mouths and seized their free hands again.

Visibility was almost non-existent as Joseph narrowed his eyes against the slashing sand and felt his way to the guardrail at the side of the bridge. The wind was so savage it nearly blew him off his feet. Tightly gripping the boys' hands, he bent over as they inched their way north toward Tilda's. To keep himself on course, he crept along with one foot on the wooden sidewalk, the other in the gutter. They had covered half a block when Joseph glimpsed a building a few feet to his right. Pulling the boys with him, he followed the line of the building, knocking at every door they passed. There was no response to his knocking, not even at a church.

Suddenly a hand tugged at his shirt. A moment later a bell rang, a door slammed, and Joseph and the boys were out of the storm.

"What are you doing out in this?" a woman asked.

Joseph opened his eyes fully. They were in the corner grocery store and the woman was Beth Hoogaboom.

"My boys," Joseph muttered breathlessly. "Had to find them." He coughed up a mixture of phlegm mixed with dirt. Looking down at the boys, he saw their hair was full of dirt, their skin bright red from the blasting sand. They still held the scraps of torn handkerchief to their mouths.

"Wait here." Beth's clothes shed dust as she dashed through the door behind the cash register. She returned with a pretty young redhead, her daughter, Patricia, she explained briefly, as they handed tumblers of water to Joseph and the boys.

"Thank you," Joseph managed, between coughs. Nolan and Cole lowered their handkerchiefs and all three drank.

When Joseph could speak again, he introduced himself and the boys.

"I've heard about you," Beth said, laughing. "The Great Henri's brother, and evidently as foolish as he is. You're lucky I was looking out the window when you passed or you'd still be out in that hell."

Joseph coughed again, hiding his surprise. What lady talked this way?

"Momma!" Patricia exclaimed.

"Momma, nothing," Beth said. "I can see it in his eyes. Wants to get home. Am I right?"

"Well, yes ... I'm worried about my daughters."

"Safe inside, I'll bet."

Joseph prayed she was right. He told himself not to worry; he knew Tilda was looking after the girls.

"Yes," he said.

Beth laughed again. "I wonder, sometimes, why so many men lack common sense."

Her laughter vanished as she looked once more through the window. "This is as bad as I've seen." When she turned to Nolan and Cole, she was smiling again. "Too bad the storm kills radio reception. *The Shadow* is on tonight!" Pretending to pull a cape over her face, she made her voice menacing. "Who knows what evil lurks in the hearts of men?"

"The Shadow knows!" Nolan and Cole exclaimed in unison, and laughed with Beth.

"This could go on for hours," she said. "You will have dinner with us, won't you?"

"Thank you." Joseph accepted the invitation gratefully.

"Terrible things these," Beth resumed, as Patricia went upstairs to their apartment to prepare the meal. "Each summer these damn storms get worse, and there are more of them, too. And if it's not the storms, it's the bloody grasshoppers."

Joseph had read about grasshoppers, too. He knew that swarms of them, miles in width, moved over farmlands, devouring crops down to the roots, and making such a mess of the fields that what was left wasn't even good enough for cattle to graze on. Grasshoppers attacked urban areas as well, gorging on carrots, beets and turnips in gardens. They even liked the residue of human sweat, so much so that they would bite at the cuffs, collars and underarms of shirts hanging on clotheslines. So dense were their formations that, in cities, their bodies coated buildings, telephone lines, sidewalks and streets. When it rained it was even worse, for then the grasshoppers clogged the drains and the streets flooded.

"Those poor farmers," Beth continued. "Christ almighty, if it's not one thing, it's another."

She went on to talk of other problems farmers faced: the odds of good crops, the number of bushels per acre and how the "sons of bitches" at the City Relief Board refused to give a few dollars to the farmers and their families who so desperately needed assistance. "The poor bastards don't even have enough money to buy axel grease to keep their machinery from seizing up in this dust. It costs them 16 cents a pound for axel grease, so they come here, buy butter from me for five cents a pound, and mix it with beef tallow. I don't know how well it works, but they keep coming back for more."

Joseph thought she talked a lot for someone who was around people all day. You'd think she'd hear so much jabbering from her customers that she'd welcome silence. But that didn't seem to be the case. She also cursed a lot. She said, "damn," "Christ almighty," and "sons-of-bitches" just as often as any man did. He saw Nolan and Cole glance at him a few times, as if they wondered why they got scolded for doing what she did freely.

Beth's conversation moved from beleaguered farmers to local goings-on. The town was too big for one person to know what everybody was up to, but she seemed to know a lot. She recognized the boys from the few times they'd been in the store.

Patricia arrived some time later with dishes of pork chops, creamed corn and mashed potatoes with gravy. Joseph jumped up to help her, but the young woman cheerfully told him she could manage. As there was no table in the store, they sat at boxes and crates which Beth brought in from the storage area. After dinner, Beth brought out a deck of cards and unashamedly lit up a cigarette. She offered one to Joseph, who had never seen a woman smoke, and he politely refused it.

"And what do you guys do for pocket money?" Beth asked the boys as she dealt out a hand of go-fish.

"Snare gophers," Nolan said.

"Where do you take the tails?"

A number of stores that sold dry goods, hardware and groceries in Philibuster acted as municipal agents for the gopher program. They stored the gopher tails until a provincial employee made his monthly rounds, collected the tails and reimbursed the agent seven cents per tail.

"We take them to Briggs Hardware," Nolan said.

"Bring them to me and I'll give you an extra half cent a tail."

"That's very kind, but—" Joseph began, but Beth interrupted him.

"And you?" she asked Cole.

"I get gophers too, and I also find magpie eggs," he told her.

Because magpies and blackbirds had a habit of getting into hens' eggs, the local government offered ten cents for a pair of either bird's feet. Kids Cole's age climbed up the branches of aspens in search of magpie eggs, for which the reward was a nickel an egg.

As Cole described the shoebox in which he kept his pilfered eggs, Joseph learned more about the ways in which his sons spent their days. They were apparently adjusting well to their new surroundings. Before school every morning they followed the bakery wagon down the street, hoping for a dropped sweet roll or two. After school they joined their new friends and fished or swam in Cree Creek, or watched baseball; the unemployed men often had a game on the go. On weekends they scrounged through back alleys, looking for bottles or metal or anything else the scrap man might buy.

Then there was the "tree trick." Nolan and Cole had heard about it from their friends, none of whom had actually tried it themselves. No one was brave enough, Nolan told his father— *or foolish enough*, thought Joseph—until he, Nolan Gaston, had come to town.

"You gotta find the right kind of tree first," Nolan said, as seriously as if he were describing a complicated surgical procedure.

The tree had to be an aspen, and a boy had to climb high enough, about 30 feet up, to be able to wrap his hands around the trunk. "When you get a real good grip, you kick off from the tree like you're meaning to jump, but you still got a grip on the trunk. Well, Nathan McCormick tells us what to do, but he won't do it himself. So I tried it and it worked! That old tree bent over like an Indian's bow. I landed on the ground, soft as a feather. And that wasn't the best part either. When I let go, the tree snapped back and rained leaves on me like I was in a ticker tape parade!"

If Nolan had expected to be congratulated on his daring, he was mistaken. He seemed unable to understand that his father's primary concern was to keep his children alive and safe. Joseph asked Nolan to promise he would not attempt the stunt again, but his son complained he would be called a sissy. It took some urging before a relieved Joseph was able to extract Nolan's promise.

As Beth and the boys continued to chat, Joseph wondered why women seemed to get on so much better with his children than he did. He remembered the two boys talking endlessly with their mother about their adventures, the conversations seeming to flow quite naturally. After Helen's death, Joseph had expected the boys would confide in him. When it didn't happen, he put it down to the children's grieving. Yet, on moving to Philibuster, the boys had opened up to Tilda. Now they were telling to a stranger things they'd never thought of telling him. Listening to their chatter, Joseph could not help but wonder where he was going wrong.

By nine o'clock the storm had subsided sufficiently for them to leave the store. As Joseph thanked the two women for their hospitality, Beth reminded the boys to come back the next Wednesday to listen to *The Shadow*. To Joseph, she said he should pass on her greetings to The Great Henri.

"Nice man," Patricia commented, when the Gastons had gone.

"Nice enough." Beth sounded somewhat offhand.

Patricia winked as she elbowed her mother.

"Don't go thinking foolishness," Beth said, putting a quick stop to any further comments her daughter might make. She was not interested in talk about love and romance. All that was far behind her, she told herself.

CHAPTER 9

When Joseph and the boys got back to Tilda and The Great Henri's, Clare and Sarah were already asleep. Tilda, who'd had previous experience with Black Blizzards, had shut the windows and doors and sealed the cracks with wet towels.

The boys were excited as they related their adventures: the wall of blackness rushing toward them, waiting for the storm to envelop them, their father hiding them under the traffic bridge, the safety of Hoogaboom's. Nolan and Cole did not notice that their aunt's smile vanished at mention of the store. They chattered happily about free soda pop, playing cards, Mrs. Hoogaboom's cursing and her offer to pay more than other stores for gopher tails. Every complimentary comment about Beth caused the lines in Tilda's brow to deepen further. Joseph willed them to be quiet, but they went on talking. When they paused to take breath, Tilda said emphatically, "Mrs. Hoogaboom is not a nice woman," and left the room abruptly. Joseph glanced at his brother, who merely shrugged his huge shoulders and returned the look with one that seemed to say, "Women—who understands them?"

When Joseph fetched the girls from the room where they were sleeping, Tilda was curt with him. He was tempted to accuse her of being unreasonable. What had she expected him to do? Refuse Beth's hospitality and force the boys back out into the storm? But he decided to say nothing; there was no point in infuriating Tilda any further. He needed her to look after his children, after all. Reluctantly, he also made a decision not to buy his groceries at Hoogaboom's, even though prices were no higher there than anywhere else. A shame, really, for Beth had been so kind.

Although the next day saw Joseph painfully coughing up mud-like phlegm, he did not allow his malaise to deter him from his search for work. Eventually he found a job as a door-to-door sharpener of knives and scissors. He paid 25 cents a day to rent the equipment—a small grinder that spun by working a foot peddle—and kept all his profits. Sadly, he barely broke even most days, for very few housewives could afford to give him cash for his services. They resorted to paying him in kind with garden vegetables or jars of preserves, when what he really needed was money.

The sawmill, Joseph thought, when he had exhausted all other possibilities. He had stayed clear of the Great West Sawmill until now. For one thing, he felt fairly sure new employees were not needed. For another, he knew his brother would have let him know of any available work. That was how the system worked. Jobs were acquired through family or friends. In fact, he'd lost the position at the dairy for that very reason. A few days earlier Henri had told him that Mrs. Westmoreland's cousin had been given the job. "I 'ear dis man know no'ting about duh dairy business. Can't even milk cows," he'd said with a wry grin.

Though Henri seemed to think it quite a joke, Joseph did not share his amusement. With only two dollars left in his pocket, and rent almost a month overdue, he needed help, which probably meant going to a charity organization.

Joseph bitterly recalled how he had been driven to ask for charity when he had gone bankrupt. The bank that had foreclosed on his farm had been so determined to get all it could from the auction of the property and its contents, that the family had had to leave their home with nothing but their clothing. Swallowing his pride, Joseph had approached the minister of the community church, who also happened to run the local charity. The minister, who maintained that Joseph was to blame for his circumstances by doing wrong in the eyes of the Lord, agreed to feed the family only on condition that Joseph sought forgiveness and admitted to being a sinner. He preached to Joseph for half an hour before granting assistance. Joseph knew the minister wanted to break him. Make him beg. Take away his dignity. He already felt like a failure for having to accept help, but the minister wanted him to feel worthless, so that he could have his soul. Desperate to feed his family, Joseph had given in to the man's demands, after which he'd promised himself never to ask for charity again.

Despondently, he trudged down dirt roads toward the sawmill. From a mile away he could hear the sounds of humming and buzzing. As he came closer, he caught the fragrance of fresh-cut pine. Pausing at the top of the riverbank, he had an overview of the whole operation.

The Great West Sawmill was the only lumber mill operating in the area. It had been set up to receive logs brought in by horse, truck and teams of oxen, or floating downstream to a catch basin at the edge of the river. A series of complex procedures resulted in finished boards, planed and piled as high as a two-storey house at the back of the sawmill. The kiln in which the wood had at one time been dried, had burned down, "nearly taking duh 'ole mill wit' it," Henri had told Joseph.

Joseph found the manager's office. "To what do I owe this pleasure?" Raven Mullens asked, shaking his hand.

Figuring Raven wouldn't be interested in idle chat, Joseph got straight to the point. "Wondering if you got any work?" he asked, clutching his hat tightly. "I worked as a log driver and in a sawmill on the French River back home. I work hard. I work fast."

Raven grimaced. "I don't have anything right now," he said ruefully. The principals of the sawmill—Raven owned less than five percent—had already stretched their resources to the utmost. Before the worsening of the economy, the plant had run six days a week, sixteen hours a day. As crops failed and industry suffered, money had become tight. The sawmill had cut back to twelve-hour and then eight-hour days. Before long, it was being shut for days at a time. It now ran, on average, only four days a week. The thirty men still employed there worked in shifts.

"Sorry to take up your time," Joseph said.

Raven felt bad. He had never gotten used to turning down the men who came looking—begging—for work. He understood that Joseph was desperate; there was the expression in his eyes, the set of the jaw, the angle of the chin, the flexed muscles in the cheeks. Like so many other men, all Joseph wanted was to work, to earn enough money to feed his family and to put a roof over their heads, to be able to afford the essentials and maybe, just maybe, to enjoy a day without having to worry about the immediate future.

"Joseph ..." Raven said unhappily, "the truth is, there isn't enough work here to warrant hiring another man. Mind you, I heard of an outfit in town needing a plumber. Have any plumbing experience?"

"No."

"How about fixing radios?"

Joseph shook his head. He had once sold radio tubes, but couldn't claim to know much about their actual function.

I cannot hire another man, Raven told himself.

"Anyway, appreciate your time." Joseph stepped toward the door.

"Wait," Raven said, surprising himself. *What am I doing?* "I can give you ... two days a week. Come back Thursday."

Joseph wondered if he'd mis-heard. Turning, he asked, "Thursday?"

"I can't give you more than that, times being what they are ..." Raven's words trailed away.

Two days of work every week! In seconds Joseph was back at Raven's desk, shaking his hand vigorously. "Thank you. Thank you."

He was elated as he walked away, thrilled at the thought of a paying job. He began to think of other ways to increase his income. He could go on sharpening knives. If Henri would lend him his mower, he could cut grass and make another 60 or 70 cents a week. With all the dust around, he could buy a 50-cent chamois and clean windows. Come fall, he could put up storm windows. In the winter, he could shovel snow for the rich folks in town.

He was on his way back to Philibuster, whistling *Pack Up Your Troubles,* when he saw Tom Wah—Tai Wah was his Chinese name—some way ahead. The man was alone. He was walking, as he always did, with his head down as if he were ashamed of himself. They were shy folks, Tom, his wife Betty, and their two little boys who were close to Sarah's age. Although Joseph had used their washing services only once, he often ran into the Wahs in the hallway or outside the rooming house. Betty's only English words were "wash-ee" and "dry-ee." On returning Joseph's bed linen, she had used her fingers to indicate the amount he owed her.

Joseph had tried to talk to Tom a few times, but the man was so timid that after a brief greeting he always found an excuse to cut short the exchange. Joseph understood why Tom avoided him; he probably took Joseph to be as prejudiced against the Chinese as so many other white Canadians were.

Joseph's beliefs were different. After the time he'd spent as a boy, working and living among the Italian immigrants in Hamilton and listening as they reminisced about their homes, he understood how difficult it was for anyone not of British descent to make his way in Canada. For this reason, he quickened his pace to catch up with Tom. He wanted to get to know Tom better.

As Joseph hurried along, he passed groups of men outside businesses and on street corners. With so little work available, there were always people passing the time in idle chatter about sports, the weather and politics. Joseph had almost caught up with Tom when he was shocked to see someone spit in the Chinese man's path, reminding him of the men in Hamilton who had abused his former co-workers. He tried to tell himself that what looked like an insult might have been an accident. But when it happened again, he knew it was intentional.

Obviously unwilling to show anger lest he invite further trouble, Tom walked faster, although not so fast as to tempt his tormentors to give chase.

Shouted insults began.

"Hurry, Chinky, Chinky."

"Go clean-ee clothes and cook-ee food."

"Walk-ee fast-ee, Ching Chong."

Joseph longed to tell the men to shut up, but there were so many of them—fifty or more, laughing and jeering. A third man spat in Tom's path, and then a fourth. They were getting closer to him, as if playing a game of some sort. Finally a bearded man spat directly at Tom, hitting him in the face with a gob of tobacco juice. "Go clean that," he yelled, and then laughed.

Keeping his eyes averted from the ruffians, Tom did not break his stride or stop to wipe the spittle from his cheek. He just kept on walking.

Without pausing to think, Joseph sprinted forward. "Leave him alone!" he shouted.

The men turned as one. The bearded man looked astonished, as if he took it for granted that all white men would naturally unite against the Chinese. "What's it to you, fella?" he demanded.

As a boy, Joseph had often imagined the things he might have said to the insolent men in Hamilton. Now, in his anger and disgust, he forgot the words he had rehearsed. "How about I spit on *you*?" he burst out, instead.

"You a Chink lover?" the bearded man asked menacingly, stepping toward Joseph. His eyes were narrow slits.

"What of it?" Joseph responded robustly.

"Don't know who your people are?"

"Not ignorant fools like you, that's for damn sure!"

"I'll mop the ground with you!" the bearded man exclaimed, giving Joseph a hard shove.

Joseph staggered backward. Evidently the other man needed to vent his frustrations and was itching for a scrap. Joseph hadn't expected the confrontation to develop into a fight, nor was he prepared for one. He hadn't so much as thrown a punch since he was a teenager.

"I'm waiting for you," the bearded man said.

Joseph's heart was beating fast as a circle of men formed around him.

"Come on, you cowardly bastard!" The bearded man shoved him again, almost knocking him off his feet.

Adrenaline surged through Joseph. Pumped with fury, he returned the shove and prepared to punch the man in the face. Joseph hesitated. This wasn't a schoolyard, he told himself. He could be thrown in jail if he was seen fighting. He had a job to go to and the children to look after. He couldn't risk it.

The bearded man taunted, "Traitor."

Joseph stared at him, holding his ground.

The man stared back, but retreated a step. Slowly the circle of men loosened, then broke up. Joseph waited until the last of them had gone, before forcing his legs to move. With the adrenaline ebbing, he began to shake.

He looked around for Tom. But Tom was nowhere in sight. Instead, Joseph saw Beth Hoogaboom watching him from her store window. Her expression was enigmatic, giving no hint of her thoughts. Joseph pretended he hadn't seen her as he turned and walked back home on unsteady legs.

CHAPTER 10

"Put away duh horses—I am 'ere to work!" The Great Henri announced dramatically, as he and Joseph joined the men behind the Great West Sawmill waiting for the workday to begin. Henri waded exuberantly into the group, slapping backs and introducing his brother. The men were friendly, yet at the same time oddly reserved, as if, Joseph thought, he represented a threat of some sort. He recognized their attitude as one he'd experienced himself in the past when a new employee had been taken on, a natural fear that someone else might be able to work faster or for less money than he could. *You will not rob me of my livelihood,* the men's demeanour implied.

Work was already underway before the seven o'clock whistle blew, the air filled with the scream of fast-moving blades. There was no conversation amongst the men, only the latent competition as to who could work the hardest. Joseph was soon sweating profusely and breathing in gasps. He began to cough, and brought up something sticky which he spat on the ground. There was no time to stop and catch his breath. Cat and Copper, the men he was working with, were fairly new at the mill too, and just as anxious as Joseph was to prove themselves valuable employees.

As his breathing grew increasingly painful and uncomfortable, Joseph struggled to get through the morning. A whistle blew at noon and the whining noise of the saws ceased. The men gathered behind the mill and relaxed on the processed lumber. Most of the men pulled out packed lunches of bread, cheese and wrinkled apples left over from the previous year's harvest. A few, like Joseph, had not brought lunch with them. Money was tight for many, and if a man missed a meal his children would have more to eat that day.

Joseph sat at the edge of the group, coughing into his handkerchief and listening to the good-natured banter around him.

"Listening to the fight tonight?"

"Yep. Yep. Wouldn't miss it."

"Who's your money on?"

"Carnera."

"He's some monster. Six foot six, 284 pounds. Anyone know anything about Sharkey?"

"Six foot, 193 pounds."

"Going to listen at Hoogaboom's."

"Me too."

Though Joseph had not been back to Hoogaboom's since the

day of the Black Blizzard, he had learned more about its owner since then. Beth Hoogaboom did whatever was necessary to keep her store going. She kept extended hours. She'd agree to open a man's favourite brand of cigarettes and sell him just one for a penny. She also exchanged canned goods for the eggs and vegetables the farmers brought in.

But Hoogaboom's biggest attraction was the compact Philco radio Beth kept at the back of her store. Many of her customers couldn't afford their own radios, and she would play whatever they requested. For the ladies, the choice might be *Women's Magazine of the Air,* or one of the radio dramas people called soap operas because the sponsors were often soap companies. Beth's male customers liked *Men of Adventure* or a baseball game. For big events, like a prize fight or the Stanley Cup playoffs, Beth would put the radio on the liar's bench outside the store so that more people could enjoy the broadcast. As for the few who had their own radios, some would come to Hoogaboom's for the chance to socialize.

"I'm listening at home."

"Wife won't let you out?"

"Worried the widow'll get her hooks into you?"

"Nah, not my kind of woman, Beth Hoogaboom. Not right, a woman wearing trousers."

"Good-looking woman, though."

"Like licking honey from a thorn, I'd say."

"She's a wild one. I don't like a dame that swears and smokes."

"Way I hear it, she's a drinker and carouser."

"I'd rather shack up with old Millie from the café. She doesn't have sharp edges."

As some of the men hooted and whistled in agreement, Joseph realized how much he had missed the camaraderie of other men, the fun of being among them, joking after work, or talking about unimportant things like boxing matches and baseball scores.

He bent over, racked by a sudden fit of coughing. A few men turned and looked at him and he stepped behind a stack of lumber.

When the cough subsided and his breathing eased, he rejoined the others. When someone slapped him suddenly on the back, he turned to see Henri, holding a lard bucket. Henri had only just arrived on the scene; as the saw-filer, he had to wait until the blades were idle before he could inspect them.

"Finished lunch?" Henri asked. And when Joseph nodded, "Coming to 'oogaboom's to listen to duh fight tonight? We can 'ave a beer after."

Joseph wondered if Henri was stupid or just crazy. His brother knew only too well how much his wife disliked Beth. In the week that had passed since the Black Blizzard, Tilda—still angry that he and the boys had sheltered at Hoogaboom's—had barely spoken to Joseph.

Joseph shook his head. "Can't make it," he said hoarsely. "I need to be with the kids."

The whistle blew just then and Joseph returned to work. Before long his coughing was bad again. His breathing grew laboured and his chest hurt. Without warning, the edges of his vision darkened and his legs turned to rubber. Next thing he knew he was on the floor of Raven Mullens's office, his brother peering down at him with a look of concern.

CHAPTER 11

"Dropped like he'd been shot," Copper said a bit later on, running his hand over his mop of red hair.

Joseph, Copper and Cat had been loading lumber onto the back of a truck when Joseph had suddenly collapsed, bringing two hundred pounds of lumber down on his leg and hurting himself. Joseph had refused medical attention, but rested a few minutes before returning to work. Not long afterward he passed out again. This time Raven, alarmed at how bad Joseph looked, insisted he go home.

At the rooming house that afternoon, Joseph was unable to rest. His leg throbbed with intense pain and his chest shook every time he coughed. Above all, his mind was in a turmoil of worry. He wondered when he would be well enough to work again. If, for some reason, he could not return to work by next week, how would he be able to make up for lost wages and feed the children?

To take his mind off his situation, he leafed through his dictionary. Coming to the word "bleak," he leaned back in his chair, closed his eyes and thought about the definition he'd just read: "barren; austere; lacking in warmth." "Bleak" was an apt word to describe his own life at present.

As his breathing slowed and his coughing eased, he listened to voices filtering through the thin walls of the rooming house. Mostly, he heard shouting.

Across the hall lived the Johnstons, Dick and Christina. Dick drove a taxi and had a contract with the municipality. As city council was unwilling to purchase a car for the police department, they employed Dick as a chauffeur. For some reason, Dick and his wife were arguing over the cost of dental cream.

Directly below Joseph lived a single mother—Ann? Annie?—whose three teenage boys were often in trouble. She'd yell at them until she was hoarse. Invariably she would break down and sob, and ask her sons why they didn't love her. The boys would be contrite and promise not to be a nuisance. For a while peace would ensue, but never for long.

The McIvors, an old couple who rarely left their room, lived beside the Johnstons. At least twice a day, Mr. McIvor would shout "Goddammit" loudly enough to be heard down the block. Joseph never knew why the old man was so angry.

The Wahs lived next door to Joseph. They spoke Chinese, of course, but so softly that Joseph heard them only rarely. Even the two little boys seldom raised their voices.

After a while the voices in the house quietened and Joseph's thoughts turned to some of the choices he had made during his lifetime. He wondered what he could have done differently. What if he'd not left school at the age of eleven? What if he'd continued his education and become an architect or a teacher? What if he had not purchased the dairy farm? So many "what ifs." But different choices, Joseph realized, would have resulted in different outcomes. Imagine if he had not married Helen! He missed his wife terribly, and could not picture life without his beloved children.

Although Joseph had returned to his job at the steel mill after the Great War, he knew he didn't want to work there all his life. And so was born his dream of owning a farm, a dream that had no chance of being realized unless he was able to come up with a great deal of money. To do that on his meagre pay, he'd had to economize and make changes, one of which was to find an alternative to the expensive company housing in which he was living. In 1920 he found a room at the home of Mrs. Emily Thompson, a middle-aged woman whose husband had died of the Spanish Flu in 1918. She rented out two rooms on the upper floor of her house to help pay for food. Of her six children, the only one still at home was her youngest daughter, Helen.

Joseph noticed Helen immediately, but the long hours he worked gave him little time to get to know her. The steel mills had a brutal work schedule, alternating seven consecutive days of eleven-hour shifts with "long turns" of twenty-four hours, followed by a week of thirteen-hour night shifts. The only break from the schedule occurred when another team worked the long turn. He returned to his room at the end of every working day, hungry, dirty and very tired. After breakfast or dinner, depending on which shift he'd worked, he slept. Only on his one day off every two weeks did he sit down to lunch with Helen, her mother and whoever else was boarding with them.

Helen was a member of the new generation of women who enjoyed a measure of freedom and independence that women hadn't experienced until then. With so many men away fighting in Europe, the women they left behind had, of necessity, took on the men's jobs. They evolved from being homemakers to being wage earners. For the first time ever, they had their own incomes, could afford to explore the country beyond the confines of their own towns and cities, and were able to develop interests outside their homes. By the time the war ended, women had become accustomed to the working world and the freedom associated with it. Although they were no longer needed to build munitions or other war materiel, women found other available work. Often the daily newspapers advertised more jobs for women than for men. There was demand for office girls, typists, factory-floor scrubbers, housekeepers and more. Some women were even becoming doctors and, having recently gained the right to vote, were running for elected positions as well.

To her mother's embarrassment, Helen attended lunches where she boldly voiced her opinions. During the Victorian era, women's fashions had been modest; they had worn skirts and dresses down to the ground and had grown their hair long. During the war hemlines had began to rise, eventually ending above the knee. Women cut their hair in the new bobbed style. Helen, who worked at a factory that manufactured dresses, often spoke scornfully of the people who criticized the new styles and demanded that fashion return to normal. "Fuddy-duddies," she called them. She laughed at newspaper articles that complained about young girls who "didn't wear enough underclothes to cover themselves decently."

Joseph looked forward to these all-too-rare lunches. He enjoyed hearing Helen's opinions on different topics. Her zest for life imbued him with some of the exuberance he'd lost during the war. He often wondered what marriage to a vivacious girl like Helen would be like. Joseph had never been confident around women, and didn't dream he stood a chance with such a lovely girl. He was amazed, therefore, when Helen suggested a picnic on one of his Sundays off. Joseph naturally assumed Helen's mother and the other boarder would be joining them. As it was, the two young people spent a glorious Sunday afternoon without a chaperone, and Joseph listened spellbound to Helen's dreams, which were so similar to his own. By the time they walked home later, holding hands, Joseph knew they would marry.

Yet although Joseph had married the woman he loved, he'd never felt quite worthy of her—not because he thought himself lacking, but because he believed Helen had been affected by the circumstances of the times. So few men had returned from the war. Of Joseph's childhood friends who had fought, none had survived. Many of those who did return were changed forever; they'd come back seriously impaired, without limbs, or with lungs badly damaged by mustard gas or faces destroyed by gunfire. Apart from Joseph himself, he knew of only one man—an acquaintance he'd worked with at the steel mill—who had made it back in decent physical shape. Soon after his own return, Joseph had gone to visit him, hoping that together they could make some sense of the horrors they had experienced and why they had been spared when so many other good men had not.

The man's wife had invited him in. She told Joseph her husband was having an "episode," and that seeing an old buddy might help him get over it. Joseph had sat with him in the living room, asked a few questions and tried to start a conversation, but his acquaintance gave no indication that he was aware of Joseph's presence in the room. He didn't move, seldom even blinked. His wife brought in tea, poured it, positioned her husband's fingers around the cup handle, and left the room. Joseph spent an hour in uncomfortable silence. When he excused himself and said goodbye, the man's wife apologized for her husband's troubled state of mind. He brooded all the time and seldom spoke, she said sadly. She hoped Joseph would come again.

But Joseph didn't have the heart to visit his old acquaintance again. Nor did he speak to anyone else about the horrors of war, not even to Helen.

Now he sat by the window with the dictionary on his lap, thinking about Helen and idly twisting the gold wedding band on his finger. Suddenly another coughing fit gripped him. His body shook. As he covered his mouth with his handkerchief, the dictionary fell and landed face down on the floor. When the coughing had passed, Joseph saw that he had brought up more muddy phlegm. Wheezing, he poured himself a glass of water and drank it. A minute later he was coughing again, so violently that he retched.

For the first time it occurred to him that he might have dirt pneumonia.

CHAPTER 12

Joseph suffered for days with an uncontrollable cough. His chest hurt, his sides ached and his throat was raw. He continued to cough up muddy phlegm and for a while he worried he would never be well again. Yet as time passed, he was relieved when what he brought up became paler and his breathing felt easier.

As his health improved, Joseph wondered whether he still had the job with the mill. True, Raven had promised he would hold the position for him, but everyone knew that in these bad times jobs were often terminated. To his enormous relief, Joseph returned to the sawmill to find that Raven had kept his word. Gratefully, he assured Raven he would work harder and faster than anyone else.

Although Joseph had a steady pay cheque and found an odd job here and there to supplement the money he made at the mill, it was barely enough to cover rent and feed the children. With every penny necessary for survival, he thought about shopping at Hoogaboom's, because he remembered Beth's prices as being slightly lower than those at Jackson's Grocery Store. But for now he stuck by his earlier decision to avoid Hoogaboom's, knowing how much Tilda disliked Beth. He needed Tilda's help with the children and had no desire to provoke a confrontation.

Joseph now knew that many things upset Tilda, most of them related to superstition. A few days after the Black Blizzard, Sarah and Clare had come down with summer colds. It took the girls two long weeks to recover. When they did, they came home with red ribbons tied around their wrists. Concerned that Clare might suck on the ribbon and choke, Joseph removed it before putting her to bed. He thought no more about it until the next day when Tilda reproached him for discarding the ribbon. Its purpose, she told him, was to prevent the baby's illness from returning, and Joseph should have left it on for a week.

Every few days Joseph learned of other superstitions that invited evil spirits or incurred bad luck: keeping a hat on a bed, entering a house through one door and exiting through another, leaving shoes upside down, pouring more water into a tumbler that already had water in it. Worst of all was allowing a white moth into the house; to do so meant death.

Tilda often reprimanded her husband, who tended to ignore the beliefs she held dear and was forever "bringing bad luck into the house." Henri apologized to Tilda every time, smiling as if she'd just told him she loved him. Joseph failed to understand how his brother could tolerate the frequent scoldings. He appreciated that Tilda's petite good looks might have appealed to Henri when he first met her, but he couldn't understand how such a cheerful man was able to remain with a woman who was so often as sour as a lemon. He could only guess that Tilda filled some deep-seated need of her husband's.

Henri had been very young when his mother had died. Although his father hadn't been the tyrant with Henri that he'd been with Joseph, he wasn't much of a parent, either. If anything, the man had treated Henri with indifference. In a sense, the boy had welcomed his father's detachment because it had left him free to explore his own world without fear of consequences, thus allowing a confident boy to discover his strengths and weaknesses without interference. At the same time, his father's attitude had deprived

Henri of the nurturing he needed. For this reason, perhaps, he had been attracted to motherly women. Tilda was perfect for his needs. Ten years older than her husband, she kept an orderly home and enjoyed caring for others. Believing that Tilda thought only of his best interests, Henri accepted her admonishments as a form of love.

Although Joseph kept away from Hoogaboom's, he didn't ban his sons from going there. Like the unemployed men who congregated around the corner grocery store to talk and listen to news, Nolan and Cole and their friends also whiled away much of the summer hanging about there. If they sold something to the scrap man—a strand of copper wire or a metal pipe—they spent the money at Hoogaboom's. Every penny found on the street went into Hoogaboom's till. Gopher tails went to Hoogaboom's too, for the boys all knew Beth was more generous than the other merchants. She put the tails in an old Amphora Brown tobacco tin below the cash register, punched NO SALE on the till, and scooped out the hard-won cash, which the boys promptly spent on orange pop or chocolate bars.

Joseph was glad his children had friends, were having fun, and had the chance to grow up normally—things he himself had been denied. He wondered now and then how Tilda would react if she learned where the boys were spending so much of their time, but he wasn't overly concerned. For one thing, Nolan, being a bright boy, had quickly grasped the wisdom of avoiding the topic of Hoogaboom's with his aunt and had convinced his younger brother to do likewise. For another, Tilda was unlikely to take out her anger on the boys, even if she did learn the truth. Harsh though she could be with adults, she seemed to love children— Joseph's in particular.

So the boys went about their business unhindered. Catching gophers became their most important concern. Despite his plan to bag 20 gopher tails a day, Nolan only managed to catch 14 during June and July. He and Cole spent long afternoons together with the other boys, watching gopher holes, placing wire nooses over the entrances, and waiting for gophers to peep out. If they happened to select a seldom-used entrance, an afternoon of patiently biding their time might yield nothing. One of the boys, Nathan McCormick, achieved more success than the others by pouring water down a hole and flushing out the gophers into the jaws of his eagerly waiting dog, Buck. Hoping to achieve the same success with his uncle's dog, Nolan borrowed Jasper. But the great beast didn't seem to understand what was expected of him, merely running around and barking at the escaping gophers, instead of snagging them.

Disappointed with his summer's catch and shamed by his younger brother's accomplishments—the more patient Cole had managed to catch 16 gophers in the same amount of time—Nolan pondered ways of making more money and recovering some of his lost pride. A shrewd idea came to him when he saw the government man stop in at Hoogaboom's, count the tails Beth had collected, and pay her seven cents for each one. Nolan decided to pay his brother and his friends six cents per tail, sell the tails directly to the government man, and reap a one-cent profit for himself. His plan came to nothing, however, when he learned that over the years others had tried the same idea without success.

Nolan's next idea was less lawful. Why not steal Mrs. Hoogaboom's tobacco tin, with its stock of gopher tails, and sell them to the other municipal agents in town? Since her till was always full, she would not miss the money. First, of course, he had to figure out how to stage his crime. The solution he came up with was to replace the stolen tobacco tin with a similar one. He would put a few gopher tails into the new tin, and Mrs. Hoogaboom would not even realize she'd been swindled. Finding a suitable tobacco tin was not a problem. The Great Henri kept one filled with bolts and nails in his shed.

The more Nolan thought about his plan, the more he liked it. Wasting no time, he pilfered the tobacco tin from his uncle's shed and threw the bolts and nails into a different container. The next step was to fill the substitute tin with gopher tails. That was simple, too: he caught two gophers himself, and borrowed two tails from Cole and five from his friends, promising to pay them all back before school started.

Switching tins was a more difficult procedure, as it entailed creating a distraction so he could act unobserved. It took him a while to come up with the perfect distraction: *The Shadow*, the radio program that was so popular with Hoogaboom's customers.

On the day he proposed to commit felony, Nolan arrived at the grocery store 20 minutes before the program was due to begin, with the replica tin hidden inside his jacket. Half a dozen adults talked and shopped and listened to the radio, but none of Nolan's pals were around yet. Now that the moment had come he was nervous, his breathing jerky and his hands clammy with perspiration. Not wanting his presence to seem suspicious in any way, he decided to wait behind the store until the time was right.

After what seemed like hours, Nolan heard *The Shadow*'s familiar theme music. He re-entered the store just as the Shadow said, "*Who knows what evil lurks in the hearts of men?*" A menacing laugh followed. Then came the words: "*The Shadow knows.*"

As Nolan moved toward the cash register and the tin of gopher tails stored beneath it, an advertiser came on air to extol the benefits of Fleischmann's fresh yeast and its ability to help a person who was tired and run-down.

The commercial over, the theme music swelled then softened, and the narrator spoke. "*The Shadow, Lamont Cranston, a man of wealth, a student of science and a master of other people's minds, devotes his life to righting wrongs, protecting the innocent and punishing the guilty. Cranston is known to the underworld as* The Shadow. *Never seen, only heard. As haunting to superstitious minds as a ghost. As inevitable as a guilty conscience. The identity of The Shadow is only known to his intimate friend and aide, Margo Lane. Today's story:* The Blind Beggar Dies.*"

The store became hushed. With the exception of Mrs. Hoogaboom and Patricia, everyone stared at the radio.

Singing Jim began: "*There are smiles that make us happy, there are smiles …*"

Then, dialogue: "*Evening, Singing Jim, chilly night tonight isn't it?*"

The sound of a coin dropping into a pail.

"*Indeed it is. Thank you, sir.*"

Singing Jim continued: "*There are smiles that make us happy, there are smiles …*"

The audience in the store listened, enthralled, as a tough guy started to threaten Singing Jim. Things did not bode well for poor Jim as he was dragged into an alley and beaten up.

Nolan, anxious to get the deed done as quickly as possible, reached too hastily for the tobacco tin and knocked a display of chewing gum to the floor. Instinctively, he pulled back his arm— just in time, too, for Mrs. Hoogaboom spun around, startled by the sound.

"Nolan?" she asked.

The boy stopped breathing for a moment. Had he been caught?

"Aren't you hot in that?" She was staring at his jacket.

"No …" he muttered.

Beth frowned as though she sensed something odd, but didn't quite know what it was.

During the next commercial several people took the opportunity to make purchases.

"*That fagged-out feeling, your doctor will tell you, is usually a sign that you're not absorbing the full amount of nutrition from your food. Fleischman's fresh yeast stimulates the digestive organs to new activity …*"

When the story resumed, Beth remained in front of the register, giving Nolan no chance to switch the tins. He was beginning to despair when a customer entered the store and demanded Beth's attention.

Here was Nolan's chance. Moving rapidly, he opened his jacket, pulled out his tin and switched the containers. Frightened that he might have been seen, he pushed his way through the crowd toward the door. As he ran down the street, an evil voice seemed to follow him: "*The weed of crime bears bitter fruit. Crime does not pay. The Shadow knows.*"

It wasn't until the next day, when the government man arrived for Beth's gopher tails, that she realized she'd been swindled. She was short by about 120 tails. And she thought she knew who had taken them.

CHAPTER 13

"Kee-rist, you should smell it!" Cat exclaimed.

It was the lunch break on a hot September day. The mill workers relaxed on piles of newly cut of lumber. Those who were fortunate enough to have food ate their sandwiches. The rest drank water.

"And the blowflies! Big as your fist." Cat held up a clenched hand. "She put enough manure on her back garden for ten acres. Been sitting there baking in this heat for two weeks!"

The men—Joseph and The Great Henri among them—roared with laughter. Cat's neighbour was Daisy Nye. Most people knew her as Dizzy Daisy. Born in Philibuster more than 60 years earlier, it was said that Addison Philibuster himself had tried to court her when she was a girl of seventeen. Folks who had known her then described her as being pleasant, kind and a little naïve, pretty but not beautiful. Then, one day, Daisy was gone. According to her parents, she had gone to live with relatives out east, a tale that usually meant a girl had "gotten herself" into trouble.

Daisy's friends insisted she had fallen in love with a man her parents didn't approve of, and had run away to get married. They claimed he was a high-stepper from Toronto or Montreal. Twelve years later Daisy had returned with a son in tow—none other than Philibuster's future mayor, Winfield Westmoreland. When asked his age, the boy would say he was nine. "Nine my foot! Eleven, more likely," people whispered. It wasn't his size that created the gossip. He hadn't been exceptionally big. But folks who'd been around town when Daisy left had done their own math.

In some ways Daisy hadn't changed in the intervening years. She was still caring and friendly, and it wasn't long before a local fellow courted her. Edward Nye, a widower, owned a small but profitable dairy farm. Having met Daisy while delivering milk, he had fallen for the cheerful woman.

They had been married for nearly 20 happy years when Edward Nye passed on. Not long after that Daisy began to get into some harmless mischief. Whether she was becoming fey or had always been that way was a matter of opinion. Winfield Westmoreland— he had kept his father's name, if a legitimate father had indeed existed—had tried to keep his mother out of trouble, a difficult feat when he had a family to support, businesses to care for and a city to run.

Most of the town took Mrs. Nye's oddness in their stride. "You know Dizzy Daisy," they'd say indulgently. "Still living in that house Edward bought her, the big old place on Deer Street, the one Addison Philibuster built. Well, you'll never believe what she's done now!" People would laugh at the most recent story, but her neighbours seldom found Daisy's eccentricities amusing.

"What am I supposed to do?" Cat was genuinely distressed. "If I complain about the smell, the mayor might set the police chief on me!"

Cat grinned resignedly as his audience laughed again. Several others shared stories about Dizzy Daisy. No one noticed Raven standing quietly to one side, waiting for the mirth to die down. Eventually he cleared his throat and the laughter quietened.

"I don't know how else to put this, so I'll just come out and say it." Raven looked uncharacteristically grim. "The mill will be running only two days a week from now on. No one will be fired and hourly wages won't be reduced, but everyone's hours will be cut in half. I'm very sorry." He did not wait for questions, but walked back to his office and shut the door.

The yard was hushed. Nobody spoke. In the silence that followed Raven's announcement, all heads were bowed as the men thought about the consequences. One day a week at two-fifty a day? Not enough to cover rent and electricity, let alone food. How will we manage? The kids can go barefoot in the summer, but what will they do in the winter? What if someone gets sick? The crinkle of wax paper was the only sound in that awful silence. Several men rewrapped their unfinished sandwiches, which would now become dinner that night. Others went on eating, figuring on making lunch their only meal of the day.

Later that evening many voiced their anger. "Been here since before Raven took over the mill," some yelled at their wives. "He should keep on those of us that's been around longest!" Others protested to friends that since they worked harder than the rest, they should get more hours. In the end, most were grateful for the little work they still had. Any fool could see the dire situation as stacks of lumber mounted behind the mill without industries to purchase them.

"Did you hear about Matt Ludlow? He shot himself in his kitchen. His wife found him. He hadn't worked in two years."

"Might have closed the mill completely."

"Raven's a good man. Kept the mill running when anyone else would have shut it down."

Over dinner that evening, Henri told Tilda about the reduced hours. As the most skilled man at the mill—it was his job to see that the saws were always in good repair—he would still be working three days per week. There was also the money he received for cutting hair. In his usual glib manner, he assured his wife they would be fine.

"And Joseph?" Tilda asked.

Henri was still of the opinion that Joseph could cope with anything. Look how well he was raising four children by himself. "Joseph will be fine too," he said reassuringly.

But Tilda was worried, nonetheless. Henri did not see the things she saw. He often seemed blind to other people's struggles. "Innocent" and "unworldly" were the words that came to her mind. Tilda knew that Joseph's children had enough to eat only because he deprived himself. And apart from food, they had little else. She had done her best to keep the children's clothing in reasonable condition, but what they owned would not last much longer. The boys' pants were patched from the cuffs to the waist; Sarah's dresses, already too small for her, were so threadbare that her underwear showed through. With a reduction in Joseph's working hours they would have even less. Worst of all, if Joseph was unable to feed his family he might be forced to move away from Philibuster, and he would take the children with him.

Tilda felt ill at the thought of losing the children, especially Sarah and Clare. Ever since she could remember, she had wanted children of her own. Even as a little girl, she had seen herself as a wife and mother. She had pictured herself having five children and had hoped at least one of them would be a girl. In her frequent daydreams, she saw herself caring for them, feeding and teaching them. Tilda felt very strongly that she had been put on this planet to be a mother.

During the years of her first marriage, Tilda had been aware that people discussed her inability to get pregnant. "Barren," was the word they most often used. Though they talked in whispers, she knew what they said. The word "barren" made her feel less of a woman—hurt and even ashamed.

Tilda was often angry. She took to avoiding births and christenings. She felt bitter when she saw baby clothes in stores or pregnant women on the street. It was years before she could even bring herself to be in the same room as an infant. In time the anger diminished and was replaced by sadness, but she never got over her distress at the word "barren."

Tilda vividly recalled the day Henri told her his recently widowed brother was moving to Philibuster with his young family. The news brought back her yearning to be a mother. Determined to derive some happiness from the new situation, she had offered to look after the children while Joseph was at work. The thought that she might lose them now, after she'd become so attached to them, was unbearable.

"Will Joseph leave Philibuster if he cannot find other work?" she asked anxiously.

"I cannot see it. No, I cannot," Henri answered between mouthfuls of stew.

Tilda needed reassurance. Her husband had told her what she'd wanted to hear, but she wasn't satisfied. Joseph would leave Philibuster if he found something better elsewhere; she would expect no less of him. Seemingly out of nowhere came the memory of the first time Clare had slept in her arms, and of the guilty thought that had appeared that first day, but which she'd managed to suppress since then. Now she allowed it free reign.

What would Joseph say if some of his children wanted to remain in Philibuster? Would he agree to leave them with her? Surely, Tilda reasoned, Joseph would understand the benefits of allowing her to ease his burden. What if she were to raise Sarah and Clare, while he kept Nolan and Cole with him? Joseph was killing himself trying to feed and clothe all four kids. She would be doing him a favour if she took two of them. Besides, what did a man know about caring for little girls?

For Tilda there would be benefits too. If she were to nurture Sarah and Clare, raising them to become paragons of virtue and intelligence, the awful whispers would finally end. To all intents and purposes, she would no longer be less of a woman than if she had given birth herself.

"God helps those who help themselves," Tilda said, quietly.

Henri was mystified. "*Pardon?*"

"Nothing dear." Tilda smiled at her husband as a plan began to take shape in her mind.

CHAPTER 14

Police Chief Montgomery Quentin left his office at the courthouse and turned south along Main Street. As he made his way with the heavy tread of authority, he felt the boards of the sidewalk bend with each step. Men moved aside and doffed their caps when he passed. He acknowledged everyone, whether a stranger or a long-time acquaintance, with a grim nod.

Monty loved being a police officer. He felt born to the role. He savoured not knowing what the day held in store for him, believing uncertainty was part of what kept his mind nimble and alert. He loved the challenge of interviewing suspected criminals and catching them in lies and half-truths, enjoyed the discipline needed to give and follow orders, and took delight in knowing he had an honourable job. Besides, in what other job would he get paid to carry a gun?

Initially, Monty had joined the force as a way of getting respect. His father, Norman—long since dead of liver failure—had been a drunkard who tended to do stupid things when intoxicated. When an idea entered his head, he persevered until he was either done with it or had passed out. More than once he'd decided to go hunting in the middle of the night. One evening he climbed over a neighbour's fence while drunk, stumbled, and accidentally shot off the big toe of his right foot. In the course of another drunken hunting escapade, he spent hours tracking and killing what he thought was a bison. When an angry neighbour kicked him awake the next morning, he discovered he'd been tracking the man's cow and had emptied a whole box of shotgun shells into the slow-moving animal. The unfortunate cow's sides had resembled ground beef.

In the middle of summer, when everything was dry, Norman once started a bonfire on a whim. When the fire was blazing he passed out, as he so often did when he'd had too much to drink. A light wind had carried burning embers into the surrounding dry grass. The fire reached the Quentins' little shack and burned it to the ground. Monty survived because the need to urinate happened to rouse him. Norman survived because he had passed out upwind from the fire.

In addition to his love of drink, Monty's father was also very lazy. Rather than work, he found it easier to feed himself by raiding a garden or stealing a chicken. Amazingly, he was smart enough not to get caught.

Philibuster was still a small town then. People knew one another, and the stories about Norman got around. Monty was only seven when the kids at school started to poke fun at him. Repeating what they had heard their parents saying at home, they would ask him when last his old man had killed any wild cows or shot off any body parts. Monty learned to stand up to his tormentors on the playground, often with words, sometimes with his fists. As he grew older and noticed the disrespect with which the other men treated his father, he began to resent his dad.

Monty didn't want to grow up to be like his father. By the time he was 18 he had a great personal need for respect, and realized that one way of attaining it would be to join the police force. But he quickly learned that the respect he craved was not an automatic adjunct of the job. People had to fear you, he decided, before they would respect you. For that to happen, you needed to throw your weight around. Once Monty learned this valuable lesson, he soon found what he coveted.

Not that the job was perfect. It bothered Monty that people tended to think of cops as lazy or apathetic because they didn't handle incidents the way the public deemed appropriate. A small town police officer was expected to perform a variety of duties. He enforced liquor laws, acted as game warden, and, when necessary, even helped out the fire department.

Other things troubled him too: seeing a man's brains splattered over his bedroom walls because of his inability to feed his family, or pulling the body of a drowned seven-year-old from the river. Yet, all things considered, he still preferred a police career to working on a farm or being confined to an office or a grocery store.

As Monty made his way through the ranks, he observed things that needed improving, in particular, the slipshod manner with which most officers treated the law. Monty had come to believe that laws were made for the general good. As a boy, his teachers had considered him a serious child who did as he was told. When Westmoreland promoted him to Chief of Police, Monty implemented strict rules, which he expected his officers to enforce. By and large, they carried out his wishes because he was a good leader. He worked longer hours than anyone else, and continued to walk the beat, although, as police chief, he could rightly have claimed he had many more pressing duties to attend to. Above all, he abided by the laws he had sworn to protect.

In fact, Monty had broken the law only twice in his life. The first time was at the age of ten, when he had helped his father to steal their sixteen-year-old neighbour's diamond-spotted calf. Monty vividly recalled the beating his father had received the following day at the hands of the calf's enraged owner. Monty had been out hunting in the woods that morning. On his return, he found the teenaged neighbour yelling at his dad for being a thief and thrashing him with an axe handle. Fearing he would be next, Monty fled back into the trees. He spent several days alone in the woods without shelter, with only berries and roots for food. Emerging at length, he was astonished to learn that his father had survived the beating and that he and the neighbour had reached an understanding. Monty never forgot the importance of being on the right side of authority—and he never forgave the neighbour for thrashing his father.

The second time Monty broke the law was far more serious, because by then he knew better. Chief of Police Emerson was retiring and city council was interviewing possible replacements. Winfield Westmoreland, already a member of city council, approached Monty, aware of his ambition to become Chief of Police. Westmoreland slyly intimated he would put in a good word for Monty in return for a few favours. How did Monty feel about Raven Mullens? Westmoreland asked. Monty candidly admitted that he despised Raven, the city's chief engineer at the time, but didn't elaborate. That was a good enough answer for Westmoreland, who didn't care about the reason. He simply gave Monty an assignment: amend a few documents, after which his name would head the list of candidates for the chief of police position.

Before long, based on the documents Monty Quentin had falsified, Raven Mullens was charged with embezzling city funds. Mullens was fired even though he was innocent of any wrongdoing. The public never learned the truth, because Westmoreland made certain the case never went to court. Raven never learned about Monty's part in the fraud. Some time after that Monty discovered that funds were, indeed, missing—but Raven Mullens was not the thief.

Monty soon realized that he did not have as much power as he'd imagined. True, the men below him obeyed his commands and the citizens of Philibuster feared him. Indeed, his old school mates often commented that authority had gone to his head. But he was at the mercy of city council, and could be fired at a moment's notice if they disapproved of his work. Thankfully, the council members—all but Winfield Westmoreland—approved of him and gave him free rein to manage his department.

As mayor, Westmoreland wasn't overly demanding, but occasionally he expected the police chief to go beyond his duties. Not that Monty had to break any more laws in order to do Westmoreland's bidding, but he did have to bend them. The one saving grace, as far as he was concerned, was that Westmoreland's indiscretions did not take place in Philibuster, making it easier for him to accept them. He could only hope that Westmoreland would not put him in an impossible position by asking him to ignore something crooked in Philibuster. Honest though Monty was, he was trapped by Westmoreland's power over him, and he could not permit scruples to destroy the success he had worked so hard to achieve. Life could be good for someone in his position, apart from which, he had a large family to support.

Montgomery Quentin walked through a small crowd into Hooper's, a café next door to Hoogaboom's. Music was playing, a song by Guy Lombardo and his Royal Canadians. A large sign over the grill promoted the "Economy Lunch." Spotting the owner, Frank Hooper, in conversation with two of his constables, Monty joined them.

"The two of them just sat right down and ordered a meal," Frank was saying, nodding his head in the direction of a pair of derelict-looking men at a corner table. "Had the meatloaf platter, coffee, pie and ice cream. When Milly asked them for 60 cents, they told her they didn't have the money and she should call the police. Said it like they were proud of it." Frank turned to Monty. "They even asked for a coffee refill," he added indignantly.

Monty believed Frank's story. It was not the first time men down on their luck had provoked the police into arresting them. Jail was not the most pleasant of places, but the inmates were given regular meals there. When the derelict men had freely admitted their guilt, they were handcuffed and led out the door.

Joseph was in the crowd outside the café when the police emerged with their charges. Chief Quentin's eyes scanned the crowd, narrowing as they stopped momentarily on Joseph. Since their unpleasant encounter on the day of Joseph's arrival in Philibuster, Joseph had gone out of his way to avoid Quentin. He had hoped the police chief had forgotten him, and felt uncomfortable when he realized he'd been recognized.

"Thieves!" yelled a man.

"Shame!" called a woman.

"Poor buggers," said a familiar voice at Joseph's side.

Startled, he turned and found Beth Hoogaboom behind him. As usual, she wore a shirt, pants and boots.

"What kind of place do we live in when a man has to get himself arrested just so he can eat?" she observed in disgust. "It's a goddamned shame."

Beth was right, Joseph thought disconsolately, as he watched the two men being led toward the courthouse and its basement jail: hunger could drive a person to do things he was ashamed of. He had been struggling for days to find an answer to his own constant hunger. He had been going without food so that the children could eat, but he knew he would collapse if he went on starving himself. Finally, he had come up with a solution, but it made him feel dirty.

"Anything I can get for you today?" Beth asked.

Joseph had not forgotten Beth's hospitality during the Black Blizzard, but he had kept away from Hoogaboom's and its owner for several months, simply to prevent Tilda's anger.

"I do need a few things," he said quietly, hiding his uneasiness.

They walked into the store, pausing as they heard the radio, and listening in horrified silence.

"... *grievances of the relief camp workers in Ottawa today. In local news, a tragedy has shocked the city of Calgary with the discovery of an aged man and his sister, dead from hunger. Another sister, close to death, lay on a plank bed. Police, who broke into the house after being alerted by neighbours, said the 64-year-old woman managed to explain the presence of $22 found in the bare cupboard: 'We were afraid to spend the money for food. We needed it for the rent.' The* *woman is now in the care of the Service to Other's Club. And* that *is your news of the moment."*

The newscast over, Joseph searched the shelves for the groceries he needed: soup and noodles for the children, an onion for himself.

"Find everything you need?" Beth asked, kindly.

Joseph nodded. Ashamed of the deed he was planning, he avoided eye contact. "Thanks again for sheltering my boys and me from the terrible storm a few months ago. If not for your kindness, we might have died," he said.

"You'd have done the same for me," Beth said warmly. Joseph had impressed her deeply some time back, when he'd stood up against the pig-headed bigots who had been so rude to poor Tom Wah. Beth believed there were only a few truly good men in the world, and Joseph had proved he was one of them.

"I should've been by before to thank you ..."

"That's all right." Beth smiled at him, as if she knew why he had stayed away.

Feeling the need to say something more, Joseph brought up the subject of the gophers. "I guess my boys were pretty successful this summer. Nolan bought a baseball mitt and a ball with the money he made. He must have brought you a lot of tails."

Seeing Nolan's purchases, Joseph had initially suspected him of stealing. Nolan had insisted he'd earned the money by catching gophers, and Cole hadn't contradicted him. Joseph had found it hard to believe his son could have snared so many gophers, but Nolan had abided firmly by his story.

Beth wondered how best to answer Joseph. She was pretty sure Nolan had stolen the gopher tails, but she was reluctant to accuse him without being certain. If the boy had been anyone else, Beth might have approached the parents with her concerns. For some reason, she couldn't do so in this instance. Having learned a little about Joseph's recent past from his brother and Raven, she didn't have the heart to cause him further pain.

Beth debated with herself while a radio commercial blared its message:

Dentists know why Dentyne is such an aid to sounder, more beautiful teeth. Dentyne's special firm consistency induces more vigorous chewing, giving your gums and mouth tissue stimulating exercise and massage ...

"Yes, your boys have been successful," Beth finally agreed.

Joseph drew the wrong conclusions from Beth's hesitation. He thought the boys must have gone elsewhere with their gopher tails. Embarrassed, and not knowing what else to say, he said good day to Beth and left the store, the little bell ringing as he crossed the threshold.

As he walked away, Joseph called himself an imbecile and a buffoon for his failure to carry on a normal conversation with a woman. He might have continued to reproach himself for hours had his thoughts not turned to the shameful task he had set himself.

He returned home to any empty room. Nolan and Cole were at school, Sarah and Clare were with their aunt. It was time to pull out the package he'd hidden behind a block of ice at the back of the cold closet. He unwrapped the meat and stared at it for a full minute. "Other people do this, too," he said aloud, as he made certain he'd locked the door.

He turned on the hot plate and cut up some onions. He placed the onions and some oil in the pan to cook, warming the room and filling the air with a distinctive aroma. Worried that the boys or the neighbours would find out what he was up to, Joseph hoped the onions would mask the smell of cooking meat. After seasoning the meat with salt and pepper, he added it to the onions in the pan. As the meat began to sizzle, he opened the door again and looked cautiously down the hall. *The boys are at school. No one will know,* he thought, as he relocked the door.

Before long, the distinctive aroma of frying meat filled the room. Joseph took a plate from the cupboard and brushed away a thin film of dust. He was surprised that although there had been no black blizzards in over a month, dirt was still settling everywhere. He flipped the meat a few times.

When the meat looked ready, he turned off the hot plate and dropped the contents of the pan onto his plate. The meat had shrunk during cooking. It appeared smaller now. He poked it with his fork and then cut off a piece.

Why shouldn't it taste good? These creatures eat grass, just like deer do. I should picture a rabbit. They say it tastes like rabbit.

For an instant he felt revolted, but then the despair caused by hunger overwhelmed him. He forced his lips apart, brought the meat to his mouth and began to chew.

Thus it was that Joseph Gaston ate his first gopher.

CHAPTER 15

"*Eaton's Department Store. Canada's largest retailer. Reliable mail order workers required for the Christmas season.*"

It was the first employment ad Joseph had seen in the *Philibuster Post* for weeks. Although he understood his chances of landing one of the five advertised positions were slim—by now he was sufficiently jaded to know that such jobs almost inevitably went to relatives or friends of the person doing the hiring—he had to make an effort, at least.

When he arrived at the rear entrance of the Eaton's store at 6:00 AM the next morning, he found that approximately 200 men had arrived before him. They lined up in the cold, their breath condensing into small clouds of vapour on the morning air. Joseph joined the line. Like the others, he was soon rubbing his hands together and hopping from foot to foot to keep his circulation going. The cold made him realize it was winter. He must stop by the coal yard to look for any waste coal with which to heat their room.

A new man took his place behind Joseph. "How long you been in line?" he asked.

"Few minutes."

"Front of the line been here since yesterday noon," put in someone ahead of them. The man who'd asked the question shook his head in disgust and walked away.

Others took his place and stayed. The men smoked as they waited. They discussed the weather and spoke of Hallowe'en pranks that had occurred a few days earlier. It was said that a ghost had been seen floating over Main Street, but investigating cops had found nothing to prove the rumour.

Joseph glimpsed Copper, his buddy from the sawmill, some way ahead of him. Joseph waved a friendly greeting and Copper waved back. Some time later, sections of newspaper were passed back and forth. Joseph managed to get a glimpse of the front page, which was dedicated to the upcoming weekend's Armistice Day Ceremonies. "LEST WE FORGET," blazoned the three-inch headline. There was information regarding memorial service sites, the names of the distinguished gentlemen who would be presiding over the various proceedings, and stories about heroes who had returned from the devastating horrors of European battlefields. One story concerned Winfield Westmoreland.

"*Mr. Westmoreland served in France as an ambulance driver. During the performance of his duties, he befriended physician John McCrae. After the Second Battle of Ypres in Belgium, he happened to see Dr. McCrae writing a poem while sitting in the back of Mr. Westmoreland's medical field ambulance. The poem, written after a grief-stricken McCrae presided over the funeral of a friend, Alexis Helmer, was to become famous as* In Flanders Fields. *After writing the poem, John McCrae discarded it. Fortunately, another officer rescued it, and it was eventually published in the magazine* Punch. *When asked for his interpretation of the poem, Mr. Westmoreland stated unequivocally that, 'our duty lay in serving our fellow man.' This newspaper says amen to that.*"

Joseph, too, had fought at the Second Battle of Ypres. He wondered if he'd come across Winfield Westmoreland there. It was unlikely he would ever know. Generally, he was reluctant to think about his time in Europe, let alone talk about it. But with nothing else to do while waiting in line, he couldn't avoid the memories that flooded back unbidden.

On August 4th, 1914, newpaper headlines read: BRITAIN DECLARES WAR. As a member of the British Empire, Canada was automatically involved—not that there was ever a question about Canada's participation. Most Canadians were of British descent and saw themselves as having dual loyalties. The Canadian government asked for 20,000 volunteers. The newspapers predicted the war would be over by Christmas, so men who did not hurry to enlist would miss out on the glory. Within two months, the Canadian army had signed up 32,000 men. Among them was Joseph Gaston.

Because the Canadian government wanted to field a force as quickly as possible, it sent the men to a hastily erected military training camp. This camp, consisting of thousands of white canvas tents, was situated about 18 miles north of Quebec City, outside the small town of Val Cartier. After a few months of training, during which he learned to march and fire a rifle, Joseph was shipped across the Atlantic to England. After landing in Plymouth with thousands of other men, he was taken by train to another tent city. There he spent the winter months training in the cold drizzle of the Salisbury Plain. Joseph's powerful physique made him stand out. Years of hard manual labour—digging trenches and carrying iron ore, coal, hot slag and pig iron—had made him exceptionally strong and sturdy. Initially trained as a rifleman, his superiors soon transferred him to a position more suited to his excellent physical abilities: communications runner.

As a runner, Joseph's function was to carry messages from platoon officers in forward positions to battalion commanders in

the rear. While carrying the full fighting kit of an infantryman—
although with fewer entrenching tools—he was still expected to
run with the speed of a jackrabbit. He had to learn the proper
etiquette for dealing with officers and was taught how to handle
carrier pigeons, read maps, use a compass, and care for his feet, as
well as how to work in pairs. He also had to learn semaphore, the
flag-signalling alphabet, and gain an understanding of landmarks.

In the spring of 1915, having proven himself competent in his
new skills, Joseph was informed that he was being sent to Belgium.
Since he didn't believe anything could be drearier than the damp
cold of the Salisbury Plain, he looked forward to the excitement
of combat.

By the time Joseph arrived in Belgium, the war had evolved
into a stalemate of trench fighting. Men shared cold, muddy
trenches with rats. They faced the enemy across narrow strips of
land covered in barbed wire and pockmarked with shell craters.
On his first day in the field, he was running a message to the front
when he came across a shell hole full of dead Brits. He stopped and
stared at bodies without arms, legs and heads. The stench of death
made him vomit. He collapsed on the ground, stunned by horror
and fear. His partner, an experienced runner by the name of Ted
Meeres, shook him to snap him out of his daze. When Joseph came
to, his friend was slapping his face. He remembered Ted saying
he would be okay, just "Do your job and don't think too hard."
Ted died a month later, when a bullet entered one eye and exited
through the back of his head, taking most of Ted's brain with it.

At the time, the Allies had recently taken the Belgian town
of Ypres. Remnants from the German occupation of the trenches
were scattered about: helmets, empty wooden crates, spent shells
and the personal effects of men who had only weeks before made
these muddy trenches their homes.

On one of his trips from the front, Joseph spotted something
shining in the mud. He picked up what turned out to be a silver
cigarette case bearing a picture of the Kaiser, and a few words

written in German. He wiped the mud and filth from the cigarette case and kept it in his left breast pocket. Weeks later, someone told him the meaning of the German inscription: "God is with us." Joseph was shocked. Until that moment he had firmly believed that the Allies were on the side of right, yet the Huns were also claiming divine protection. It made Joseph wonder about the men fighting on the German side: were they all truly evil, or had they also been torn from their homes and families and been thrust into this terrible war because they were lied to?

As Joseph grew more experienced, he did more than carry and interpret messages. Because he knew the terrain well, having run across it many times, he often had to lead men to forward positions or help take the wounded back to the medical unit. He was leading a group to the front during the Battle of the Somme in August of 1916 when he was hit for the first time. In the moonlight he saw wild shots throw up dirt, and the occasional bullet whistled past his ear. But Joseph had become so accustomed to this kind of thing that he didn't take much notice of it. Suddenly something punched him in the chest and he fell to the ground, unable to catch his breath. A few of the men he'd been leading saw him fall and attended to him right away. They tore open his jacket and ripped off his shirt, intending to inspect the wound and stop the bleeding. To their surprise, there was no blood. The silver cigarette case Joseph had kept in his left breast pocket had prevented the bullet from penetrating his heart. He was bruised, but otherwise unharmed.

Two months later Joseph was shot in the leg. Seven months after that, he took a bullet in the arm. Every time he was injured he wondered whether he would be sent home, but he was always returned to the front. With the war in its third year, there was a shortage of men. Command determined that if a man was able to walk and carry a rifle, he was able to fight.

Joseph's last injury occurred at Passchendaele, an area of Belgium that was flat and low, swampy even when there was no rain. By the time Joseph was assigned there, three years of heavy fighting had already taken place in the vicinity. The ground had been churned up by millions of artillery shells. In 1917 the heavy autumn rains had come early, turning the battlefield into a sea of mud. Instead of running through trenches, Joseph had to run over exposed wooden walkways, nicknamed duckboards or bathmats. Slipping off a bathmat meant falling into a quagmire of mud. Without help, a person could drown in the swamp.

Joseph and another runner were taking a message to the front when they heard the scream of artillery and were splattered with mud. Looking down, Joseph saw sparks where an enemy shell had plunged into the mire. There was no time to jump out of the way. Joseph and the other runner exchanged a brief glance—nice to know you—before the shell exploded.

Everything was suddenly quiet. Joseph felt no pain. *So this is what it's like to die,* he thought. It was a few minutes before he realized that he was still alive, although not in good shape. He was on his back, covered in mud, bleeding from the ears and staring into a cloudless sky. The shell was so deeply buried in the Passchendaele mud that Joseph and the other runner had been buffered from the explosion. Joseph escaped with severe bruising and a temporary ringing in his ears. He served as a communications runner until the war ended.

Waiting outside Eaton's, Joseph was brought out of his wartime reverie when he heard Copper speaking. "I hate these damn lines," he was saying. "Not a hope of getting taken on here, anyway."

When Joseph had taken his place in the line, Copper had been a good 20 feet ahead of him. By now, the line had compressed somewhat, and Copper was less than half that distance from Joseph.

"It's not worth waiting like this in the cold," he went on.

Some of the men within earshot grumbled and agreed.

"Still, better than a work camp," said a man directly behind Joseph.

He wore the uniform of a person who had been in a relief work camp: khaki sweater, army pants and black boots. The government had set up the camps in areas remote from towns or cities, supposedly to help homelesss men survive the frigid winters. Run by the military, the camps housed tens of thousands of single, unemployed men. The real purpose of the work camps, it was speculated, was to hide unemployed men in outlying areas, where they would be unable to organize or make trouble.

"Rather freeze to death here than go back," the relief camp man said.

"That bad?" Copper asked.

"Three meals and twenty cents a day, and you're treated like a dog."

"At least you were fed," a grey-haired man pointed out. He was bent over and gnarled, like an old tree that had been deprived of rain and sun for too long.

"Just enough to keep you on your feet. Everything's doped with enough saltpeter to make you sick," the relief camp man protested.

Joseph had heard stories of camps where men spent eight hours a day clearing brush and piling stones. The workers could have been employed productively, cutting timber to make houses for the poor, or constructing public buildings, but for the fact that some big contractor or lumber company with political connections would raise a stink. Free labour would kill their businesses. The rich knew how to stick together.

"Gave you clothes and shelter, didn't they?" the grey-haired man demanded.

"Sure," agreed the relief camp man. "But it wasn't the work, mister, or even the food. It was what happened the rest of the time. Nothing to look forward to at the end of the day. Just sit in your bunk, stare at a blank wall and think about life outside the camp. Day after day doing nothing but thinking and worrying and fretting that your life was amounting to nothing, that no one gave a damn whether you rotted or just up and died."

Other men were listening now. "It eats at your mind. You just think and think and think. And you get so antsy you can't sit still. All you want is something to take your mind off things, but there's nothing to read, no radio to listen to, no hockey rink or baseball diamond to play on. You can't even walk down the street to bum a beer off your buddy or sit on the sidewalk and watch some tomato walk by. There ain't a broad within a hundred miles of the camp. Drives a man crazy."

"Drives a man crazy in Philibuster, too. I haven't seen a whore since I got here," Copper said.

"Run out of town," the grey-haired man explained.

The relief man stared at him. "The hell, you say!"

"It's true," agreed a short, skinny man with spectacles. "Not even the Buffalo Hotel can help you out anymore. Wasn't so long ago you could talk to the front desk manager. Acted as the business manager for a couple of ladies who worked out of the second floor."

"My grandpa once told me that in his time each town had its own districts of cathouses," Copper said.

The grey-haired man gave a short laugh. "In my day we called the women 'languid ladies.' You youngsters wouldn't remember. Philibuster had its own neighbourhood of bawdy houses. We called it the Maze, a place where a man could lose himself. Still here, of course, and not the most reputable, but it's changed. There was a time, not so long ago, when the local waiters or livery operators would point you in the right direction. Don't do that now."

"Wasn't that long ago that a taxi driver could tell you where to go," another man put in.

"Philibuster use to have the best damn house of ill fame in Canada." The grey-haired man was well into his subject. "One madam made her place like a classy Parisian bordello with tapestries, velvet hangings and French wine. Girls in flimsy kimonos waving from the windows. You could hear singing and shouting for miles. Mostly families in Philibuster now, but when I first came west there wasn't nothing but carpenters, blacksmiths, labourers and men breaking the land here. And when you find single men with time on their hands and money in their pockets, many women will oblige. Addison Philibuster himself used to walk into a brothel like he was visiting a dry goods store. No guilt about it. Wasn't done secret-like, either, just a part of daily life."

"Not any more," Copper said.

"Nope. Everyone got all civilized." The grey-haired man sneered. "Westmoreland promised to get rid of them lovely ladies and he done just that. Sicked the police chief on them. Man's got to go pretty far to find a languid lady now."

"Who's got money for a lady these days, anyway," the relief camp man said. "No wonder they're all gone."

"Don't think so," said a new voice. The speaker was a swarthy, brown-eyed fellow. "Late one night I seen a lady go into a dark house in the old Maze district. She wasn't there for choir practice neither. Done up like she was ready to squeak bed springs. Should've —"

His words trailed off as the Presbyterian Church bell chimed nine o'clock. A man in a well-cut suit appeared in the doorway at the back of the Eaton's store. Two tough-looking characters took up their positions, one on either side of him. Joseph was pretty sure the name of the man in the suit was Harmon Kingston.

"I expect an orderly line. Anyone not behaving will be removed from the premises. Start any trouble, and we'll finish it," Kingston threatened, nodding at the toughs.

The men eyed one another uneasily. Although they were insulted, nobody answered back. All were desperate for work and would tolerate abuse if it came with a paycheck. Joseph saw Copper make a rude gesture, surreptitiously, so that Kingston and the toughs didn't see it.

For the next hour the line moved slowly until, just before ten o'clock Harmon Kingston appeared again with his bodyguards. The jobs had been filled, Kingston said, and he ordered the men to leave. The two toughs followed him back into the building, slamming the doors behind them.

The line dispersed slowly. Some of the men walked away in ones and twos, heads down, obviously dejected. Others, with nowhere else to go, gathered in groups. Joseph heard angry talk about Harmon Kingston.

"God damned, if he's not a horse's ass!"

"Hope I run into him in a dark alley some day."

Joseph empathized with them. The insolent treatment had been unnecessary. It didn't take much effort to be pleasant.

"Like to make him guest of honour at a necktie party," Copper said, picking up a stone and hurling it at the receiving door. The stone hit the handle with a metallic ping before falling to the ground. "Don't want your damn job, anyhow!"

Some of the departing men turned their heads.

"A man waits in line in the cold for hours and hours, without even a thank you!" Copper shouted, realizing people were listening. He hurled another stone. "All these damned long lines—and for what? A job mailing toys to rich kids? I'm a chemist, for Christ's sake! I trained as a chemist!"

The departing men returned to the Eaton's parking lot. Agitated and disturbed, they began to call out their own occupations.

"I'm a draftsman!"

"I'm a printer!"

"I'm a carpenter!"

They uttered oaths and threw stones. Joseph felt the tension around him as an eruption of pent-up resentment and rage.

"Bennett!" Copper spat the prime minister's name with disgust. "If it weren't for him, we'd all be working. He's just a rich man, protecting the rich man's interests!"

The door opened suddenly. Out came Harmon Kingston and his toughs. "What's the meaning of this?" he bellowed.

The crowd grew quiet. They stood motionless, hands clenched around rocks and stones. Joseph held his breath, as if to prevent something bad from happening. Harmon Kingston must have sensed the tension, too. He looked as if he was about to say something more, but then thought better of it.

Joseph saw Copper bend down and pick up another stone. When he straightened, his eyes were fixed on Kingston. Joseph caught his arm and hissed, "Don't!"

As if shaken from a trance, Copper dropped the stone and broke free of Joseph's grip. "Damn all these long lines!" he yelled at the men near him. "It's all Bennett's fault! I'm gonna kill him!" Then he stormed off.

Joseph breathed more easily as the tension lessened slightly. Perhaps the other men in the crowd felt as he did, for they began dropping the stones they'd picked up minutes earlier.

"Disperse immediately or I'll call the police!" Harmon Kingston ordered, his bravado returning.

The crowd stirred, muttered and slowly departed, but their anger at the situation remained. It festered and brewed and would soon find a violent outlet.

CHAPTER 16

More than a month had gone by since Tilda had decided to make Sarah and Clare her own children. Her plan was simple: the girls had to want to be with her rather than with their father. If Joseph decided to leave town, it was important for him to understand that the girls felt closer to her than to him. That being the case, he might allow them to remain with her. Of course, it was important that she keep her intentions secret from Joseph. He must never know of her designs on his family.

Tilda began to set her plan in motion by indulging Sarah whenever possible. Out of Nolan and Cole's sight she encouraged the child to eat whatever she wanted. Breakfast might consist of buttered toast sprinkled with sugar and cinnamon rather than porridge, and lunch would be supplemented with penny candies. This was just one of the kindnesses Tilda hoped would lead Sarah to love her aunt more than she loved her father.

As for Clare, Tilda kept her close all the time. At first she had carried the baby whenever she could; Clare had even napped in her arms. Clare was now crawling and showing an interest in walking, but Tilda believed she still needed to provide as much physical intimacy as Clare was willing to accept.

Another part of Tilda's strategy was to reduce, as much as she could, the amount of time the girls spent with their father.

"You're going out tonight," she informed Joseph late one afternoon, when he arrived after another day of fruitless job searching. He was to join Henri at his usual watering hole. Although Tilda disliked her husband's habit of spending his money in beer parlours, getting Joseph to act as chaperone was a good way of keeping him away from his children.

"I really would like you to mind Henri," Tilda begged, when she saw Joseph's reluctance. "Please, be a dear and do it for me."

Much as Joseph disliked Tilda's suggestion, he felt he could not refuse her request after all she'd done for him. Perhaps it was true that his brother was over-indulging, in which case agreeing to spend one evening keeping an eye on him was not unreasonable.

Henri was delighted to have Joseph join him for a beer at the Buffalo Hotel. Officially called McCulloch's after its owner, Bruce McCulloch, the patrons spoke of the beer parlour as "the Hole," because its door was located at the dirty rear entrance of the building. The place actually had two entrances leading to two separate rooms: one for men, the other for women. Temperance leaders insisted the two sexes could not share the same space lest improper behavior result, and the threat of arrest by the local constabulary kept them separate.

Entering the bleakest bar he had ever seen, Joseph was hit by the smell of sour beer, body odour and dense smoke. Men sitting at plain wooden tables were drinking beer while they played cards or dominos. There was no standing, no entertainment, no food and no singing. A sign above the bar read: *Absolutely no credit given here.*

Henri spotted Raven and Copper playing cribbage at a centre table. As he and Joseph joined them, Joseph marvelled at the ease with which Raven could switch from his managerial status to being just one of the men.

"Copper." Henri's voice could be heard across the place. "What are you doing 'ere?"

"Having a beer."

"I 'eard you were t'reatening to kill Bennett dis morning. Said duh long lines were 'is fault."

Some of the men laughed, enjoying Henri's joke.

"Well? Did you kill our prime minister?"

Copper was embarrassed by his loss of temper, but his comeback was quick. "I couldn't. That line was twice as long."

To more laughter, Henri ordered beer. He wanted to buy Joseph one too, but his brother declined the offer. Henri wondered if Joseph disapproved of alcohol, which would explain his usual reluctance to join him at the Hole. But if that were the case, why had Joseph agreed to join him this evening? What Henri did not know was that Joseph felt it was wrong to have a beer, even a free one, when he struggled to feed his children.

As the brothers sat down with Raven and Copper, the talk turned to a fire that had occurred two nights earlier and had destroyed four buildings, one of which was owned by Winfield Westmoreland. The *Philibuster Post* had blamed the fire on an opium den operating in the basement of one of the buildings. Apparently, an overturned oil lamp had caught some bedding on fire before spreading quickly to wooden floors and walls. The newspaper's information source was unknown. According to Raven, the building had been vacant and no one recalled even a whiff of the distinctive fumes of opium.

Regardless of the story's accuracy, the article stirred up negative sentiments toward Philibuster's Chinese population. *Who smoked opium other than the Chinese?* asked indignant town residents.

The day after the fire, Chinese-owned laundries and restaurants were attacked. Windows were broken, signs were smashed, kitchens were destroyed, cash registers were looted and the owners of the establishments were beaten. The *Philibuster Post* ran another story, cautioning its readers not to sympathize with the Chinese whose businesses had been ruined. "After all, those heathens got what they deserved." Tom and Betty Wah were so anxious about their children's physical safety that they decided to keep them inside for the time being.

Any support for the Chinese community in Philibuster—and some did exist—was non-verbal. The Chinese themselves did not dare to fight back. The federal government, in a transparent attempt to reduce the Chinese population of Canada and to cut down on relief costs, was threatening to deport anyone deemed indigent or subversive. Joseph thought the idea ridiculous. In his six months in Philibuster he had never once seen a Chinese person asleep on a park bench in the middle of the afternoon, or playing chess in the park or hanging about idly on some street corner. And in the rare event of any Chinese person receiving relief, the amount paid out was exactly half the amount given to a Caucasian.

He was still thinking about the fire and its aftermath, when the bar was suddenly silent and all heads turned toward the door. The police chief stood in the doorway, gazing silently around him. Only when he walked over to speak with the owner did the men resume their conversations.

Chief Quentin's appearance reminded Henri of an incident earlier that day, when he'd witnessed Arthur "Slim" Evans, a notorious labour organizer, being handcuffed and hauled away by the police chief himself.

"I swear it was 'im," Henri insisted with something like reverence. "Skinny guy walking wit' a limp."

"Jesus, who isn't skinny these days?" Copper observed cynically.

"No, it was 'im, Evans. I am certain. Short, dark-'aired fellow. Looks just like 'is pictures in duh papers."

Most people at the Hole that evening knew about Slim Evans. As leader of the Workers' Unity League, or WUL, Evans had spent 20 years battling to unionize Canadian and American workers. He had begun his fight for North American workers in 1911, when he'd taken part in a demonstration by the International Workers of the World. Arrested, he'd been jailed for a year. His crime: reading aloud the Declaration of Independence. In 1913, during a strike in Ludlow, Colorado, he was injured when strikebreakers hired by John D. Rockefeller opened fire, leaving him with his life-long limp. Most recently, he'd been jailed for helping coal miners strike for higher wages in Princeton, British Columbia.

"Henri is right," Raven agreed. "Evans was handing out leaflets for the WUL when he was arrested. I guess he was trying to help the poor buggers in the relief camps get better food and shelter. Quentin tossed him in jail."

Not long before, Prime Minister Bennett had enacted a controversial law that enabled the police to incarcerate anyone for attending labour union meetings, publicly speaking out in favour of leftist organizations or handing out literature advocating such associations. Westmoreland fully supported the law.

"Arrested for handing out flyers?" Copper asked disbelievingly.

"That's correct," confirmed a deep voice. "Evans was arrested for handing out flyers."

The men at the table turned as one. Chief Quentin stood behind Joseph.

"Evening, Chief," Raven said, cordially.

"Evening, Mullens," the police chief responded coolly.

Joseph did not turn to look at the man, but he sensed a menacing stare through the back of his head.

"You honestly thought it necessary to put Evans behind bars?" Raven asked.

"Sure. He's a filthy communist."

"He's fighting for the common man."

"Trying to subvert our country," came the police chief's angry response.

Raven shook his head. "I don't agree. Evans only wants workers to band together. If we let the rich dictate the rules, no one will ever earn a decent living again. You should know that better than anyone, Chief."

Everybody was listening to the exchange. Although most of the men were afraid to speak their minds, they were extremely interested in what unions were promising. They were all desperate for the livable wages, safe working conditions and benefits that strong associations such as the WUL might be able to deliver. Unfortunately, unions had become associated with communism, a word the press had made blasphemous. No one wanted to be branded a communist.

"We need to be more open-minded. We shouldn't blindly believe what the newspapers tell us," Raven said evenly.

Chief Quentin was offended. "Newspapers don't tell *me* what to think."

Raven tried to explain his theory that the wealthy dominated the press, thereby controlling what people could read.

"What exactly do you mean?" Chief Quentin sneered.

The normally composed Raven jumped to his feet and declared loudly, "Men like Westmoreland pay their employees slave wages while they line their own pockets!"

Joseph had never seen Raven so upset. He wondered whether things were about to get out of hand, but Raven sat down again and spread his hands on the table. His tone only slightly less loud, he said, "Talking to you, Chief, is like riding a freight train. You're stuck on your rails and can't see any other path."

Chief Quentin's face darkened. "Keep this up, Mullens, and you'll be joining Evans."

The two men stared at each other for a long moment. "Thought so," Quentin sneered when Raven did not answer the threat.

The police chief left then, and for a while the room was quiet. Gradually, however, people began to talk once more. Beer was ordered, glasses were clinked and cards were dealt. Still, the atmosphere was not what it had been before Quentin's unsettling visit.

To lighten the mood at the table, Copper mentioned that a ghost had been seen floating above Main Street on Hallowe'en night. Joseph recalled having heard about the incident, though he hadn't given it any thought since then. Raven and Henri exchange amused glances, then Henri told the other two how he and Raven had made a "ghost" out of a white sheet and attached it to a wire that stretched from one rooftop to another. Whenever someone approached, they had hauled on a pulley and made the ghost float across the street. They had dismantled the thing before the police could investigate.

The story made Joseph think back to the pranks he had played on his relatives so many years earlier. His high spirits had earned him beatings, whereas his brother's brought him laughter. He was about to recount one of the pranks when his brother began to tell another story, "a real ghost story," Henri said.

"It 'appened five years ago," he began. "It was January. Dare 'ad been an enormous winter storm duh day before, lots of blowing snow and 'uge drifts. It was really terrible out. I was 'eading 'ome when I see a funeral procession coming down duh street. I say to myself, 'Oo would 'ave a funeral on a terrible day like dis? 'Postpone it,' I say to myself. 'The corpse isn't going to get any deader.' Well, I just watch 'doze old 'orses wit' dare fancy 'eaddresses traipse on by tru' duh snow. As cold as it was, I stood and waited until duh procession passed before making my way 'ome—dis being duh proper t'ing to do, you know.

"Den I see Ambroos 'oogaboom sitting on top of duh last of duh wagons. Strange to see 'eem up dare, since he rarely leave duh store. I figure duh corpse must be a relative of 'is. I didn't want to disturb 'im, seeing as 'ee was looking so solemn. But it was 'ard not to be surprise, so I wave at 'im. 'Ee just stare straight ahead. 'Ee geeve no indication 'ee see me.

"But after dat wagon pass by, 'ee turn 'is 'ead to look at me. 'Is eyes were all white. No coloured part or black centre—just ghastly white. 'Ee keep on looking at me as duh procession went fur'der down duh street. Den 'is 'ead start to turn too far backwards. I t'ink I must be seeing t'ings because it look unnatural wit' 'is body not turning at all. Finally, I lost sight of dem in duh storm.

"My nose and checks were tingling sore, like I was getting frost-bit, so I went 'ome. I woke duh next morning wit' chills and fevers. I stayed 'ome and only went into work duh day after dat. Later, I found out Ambroos 'ad gone out looking for 'is daughter's black lab pup. Dis pup, it wander out onto duh river. Duh ice wasn't frozen solid and Ambroos fell tru' a weak spot. We drag duh river for t'ree days. Four days later, we bury an empty casket in Memorial Cemetery. Duh procession was just like duh one I see five days earlier in dat snow storm."

The men were still.

Joseph had known the cause of Ambroos Hoogaboom's death; he had not heard the rest of it. "That story gives me the shivers," he said, speaking for the first time that evening.

CHAPTER 17

Grey December clouds hung oppressively low over Philibuster, stretching to the horizon and blocking out most of the dying winter afternoon light. Pedestrians paused in the foyers of open buildings to kick the light snow from their shoes and to spend a few minutes warming up. Fur hats were pulled down over ears, collars were turned up. Mailmen wore raccoon coats, the rich wore beaver coats. Pink stains showed here and there through packed snow, where frozen radiator hoses had broken.

Joseph stood in front of a pawnbroker's store, his shoulders hunched and his knees aching from the bitter cold. Reluctantly he pushed open the door and entered. A variety of musical instruments—trombones, violins and flutes—hung on the walls. Washing machines, dryers and odd pieces of furniture crowded the floor. Light sparkled on a pile of watches, earrings, bracelets, pendants and gemstones beneath a glass counter top. Eyeing a small collection of rings, Joseph tried to find a wedding band similar to his own, knowing full well that its true mate lay beneath six feet of dirt in an Ontario graveyard.

The pawnbroker, an odious man, looked at Joseph's wedding band without much interest. "I can give you eight, maybe nine dollars," he offered. He held the gold band between his thumb and his index finger, keeping his other fingers well clear of it, as if it were unclean.

Joseph tried to read the man's thoughts. Was he suggesting he had no use for the band, and that there was no point in him asking for more? And if he did decide to accept less, would he also have to pay proportionately less to buy it back? Not that there was any reason to think he'd ever have the money to retrieve it. Once the band was sold, Joseph would have nothing tangible left to remember Helen by.

Sadly, Joseph lacked other options.

"Make it ten," he said, without much hope.

The pawnbroker shook his head and frowned. "Nine-fifty, highest I'll go."

Joseph realized he had no alternative but to agree to the man's price. He held the band in his hand a long moment. Closing his eyes, he pictured the woman he had loved so much. *Forgive me, my darling*, he whispered to her silently. Then he put the band on the counter, took the pawnbroker's money and walked out into the cold.

When he reached Hoogaboom's, the store was warm and crowded with people picking up Christmas orders—holiday food Hoogaboom's didn't carry the rest of the year: ham, Christmas chocolates, walnuts, pecans and Brazil nuts. Joseph looked around him, wishing he could enjoy the festive mood in the store. People greeted each other gaily, calling out "Merry Christmas," and spoke of the weather as crisp rather than cold. Beth's other daughter, Ina, a student nurse, was home for the holidays. While Ina grabbed orders from the back of the store, Patricia cut meat and Beth worked the cash register. Joseph found what he needed then waited in line to pay.

"Joseph," Beth said with a smile, when he reached the till, "I was hoping I'd see you. There was something I meant to ask you. Have you ever worked in a lab?"

"No. Why?"

"I heard the dairy needs someone to run tests on their products, and you're a smart man."

Joseph flushed, gratified at the compliment. "Thanks, but I don't have any experience."

"Too bad." Beth seemed about to say more, then she seemed to think better of it.

They stood and looked at each for a few tension-filled seconds. For some reason, Joseph was unable to move. The expression in Beth's face captivated him. He had seen that look before, enigmatic yet friendly, and still had no idea what it meant. He was the first to look away. The tension passed. He paid for his purchases, wished Beth a merry Christmas and hurried away.

As Joseph walked through the streets carrying his small bag of groceries, he thought about the job Beth had mentioned. How nice it would be to work indoors, wearing a clean white coat and not having to worry about the weather. A brief thought passed through his mind, a momentary awareness of ideas that were connected in some way. He rubbed his forehead, hoping to bring back the thought, but it was gone. Putting his free hand inside his pocket for warmth, he touched the roll of one-dollar bills he'd received from the sale of his wedding band, and wondered whether he should get something more for the children.

A few blocks further on, tempting displays of toys filled department store windows, everything from electric trains on tiny tracks, smiling dolls and toy soldiers to Meccano sets, Tinker Toy castles and puzzles.

Joseph looked longingly at a display of boys' and girls' skates. How the three older children would each love a pair. They would think him the greatest dad in the world. Sadly, he walked further.

He was looking at a pile of boxed microscopes and chemistry sets when he remembered the thought that had eluded him earlier—the long line of men outside Eaton's a few weeks earlier and Copper calling out that he was a chemist. Copper was probably qualified to apply for the job at the dairy.

He left the store, not knowing what to do. He could keep quiet about the position. He didn't owe it to Copper to tell him about it, and the man could suffer with the rest of the unemployed. At the same time, he understood himself well enough to know that if he allowed envy to get the better of him, his conscience would trouble him. Without further hesitation, he set out in search of Copper.

On the day before Christmas, Joseph spent the afternoon doing chores around the house for his brother and Tilda. Tilda thought he looked weary, but he insisted he was fine. She also noticed he was no longer wearing his wedding band, but decided not to question him.

It was so cold that night that the children wore their coats indoors, but they were so cheerful that they didn't seem to mind the discomfort as they hung up the ornaments they'd made at school. They didn't have a tree so they improvised, stringing a rope of coloured paper rings and a couple of smiling paper snowflakes behind the parlour stove. They put their stockings—hole-free thanks to Tilda—at the foot of the stove.

Joseph was saddened by the meagerness of the Christmas setting, but Cole and Sarah talked excitedly of Santa's visit and the feast they would have at their aunt and uncle's the next day. Nolan, more worldly-wise than his siblings, played along with their anticipation of Santa Claus. Joseph waited until the children were asleep before putting a single gift inside each stocking. It distressed him to imagine their disappointment.

Next morning the kids hurried to see what Santa had left for them. To Joseph's surprise, they were thrilled with the orange each had received, and even discussed whether to eat them right away, or to keep them to show their aunt and uncle. Temptation got the better of them and they peeled the oranges and happily exchanged slices.

A stranger might well have taken Henri and Tilda's house to be the happy home of four children. Joseph and the children were welcomed by a crackling fire and the wonderful aroma of roasting turkey. A Christmas tree stood in a corner of the living room, decorated with garlands of popcorn and wooden and glass ornaments. A tinfoil star sparkled at the top of the tree. Two presents for each of the children lay beneath its lower branches.

Tilda had been busy. She had knitted them scarves and caps and had sewn trousers for the boys and dresses for the girls. The three older children received nuts and hard candy. Joseph had no idea that Tilda's efforts to make Christmas perfect—to the extent that she had spent more than she and her husband could comfortably afford—was part of her plan to acquire the children's affections. She was determined to convince them that she was more generous than their father. Joseph supposed that Tilda and Henri could afford the extravagances because they had never had to support children of their own.

It was so cold that Henri was unable to attach Jasper to a sled, as he had promised. Instead, he stoked the fire and showed the children how to roast nuts. While they waited for the nuts to get hot, he brought out his accordion. "I only know two Christmas songs," he said boisterously. "One is Jingle Bells and duh u'der isn't."

To the children's delight, their uncle also remembered French songs from his boyhood, some of which he taught them now; *D'où viens-tu, bergère,* and *Cantique de Noël.* Tilda emerged unexpectedly from the kitchen and showed the children how to waltz. The fragrance of roasting nuts filled the living room as they all danced and laughed and raced around with Jasper.

Despite the good smells and laughter, the house felt stuffy to Joseph. Unable to shake off a feeling of sadness, he put on his shoes and coat and snuck out the door. Ignoring the cold, he sat down on the front steps and wondered why he felt like an outsider around his own children, as if he were merely an uncle who had dropped in on his brother's family to share the joy of Christmas with them. Grateful though he was to Tilda and Henri for their generosity, their gifts to his children made him feel even more embarrassed than he had been that morning about his own meagre offerings. But what upset him more than anything else was the fact that Helen was not with them.

He vividly recalled the day after Helen's death, just over a year ago. He remembered looking at her possessions: her favourite chair, her clothes in the closet and her shawl on the bed. All just objects. Out of place. He remembered needing to get away from the house, lurching through the door and staggering out into the bare winter fields. The sky had seemed vaster than usual that day. He had stood there a while, feeling as though some catastrophe had taken place and he was the only person left on earth. He remembered not caring about anything, not even the children.

Two days later he had accepted a kind neighbour's offer to care for the children while he did a few errands in town. Walking along the streets, he had found it unfathomable that people were talking, smiling and even laughing. He felt an unreasonable anger that all these strangers were still living their lives as if nothing momentous had happened. They had seemed disrespectful. In some illogical part of his mind, he had expected the world to end with Helen's death. It was inconceivable that things should continue as if nobody cared.

And now, thought Joseph, the children no longer appeared to care either. Nolan, Cole and Sarah seemed to be getting over the loss of their mother. Although he knew it was good for them to move past their unhappiness, the fact saddened him all the same.

The children had all reacted differently to the tragedy. At first, Sarah had asked many questions. *Does everybody die? Will I die? Will you die?* She had asked them again and again. Cole had experienced guilt of some sort. Unfortunately, he and his mother had had an argument shortly before Clare was born, leading poor Cole to blame himself for Helen's death. Nolan had seen cows die giving birth; he simply wanted to know the details.

What disturbed Joseph almost more than anything else was that he was finding it increasingly difficult to remember Helen's face clearly. Even the pain of his grieving was not as acute as it had been. In a way, it had become like a bad mental bruise that only hurt when he applied pressure to it.

"Merry Christmas," someone said, startling Joseph from his memories. Looking up, he saw Copper at the fence, smiling broadly.

"And to you." Joseph stood up, went to the fence and shook Copper's hand.

"I came by to ask The Great Henri where you lived. I guess you've saved me a trip," Copper said cheerfully. "I wanted to thank you for telling me about the job. I start work at the dairy tomorrow."

Copper said how good it would be to do work he'd been trained for. Listening to him, Joseph was glad he'd been able to help his friend. They wished each other a merry Christmas again, and then Copper walked away, whistling.

A light snow began to fall. As Joseph turned his eyes skyward, a snowflake dropped onto his lips. He felt a momentary coolness and then it was gone. Suddenly, in the west, he saw a Chinook arch. A sliver of blue sky along the horizon, it was a welcome herald of warming winds and better weather. Joseph stood there a minute longer, taking in the sight of the arch, before turning toward the house. As he opened the door and stepped inside, a little warmth crept into his heart and a smile appeared on his face.

CHAPTER 18

The warm Chinook winds that had blown in the day after Christmas were gone by the New Year. The frigid cold returned and frost clung to evergreens and naked poplar trees. Coated by the white ice crystals, the dead grass crunched underfoot as Joseph and Henri walked into the woods.

Joseph heard the sound of cows in the distance. After years of working with cattle, he understood what they were saying as surely as a mother knows her infant's varied cries. There was the quick moo with which a mother might call to her wandering calf. There was the lower-pitched moo of a mother warning its calf of imminent danger. But what Joseph heard now was quite different. These cows were bawling, a raspy, drawn-out sound. The cattle were hungry; they had nothing to graze on.

What the heat and dust had not killed in the past summer, swarms of grasshoppers had destroyed. Some farmers had had the foresight to harvest Russian thistle for their cattle's winter food. There was also the generosity of farmers in eastern Canada who had shipped in bales of hay with the assistance of the Canadian Pacific Railway. Nevertheless, although a few thousand head of cattle had been saved, many more had died of starvation.

"Cold as a bear's ass." Henri slapped his hands together, the sound echoing off the trees.

The brothers hauled 15-foot-long logs out of the bush and laid them on a sawbuck beside the closed-cab truck they had borrowed from Raven. The logs had been felled the year before. Like the truck, the land and the wood also belonged to Raven. The deal was that Joseph and Henri would cut the wood, and each man would keep a third.

"Don't rip off my arm," Joseph warned as he and Henri began to cut the first log with a lance-toothed two-man saw. "Not so fast, Henri. Just keep it nice and steady. You'll sweat otherwise, and once the cold freezes the sweat, I won't be able to lift your big carcass into the truck."

"Don't you worry—I'll warm up duh outdoors wit' my own steam," his brother responded with a laugh. But he slowed his pace.

They worked steadily, cutting the logs into usable lengths for their stoves and fireplaces. After four hours of ceaseless labour and a steady stream of talk from Henri, they stopped for a break. Henri pulled out the lard pail containing his lunch. Observing that his brother had nothing but a milk bottle filled with water, Henri insisted that Joseph take half the lunch. When Joseph declined, Henri put his own lunch back in the truck, uneaten.

They were resting on the tailgate of the truck, passing the water back and forth, when Joseph pointed. "Look, Henri—a deer. Fifty yards."

The men watched the grazing animal a few minutes, until Henri said, "I've not 'ad deer meat in a mont' of Sundays."

"Wouldn't mind a deer steak myself," Joseph said wistfully.

With his mind filled with a picture of a warm and tasty meal, he didn't notice when his brother climbed into the truck. Suddenly, a rifle shot split the air. A second later, the deer fell to the ground.

Joseph spun around. Henri, still holding the rifle, was eyeing the fallen animal.

"Jesus H. Christ! You scared the hell out of me!" Joseph shouted.

Henri rested the rifle against the tailgate and raced to the deer. "Right between duh eyes!" he yelled in excitement.

"Whitetail! Henri, it's out of season!" Joseph exclaimed in dismay.

"Raven won't mind. 'Ee will be 'appy to get 'is share."

"It's the law I'm worried about!" Joseph said. "Someone could have seen us."

"Nobody around. No one will know."

Henri felt bad. He hadn't meant to upset his brother, but he was a man who followed his impulses. Seeing the buck, he had thought immediately of deer stew.

"We got to hide it, Henri."

"No. No, Joseph. I 'ave a friend who will dress and cut it for us."

"We can't just rope him to the grill," Joseph protested.

Henri glanced around. "We'll put 'im in back of duh truck and cover 'im wit' duh wood."

Joseph shook his head.

"No one will know," Henri reassured him. "Besides, 'ee is dead now, Joseph. Why let 'im go to waste?"

His brother was right, Joseph realized. If they abandoned the carcass, the buck's death would have been in vain. Besides, his own share of the animal could feed his family for months. Reluctantly, he agreed to his brother's plan. The two men finished cutting the logs they had already pulled out of the trees, heaved the deer into the bed of the truck and piled wood on top of it.

"We need turnips, peas and potatoes for duh stew," Henri said enthusiastically, as they drove back to town and made for Hoogaboom's.

"Let's get the buck to the butcher first," Joseph suggested.

His brother grinned at him. "It's out of our way. Best to get duh vegetables first."

They parked in front of Hoogaboom's and Hooper's Café, and Henri ran into the store. Joseph told himself to relax as he waited outside. Soon the buck would be safely in someone else's hands, and he could look forward to months of tasty, belly-filling meals.

He stiffened suddenly. The police chief had just walked out of Hooper's Café. Joseph's throat tightened, as if in reaction to a baton choking him beneath the chin. Instinctively, he touched his neck. As Chief Quentin paused to do up the buttons of his heavy buffalo coat, his eyes met Joseph's. Tensely, Joseph asked himself how an innocent man would act in the same circumstances. He figured it was better to stare back than to avert his gaze. A mistake, as it turned out. As Henri came out of Hoogaboom's and got back into the truck, Chief Quentin was already approaching them.

"What have you boys been up to?" he asked.

"Cutting firewood," Henri told him.

"Awful cold to be cutting wood. Smarter to do it in the summer."

"Yes, but den I'm not as sharp as you," Henri said with a smile.

Joseph held his breath. Did his brother have to pick this moment to be a wise-ass?

"Raven Mullens's truck?" Chief Quentin asked.

"Sure, I stole 'er. You want to run me in?"

"Keep talking like that and I will. I think you'd better get out of that truck."

"Why?"

Chief Quentin raised his voice. "Now!"

"Just do it," hissed Joseph and opened his door.

A number of people shopping at Hoogaboom's watched the scene from the window. It was growing dark and the interior lights of the store illuminated their faces. Beth appeared and stood on the wooden sidewalk, arms crossed in an effort to keep warm.

"You know, Chief Grumpy," Henri began, appreciating that he had an audience. "I don' know which I'd rah'der 'ave—a million dollars or your nose full of nickels."

Joseph flinched in shock. Why was his brother taunting the police chief?

Chief Quentin looked ready to belch smoke and fire. "I don't think I like you, Henri Gaston, and I sure don't like your brother."

"Better not look under duh wood pile, in dat case. You really won't like what you'll see."

Joseph eyes widened.

"Your brother looks frightened—makes me think I should take a look. What do you have there, anyway?"

"A whitetail," Henri said calmly. Joseph almost choked.

"Wouldn't put it past you." Chief Quentin poked Henri in the chest. "Bet if I moved that wood, I'd find a deer."

Joseph heard himself speak before he knew what he was saying. "You can move the wood if you want to," he said loudly, "but when you don't find a deer under there, you'll be piling the wood back up in front of all of these people. And won't you look stupid doing it."

Hoogaboom's customers must have heard Joseph's words, for they looked astonished. The police chief was silent for at least a minute. Then he went up to Joseph, whispered something in his ear and walked away.

When Chief Quentin had gone, Beth came up to Joseph. "Great Caesar's Ghost! What did he say to you?"

"Told me to have a nice day," Joseph told her, and climbed back into the truck.

Joseph sat in silence on to the drive to the butcher's. Though he was mad at his brother for getting him into the situation, he was more upset with himself. What had induced him to be so insolent to the police chief? He had let his self-control slip, just for an instant, and now he would pay for it.

"Strike two," Chief Quentin had whispered to him. Joseph wondered when the next pitch would come, when he'd hear the chief call him out.

CHAPTER 19

By mid January the brutal cold began to subside. It had not snowed for a while, but Joseph knew more was expected. Once it started, it would go on for days. Wind blew the existing snow into drifts five feet deep, blocking doors and covering cars. Icicles as long as a man's arm hung from eaves.

Clare came down with a bad cough. At first Joseph tried to care for her himself. Taking Tilda's advice, he rubbed goose grease on Clare's chest, followed by hot poultices. The treatment was unsuccessful. The cough worsened and Clare began to pant. When Joseph, now thoroughly alarmed, noticed red flecks in Clare's phlegm, he sent the three older children to stay with their aunt and called for the doctor.

Dr. Graham arrived promptly. Putting his stethoscope to the little girl's chest and back, he heard a worrying rattle. When she coughed, the doctor saw the redness in her mucus. He was deeply concerned, but tried not to show it; there was no reason to make poor Joseph even more worried than he was already. He did not tell him that the child had little chance of survival.

"Your daughter has a bad case of pneumonia. She needs to be treated with hot air in an oxygen tent and must take something for the cough," he said with professional calm. He wrote a prescription for a mixture that included, amongst other things, black cohosh, bloodroot and lobelia, and told Joseph how to administer it. Privately, he wondered whether Joseph would have the prescription filled, and, if he did, whether it would be enough to help the little girl.

When the doctor had gone, Joseph bundled up Clare against the cold and walked through knee-deep snow to the pharmacy. Handing the prescription to the pharmacist, he enquired nervously about the cost. The man, elderly and balding, briefly studied the doctor's list before giving Joseph a figure. Joseph swallowed hard when he heard it. Most of the money he had received for his wedding band was gone, spent on the basics of rent and utilities. Thirty cents was all he had left in his pocket.

"Is there something less expensive?" he whispered.

Pursing his lips, the pharmacist shook his head.

Leaving the pharmacy without the mixture, Joseph carried Clare to the hospital. *Let her be admitted to the charity ward*, he prayed. But that hope was dashed when an admissions nurse pointed down the hall at the line of waiting men, women and children, many of whom were coughing and moaning. There were no spare beds, she told him.

"But my baby is sick," Joseph said despairingly.

"So are they," the nurse responded. Seeing his despair, her face softened and she went on quietly, "If I can give you some advice, sir—the air in here is full of germs. You'd be better off taking the child home."

"Can a doctor look at her, at least?" Joseph pleaded.

"I'll see what I can do," the nurse said kindly.

Joseph waited in the crowded hallway, keeping his handkerchief protectively over Clare's face to ward off germs. A doctor examined the child three hours later. His recommendations were the same as Dr. Graham's had been earlier. The little girl needed an oxygen tent in which she could be treated with hot air. But none were available, and others were already waiting their turn. He could only repeat the instructions Joseph had received already.

A disheartened Joseph took Clare home and kept the fire well stoked. He sat near the stove, holding the child in his arms, rocking her and trying to make her as comfortable as possible. Clare coughed all night, a loud wet cough. In between fits of coughing, she gasped for air. It was agonizing to hear. Very early, before the sun was up, Joseph wrapped Clare in every blanket he had and carried her to his brother's home. He managed to catch Henri before he left for work.

"Clare has pneumonia," Joseph said awkwardly. "I wouldn't ask if I didn't have to, but …"

His brother was concerned. "'ow much do you need?"

"If you can see your way to … I know it's a lot, but …can you spare a dollar?"

"Let me see what we 'ave."

Joseph waited in the hallway while Henri went upstairs. The other children were already up and ecstatic to see their father, especially Sarah, who wanted to run into his arms. He was glad, too, but afraid Clare might infect them, so he insisted they talk to him from the kitchen doorway.

Henri was back quickly with the money. For a moment Joseph hesitated about taking it, until he remembered how badly he needed it. He promised to pay his brother back when he could. It was hard for him to say goodbye to the children, but he had to tell them, quite firmly, not even to visit until he came for them.

After getting the prescription filled, Joseph gave Clare a spoonful of the medicine. She soon began to scream, shake and vomit. Joseph spent the next two hours carrying her around the tiny room, trying to soothe her. Realizing she had thrown up most of the first dose, he gave her a little more medicine when she was finally settled. The result was the same as the first time: Clare was soon in distress again. Obviously, the medicine was harming her somehow.

By nightfall, Clare's cough had worsened. Her little body shook like a dog's toy. Whenever there was a lull in the coughing she lay inert, her little chest rising and falling rapidly with the effort to bring some air into her infected lungs. Again, Joseph took her to the hospital. Again, he was greeted kindly but without much hope. The charity ward was full and there was no space for Clare. Joseph pleaded with one of the weary doctors, who said he couldn't conjure an oxygen tent out of good intentions. Back home, watching the small body alternating between coughing and frightening stillness, Joseph wondered how long his beloved child might have left to live.

For two days Tom Wah had been hearing Clare's frightening cough through the thin wall that separated him from the Gastons. He understood its progression for he had experienced similar illnesses many times in the past. He realized that unless Clare received immediate help, she would not survive.

Tom was well versed in coughs, colds and all manner of other illnesses. When he was a young man his grandfather had taught him traditional Chinese medicine. He knew about yin and yang, the five-elements, the vital energies of the body and the pathways they travelled. He had spent years learning how to diagnose patients through careful questioning, as well as by observing a patient's posture, voice, gait, face, eyes, ears and tongue. He was educated in the various odors patients emitted, the different pulse types, and how to feel for tenderness and relative temperatures in different parts of the body. But even after ten years of study, Tom still did not feel he fully understood the complexity of symptoms and dynamic balances of the human body.

A conscientious student, sensitive to his patients' injuries and illnesses, Tom lacked only confidence. Despite his talent for diagnosing and treating his patients, he had had a bad habit of second-guessing himself, to the point where he questioned his skills and, therefore, his ability to help his patients. That shortcoming might have been remedied in time, but in 1917 Tom's medical training had been interrupted when he was forced to join the Chinese Labour Corps.

Tom was one of nearly 140,000 men from the Chinese provinces of Hebel, Jiangsu and Shandong, who were voluntarily, and, in some cases, involuntarily recruited by the Chinese government and "loaned" to the Allies during the Great War. Because China wanted to remain neutral during the conflict, the country did not actually allow its men to fight in Europe. By 1916, however, when manpower was greatly needed, China agreed to contribute non-military personnel—the Chinese Labour Corps—to help repair roads, manufacture munitions and unload ships.

Those who joined the Chinese Labour Corps were offered reasonable pay and were promised they would not be given hazardous duties. Many poorer Chinese took the opportunity to provide for their families and signed up. The problem was that with so many Chinese men unable to understand either English or French, it became necessary to force men who could speak and translate these languages to also join the labour corps. The British missionaries who had taught Tom to read, write and speak English and endowed him with his British accent remembered his language skills and told local authorities about him. Tom was asked to join the corps. When he refused, his family was threatened with punishment.

The day after Tom "volunteered," he was marched from his hometown to the port city of Qingdao. There, he and the other recruits were medically examined and rejected if they had tuberculosis, bad teeth or a venereal disease. Their heads were shaved, they were given khaki uniforms with numbered wooden clothing tags, and identifying brass bands were affixed to their wrists. They were then placed in cargo holds and shipped across the Pacific on a 21-day journey to Vancouver, British Columbia. Upon reaching Vancouver, they travelled by ferry to the nearby William Head quarantine station on Vancouver Island. After clearance by the authorities at William Head, they were ferried back to Vancouver under armed guard. There they were put in sealed freight trains—

to prevent them from escaping to any perceived "freedom"—and hauled across vast expanses of mountains, prairies, forests and lakes to Halifax, Nova Scotia. The press was forbidden to write about the crossing, so the public never learned about it.

Nearly 84,000 of the 140,000 Chinese Labour Corps members serving in Europe underwent the cross-Canada journey. Tom still remembered it well: the over-crowded boxcar, the tipped-over latrine bucket that spilled effluent everywhere, the inadequate ventilation consisting of just a small window at the top of one corner, with the men fighting to be near it. The conditions were unbearable.

Thankfully, Tom had found himself a crack between two wooden slats. With his face firmly pressed against it, he was able to observe the passing scenery. Occasionally, he spotted deer, moose and bison grazing near the tracks, and people, when the train passed through cities. But the great stretches of land between the cities looked unpopulated. Canada, it seemed to Tom, was a country in which a man could live freely without interference, a veritable paradise.

Arriving at Pier 21 in Halifax, the men were loaded onto the SS Temple. The ship took them to Southampton in England, where they were again quarantined. Only after being certified fit for duty were they shipped to France and Belgium to perform the duties for which they had signed on.

Although Tom was valued as an interpreter, he was still expected to do physical work ten hours a day, seven days a week. When his language skills were not required, he filled sandbags, dug trenches and helped repair roads. The British officers in charge were generally decent men. Tom and his group were treated fairly well: two meals a day, adequate clothing, good care if they were ill. Notwithstanding these benefits, Tom knew the Europeans considered them inferior, for they were never allowed out of the camp to visit the nearby town of Loos-en-Gohelle.

With nothing on which to spend his daily wages of two and a half francs—apart from gambling, which was not to his taste—Tom sent his pay back home to his family. Every month he received letters from his father or grandfather, giving him news of the village and thanking him for the money that made their lives a little easier.

Although the men of the Chinese Labour Corps had been promised hazard-free duties, there were still many deaths. Nobody escaped the bombings, and those near the front were affected by the German mustard gas attacks. But the overwhelming cause of death was the unsanitary conditions in the trenches; overflowing cesspits, rats, lice and the rotting bodies of their dead comrades, all of which combined to create ideal breeding grounds for disease and infection.

Eventually, although reluctantly at first, Tom tried to treat the men who became ill. Without access to necessary herbs, he still performed successful acupuncture. After hostilities officially ended on November 11th, 1918, he and many other members of the Chinese Labour Corps were kept in France to carry out certain clean-up chores—filling in shell holes, collecting corpses and body parts, and clearing the battlefields of live ammunition, unexploded bombs and landmines. The undertaking to keep the Chinese Labour Corps free from hazardous duties was flagrantly disregarded.

It was in France after the war that Tom faced a disease that left him more unsure than ever of his medical skills: the Spanish Flu. Almost a third of the world's population caught the flu and close to 50 million people died. It wasn't just the sheer number of affected people that confused Tom and many other healthcare providers. What was most difficult to understand was why an illness that typically killed infants or the elderly, was, in this instance, most frequently fatal to young, healthy adults. Nothing Tom and his colleagues did was ever enough.

As a contract labourer, Tom continued to work during the day at translating, filling in trenches and removing barbed wire. In the evenings he tended to his sick countrymen, trying to ease their discomfort. He did his best. So many men requested his assistance, but a disheartened Tom felt he was doing little for them.

Tom lost contact with his family in China during this time. He continued to send his pay home, yet received no response. Anxious though he was, he made himself believe that the absence of family correspondence was caused by a failure to deliver Chinese men's mail, rather than by any problems at home. But seven months to the day after his grandfather's last letter, he finally heard from a neighbour in his village. Tom's entire family, including his grandfather, his parents and his three sisters, had died of the Spanish Flu—which, it was later determined, had actually originated in China. The neighbour said he would have written earlier, but hadn't known how to get hold of Tom. Already distressed by what was happening around him, Tom was devastated by the information that not a single member of his family was still alive.

Soon thereafter, Tom was told he was being shipped home. His return to China was much the same as his earlier journey to Europe had been, but in reverse, a circuitous route that took him from France back to William Head, by way of Halifax and Vancouver. At William Head he waited with eight thousand other men for ships bound for China and repatriation.

A riot broke out one night. In the ensuing panic, Tom suddenly became aware of his real situation. Because he had no family to return to, nobody would lose face if he broke his contract and did not return to China. He was in a new country and could, therefore, start a new life. When the opportunity occurred, he tried to escape with two thousand others. Most of the escapees were caught and returned to William Head, but Tom was one of the few who eluded capture and slipped into Victoria's Chinatown. There he lived off garbage until he found a dishwashing job in a Chinese restaurant. He used his paltry salary to pay a man to forge documents, changing his name from Yuan Chu to Tai Wah.

The documents gave him the freedom to move from Victoria to Vancouver, a city with a large Chinese population where he hoped authorities would have no reason to look for him. The move was a success. Tom spent the next five years working in Chinese-owned laundries and waiting on tables in Chinese restaurants.

Things changed when a restaurant owner found out about the skills Tom no longer used—his training in traditional Chinese medicine—as well as his excellent English. Believing Tom had only recently arrived in Canada—why else would such a man wash dishes?—he thought him a good potential match for his daughter. The father could well afford to be selective, because restrictive Canadian immigration polices had ensured the ratio of Chinese men to women would never be equal. In 1925, when a lonely Tom agreed to a marriage arrangement, Chinese men outnumbered Chinese women by ten to one.

With a wife and, in time, Tom hoped, a family, it was important that he become a good provider. Five years after his escape from the William Head quarantine station, he thought it was time to become more venturesome. Leadership of North American Chinatowns rested firmly in the hands of the wealthier Chinese merchants. In order to start or run a business, one needed the backing of such men. His father-in-law's influence allowed him to practice traditional Chinese medicine. He spent four years building his practice, during which time Betty gave birth to two sons, a year apart.

All went well until a prominent man sought Tom's help for his firstborn son, a two-year-old child who was ill with pneumonia. The father had taken the boy to other practitioners, but in vain. Tom did what he could, but the boy's illness was already advanced when he saw him, and the child died while in his care. Overcome with grief, the father blamed Tom for his loss and convinced the close-knit Chinese community in Vancouver that Tom was incompetent. His credibility was destroyed instantly. Even worse, Tom, who had always lacked confidence, came to believe himself responsible for the child's death. He had never practised since.

As the community turned against him, Tom could no longer find even menial work. Unable to provide for his family, he had no option but to move away from Vancouver. He'd heard there was lots of work for the Chinese as laundrymen, cooks and domestic servants in the new cities of the prairies, where anti-Chinese sentiment was said to be less pervasive than in British Columbia. These stories led Tom and his wife to Philibuster, where the Chinese community was tiny and nobody knew him.

Sadly, Tom's information proved false: anti-Chinese sentiment was as bad on the prairies as it had been on the west coast. In Philibuster he was called names and pushed around, and he walked with his head bowed in order to avoid eye contact with Caucasians. His sons had no friends, because there were no other Chinese children their age and white parents discouraged their children from playing with them. The Wahs were lonely. Tom and Betty often spoke of moving again, but their tiny wet-wash business earned them barely enough to live on, let alone money for savings.

Tom fought with himself as he lay sleepless, listening to the coughing of Joseph Gaston's little girl. Hearing the child struggle for breath, he realized her condition was steadily worsening. On one hand, he wanted help her; on the other, he thought of the little boy who had died in Vancouver, and of the men he had been unable to save from the Spanish Flu in Europe. After these failures, as Tom mistakenly considered them, he had promised himself never again to risk hurting another human being, least of all a child. At the same time, as he listened to Clare, he was overcome with a desire to help.

It was on Tom's conscience that he had never thanked Joseph Gaston, the only person in Philibuster who had treated him with respect, for standing up to the men who had abused him in the street. Could he let this good man's daughter die without trying to help her? Or was he a fool to think there was anything he could do for her? Perhaps even his highly-skilled grandfather would not have been able to save the child's life at this point.

A weary Joseph had just laid an inert Clare on the bed, when he heard a knock on the door.

"Your baby is very ill," Tom began tentatively. "Perhaps I can help."

"Thank you, but …" Joseph said, wondering what Tom could possibly do for Clare.

Tom saw the doubt in Joseph's face. "I've heard her kind of cough before," he said, and told Joseph briefly of his medical training.

Joseph was desperate. The hospital had turned Clare away again, and the costly medicine had only made his little girl worse. Without a word, he stood aside and let the other man inside.

Tom tried to hide his nervousness as he bent over Clare and began to take a thorough history of everything that related to her illness. Joseph answered his questions as best he could. Then Tom proceeded to examine the child.

First, he smelled Clare. Then he held her little wrists, feeling for the pulses that corresponded to her internal organs. He examined her hair, skin, eyes, fingernails and tongue. Observing the rattle in her chest, the blueness of her fingertips, and the coldness of her limbs, he deduced she was no longer getting enough oxygen. He doubted she had long to live. But they could not give up hope.

"I may have something for her," he told Joseph, promising to return quickly as he left the room.

Ideally, Tom would have liked to perform acupuncture on the little girl, but he doubted a westerner would consent to the procedure. Instead, he brewed a tea made with raw herbs, which he gave the haggard-faced father together with instructions on how to administer it. "Keep her warm," he advised, " but put her beside an open window."

Doubtful though he was that Clare would respond to Tom's brew, Joseph followed the man's advice. Later that night, Clare's breathing became so slow that Joseph knew he was losing her. Holding her tiny hands in his, he whispered desperately, "I love you so much, Clare. Please don't leave me." Then he sat with the child in his arms, trying to will his own strength into her small body.

Joseph thought he was dreaming when he felt Clare squeeze his hand. He opened his eyes to see her smiling up at him. It was as if she were fully aware of what was happening and was saying goodbye to him.

"Don't you dare die!" he pleaded.

A moment later, she shut her eyes again. Holding his precious child close, waiting for her to take her last breath, Joseph blinked away tears.

CHAPTER 20

Joseph wished there was something worthy he could do for Tom in return for healing his beloved child. As it was, he felt inadequate. Tom's specially brewed tea had helped Clare get over her cough. After coming by every day to examine her, he had finally said Clare was going to make it.

Tom had not wanted thanks. Mystified, Joseph had watched him leave. He had a thousand questions for the Chinese man, but he respected the fact that Tom was an intensely private person, and he knew better than to ask. At the same time, he was determined to find a way of repaying Tom. There had to be something more he could do besides thanking him profusely and saying, "If ever you need anything, you must tell me. Anything at all."

Not long after Clare's return to health, Joseph came across an interesting advertisement: *"Elderly person needs looking after. Room in exchange for wages. Family preferred."*

Perhaps, Joseph mused, the advertiser had no family nearby to help out around the house and to act as caregiver, which happened sometimes when adult offspring were unable to look after their elderly parents. The position had a certain appeal. On one hand, of course, it did not state the type of help required; it could be anything from chopping wood and starting fires to looking after the bodily needs of a person with dementia. On the other, it provided an irresistible opportunity for free accommodation.

Joseph wrote a letter outlining his qualifications. A reply arrived a few days later, granting him an interview. To his surprise, the advertiser was none other than Mrs. Daisy Nye—Dizzy Daisy, Mayor Winfield Westmoreland's mother.

When Joseph told his brother about the position, Henri promptly launched into a few hilarious Dizzy Daisy stories. Raven's response was more circumspect. "You know your own business," he said gravely, "but I would think twice about this caretaking situation. By all accounts, Daisy Nye is a kind-hearted woman, but her son is a ruthless bastard."

Raven told Joseph about the first dairy manager of the Philibuster Dairy. Supposedly, the man had spoken the word "dizzy" within earshot of his boss. Westmoreland assumed he was referring to his mother. Minutes later the manager, together with the contents of his desk, was on the sidewalk. A day later he was arrested and charged with embezzlement. He was eventually found innocent, but his reputation had been tarnished.

Joseph had his own memories of Westmoreland's callousness. He still thought him a son-of-a-bitch for denying him the job he had been promised. But son-of-a-bitch or not, the fact was that Joseph did not earn enough to pay rent in addition to feeding his children.

On the day of the interview, Joseph dressed his daughters in the clothes Tilda had given them for Christmas. Clare was fussy that day and Joseph considered leaving her behind. But remembering that the advertiser preferred families, he decided to take her along anyway.

The interview took place in a huge three-storey house on a quiet, tree-lined street backing onto Cree Creek. A beautiful house, Joseph saw, painted dark green with white trim around the windows and doors, and with a widow's walk, and a veranda extending the length of the house and along one side.

On the porch, he paused to give Sarah some last-minute behavioural instructions then pulled on the lion-head brass knocker. A rather dowdy-looking woman answered the door. She wore a plain brown dress, her graying hair was tied in a bun, and she held a stenographer's pad in her hand. Joseph drew in his breath as he remembered meeting her on his second day in Philibuster: Winfield Westmoreland's assistant.

"Afternoon ma'am," Joseph said, lifting his hat. "My name is Joseph Gaston. I was told to come here today."

"We've been expecting you. Please, come inside," she said, and introduced herself as Mrs. Brown. It was clear that she did not recognize Joseph.

Joseph made certain the children's shoes and his own were clean before they entered the house. Walking into a wood-panelled foyer easily twice the size of his own room, he felt over-awed. He had little time to look around, however, as he followed Mrs. Brown into what he took to be a sitting room. As the woman invited them to sit down, he was glad to see Sarah behaving decorously. Clare settled herself on his lap. From somewhere above him, he heard a scraping noise, as of furniture being pushed across floorboards.

As best he could, he answered Mrs. Brown's questions, giving her first a few personal details and then something of his work history. He watched her face anxiously as he spoke, sensing she preferred girls to boys, and hoping that having sons would not count against him.

He was concentrating on some of his personal qualities—kindness, competence, honesty, a non-smoker and non-drinker—when Clare, who'd been growing restless, passed gas loudly. Sarah giggled and covered her nose. Mrs. Brown continued to gaze impassively at Joseph, as if nothing out of the ordinary had occurred. Joseph thought it best not to acknowledge the sound and spoke of the farm he had owned back home in Ontario.

The scraping sound from the upper floor came again a few minutes later. Mercifully, it drowned out the recurring sound of Clare's flatulence, though it did nothing to hide the smell. Sarah moved ostentatiously away from Joseph and the offending Clare, still holding her nose, while Mrs. Brown continued to pretend nothing was amiss. Ignoring both girls, Joseph talked faster.

"I can repair most anything. I can cut wood. I can cook. I can iron. I can clean windows and floors ..."

When Clare passed gas again, very loudly, and Sarah giggled uncontrollably, Joseph couldn't help laughing at the sheer inappropriateness of the situation.

"I'm very sorry about this," he apologized, just as another woman appeared at the bottom of the stairs.

Joseph's laughter died as he got to his feet. The woman—Mrs. Nye?—blinked through thick glasses at the strangers in her house. She was very pale, as if her frail elderly body lacked enough blood. Over the pallor her cheeks were heavily rouged, giving her a clown-like appearance. Joseph had the odd feeling that if he were to touch her face, he would encounter wax. "I thought I heard giggling," she said.

When Mrs. Brown had introduced him, Joseph said, "It's a pleasure to meet you, Mrs. Nye." He motioned for Sarah to stand. "And these are my daughters, Sarah and Clare."

"It wasn't me," Sarah said. "Clare's hiney burped."

"Sarah!" Joseph exclaimed.

Mrs. Nye seemed unfazed. "I'm sure it did. And are you applying for the position of caretaker?" she asked Sarah.

Sarah smiled at her. "Nooo. I'm a little girl."

"Does your father want to be the caretaker?"

"Yes. Daddy says we need a clean place to live and not be cold. He said I need to behave myself so he can get the job."

Joseph groaned inwardly.

"Are you cold now, dear?" Mrs. Nye asked.

"No," Sarah said.

"That's good."

"You have bad breath," Sarah accused the old woman.

"Sarah!" Joseph exclaimed again. Any hope he might have had of getting the job had vanished now.

Mrs. Nye smiled at Sarah. "Better to have bad breath than no breath at all. Would you like a cookie?"

"Yes, yes, yes!" Sarah squealed with delight.

"Come with me."

They were back again quickly, Sarah carrying a small paper bag with grease stains showing through the bottom. "I've given her some cookies for later," Mrs. Nye told Joseph.

Joseph thanked her, after which they all stood for a few moments without speaking.

Mrs. Brown broke the silence. "I will contact you in a few days and let you know what's been decided," she said, and showed Joseph to the door.

Joseph waited until he was out of sight of the house before he smacked his forehead a few times. What an idiot he had been to bring Clare along when he'd known she was uncomfortable. And why had he thought Sarah would behave herself? Then, despite the likely loss of a good job, he recalled the events of the last few minutes and laughed out loud.

His laughter stopped abruptly when he saw Sarah put the bag Mrs. Nye had given her on a fence post.

"What are you doing?" he asked, sharply.

"I don't want them," Sarah said.

"Why not?"

"They look yucky."

"I'll eat them, and so will your brothers," Joseph said, annoyed that his daughter was such a picky eater.

He opened the bag. It took him a moment to understand what he was seeing: sugar, butter, peanut butter, flour, baking soda, baking powder, salt and an egg still in its shell: all the necessary ingredients for two dozen peanut-butter cookies.

CHAPTER 21

Joseph had learned to live with the persistent rumour that the Great West Sawmill might close. The rumour, which had been circulating when he'd started work there, still persisted. With scant construction going on in and around Philibuster, lumber continued to stack up outside the mill. Joseph's co-workers tried their best to hold on to the hope that the economy would turn around soon and that things would get back to normal; it was a hope very few really believed.

Sadly, the rumours proved to be correct. A large Ontario outfit, Canadian Sawmills Inc., bought the Great West Sawmill on February 19th, 1934. The new owners immediately reduced the workforce from 30 men to 12 and cut wages by a third. Raven and Joseph both lost their jobs. Henri was retained, although at much reduced wages.

Fortunately for Joseph, Mrs. Nye offered him the position of caretaker. He and the children at least had a place to live.

On the day they moved in, a new black 1934 Cadillac Fleetwood was parked in front of Mrs. Nye's house. Philibuster's mayor waited at the front door. Joseph introduced himself with a smile.

"Winfield Westmoreland," the mayor said, shaking Joseph's hand. It was clear from his manner that he didn't recognize Joseph. "You've spoken with my assistant, so you know what I expect of you."

Mrs. Brown had, indeed, explained Joseph's duties and responsibilities. He was to keep the house operating well—lighting fires, shovelling walks, mowing lawns—and to perform any other regular maintenance the place might require. The main floor was for the use of Joseph and his family. The upper floor was exclusively Mrs. Nye's. Alcohol use and coarse behavior would not be tolerated. If Joseph failed to satisfy Mr. Westmoreland's expectations, his position would end right away.

"Let me make it very clear," Westmoreland said. "You have been placed in a position of great trust and must, therefore, behave in an exemplary manner. Mrs. Nye has—how shall I put it?—spells." He uttered the last word with disdain, as if his mother had a deficiency that reflected badly on him. "These spells must be treated delicately. It is your job to see that she does not embarrass herself. You will speak of nothing that goes on in this house. And you will bring any trouble to my attention immediately."

Joseph acknowledged that he understood his responsibilities and would carry out his orders properly.

"Always remember," Westmoreland intoned before leaving, "that you work for me."

After Westmoreland had gone, Joseph began to explore the house. He started with the main floor. Apart from the large sitting room, which he had already seen, the level consisted of a formal dining area, a library, a washroom, a large kitchen and four bedrooms. The bedrooms and library still contained clothing and personal articles, which, Joseph guessed, had not been used in ages. There were fireplaces in the library, dining room and sitting room, and ornate pot-bellied stoves in the kitchen and bedrooms. Every room had hardwood floors and elaborately carved crown moldings. All in all, the house was as beautiful as Joseph had first thought. At the same time, it needed attention. Paint was peeling everywhere; varnish was fading and nails protruded in places.

In the basement—a vast windowless room of exposed beams with a moist dirt floor—Joseph found steamer trunks, piles of odd-sized lumber, a number of tools and rotting towers, 15 to 20 years old, of the *Star-Phoenix,* Saskatoon's daily newspaper. On a workbench in a corner, Joseph found a Smith & Wesson .455 with a Sam Brown belt and holster. Having used the identical weapon during the war, he wondered if Westmoreland had owned this revolver. For safekeeping, Joseph decided to put it in the room that was going to be his.

On the kitchen table he found an invitation, addressed in careful calligraphy He was to join Mrs. Nye for tea at three o'clock that afternoon. It was almost that time now, he realized. He carried the family's meagre possessions into the house, then went upstairs and knocked at the door of Mrs. Nye's personal sitting room.

She welcomed him cheerfully. "I thought we should become acquainted, since we'll be sharing the same roof. Do make yourself at home while I get the tea."

Joseph looked around him while Mrs. Nye went out to get what she needed. The room was sparsely decorated with a burgundy rug, two small chesterfields, a grandfather clock and a single painting of an ocean scene. A radio played music from the same local station Beth Hoogaboom enjoyed.

Mrs. Nye returned to the room, wheeling a teacart bearing a silver tea service and a tiered stand holding several cakes. "The tea is steeped," she said, pouring it into two cups and handing one to Joseph.

Nervous of making a mistake in etiquette, Joseph decided to follow his employer's lead as he partook of the elegant spread. Mrs. Nye's gracious manner soon put him at ease. He was about to ask her why she had engaged him when she volunteered the information herself. She had made her decision based on her brief meeting with his "delightful" daughter Sarah, she told him. Her son, whom she spoke of as Winny, had had someone else in mind for the position of caretaker, but she had insisted on hiring Joseph. As to why she had wanted a family in the house, she told Joseph that she enjoyed having children around because they made her feel alive.

Joseph promised Mrs. Nye that he and the children would not interfere with her privacy and that he would always be at her disposal. They discussed the work the house needed, although Mrs. Nye assured Joseph that nothing was urgent. "Get settled first," she insisted. He was to pack any of her personal possessions from the main floor into the steamer trunks in the basement. And he was to feel free to use the vegetable garden in the spring. "I know you and Winny will hit it off perfectly," she added, as if the two men were children about to start a new school year together.

Joseph was careful not to overstay his welcome. When the clock struck four, he rose and excused himself. Mrs. Nye said she had enjoyed his visit and looked forward to repeating it. Everything about her manner was well-balanced and friendly. As he went back down the stairs, Joseph wondered whether all the stories he'd heard about her were really true.

Joseph worked diligently at the Nye house in the days that followed. He removed snow, chipped ice off the walkway, repaired fences, and oiled the hinges of the front and back gates. Whenever Westmoreland came to check on his mother, he seemed, in his brusque way, satisfied with Joseph's work.

Mrs. Nye was a delightful employer. She often came downstairs and played with the children—not only the girls, but also the boys, for whom she seemed to have special understanding. Occasionally, she even invited them all for tea in her apartment.

She only complained when her hands bothered her in cold weather, making it difficult for her to get her washing done. Joseph offered to do it for her, and when she refused to let him touch her dirty clothing, he thought of the Wahs' wet-wash service. To his delight, his employer took an immediate liking to Tom and Betty. Joseph was glad he was able to find some business for his former neighbours, although it was hardly enough to make up for the debt he owed Tom. He was even happier when Mrs. Nye discovered Betty's skill with a needle and asked her to embroider some cushions with an elaborate Chinese design.

As time passed, Joseph felt happier and more at ease every day. He had a free home—including heat and electricity—for his children, and a garden in which he would grow vegetables in the summer. Mrs. Nye seemed fairly clear-headed and the big old house was much healthier for the children than the cramped rooming house. Maybe, Joseph thought, luck had finally turned in his favour.

CHAPTER 22

The beginning of March was usually an ugly time of year in Philibuster. Most of the snow had melted; the roads, alleys and walking paths were muddy, and the naked trees and dead grass made the city look dingy.

One bleak evening, Nolan, Cole and their friends were at Hoogaboom's listening to an episode of *The Shadow*. As the boys shoved each other playfully between commercials, Nolan happened to find himself near the cash register. Since his theft from Beth's store, he had temporarily lost the nerve to steal. The belief that his father was onto him, asking to see the gophers he had caught, had kept him honest for a while. But a few days before Christmas Nolan tried his luck again, this time making off with two Hershey chocolate bars from a busy Eaton's store. Another attack of conscience kept him honest for three months after that.

On this particular day Nolan had not planned to steal again: when he did, it happened very quickly. Mrs. Hoogaboom had gone to the back room to fetch an order for a customer and Nolan snaked out a hand for a pack of Wrigley's gum. When Mrs. Hoogaboom returned with the woman's groceries, she rang up the purchase and went on serving other people. She appeared unaware of Nolan's theft.

The radio program ended and Nolan was about to leave the store with his friends. He was congratulating himself on his sleight of hand, when Beth touched his shoulder. Suddenly anxious, he did not protest when she steered him back inside and told the other boys to go home.

Beth asked Nolan to wait while she went on with her work. Standing nervously near the cash register, he tried to ignore Cole and the others who were staring at him with their faces pressed to the window. He also tried to keep his eyes away from the men by the radio, who looked at him as if they knew what he'd been up to.

Nolan wondered what his dad would do to him. He had only been spanked twice, both times when he was seven years old: once for socking Cole in the nose for breaking a model airplane; the second time for letting the cows out of the pen. Mostly, when Nolan misbehaved, his father just raised his voice or told him he was disappointed in him. But stealing was not ordinary misbehavior; it was a crime.

As he waited for Mrs. Hoogaboom, Nolan wondered if his father would have him sent to reform school. He had heard about the horrors of the place from Peter McCormick, Nathan's 15-year-old brother, who had been committed there after a number of crimes. Peter's stories about dreadful punishments for a variety of misdemeanors were frightening: cruel beatings with leather straps by guards known as night owls; having to stand for hours on end without moving; food deprivation for days at a time. It sounded like the worst kind of purgatory. Peter McCormick was the toughest kid Nolan knew, yet Nathan told of his brother's sobbing every night for a month after his return home. Half a year later, he still had nightmares.

Nolan felt ill at the very thought of reform school. He wondered whether Mrs. Hoogaboom planned to make him wait for hours before dealing with him. Meanwhile, she calmly went on serving her customers.

A new thought struck Nolan: what if Mrs. Hoogaboom decided to call the police instead of his dad? Maybe she already had. Why, they could be on their way to the store even now. It didn't take much imagination for him to picture two cops arriving, twisting his hands behind his back and slapping handcuffs on him. There would be no need for a trial. He still had the gum in his pocket and would be found guilty on the spot. His nervousness increased by the minute.

When the last of her customers had gone, Mrs. Hoogaboom led Nolan to the back room. Surrounded by bags of potatoes, cases of soda pop and cartons of canned goods, she confronted the shaking youngster. "Want to tell me what's in your pocket?" she asked.

Terrified at the thought of reform school or even jail, Nolan had worried himself into a frenzy. "I never stole any gopher tails," he blurted out.

Beth got Nolan to confess to all his crimes: the theft of the gopher tails, the sale of the tails to other stores and the things he had purchased with the money, shoplifting at Eaton's and, finally, the pack of gum in his pocket.

"Will you send me to jail?" Nolan's lips trembled.

Beth concealed her amusement. "Not this time, no. But I will have to speak with your dad."

As a chastened Nolan left the store, Beth debated with herself how to handle the matter. Should she even mention it to Joseph? Without knowing him well, she guessed he would be embarrassed. Indeed, Joseph could hardly look her in the face when he learned what had happened. It was almost as if he'd committed the deed himself.

"He's not the first boy to try stealing," Beth tried to console him. "My own girls also had to learn the lesson."

Beth's sympathy did not help Joseph feel better. "How much does my son owe you?" he asked, wondering what Beth must think of him.

Four dollars, she told him. In reality, Nolan had probably gotten away with at least double that amount, but Joseph was an honourable man and would insist on repaying eight dollars, even though it was far more than he could afford.

He reached into his pocket. "I can give you seventy-five cents now. I'll give you the rest as soon as I can."

Beth had no intention of letting Joseph pay for his son's misdeeds. "I have a better idea," she told him. She needed some help in the store. Nolan could work off his debt by delivering groceries for her.

Much relieved, Joseph agreed to the plan, and he and Beth shook hands on the deal.

For the remainder of the day, Joseph thought about what to say to his son. Knowing how much Nolan enjoyed comics about outlaws and stories of American gangsters and Canadian bootleggers, he wondered if the boy had romanticized these bandits in his mind. Nolan wasn't much of a student, mostly barely managing to pass his classes, but he relished his popularity as the class jokester. In the past he had taken pride in his daring, throwing spitballs at his teachers and bringing his slingshot to school—offences which had earned him strappings by the principal. Joseph often worried where Nolan's audacious impulses would lead him, and how he could prevent the boy from coasting along a path with no future. How close was he already to getting into the kind of trouble that would result in police charges? Would his irresponsible actions affect Cole? True, Cole was an excellent and obedient student, but he worshipped his brother and could well be influenced by him.

Instead of castigating Nolan with a prepared lecture, Joseph spoke passionately and from the heart. "Cole idolizes you," he said. "He will follow your lead so you need to set a good example.

This will surprise you, Nolan, but I stole, too. Know what my Uncle David did when he caught me? He beat me till I was covered with bruises. Thing is, I don't believe in hitting. Not when I can reason with a man. And you'll be a man soon, Nolan. You'll need to be responsible for yourself, and that starts with paying back Mrs. Hoogaboom for everything you've stolen." He paused a moment before concluding. "Mrs. Hoogaboom and I have come to an agreement. You'll be delivering groceries for her after school until she considers you're square."

Nolan remained silent during the scolding. He stared at his shoes, never once making eye contact with his father. Joseph had no idea whether his words had made an impact on his son, and he resolved to keep a close eye on him in the future.

Nolan knew he was being observed. For a while he behaved very well, refraining from stealing, or fighting with his brother, or giving way to his impulses. Before long, however, as Joseph again became ever more preoccupied with matters of survival, his watchfulness waned. When that happened, Nolan soon reverted to his old ways.

CHAPTER 23

March was passing and the days were getting longer. It was nearly eight o'clock before the sun dipped beneath the horizon. Extra daylight and warmer weather enabled Joseph to spend more time working out of doors. When he was chiselling away at the rotting windowsills one evening, Copper appeared in what looked like a racing car.

"Bought it when times were better," Copper said, as Joseph put down his tools and walked around the vehicle. The car was a long, red 1920 Napier with bright spokes, no doors and no roof. There was a single seat in the middle of the car, and the number "4" was painted on the front grille.

The car's owner grinned proudly. "First time I've had it out in years. Couldn't afford the gasoline until now."

Joseph invited Copper into the house. Mrs. Nye and Sarah were having a tea party in the dining room, while Clare toddled around, grabbing whatever she could from the edge of the table. Joseph introduced his friend to Mrs. Nye and the girls, then took him to the kitchen and offered him a brew made from dried barley which had been roasted and ground. He tried to pass the stuff off as coffee, since it was the closest he could come to the real thing. Copper tactfully refrained from commenting on the harsh taste, and even pretended to enjoy it.

Initially hired as a junior technician at the dairy, Copper was now the assistant to the chief technician. "There were three other people in the lab when I started," he said. "Only two of us there now."

"What happened?"

Copper shrugged. "Business. Why pay four guys when two can do the work?" He had been kept on because he earned less than his co-workers. It did not matter to Westmoreland that for two people to get the job done, they were forced to work seven days a week.

One of Copper's responsibilities was to have a good active cheese culture available every day—no mean feat, as even the slightest contamination or mishandling was enough to prevent the culture from growing and the cheese from being made. If the cheese-maker mishandled the cultures, as sometimes happened, and the cheese did not develop correctly, Copper would be blamed. For this reason, he was always careful to have several cultures ready for use. "Nobody knows I spend Sunday nights in the lab, making sure I have cultures ready for Monday morning," he told Joseph.

"You'll want to know why I came by," Copper said. "I wanted to tell you there might be something for you at the dairy. I heard Westmoreland cursing out one of his deliverymen. The way I hear it, the man drinks. The boss said he was going to get someone else for the south side route." He looked at Joseph. "But maybe you already know that, seeing as you're looking after his ma's house."

Joseph shook his head, without admitting that he'd barely shared twenty words with Westmoreland in the time he'd been at the Nye house.

"It might bear investigation," Copper said, and asked Joseph to keep the source of his information a secret, as news of the route was not yet public. "I don't want to be on the wrong side of a man like Westmoreland."

When Copper had gone, Joseph sat thoughtfully at the kitchen table. *A conundrum,* he thought, recalling the word he'd recently found in the old dictionary. Should he wait for the ad to appear before applying for the job? Or was it best to do something about it right away? After thinking about it a few minutes, he decided to waste no time going after the job.

From the dining room came the boisterous sounds of Sarah and Clare being chased around the room by Mrs. Nye. It was almost nine o'clock and the girls should have been in bed. If not for his employer's occasional "spells," Joseph would have felt comfortable leaving Sarah and Clara with her. The girls had really taken to Mrs. Nye, even more than to Tilda in some ways. Yet Joseph could not be quite certain that his employer might not forget the children and go off somewhere. Not wanting to disturb Tilda at this hour, he left Nolan in charge and set off to speak to Westmoreland.

At the top of the hill, he paused to look at Winfield Westmoreland's house. Although not as big as his mother's, it was impressive nonetheless, a modern, two-storey brick structure with a low-pitched roof, central chimney, double garage and a garden with well-kept lawn. Trying to shake off a feeling of apprehension, Joseph took a breath, straightened his shoulders and went on walking.

At the door, he paused to review the things he planned to say. When it was too late to change his mind—he had already knocked—he wished he had made an appointment to see

Westmoreland instead of arriving unannounced.

He attempted a friendly smile as the door was opened by a woman who would have been pretty but for the raw welt on her cheek. Joseph's smile froze as he wondered if she had been struck by a whip.

"Good evening," he said, recovering quickly. "My name is Joseph Gaston. May I speak to Mr. Westmoreland?"

Putting a hand over the ugly mark on her cheek, the woman showed him into a hallway and told him to wait. Joseph wondered if this was the mayor's wife.

He had just enough time to notice the modern furnishings in the rooms leading away from the hall when Westmoreland appeared, dressed as if for work.

"What do you want?" he demanded.

"I'm Joseph Gaston," he blurted out, at that moment regretting the impulsiveness of the visit.

"I know who you are," Westmoreland said curtly.

Westmoreland must think him an idiot, Joseph thought. After all, he was the one who'd hired him to look after his mother's house!

"I won't waste your time, sir." Nervousness made Joseph speak too quickly. "I understand you may need a man to run your south side route."

Westmoreland stared at him, clearly irritated. "And how the hell do you know that?"

Joseph had to be careful not to get Copper into trouble. "Heard it around, sir," he mumbled.

"Is that so?"

"Yes, sir."

Westmoreland looked at him so probingly that Joseph wondered if he'd jeopardized his position as Mrs. Nye's caretaker.

"What makes you think you manage the route, Gaston?"

When Joseph had finished telling him about his dairy farm in Ontario, Westmoreland wanted to know what had happened to the place. "Not much of a businessman, are you?" he taunted, upon hearing that Joseph had gone bankrupt.

"No, sir."

Westmoreland knew Joseph didn't have a paying job, and that the shabby clothes he'd worn for this interview were probably his best. He also knew it made good sense to employ desperate people, as they were easier to control.

"The route pays twenty dollars a month," he said flatly, watching closely for Joseph's reaction.

Joseph was aghast at the paltriness of the offer. Twenty dollars a month was a third of what the job was worth, half as much as Joseph had been promised for a similar position when he'd first come to Philibuster. He quickly considered the pros and cons of the offer. Would he be risking his situation with Mrs. Nye if he took the job? Could he look after Daisy and also manage the work at the dairy? And if he did, why work for slave wages?

"I'll do it for thirty," he said.

Westmoreland was unbending. "Twenty."

Surely, thought Joseph, the last man had not worked for so little? He wondered whether Westmoreland was simply a hard bargainer or if, in fact, he would absolutely refuse to go higher.

"You know the job's worth sixty," he said finally, "but I'll accept twenty-eight."

"Twenty."

Joseph hesitated before saying regretfully, "I can't do the job for that salary. I'm sorry to have taken up your time."

"Suit yourself."

What have I done? Joseph wondered, as he left the house and began to walk home.

CHAPTER 24

Winfield Westmoreland stood at the window and watched Joseph leave. His mother's lowly employee was probably feeling disheartened at the thought that the mayor did not think him suited to the job of dairyman. He could not know that this was, in fact, not the case; it was simply the way Westmoreland did business. His dictum was "keep your cards as close to your vest as you can and don't let the other guy know what you are holding." Every shrewd businessman knew that.

The truth was that Winfield experienced regret the moment he closed the door behind Joseph. Even more than regret, he felt anger that Joseph hadn't jumped at his offer. Clenching his teeth, he slammed his fist on the desk. The sound echoed ominously through the house, warning his wife and son to avoid him.

Westmoreland had fired the last deliveryman, his wife's stupid cousin, without a ready replacement. Now he was paying a lot of money to temporary workers to keep the small dairy farm functioning and the delivery route operating. Joseph Gaston would have been the perfect replacement, but the thought of paying him those few extra dollars was galling. Perhaps because he already had enough other problems to deal with, the confrontation with Joseph had made him angrier than it might have done otherwise— so angry that he was tempted to pay a visit to a whore.

Gideon Westmoreland, Winfield's father, had introduced him to his first prostitute. Winfield was just 14 when he left his mother and his home in Philibuster in search of his father. He found him in Saskatoon, Saskatchewan—the town Daisy and Winfield had fled five years earlier to escape Gideon's abuse.

Winfield had not known quite what to expect. A fatherly welcome, perhaps? What he had not anticipated was that his father would take him to a cathouse. Years later, Winfield still remembered his father leading him through a dark back alley and knocking harshly on a large steel door. A slot opened and a pair of eyes looked them over. Seconds later they were admitted into the building, where Gideon nodded at a huge man guarding the entrance. He led his son down a hall and up a long staircase to a large, open room furnished with overstuffed chairs and low tables.

The innocent boy was astonished to see men in suits and women wearing what looked like undergarments. Most had drinks in their hands. Sitting on the men's laps were all manner of women. Ranging from thin to buxom, adorned with heavy makeup, many of the women were excitingly exotic.

A man behind the bar greeted Gideon, who nodded in return. Only when Gideon asked Winfield if there was a girl he fancied did it dawn on the boy that his father expected him to choose a woman to have sex with. Although Winfield and his friends often boasted to one another about prostitutes and intercourse, the fact was that he knew nothing about women and had never been intimate with one. Unwilling to acknowledge his inexperience to his father, who might take that as a sign of weakness, he pointed to the most modestly dressed woman in the room, a girl named Chelsea. Summoned by the barman, she took Winfield's hand and led him down a hall to one of a row of doors.

Winfield remembered the encounter as horrible, devoid of any excitement. Kissing the prostitute was no more pleasurable than kissing a piece of meat: worse in fact, because he felt soiled afterwards and wished there was a way of retrieving his innocence.

The half hour with Chelsea was Gideon's way of acquainting his son with his business. The brothel was one of two that he owned and operated. The men who frequented Gideon's establishments liked them because they didn't feel like whorehouses. "Classy operations," some people called them, clean places with good booze and women who seemed satisfied with their situations. Customers approved of Gideon too. He dressed well, addressed everyone with respect, and his employees seemed fond of him. For the customers it was a little like a gentlemen's club, with benefits.

The reality, of course, was quite different from the way things appeared on the surface. Behind closed doors, Gideon ran his brothels ruthlessly. The girls he employed were forced to cut all ties with their families and friends. They were expected to work six days a week. Their one day off was strictly controlled. Gideon had to know where they went, whom they saw, and what they did. He so intimidated his employees that his deliberately erratic and volatile behaviour was enough to keep them in line. He did not hesitate to make an example of the rare woman who might anger him by being disrespectful, by bringing in too little money, or by trying to escape. Such misdemeanours incurred physical punishment, anything from a painful slap in the face to a brutal whipping. Gideon knew and bribed all the cops in town, so he was never arrested for assault.

Before long, Winfield was helping his father run the brothels. His previous sensitivity and scruples vanished remarkably quickly. Learning by example, he soon treated the women as his father did, and violence became a normal part of his life. Over time, he found that treating the girls roughly actually gave him a sense of serenity and clear-headedness that nothing else could provide.

After Winfield left his father and the whorehouses of Saskatoon for other ventures, he found he still needed prostitutes, never more so than when he was having a particularly bad day. At such times his only way of calming himself was by knocking around a whore—which created a problem for a man whose election platform had emphasized the importance of making Philibuster a family town and eliminating prostitution.

Westmoreland knew his philandering would not go over well in conservative Philibuster. When the occasionally nasty rumour surfaced about Winfield Westmoreland, a well-placed newspaper article or anonymous letter—usually by one of the city councillors with ownership in the *Philibuster Post*—mentioned the mayor's good deeds or generosity, thereby laying the rumour to easy rest.

He also understood that it took more than printed compliments to safeguard his reputation, and that it was important for him to be careful. In order for him to continue his enjoyment of prostitutes, he needed a third party to schedule his arrangements, a man he could trust, and over whom he had power of some sort. That person was Chief Quentin. After a quick call from Winfield, the police chief would call his counterpart in Calgary or Edmonton, the two largest nearby cities. He would learn which cathouses were safe from impending raids and which girl to ask for. When Westmoreland had the necessary information, he would drive three hours to the anonymous rendezvous.

Sitting at the desk in his well-appointed home office, Westmoreland was tempted to call Chief Quentin. His fingers were on the phone, ready to dial, when he decided to do something else first.

He drove to his mother's house. After spending a few perfunctory minutes with Daisy, he made jovial, inconsequential conversation with Joseph. Almost by way of an afterthought—or so Joseph was meant to think—he offered the man the job he'd sought, for twenty-four dollars a month plus sales bonuses.

Joseph jumped at the offer with such alacrity, that Winfield sensed the man had had a change of heart. Indeed, had he repeated the original salary of twenty dollars a month, Joseph might well have accepted it. Irritated that he had failed to read the situation correctly, Westmoreland felt it necessary for Joseph to understand who was in charge.

"Remember," he said aggressively, "I expect you to do a good job looking after my mother's place as well as managing the route. If you don't, you'll lose both jobs."

"I can manage," Joseph said quietly.

"See that you do. I'll meet you at the barn at five tomorrow morning."

CHAPTER 25

Some hours before dawn, Joseph left the girls with Tilda and made for Westmoreland's dairy farm on the eastern edge of town. Sarah would start school in another year and a half, and maybe Clare would be able to come to work with him by then. He looked forward to the day when he would no longer have to rely on Tilda. Grateful though he was to her for taking such good care of the children, since Christmas he had been unable to shake the feeling that he was losing his daughters to his sister-in-law. He felt intensely troubled at the thought that he was being—what was the word he had recently learned?—supplanted.

The streetlights stopped at the edge of town, but the stars and a sliver of moon lit up the gravel road so that he could see the way. At a bend in the road he turned onto a dirt drive from where he could make out the black forms of a barn, a garage and a farmhouse. His footfalls were quiet, yet audible enough to alert the cattle, who began a sleepy lowing. Out of long habit, the cows ambled slowly toward the barn to be milked. Joseph was inclined to get on with the day's work, but he decided it might be better to wait for Westmoreland.

Half an hour later, the cows sounded more urgent. Milk filled their udders, but there was still no sign of Westmoreland. Seeing the lock hanging loosely on the barn door, Joseph thought he would investigate. He opened the door, turned on lights and looked around. The place, he saw right away, was an old-fashioned hand-milking operation, with no pumps or machinery to speak of, but there was a small bottling room that was no longer used. The once-independent dairy farm had become a small part of a larger one. The milk was destined for the plant, where it would be pasteurized and bottled.

Joseph was concerned when 20 more minutes had passed without him seeing Westmoreland. He knew how important routine was for the health and milk production of cattle. In addition to milking, his duties would include feeding the calves, delivering the milk to the dairy plant, picking up the cheese, butter, bottled milk and other products for his run, doing the route, cleaning the barn, and milking the cows again in the evening. It was difficult for a man to handle more than a dozen cows on his own, let alone 25, which he figured there were here. In light of all this, his monthly salary looked even skimpier than before. But this was no time to brood: Joseph figured he should begin without Westmoreland.

He found everything he needed: cleaning solutions, ten-gallon milk cans and a pail. He moved the first cow into place and washed its teats. Listening to the familiar, hollow sound of the milk as it hit the side of the pail, he quickly got into a rhythmic stride.

"Good, you've started," Westmoreland said suddenly, from behind him. Concentrating intently, as he always did when he was working, Joseph hadn't heard his employer's approach.

Westmoreland gave him a quick tour. "You're responsible for everything on the farm. Milking, delivery, livestock and upkeep. When you get to the factory with the milk, the pickers will already have today's stock ready for your route. South side from Hastings and 45th Avenue to the edge of town. If you need any help, you'll pay for it yourself."

Westmoreland added a few details Joseph needed to know. "Anything else?" he ended brusquely. When Joseph had no questions, Westmoreland handed over the keys to the barn and the garage and departed abruptly.

Joseph finished milking as quickly as he could before going to the garage to find the delivery vehicle. It was an old horse-drawn wagon, essentially a white-painted box on four wheels. The cab was open but covered, with a door leading to the rear where the milk was stored. Lamps were suspended from the front and back corners of the roof, and metal mud flaps hung over the wheels. *PHILIBUSTER DAIRY* was painted in red on each side of the wagon.

Outside the garage, a horse waited by the gate. Joseph wished he had an apple or a carrot for the animal; he would remember to bring something the next day. After feeding, watering and harnessing the horse—a gentle old creature—he loaded the milk into the back of the wagon and hitched the horse to the front. He was already on his way to the dairy pool when dawn lit the eastern horizon and birdsong filled the air.

Joseph led the horse and wagon to one of the loading chutes to drop off the milk and be loaded with the day's deliveries. He introduced himself as the new route driver to the dock-worker, a surly, bearded man with short dark hair who looked oddly familiar. The dockworker muttered something incomprehensible in return. Joseph watched him move with a slowness that looked deliberate. Worried about the precious wasted minutes, he offered to assist, only to be met with a rude response: "Don't need any of your damned help!"

When the rig was finally loaded, Joseph requested a list of delivery addresses. Once more, he was taken aback. "Don't have one."

"You don't? There must be a list …"

"There was only one, and someone lost it." A mean grin accompanied the words.

Joseph was exasperated. "How am I supposed to know who gets what?"

"Not my concern." That same ugly grin. "Why don't you ask your Chink friend for advice?"

Suddenly Joseph knew why the dockworker looked familiar. His name was Mack Fisher, and he was the man who had spat at Tom Wah some time ago. Joseph would have liked to grab the ignorant bastard by the throat, but stopped himself. The man was quite obviously itching to continue the previous altercation and Joseph knew better than to risk his new job for the sake of personal satisfaction.

Without another word, he shut the wagon, pulled it to the front of the dairy, engaged the brake, and walked into the office. The receptionist was polite, but could not help him. She had a note of the customers on the route, but did not know their addresses and requirements. What Mack Fisher had said was correct. There had only been one daily delivery list, and she did not have it.

Joseph thought only briefly of enlisting Westmoreland's help. The hostile Mack Fisher might well insist he'd given the list to Joseph, and that Joseph must have lost it. It would be the trouble-maker's word against his own, not a good way to start his first day of work.

Joseph also understood that his employer was unlikely to toler-ate excuses. Westmoreland would expect the work to be completed properly and in good time. So Joseph had only one option: start on Hastings Street and stop at every house until he had delivered everything in the wagon. He had no idea how he would manage to finish the route and still make it back to the farm for the evening milking. He felt ill at the thought that he might lose his job on the first day, and, with it, possibly his situation with Mrs. Nye.

At the first house on Hastings Street, Joseph got out of the rig, engaged the brake—a short chain with hooks on either end that kept the wheels from turning—ran to the door and knocked.

"Do you get milk delivered?" Joseph asked the woman who answered the door.

"Yes. You're new—but didn't you get yesterday's order card?" Looking puzzled, she handed Joseph a piece of cardboard the size of an index card. He glanced at it quickly. The card listed the dairy's products with check marks indicating the customer's wishes for the next day.

He looked up and smiled. "Thank you. Yes, I'm new, but I do have your order." He took the card and the empty bottles, picked up the customer's milk and cheese, and carried them to the house.

Returning to the wagon, he was surprised to find the old horse already starting to move. Fortunately, the brake was in place, so the wagon stayed put: but he now realized that if he did not use the brake every time he left the rig, the horse might bolt.

The horse proceeded to the next house. Joseph was about to pull on the reins, but the horse stopped of its own accord. The woman of the house gave him her order card and said she wanted milk, butter and cream. When Joseph returned to the wagon after doing the delivery, the horse tried to move off again, making him wonder whether the animal was going to be a problem.

The pattern repeated itself all the way down the street. The horse seemed to sense when Joseph wanted to stop and moved its hooves in a type of dance until it was time to go further. As Joseph carried two quarts of milk and a block of cheese to the last house on Hastings, he wondered what he should do next, cross the intersection and continue down the same side of the street, or turn around and do the other side? Which way would be fastest? Leaving the milk and the cheese at the house, he turned back to the street. "Shit!" he exclaimed when he saw the wagon was gone.

He looked up and down the street, but the horse and wagon were nowhere to be seen. In his haste, he had forgotten to hook up the brake.

To his relief, he spotted the horse and wagon around the corner, waiting patiently three houses down a new street. Joseph engaged the brake before running back to the two houses the horse had bypassed: nothing was wanted at either of them. The owner of the third house, the one outside which the horse had stopped, wanted milk.

Suddenly Joseph understood. The horse knew the route! Left to itself, it clopped down the street to particular houses, stopping while Joseph did deliveries and dancing in place until they were ready to move on. Joseph spent the rest of the morning taking his cues from his new friend.

After completing the route, Joseph dropped the empty bottles and order cards at the dairy pool, then returned to the farm to do the remainder of his chores.

Without direction, the horse pulled the dairy wagon into the garage and waited patiently to be unharnessed. Then it walked to a stall in the barn, stopped and did its little dance. Understanding what he had to do, Joseph checked the horse's hooves, dug out a few stones, bathed the hooves in oil, then fed, watered and brushed the animal. When he had finished, he patted the horse affectionately and watched him amble out to pasture.

"Thanks, Dancer," Joseph called, smiling when the old horse whinnied in response.

CHAPTER 26

Joseph didn't miss any deliveries that first day, nor on the days after that. When he loaded his rig in the mornings, he made sure not to choose a loading chute operated by Mack Fisher. He also started bringing Nolan and Cole with him. The boys helped him move the cows, empty pails, set up cans, load the wagon and care for Dancer. On his way back into town he'd let the boys take turns driving the wagon—although Dancer needed no direction—and then dropped them at their aunt's for breakfast before they went off to school.

The day he received his first pay envelope, Joseph hurried through his chores, arriving at Tilda's earlier than usual. The children were so excited when they learned they were going for treats, that Nolan and Cole bounded along, whooping, hollering and jumping off the bases of lampposts. Affected by her brothers' high spirits, Sarah imitated them. Clare was content to toddle along at Joseph's side, stopping now and then to inspect something on the ground and bring it to her mouth: an ant, a pretty stone, a piece of paper.

When they reached Hoogaboom's and Hooper's Café, they found a crowd gathered outside. Joseph wondered if another poor unfortunate soul had ordered a meal and refused to pay. As he got closer, he heard a radio blaring out the play-by-play of a hockey game, the fourth game of the Stanley Cup finals between the Detroit Red Wings and the Chicago Black Hawks. The radio sat on the liar's bench, with a number of extension cords, one plugged into the next, leading into the grocery store. As the legendary Foster Hewitt announced that just two minutes remained in the second period, Joseph stopped to listen.

"*Thank you for listening to the General Motors Hockey Broadcast*," said Hewitt when the period ended. "*Please stay tuned to your local station.*"

During hockey game intermissions, the national broadcast reverted back to the local affiliate stations. In Philibuster, the break was filled with local ads and a quiz show that was known for trying to trick its contestants. The Detroit fans were discussing that team's chances of winning the series and the coveted Cup. Detroit was down two games to one in a best-of-five series, and the present game was still scoreless. Other people preferred to listen to the quiz show.

As the boys ran off to join their friends, Joseph spotted Raven and Henri.

"Just get off work?" Joseph asked his brother.

Henri put a finger to his lips. Joseph understood. His brother did not want Joseph to tell Tilda he'd been at Hoogaboom's, listening to the game.

"We're having ice cream!" Sarah exclaimed, and went on to tell her uncle how much she planned to eat.

Leaving the girls with their uncle, Joseph entered the store. He grabbed a brick of vanilla ice cream, exchanged a few words with Beth—who told him Nolan was doing an excellent job—then joined the line-up at the cash register. He was startled when Raven burst into the store and hollered, "Joseph, get out here!"

Thinking something had happened to one of the children, Joseph dropped the ice cream on the counter without paying for it and hurried outside. Raven nodded at the radio and said, "Dizzy Daisy."

Joseph listened uneasily as the show host asked, "Now, Mrs. Daisy Nye, please tell us where you live."

"In my house," she answered, in a way that made Joseph realize she was speaking on her phone at home.

Around the radio, everyone chuckled.

"Pardon me, ma'am, I meant in which town do you reside?"

"Philibuster."

"Right here in Philibuster. Well, well. Now, Mrs. Daisy Nye of Philibuster, do you know how to play our game?"

"I think I do, dear."

"For our audience at home, let me repeat the rules. I will ask you a skill-testing question. If you answer it correctly, you win our prize—a year's supply of Rinso Detergent. You use Rinso, as I'm sure you know, to make your colours come out fresher and brighter. Are you ready Mrs. Nye?"

"Yes, I am."

Somebody in the crowd laughed and said, "This could be good."

Joseph was nervous as he looked around to see who had made the remark. An important part of his job with Mrs. Nye was to keep her out of trouble. He could only pray there would not be any.

"The question is: Which weighs more, a pound of feathers or a pound of lead?"

"That's easy," Mrs. Nye said confidently. "A pound of lead."

Again, there was laughter.

"I'm sorry, Mrs. Nye. Your answer is incorrect. In fact, a pound of feathers weighs the same as a pound of lead."

Mrs. Nye snorted in disgust. Raising her voice, she declared, "Well if I hit you over the head with a pound of lead, I bet you'd know the difference!" Whereupon, she slammed down the phone in evident disgust.

Joseph was unable to hear the host's response over the crowd's loud laughter.

The ice cream was forgotten as he hustled the kids back home. Just as he was about to run up the stairs to check on Mrs. Nye, a car skidded savagely to a stop in front of the house. Joseph opened the front door just as Westmoreland leaped out of his Cadillac.

"Fool! Idiot!" Westmoreland yelled at Joseph. "I told you to watch her!" Pushing past Joseph, he deliberately knocked over Sarah, who began to cry.

Joseph picked her up and soothed her gently. When Sarah was calm, he shooed the children into the kitchen and returned to the foyer. He stood there for ten minutes, listening to the muffled voices of Westmoreland and his mother. As he waited, he struggled with his need for work and shelter and the desire to hit the callous bastard. Westmoreland came tramping down the stairs at last, saw Joseph and shoved him hard with a closed fist. Joseph stumbled, but managed not to fall.

"If anything like this happens again, I'll fire you. I'll evict you on the spot, you stupid son-of-a-bitch!" Westmoreland screamed, his face a bright, unhealthy red. "You have something to say?" Spittle flew from his lips.

Joseph bit his own lips hard to keep back a furious retort.

His slave cowed, Westmoreland stomped out of the house and drove off in a shower of gravel.

As the Cadillac sped down the street, Joseph's anger spiralled to new heights. Over and over, he imagined punching Westmoreland in the face, sending him to the ground bleeding from his nose and mouth, and begging for mercy. He held on to his fantasy for some time. Sadly, he knew such a thing would never happen. He would always be beholden to men like Westmoreland That reality made him even angrier.

CHAPTER 27

The Sunday began like any other for Nolan and Cole. They and their friends gathered together after lunch. Each boy had brought a pack of wooden matches from home, with the exception of Nathan McCormick, who provided brass rifle casings. His brother Peter had told him how to make homemade ammunition. Nathan's friends were now eager to make some too.

First they had to cut the heads off the matches. That done, they packed the match heads gently into the hollow brass rifle casings—an exacting task, for if the match heads were packed too tightly they might flare sooner than they should. Lastly, they carved wooden plugs to seal up the casings. The ammunition was now ready to be used.

Guz, one of the group, was home alone that afternoon, giving the boys a chance to test their ammunition at his house. They fired up the wood stove in the kitchen, waiting impatiently until it was hot enough to put the rifle casings on top of it. The heat performed as expected, igniting the match heads inside the rifle casings and sending off the wooden stoppers like rockets. The excited boys whooped with joy whenever a wooden plug hit the ceiling.

By the time all the bullets had been fired, the boys were so pumped with adrenaline that they needed something else, preferably something dangerous, to amuse them. Somebody brought up the tree stunt. A tall aspen grew a little way down the street from Guz's house. In no time, challenges were thrown back and forth.

Not surprisingly, Nolan was the first to accept Nathan McCormick's dare. A frightened Cole tried to talk him out of it, but his daredevil brother refused to listen.

Seven boys looked up nervously at the big aspen. The tree was taller than they'd realized, easily twice the height of any other tree on which the stunt had been performed in the past.

"You're gonna catch a beating," Cole warned pleadingly.

Nolan sneered at him. "Only if you tell Dad, you little snitch."

Nolan knew very well that he had promised his father not to try the stunt again. But that promise had been made a lifetime ago; he could not be held to it now. The idea of a potential beating did not bother him. Even after the theft from Hoogaboom's, his father had only spoken to him sternly. What he was uneasy about was the height of the tree, not that he would have admitted this to a soul.

"Am not a snitch!" Cole exclaimed indignantly, upset to be so insulted in front of the others.

But Nolan had more to worry about than his brother, who looked hurt and embarrassed. For now Nathan was eyeing him tauntingly. "I think you're scared."

"I am not!"

"Oh, sure. Likely you ain't got no intestinal fortitude."

Nolan didn't know the meaning of "intestinal fortitude," but he was well aware that he was being goaded. Not that it mattered. He had taken on the dare in front of all his friends and he could not possibly renege without potential ridicule.

"Don't go too high," Cole begged.

"I'll go as high as I got to," Nolan retorted sharply, and began to climb the tree.

At 20 feet up, he planted his feet firmly on a couple of sturdy branches. Looking down, he shook the tree with his weight, testing to see how far it would bend. The tree swayed, but not as much as Nolan had hoped. At 30 feet he tried again, but still the sway was insufficient.

"Nolan, come down!" pleaded Cole from the foot of the tree.

"Nolan come down, Nolan come down," Nathan repeated mockingly. The other boys laughed.

It was one thing for Nolan to tease his brother: quite another for others to do it. "Shut up, Nathan!" Nolan yelled down. Caught by the anger in his friend's tone, Nathan did not mock Cole again.

More than anything, Nolan wanted to be back on the ground. Yet if he went down at this point his friends would razz him, and he couldn't tolerate that. Had he been thinking clearly, he would have buffaloed his pals with some excuse about the tree not being the right kind for the stunt. But by this time he'd become completely engrossed in Nathan's challenge and would have done anything to avoid being called a coward.

By the time he was 50 feet up, few of the remaining branches were large enough to bear his weight. He was worried that one of the boughs would snap and drop him to the ground. In spite of his concern, he climbed a little higher before shaking the tree again. The tree bent. *Now or never*, he thought wildly. Gripping the trunk tightly with both hands, he closed his eyes and kicked his legs forward, out into the air.

Up to this point, Nolan had done everything correctly. The one problem he could not have foreseen was that he didn't weigh enough. He was still nearly 30 feet from the ground, with his legs dangling in the air. Looking down, unable to move, he felt a thousand feet up.

"Oh, shit!" Nathan McCormick exclaimed, mouth wide open.

"Nolan, don't let go!" Cole yelled up at his brother.

"Get a ladder!" Nolan shouted back, as he kicked and twisted without result.

Guz ran off, while the others came up with smart ideas.

"Call the fire department."

"We need a mattress under the tree."

"Pile up the dead leaves."

Nolan stopped kicking, but continued to twist back and forth. His hands were now so slick with sweat that he didn't know how much longer he could hold on. "Hurry!" he howled when he saw Guz returning with a ladder.

The boys positioned the ladder directly beneath Nolan, but it was far too short to reach him.

"Jump!" Guz called.

Nolan's grip was weakening. "Get the ladder out of the way!" he yelled.

"I'm coming, Nolan," Cole cried suddenly.

To the amazement of the older boys, Cole scrambled up the tree, ignoring the branches scraping his arms and face as he climbed, quick as a monkey, toward his brother. "I'm coming," he kept calling.

Finally on a level with Nolan, Cole crawled out onto the largest branch and extended a hand toward his brother. But Nolan was out of reach.

"I can't hold on!" screamed Nolan.

"Climb further, try and bend the tree more," Guz called.

"Hurry," Nolan pleaded.

Cole worked his way back to the tree trunk. He climbed higher, this time hugging the outside of the arc.

"It's working," Nathan called.

The tree had bent somewhat in response to Cole's weight. Nolan saw he was closer to the ground than before, but still too high to fall safely. As his hands began to lose their hold, he closed his eyes in concentration.

The boys cheered Cole on as he continued to climb. He was already 45 feet up, trying his best to bend the tree still further.

"I can't hold on!" Nolan yelled suddenly.

Seconds later he fell to the ground, landing safely, thanks to Cole. Poor Cole was not as lucky. Without Nolan's weight, the aspen straightened itself violently, catapulting the boy into the air.

CHAPTER 28

The Great Henri laughed until his sides hurt when Tilda told him the story in bed that night. After being propelled into the air, Cole had landed in a lilac bush 70 feet from the tall aspen. Though screaming in pain, he had been able to walk home. When Joseph got back from work, he carried the moaning child to Dr. Graham's. The result of the accident was a broken radius that would keep his forearm in a cast for six weeks.

"It really isn't funny," Tilda scolded, annoyed that Henri was so often unconcerned when serious things happened. "Cole could have broken his neck!"

"But 'e did not—duh boy is fine." Still laughing, her husband made an arcing movement with his index finger, as if in imitation of Cole's flight.

"Cut out your foolin'!" Tilda exclaimed. She sat up straight against the headboard with her arms crossed over her chest.

When her husband stopped laughing, she decided to tell him what had been on her mind for some time.

Since resolving to take away the girls from Joseph, she had devoted herself almost obsessively to winning their love. To her credit, Tilda knew she was being manipulative and occasionally experienced remorse, although not to the point of halting her efforts. By and large, she was an honest woman who would return to a store if a cashier had given her too much change. Deceiving Joseph had caused her many sleepless nights. Indeed, she'd often wished there was another way, but if there was, she didn't know what it might be. One of her favourite dictums was *God helps those who help themselves*. Now that the girls were essentially hers, it was time to convince Henri that they should become Sarah and Clare's permanent guardians.

"Those kids need a good home," she said.

"What kids?"

"Joseph's, of course!"

"But already dey 'ave one."

"No, they don't," Tilda protested resolutely. "Think about it, Henri. Those poor kids get moved around from Joseph's place to ours like they're train freight. Joseph wakes them early every morning to bring them to me. They sleep a few hours and then wake up cranky and confused. By the time Joseph takes them home, it's already way past their bedtime. Those kids get sick because they don't get enough good rest. One of these days, they'll get an illness they can't shake."

"Tilly! Surely you exaggerate."

Tilda looked at him angrily. "I do not! And then there's that crazy Daisy Nye. Everyone knows she's not in her right mind. She walks around town mumbling to herself and doing all sorts of odd things. Why, just before Joseph started caring for her, I saw her pounding nails into a birch tree. She said she was getting syrup for her flapjacks. What if one day she takes after the girls with that hammer?"

"Joseph says she's a real gentle woman, and duh little ones adore 'er."

Tilda shook her head. "But what if she has a spell one day when she's alone with them? She's capable of anything! It's not a risk I would want to take."

Henri lay back and closed his eyes. In his opinion, Joseph was handling his affairs well.

"I think they should live with us permanently," Tilda said, after a few moments of silence.

Her husband opened his eyes. "Joseph an' duh children?"

Tilda hesitated once more. "No, not Joseph."

Henri rolled on his side and gazed at his wife.

Tilda understood the need to tread carefully. "Maybe Joseph could at least let the girls live with us. I'm sure he'd be relieved to let someone else—someone who loves and cares for them—be responsible for them. Joseph is killing himself trying to feed and clothe all four children. He pretends he's not hungry so he can fill their plates. His winter clothes aren't warm enough for a summer's day. And have you looked at his shoes lately? Why, they're held together by baling twine."

Henri listened in astonishment to his wife's speech. All he could think of by way of response was that Joseph's new job would enable him to cope with his expenses more easily.

"Yes, he has a little more money," Tilda acknowledged reluctantly, "but it's still only enough to feed himself and the boys. And with the long hours he works, he can't give the girls the attention they need. Who's to say Sarah mightn't climb a tree and fall? Cole was lucky, he was only injured, but Sarah could get killed. Wouldn't it be better if she and Clare were with us, where we could watch out for them and protect them?"

"I don' know," Henri said thoughtfully.

To Tilda's disappointment, she was not persuading Henri as easily as she'd hoped. Clutching the top of her blanket, she spoke as convincingly as she could. "Joseph is feeling overwhelmed. Taking care of four children is too much for him. He told me so. I'm certain he would like someone to take the girls, but he feels it would make him look bad if he were to give them up. He doesn't want you to think poorly of him."

Henri looked astonished. "And 'ee 'as said so?"

"Just the other day. But don't say I told you. He told me in confidence."

Henri did not answer. Tilda knew she'd made an impact on him. She could almost see the wheels of his mind slowly turning. She added a little more weight to her argument. "You've always said that you wished you'd had your momma around longer, Henri, and you're a man. How do you think two little girls must feel? They need a mother."

Henri nodded, but remained silent as he stared at the ceiling.

"I'd better get some sleep. The girls will be here in a few hours," Tilda said, satisfied with her night's work. She kissed her husband's cheek before turning off the light.

Tilda was soon sleeping, but Henri remained awake a while longer. His wife's words had made him think about what it would be like to grow up without a mother. Children needed a father, but perhaps, even more, they needed a mother's gentle, caring touch. He knew how much his brother loved his children, for he spoke about them all the time. Yet maybe it was also true that Joseph needed help. If so, it was Henri's duty to help him. After all, how often in the past had Henri himself—young, penniless and hungry—received money and emotional support from his older brother?

He stayed awake thinking for more than an hour. When he finally fell asleep, he had a smile on his face and a plan of his own.

CHAPTER 29

On May 4th, 1934, the Civic Relief Board, an autocratic group made up of the mayor, most of the city council and a pastor, put into place a number of uncompromising decisions in an effort to reduce the amount of money being paid out of the municipal coffers.

The first regulation increased the minimum residency requirement. For the past four years, the relief board had required adults to be residents of Philibuster for at least 12 months before they could receive financial assistance. The board's new determination doubled the requirement to a minimum of 24 months.

At first, the general public did not know about the new regulation. The Civic Relief Board normally met in private and made its decisions without public observers. Only when men began to turn up for their food and rent vouchers, did they learn of the change. More might have been made of the new rule, but it affected only a small number of families.

A far more invasive new law allowed board members, police officers or those reporting to the board, to enter the premises of a person or family collecting relief, without prior warning. If alcohol or an excess of worldly goods were found—the definition of excess never being clearly stipulated—people lost their relief. Thanks to Raven Mullens, who refused to reveal his informant, it soon became common knowledge that the board rewarded police officers with two dollars whenever they were able to get someone off the dole.

Unlike the increased residency requirement, this draconian new bylaw encountered some resistance. A group of 153 women and children staged a sit-in at the courthouse to protest the suspension of relief payments due to their "excess" of worldly goods. The women claimed their relief payments had been suspended because they owned wedding bands or even small cameos, jewelry often handed down for generations, which people should not be forced to sell. Surprisingly, the protestors were not forcibly removed. Instead, they were permitted to occupy the council chambers at the courthouse. Sympathetic merchants sent food and bedding to the group on the first night of the sit-in; Beth sent toiletries. But the protestors never received the donations as the police, on the mayor's orders, kept them from the group. After a few days without food, the discouraged protestors left the courthouse of their own accord. The *Philibuster Post* did not mention the incident in its pages.

A few days later, 250 men showed up to apply for two temporary positions at the Philibuster Dairy. Although the men behaved in an orderly manner, Westmoreland was nervous. In recent weeks clashes between unemployed men and police had broken out across Canada and the United States. In Vancouver, jobless men had taken over the post office to protest the degrading situations in the work camps. After being forcibly removed from there, they marched through the city, smashing department store windows and causing $35,000 worth of damage.

When Westmoreland observed a few of the waiting men sitting on the ground—from weariness rather than in protest—he became even more concerned. He did not want a repeat of the recent events at the courthouse, nor could he afford a disruption of his dairy business. A quick call to Chief Quentin resulted in the arrival of Philibuster's entire 19-man police force to control the unemployed—who, at that point, needed no controlling. Passersby, seeing the large assembly of police and seated men, assumed a protest rally was under way. Word spread quickly.

Throughout Philibuster that day, as on most other days, men walked the city streets in search of food and work, or sometimes just as a way of passing time. Many went door-to-door looking for jobs picking rocks, cutting wood, weeding gardens or mowing lawns—anything that would allow them the dignity of earning wages. Some had lost hope of finding honest work and were reduced to begging for crusts of bread, slivers of meat and bowls of soup.

The humiliation was unbearable for people who had been raised to believe in the virtues of honesty, industry and self-reliance, and who now found themselves living a nightmare of near-starvation. When these hopeless men heard about the gathering at the dairy, they joined the crowd already there, swelling the numbers to over a thousand. Beth Hoogaboom later claimed that for the first time since 1930, the liars' bench in front of her store had "not an ass warming the wood—and no one sitting there either."

Unaware of the reason behind the protestors' demands, Chief Quentin tried to find out who was leading the group. When no such person was found, he tried to persuade the crowd to disperse. He announced through his bullhorn that the men had made their point and should go home. When his words had no effect, Westmoreland demanded that the police chief lay down the law. Accordingly, Chief Quentin issued a stern warning: "This gathering is illegal. Anyone still in the area in ten minutes will be arrested."

Instead of scaring the men away, the warning actually provoked them. The crowd had grown beyond the ability of Chief Quentin and his small police force to control. The fact that the men in the crowd were confused did not make things easier. They believed they were taking part in a protest, but had no idea what exactly they were protesting against. To make matters worse, they were now angry at being asked to leave what had begun as a peaceful gathering. The police officers, who mostly dealt with drunks and stray dogs, had neither the skills nor the training to deal with such an irate gathering. The mass of restless, unemployed men was a powder keg waiting to erupt. A single spark would cause an explosion.

That spark came from Slim Evans, leader of the Workers' Unity League. Evans had already been arrested twice by Chief Quentin, once for handing out leaflets and once for trying to start a union in Philibuster. Although he'd been warned not to show himself in

Philibuster again, he'd ignored the warning and was in the crowd now. Thus far, he had remained inconspicuous. But now, taking everyone by surprise, he suddenly bellowed, "Every man a king."

The phrase "every man a king" had become the rallying cry of United States senator Huey Long. Long had recently proposed that wealth should be taken from the hands of the few and be redistributed amongst the general population. Long's premise was that by erasing poverty and enabling every man to enjoy a comfortable standard of living, the distress caused by the Depression would be eliminated and crime would be reduced.

The strident slogan frightened Westmoreland. He had no intention of sharing his wealth, and would protect all that was his. Without hesitation, he gave Quentin the curt order: "Tear gas!"

At Quentin's command, and standing back for their own safety, police lobbed canisters of the noxious gas into the throng, which by now had grown to fifteen hundred. But with the wind gusting in the wrong direction, the gas quickly dissipated without having the desired effect.

Westmoreland then summoned the fire department. "Turn the hoses on 'em," he demanded furiously. With obvious reluctance the firemen obeyed. As the great blasts of water tore through the crowd, the gathering finally dispersed.

Westmoreland thought he had won, but his triumph was short-lived. His orders had enraged the men even further. Angry groups stalked the streets, venting their frustration on anyone and anything in their way. They shattered store windows and looted businesses. They overturned cars and set them on fire. The largest groups taunted the police, jeering as they pelted them with bricks, rocks and sticks. The officers responded with nightsticks and gunfire.

Joseph knew nothing of events until late in the day, when he had finished his route and completed the six o'clock milking. Early that morning he'd noticed the long line of men outside the dairy, but had thought nothing of it other than to pity the poor buggers, most of whom had no chance at all of finding a job. He saw the first evidence of hostilities when he reached downtown and was startled by the sound of breaking glass; crazed men downed bottles of beer and swigged from wine jugs pillaged from the government liquor store. Within minutes he was caught up in the tension all around him, the desperate energy of men who had found an outlet for their grievances and frustrations.

Thoroughly worried about his children, he hurried to Tilda's. As he ran through the streets, he marvelled at the speed with which the calmness of his world could be shattered by acts of violence. His relief at finding the girls safe turned to fresh anxiety when he learned the boys had gone home to pick up Nolan's baseball glove. Unaware of the disturbance, which had not reached the residential areas, Tilda had given them permission to go.

Joseph sprinted through yards and back alleys, praying as he ran: *"Please be home. Please be home."* Arriving at Mrs. Nye's, he shouted his sons' names as he searched the house. He found the boys in Daisy's room, staring out the north window toward downtown.

"Daddy, there are fires everywhere!" Cole exclaimed.

"I know. People are rioting," Joseph said.

"Can we go see?"

"No. And why are you in Mrs. Nye's apartment? Where is she?"

"She told us we could watch from here. And to wait here till you got home," Nolan said.

Joseph felt a sudden shiver of fear. "Where *is* Mrs. Nye?"

"She went to see what was going on."

"She left the house?"

The boys nodded.

Joseph forced himself to take a deep calming breath and began to think more clearly. He would take the boys to Tilda's and then search for Mrs. Nye. Tersely, he said, "There are a lot of angry men out there. We need to avoid them. Stay close to me. Understand?"

The boys could see their father was serious and didn't question him. Joseph scribbled a quick note, letting Mrs. Nye know he would be home soon and telling her not to go back out. He left the note on the kitchen table before rushing out of the house with his sons.

By now the riot had spread from the downtown core toward the suburbs. Joseph realized he wouldn't be able to take the most direct route to his brother's house. He and the boys had to double back several time to avoid mobs of drunken men who were setting fire to garbage cans. When they reached the house, they found Henri home from work.

Joseph explained hurriedly. "I have to find Mrs. Nye."

"Don't go," Tilda begged nervously. She had seen a group of passing men attack someone further down the street.

"I'll go wit' you," Henri said.

"No!" Joseph exclaimed. "Stay here and protect my family." Then he dashed out of the house in search of his employer.

CHAPTER 30

Joseph was frantic. Where could Mrs. Nye have gone? Had she made it home safely? Hurrying back to the house, he searched it quickly. No sign of her there. Back he went to the streets. Starting with the nearest roads, he worked his way systematically toward downtown and the most dangerous areas.

The further he went, the more destruction he found. As well, an odd sense of carnival permeated the town. Men roamed everywhere, clutching looted clothing, appliances, hardware—anything they could lay their hands on and carry. They rampaged through the streets, holding bottles aloft and yelling, "Burn! Burn!"

Men bled from head wounds. A few held broken arms close to their bodies. In an empty alley, Joseph came across a body. He rolled it over and saw the face of a dead man, torn and broken, frozen into twisted pain. Beside him lay a bloody brick. Frightened, Joseph hurried further.

He spent two agonizing hours dodging in and out of alleys to avoid gangs of anger-crazed men. Realizing he might look all night and still not find Mrs. Nye, he decided to return home and call Westmoreland for help. Suddenly he saw her walking quite casually along Main Street. Running to her, he wondered at her state of mind. In the few months he had known her, she had been clear-headed except for a time when she'd had one of her spells, and then she'd behaved with the obstinacy of a two-year-old.

Taking her arm, he said, "Let me take you home, Mrs. Nye."

She turned a calm gaze on him. "Why, dear?"

Close by, a car burned; the windows of the nearest buildings were shattered. His employer was not completely lucid, Joseph realized. "It's getting late," he said gently.

"But I'm not done my shopping." She was polite but stubborn.

A dangerous-looking pack of men, armed with sticks, was approaching them. "It's not safe here, Mrs. Nye. We have to get home," Joseph implored, and promised himself to buy bullets as soon as possible for the Smith & Wesson that was still in his closet.

Mrs. Nye smiled cheerfully at the oncoming mob. "Just boys letting off steam," she insisted.

Joseph knew there was no point in arguing with her. Firmly, he manoeuvred her homeward, careful not to cross paths with the rioters. Reaching the house, he sighed with relief at the fact that all was well—until Mrs. Nye emptied her shopping bag on the kitchen table and said proudly, "Shoes for your tired feet."

Joseph stared in dismay at the haphazard pile of a dozen or more shoes. "Where did you buy these?" he asked uneasily.

Mrs. Nye looked at him, her lips pursed.

"Mrs. Nye?"

"There were so many people," she told him, "breaking windows and going into stores. I never broke the windows ... and the shoes were just sitting there."

"You stole them," Joseph said flatly.

She looked upset. "You need new shoes. There's nothing left of yours."

Joseph explained that he could not keep the shoes—that he had to return them, and so he needed to know from which store she had taken them. He must have gotten through to her, for she gave him the information he needed.

"You're a good boy," she said, and touched his cheek. "You need to take better care of yourself, so you can take care of your children."

Her hand was warm and soft; in spite of his agitation, Joseph took some pleasure in the motherly touch.

When Mrs. Nye had gone upstairs Joseph gazed at the stolen shoes and thought how nice it would be to wear something new. He picked up one and looked, without success, for its mate. As he looked a bit longer, the truth hit him and he chuckled quietly. The shoes were store window models. Even if he'd wanted to keep them, he couldn't have worn them: each shoe was for the left foot.

CHAPTER 31

The riot lasted through the night. More and more people joined the skirmishes. The anger had no real focus. Many rioters were destructive simply for the joy of it. Although some of the participants were ordinary residents, most were men who were frustrated with their inability to provide for themselves and their families. The Philibuster police force did not have enough officers to stop the riot, so they did the next best thing: they split up into two groups. One contingent patrolled the area between the dairy, the department stores and the newspaper offices, in the hope of protecting the more important business concerns. A second, smaller party of officers safeguarded the homes of the mayor and the city councillors on the east side of the town.

Nearby municipalities offered to help by providing extra policemen. Westmoreland and the council would have accepted the help gladly had the rioters not run out of energy. But by morning, the streets of the town were relatively calm, with only remnants to be seen of the riots, broken glass and wrecked automobiles. The front page of the *Philibuster Post* bore a single word in large capitals: RIOT! The accompanying article blamed communist agitators for the disturbance. Three officers had been hurt by sticks and stones, twelve men suffering from various injuries had been arrested, and two men had died.

Before the morning milking, Joseph tossed the stolen shoes through the shattered window of Eaton's. After work, he purchased some ammunition for the Smith & Wesson.

For several days after the rioting, Philibuster's citizens, Joseph amongst them, waited for something more to occur and were relieved when nothing did. It was as if the city, like a giant geyser, had let off enough steam to prevent another eruption—for the time being, at least. With the newspaper spreading stories of communist uprisings, the town settled back into an uneasy peace.

By Sunday, the atmosphere was calm enough for Joseph to allow the boys out of the house to play with their friends. After the morning milking, Henri invited him to go fishing. Joseph had been looking forward to spending time with his daughters, but Tilda persuaded him to accompany her husband. She and the girls were going to be making kites and, "You two will just get in our way."

Henri slung two fishing poles across his shoulders. He wore a long dark coat: too warm for the weather, as far as Joseph was concerned. They made their way through town to the sawmill, to a spot Henri knew on the Elk River.

Henri had thought a great deal about Tilda's words a few nights earlier. Although he had never heard Joseph so much as hint at the possibility of giving up his daughters, perhaps his wife was right. Perhaps Joseph, overwhelmed by having to take care of four children, really did need help. Unlike Tilda, Henri had his brother's best interests at heart, and so his ideas differed from hers. He figured the four children really needed a momma: it made sense, therefore, that Joseph should remarry, rather than break up his family.

Henri reckoned, quite reasonably, that Joseph might find a potential wife at a dance, where he could interact with women. The regular Saturday night dances, wild parties frequented mostly by a younger crowd, were unsuitable. The right occasion would be one of the big family dances which were held twice a year, one at Christmas, the other at the beginning of May.

Careful to avoid any mention of a potential wife, Henri told Joseph of the fun they'd have at the big May Day Dance, to be held soon. "A real wingding," he said. When Joseph indicated his lack of interest in dancing, Henri was disappointed. But, he consoled himself, at least he'd planted the idea in Joseph's head. Best wait a while before broaching the subject again.

The first thing Joseph saw at the fishing spot was a shoal of strange-looking fish swimming near the shore. Sturgeon, Henri told him, as he put down his gear and took off his coat. Sturgeon were rare in the Elk River, but he knew them well from his commercial fishing days on Lake Winnipeg. The eggs of the females, which were just spawning, were valued for a delicacy called caviar.

After casting a few lines they sat down on the riverbank to wait. As the minutes passed without a bite, Henri became impatient: it would be quicker to jig the fish, he decided. Leaning over a shallow stretch of river filled with sluggish sturgeon, he dangled an unbaited hook several inches below the water. When a fish swam over the hook, he jerked the line up quickly, embedding the hook in the fish long enough to haul it out of the water before it could wriggle loose. Joseph copied his brother. In no time he, too, was successful.

Suddenly Henri spotted two men upstream. In a flash, his manner changed. Hurriedly he pulled in his line, instructed Joseph to do likewise, and stuffed the sturgeon they had caught into large pockets sewn to the coat's inner lining. Joseph was about to ask questions when Raven and Copper arrived on the scene.

Joseph looked at them in surprise. "What are you doing here?"

"Saw you heading this way. Thought we'd warn you," Cooper told him.

"About what?"

"A couple of constables saw you walking through town with those fishing poles. You look puzzled, Joseph. Don't you know it's illegal to catch sturgeon when they're spawning?"

Joseph turned to Henri for clarification. His brother only shrugged, as if to say, "So what?"

"Jigging isn't legal, either," Raven added. "If the cops find you, they'll know darn well the two of you aren't after pike or walleye."

This, then, explained the reason for the coat: Henri needed to carry his fish home without being seen. Joseph shook his head. He should know better by now than to fall in so gullibly with Henri's suggestions. Bending or breaking the law was like a game for his brother.

"I'm going back to the sawmill. I'll catch up with you boys later. If I see anything I'll whistle." Raven turned back upstream, leaving Copper behind.

"You really think someone will investigate?" Joseph asked nervously.

"Raven's a bit jittery about the law," Copper explained. "He wants to be mayor so bad, he doesn't want to be around if the cops turn up here. He's scared to do anything wrong." Addressing Henri, he went on, "If you don't mind, I'd like to get myself a sturgeon or two."

Joseph handed his rod to Copper, then turned to glare at his brother, who just grinned back, unabashed. Sitting back against a rock, watching the two men fish, Joseph realized how little he knew about the people who lived in Philibuster. His brother, for instance. What drove him to be so reckless? And Raven. What was his story?

As if he could read Joseph's thoughts, Copper chuckled. "Know how Raven got his name?"

Joseph leaned forward as Copper began the story. "Our Raven has a bit of a temper. Let it out once, too. Back in 1907 times were tough. Maybe not as tough as today, but pretty bad, all the same. Food was short and there wasn't much being shipped in. If you were lucky enough to have a pig to slaughter, you made sure you ate everything, including the squeal. Raven's pa left him a farm, 160 acres with some cows and chickens. He was only a pup when his father died, 16 or so. His mother was already in the ground by then. Apart from Raven, there were four younger ones. He did his best to keep the farm going and the little kids fed. They survived on the milk and eggs their animals produced."

Joseph thought of his own situation. "Couldn't have been easy."

"It wasn't. Come the first spring, one of the cows had a calf with a massive white diamond on its black side. Raven knew what to do and the calf survived. But he forgot to brand it. One day the calf strayed. It walked right onto George Quentin's land."

Joseph must have looked surprised, because Copper chuckled. "That's right. George Quentin, Chief Grumpy's father. The man knew full well the calf belonged to young William Mullens. Hell, everyone did. But George Quentin was a mean-spirited son-of-a-whore, and he branded that diamond-sided calf. Raven found out the calf was at George's and went there to get it back. George claimed the calf was his. Had the gall to show young Mullens the brand."

"What happened?"

"Good question. Angry enough to chew nails, our boy goes to the local constabulary and complains. The Mounties tell him if the calf is branded with George Quentin's mark, there's nothing they can do. So he heads back to his farm with hate in his heart and frontier justice on his mind. He gets himself an axe handle and heads over to George's again. Hits the door with that axe handle and demands the calf back—or else. George comes out of the house with a knife in his hand, says the calf is his, and if the boy doesn't like it he can go jump in the river."

"Bastard!"

Copper grinned. "Like son, like father, right? But George Quentin underestimated young William. The boy went at him, yelling and screaming and swinging that axe handle like it was Thor's hammer. Of course, George fought back hard as he could. When it ended, George lay on the ground, not moving and covered in blood. Beside himself with remorse, the boy turned himself in. Told the Mounties he'd killed a man. They sent out an officer to take a look. Found George bleeding but alive, and took him to the hospital. When George got out, Mullens visited him and asked for forgiveness. By then, George must have seen the error of his ways, at least where young William Mullens was concerned. He forgave him, saying, "You were stark ravin' mad. I should have known better.""

The three men were laughing at the story, when they heard a piercing whistle. Looking upstream, they saw two policemen running toward them, one of them Chief Quentin.

"Copper, take duh rods!" Henri ordered. "Joseph, put on duh coat."

"No," Joseph said.

"Copper will take duh rods an' run downstream. You take duh coat and 'ead into duh trees. I wait 'ere for duh cops. It's me dey want, anyway. And 'urry! D'ere getting closer!"

"No," Joseph said again.

The Great Henri had no intention of accepting his brother's refusal. Tossing the coat at him, he shouted, "Beat it!"

Joseph saw no option but to heed Henri's orders. Using the heavy coat to keep thorny branches from scratching him, he fled into the bush. When he'd gone about a hundred yards he turned to see what was happening. His gut knotted when he saw Chief Quentin making straight for him. Desperate to not be caught with the fish, Joseph put down his head and ran as fast as he could through the undergrowth. Dry twigs snapped underfoot and branches broke as he went. Fearing the noise would attract the police chief to him, he plunged into a dense thicket of fir trees and bush. There he lay on the sturgeon-filled coat, trying to breathe quietly.

From his hiding spot, he heard the thudding of Chief Quentin's heavy steps. When the noise lessened, Joseph hoped Chief Quentin had left the area. But his hopes were soon crushed, for within minutes the police chief approached again, sniffing loudly. Realizing that the smell of the fish might reveal his location more clearly than any noise he might make, Joseph knew he was in trouble. He considered coming out of hiding and throwing himself on the mercy of the police chief—until he remembered the two strikes he already had against him. When Chief Quentin finally gave up and left the bush, Joseph's relief was immense.

He hid for more than two hours before deciding it was safe to leave the thicket. Henri was waiting for him when he got back.

"Where are duh sturgeon?"

"In the damn bushes!"

"You t'rew dem away?" Henri stared at him disbelievingly.

"I wasn't going to jail for a bunch of fish!"

"Oh, Joseph, 'ow very foolish you are." Henri sounded surprisingly cheerful. "If Quentin 'ad put you in jail, I'd 'ave freed you. Surely you know dis?"

But Joseph was in no mood for his brother's humour. "Never involve me in your stupid pranks again!" he roared. A week went by before he spoke to Henri again.

CHAPTER 32

The heat wave started in Mexico in late June of 1934. From there it spread north into the United States. By early July the temperature had reached 110 degrees or higher in 16 American states. In Kansas and South and North Dakota, it was significantly hotter. Nebraska, where the thermometer recorded 124 degrees, was worst off. By mid-July, Canada, too, was experiencing the blistering hot weather; people in most of the country were living with daily temperatures of 100 degrees. In some places the heat was so severe that soil temperatures almost reached the boiling point of water, effectively sterilizing the soil.

The intense heat ruptured water lines and buckled roads. People took to sleeping outdoors, returning to their stifling homes only when they could no longer tolerate the mosquitoes. The high temperatures killed dogs, cats and birds. The deaths of 20,000 head of cattle and 500,000 fowl were attributed to the heat. More frightening still were reports of polio and sleeping sickness. Newspapers across the country reported hundreds of human deaths. Even though the *Philibuster Post* maintained that no deaths were occurring in the city, Joseph worried about his children and watched for symptoms of dangerous diseases.

For many kids, the most significant news was the imminent demise of the Grab the Gopher campaign. In light of the scientific finding that gophers could carry sylvatic plague, federal and provincial governments were determined to stop humans from handling the animals. The end of the campaign was a blow to many prairie children, for whom catching gophers had been their primary income. Fortunately for Nolan and Cole, the news was not quite as dire as for most of their friends and classmates. Nolan had, by this time, paid in full for his misdemeanours at Hoogaboom's, but Beth had been so pleased with the manner in which he had delivered groceries after school and on Saturdays, ably assisted by Cole, that she had offered the boys full-time summer employment.

Not surprisingly, Tilda disapproved of the arrangement. Every once in a while she remarked that Hoogaboom's was an unhealthy environment for the boys. She "feared" Nolan and Cole would be "soiled by that woman." If one of the boys was heard cursing, she blamed the profanity on that "foul-mouthed Hoogaboom woman." According to Tilda, the people who hung around the liar's bench in front of Hoogaboom's were "layabouts and criminals," and "poor, innocent Nolan and Cole haven't a chance of growing up decent around people like that." Tilda even blamed Beth's store for Sarah and Clare's illnesses. "The boys probably picked up something from that place and brought it home," she insisted. Joseph knew better than to defend Beth and her customers to Tilda. She would only become irate and give him the silent treatment, as she did with anyone who disagreed with her. For the sake of peace, Joseph let her express her opinions without contradicting her.

Joseph had his own concerns about his sons working for Beth, but his reasons were altogether different from Tilda's: he needed their help himself. As Joseph got to know the customers on his dairy route, he often found himself in long conversation with them, even at six in the morning, conversations that he couldn't end abruptly without seeming rude. Although these delays had the advantage of increasing his sales—the more his customers talked, the more they tended to remember something they might want the next day—it meant he got home much later in the evenings.

In the end, Joseph found a solution. He used a portion of the money he was earning from the increased sales to pay for some part-time help. In gratitude for saving Clare's life, Joseph offered the job to Tom Wah, who took it on with some initial reluctance. Though Tom had no experience with cattle, he was extremely bright, an excellent worker, and could soon perform every chore as well as Joseph.

Joseph's only complaint, if indeed it could be called that, was Tom's unwillingness to enter into any kind of friendly conversation. Joseph would have liked to know a little more about Tom: where he had learned English, how he had gained his medical knowledge, and where he had come from. He tried various tactics—current events, jokes, a little gossip—but Tom would not be drawn out.

Joseph did not understand that trust was difficult for his assistant. Tom had been careful to hide his true past for so long that he censored every word before uttering it, and was nervous to answer even harmless questions for fear of letting down his guard. In fact, Tom looked forward to coming to work each day. He also enjoyed Joseph's friendship, which was something he had not experienced since the time he'd spent with his countrymen in France during the Great War. Not understanding Tom's reticence, Joseph finally gave up on making small talk and the men worked together in companionable silence.

To people's relief summer finally turned to fall, bringing cooler temperatures. Sadly, though, there was no break from hardship. What the scorching summer temperatures had not destroyed, grasshoppers and Black Blizzards had seen to. With the failure of the crops, livestock had nothing to eat and died of an illness the farmers called "hardware" disease. So desperate for food were the cattle, that they resorted to filling their empty stomachs with gate hinges, pieces of iron and doorknobs.

Farm folks were driven almost to the same desperate measures as their animals. Difficult as it was to find relief in the urban areas of Canada, farmers and their families had no assistance to fall back on. Rural residents were ineligible for any form of civic assistance, no matter how much they pleaded. Farm kids took turns eating, having dinner on different days from their siblings. Children as young as ten and eleven left school to sell newspapers and shine shoes. Some even worked in factories and mines to help support their families.

Privation drove some people crazy. Chief Quentin caught a poor farmer driving his tractor and pulling a swather down Main Street, as if he were harvesting his wheat. When he was hauled off his tractor, he kept crying out, "Whad'dya doin'? I got to bring 'er in! Best crop I ever had!" No one knew what befell the old farmer after that.

Joseph was able to feed his children, but he still often went without food himself. There always seemed to be something more important he had to purchase with his meagre salary. The children had grown out of their clothes. With Tilda's help, he was able to mend Nolan's overalls and hand them down to Cole. However, Cole's overalls were too threadbare to pass on to Sarah, whose dresses, in turn, were too thin to pass on to Clare. Nolan and the girls simply had to have new clothes.

Then there were the children's teeth, neglected for too long. Joseph figured he could afford to get the children to the dentist, one at a time, over the fall months. Nolan needed the most attention and was the first patient. When it was Cole's turn to have his teeth seen to, he refused to go. He wasn't going within 50 miles of a dentist, he insisted. It took some time for Joseph to find out that Nolan had frightened his younger brother with a stomach-turning description of his own experience.

Joseph finally convinced Cole that his brother was making up silly stories and persuaded him to go to the dentist. Cole even got into the dentist's chair. However, when he saw the dentist pick up a small sickle-shaped probe, Cole closed his mouth tightly and refused to open it again. Nolan's story had achieved its desired effect.

Nolan did more than torment his brother. At Hallowe'en, when Joseph was returning from the evening milking, he overheard some men talking about a lion that had been seen roaming the streets. Since it was too late in the year for a circus, Joseph attributed the wild comments to drink. He was not far from home when he saw a crowd of children, as well as what looked like a small lion. Controlling the beast was none other than Nolan, dressed as a lion tamer with a top hat and a whip. *What was the boy up to this time?* Joseph wondered. Drawing closer, he saw the "lion" was actually Jasper. Nolan had used his uncle's scissors to trim the dog's furry body, shaving Jasper everywhere apart from his neck, chest and the very tip of his tail. Joseph was upset with his son, but The Great Henri was very amused.

Despite the tough times, the *Philibuster Post* gave the impression that good things were happening in town. Westmoreland had enticed yet another large grocery store as well as a new car dealership to open their doors. Furthermore, building permits were on the rise, with 48 having been issued in October and 52 in November, in stark contrast to the previous year, when only 16 permits had been applied for during the same two-month period.

The *Post* also talked of improved prospects for people in need of relief. Apparently a shake-up had occurred in the city's special relief department. Four relief inspectors had been suspended. The department manager was unable to release any pertinent information, but Mayor Westmoreland was quoted as saying the inspectors would not be replaced. Instead, their salaries would go toward helping families in need.

December arrived, bringing snow and talk of holiday events. Parents hoped to see their children perform in school plays, churchgoers looked forward to hearing their choirs and children happily awaited Santa's visit.

The big December event was, of course, the Christmas Dance at the Queen Victoria Royal Community Hall. Popularly called the Royal, the place was normally the scene of bingos, whist drives, weddings, local theatre performances and meetings of the Kiwanis and Rotary Clubs. But twice a year, on the first week in May and the last Saturday before Christmas, huge dances filled the hall to capacity.

A festive air filled the Royal on dance nights. Crepe paper flowers and colourful streamers brightened the massive wood-paneled hall, and on cold winter nights, two coal-burning furnaces kept the place warm. Men wore ties and women their best dresses. Single men congregated in groups, pretending not to stare at the single women who sat straight on their chairs, hoping some nice-looking guy would ask them to dance.

A professional band played dance music that people enjoyed, from polkas, jigs and waltzes to the more contemporary foxtrot and Charleston. When the music played, children danced around their parents, but when the band took breaks the dance floor was cleared so that little boys could run and slide across the slick floor on their knees or in their stocking feet.

No alcohol was allowed on the Royal's premises during dances, but a nickel would buy a soft drink from an ice-filled washtub. The more daring dancers might smuggle in a flask containing liquor, in a purse or jacket pocket, to be poured into a half-empty pop bottle under a table. If caught, the penalty was instant removal from the hall or even, on occasion, banishment from the next dance. Most people found a way around the rule. After a song or two, men, and sometimes women, would step outside for some air. Conveniently, they'd find a bottle of booze in a paper bag behind a garbage can or in a nearby bush.

Although Joseph had been unwilling to attend the May Day Dance, Henri convinced his brother to attend the Christmas Dance. Tilda was concerned on hearing the news. She wondered whether Joseph was finally getting over his loss and moving on with his life. What if someone took his fancy and he were to remarry? What would happen to her plans for taking his girls? Realizing that she could not stop Joseph from going to the dance, she arranged for a friend to baby-sit the children for the evening, so she could accompany the two men to the Royal.

Almost immediately, Tilda began to introduce Joseph to eligible women, making sure they were women he was unlikely to be attracted to. Joseph was taken aback at the onslaught of introductions, made in so blatant a way that he found himself forced to dance with Tilda's friends. He did not enjoy himself. If only, he wished, Tilda would not be so persistent. He was glad when the band took its first break, for it was stiflingly hot in the hall by then and he needed some time outside.

When the second set of dances began, Joseph went back into the hall. He was looking for a place to hide from Tilda when he saw Beth Hoogaboom. She looked so beautiful in a fashionable white dress, with her dark hair dropping smoothly over her shoulders and her mouth luscious with red lipstick, that he could only gape at her. She sat with her back straight and her head held high, as if posing for a portrait.

In the time he had known her, Joseph had often experienced a sense of déjà vu, as if he had met Beth some time in the past. Now, for the first time, he understood why she seemed so familiar: she resembled the woman in the tattered pictures the Italians in Hamilton had had on their walls. Joseph even remembered the name of that woman: Mona Lisa.

He remembered one of his roommates explaining the portrait's importance. More than the woman's beauty, her enigmatic expression and her air of mystery had made the Mona Lisa famous. Joseph had never been able to read Beth's expressions. It came to him now that she, too, looked like a woman of mystery.

Joseph saw Tilda coming purposefully toward him, a rather plain-looking woman following close behind her. Tilda's aim, most likely, was to get Joseph to dance with the woman. But Joseph had other plans. Ignoring his sister-in-law, he walked toward Beth. He was about to ask her to dance with him, but someone else asked her first. Disappointed, but not discouraged—there would be another opportunity—he kept going, bent on escaping Tilda.

Joseph was about to leave the hall once more when he spotted Raven. About to say hello, he saw that Raven was talking to a stranger. Not wanting to intrude, he waited a little distance away. In a break between one dance and the next, he overheard the conversation without meaning to.

"Looking for some company, are you?" Joseph heard Raven ask. And when the other man nodded: "You might like to meet Lisa."

"Is she pretty?"

"Pretty as a picture."

"Is she … ah … unattached?"

"No," Raven said, "but her husband is a salesman. On the road most of the time. I happened to know he's away now."

Listening in astonishment, Joseph took a half step closer to the men.

"Where would I find her?" the stranger asked.

"At her home on Thompson Street." Raven winked. "Care to have dinner with her?" His meaning was unmistakable.

"Sure!"

Joseph walked away, his mind racing. Could he have misunderstood the exchange? Surely Raven was not some prostitute's business manager. He was not that kind of man.

Shortly thereafter Tilda caught up with him. Joseph found himself reluctantly back on the dance floor. When he finally broke free of his latest partner, he looked for Beth, but she was nowhere to be found.

That night Joseph lay sleepless. He could not stop thinking about the dance. His thoughts veered back and forth from Raven's astonishing conversation with the stranger to Beth's loveliness.

Suddenly a gunshot rang out and Joseph jerked upright. Had another riot started? He opened the window and listened. He heard distant yelling.

Grabbing the Smith & Wesson from his closet, he loaded it quickly. The yelling came nearer. A man ran down the street shouting, "Help me! Help me!" Joseph was about to go to his aid when the police chief ran by, seconds later. Though Joseph remained awake a while longer, he heard nothing more. As he finally drifted off to sleep, he wondered whether Chief Quentin had been going to assist the screaming man, or whether the man had been running from the police chief.

CHAPTER 33

Unlike the previous year, Joseph was looking forward to this Christmas. Settled in Mrs. Nye's comfortable house, with enough money to afford a decent meal for the children, life was easier than it had been in a long time. Sadly, an unexpected bout of flu put an end to his plans. Barely able to move, let alone do his job, he was forced to spend the festive day in bed.

Just when he was beginning to feel more confident, the illness brought home to Joseph the insecurity of his situation. If he were unable to milk the cows and run his delivery route, he would lose his job at the dairy. The solution, of course, was to teach someone else to take over for him if necessary. Immediately, he thought of Tom. Until now, Tom had only helped with the morning milking, but Joseph knew he was dependable. He asked Tom if he wanted to learn the route, and Tom eagerly said that he did.

The day after Christmas, Tom and an ailing Joseph completed the milking before riding into town together. After a quick stop at Joseph's to pick up some stones he had left to heat in the fire the previous evening, they dropped the morning's milk at the dairy and loaded the deliveries for the day. His mind fuzzy from the effect of the flu, Joseph—unlike Tom—did not notice how oddly the men at the plant eyed them both.

Tom ran up and down the walkways of the route, while Joseph remained in the wagon with the hot stones warming his feet and blankets covering his lap. Tom kept a careful note of the various house numbers as well as the products the homeowners received. Joseph told him he had a list and besides, Dancer knew the route. Tom smiled, nodded and went on making his own notes in tidy Chinese characters.

By the time the deliveries had been completed, a feverish Joseph was exhausted. Handing over the reins, he asked Tom to take the wagon back to the farm and to do the evening milking. Tom was smiling as he drove away.

Next day, Joseph told a disappointed but understanding Tom that he felt well enough to do the route himself again. He was picking up his supplies when one of the dairy dockworkers said Westmoreland wanted to see him. Surprised that his employer was already at work, Joseph quickly finished loading his wagon before knocking on the man's door.

"You got a Chinaman working for you?" Westmoreland asked, without waiting for Joseph to close the door.

So that was it. He should have known, of course. Fearing the worst, he nodded.

"Not any more, you don't," Westmoreland said, sharply.

"But ... Mr. Westmoreland, with respect, I need help with the route."

"Find someone else, in that case."

Joseph was about to plead his case, to explain that Tom was a competent worker and a good man, but the look in Westmoreland's eyes stopped the words in his throat. He recognized that look. He had seen it in Hamilton, in the faces of the bigoted men who had abused his Italian friends, and in Philibuster, in the faces of the men who jeered at Tom and his countrymen—a look of racial hatred and derision.

"Do you understand me?" Westmoreland asked coldly.

"Yes, sir," Joseph said quietly. He left the office without another word and went off to start his route.

After putting the children to bed that evening, Joseph sat in the kitchen, watching a candle burn down to a nub. With the dictionary open in front of him on the table, he pondered the word "indebted." Over and over, he asked himself the same questions: how much did he owe Tom for saving Clare? And at what point did the well-being of his own family take precedence over his indebtedness?

It had been so easy to give Tom work when Joseph's ability to feed his family had not been affected. But things had changed. His livelihood was now being threatened, for he knew, quite certainly, that Westmoreland would fire him if he defied his orders. That being the case, how important was loyalty? As Joseph watched the candle gutter out, he found himself wondering how Beth Hoogaboom would answer the question.

CHAPTER 34

Joseph could not do it. He could not fire Tom. He wouldn't be able to live with himself if he did. He would keep Tom on, but he would not go about it stupidly. He told Tom that Nolan and Cole were going to help him with the morning chores, but only for a while, after which he would ask Tom to return. The man took the news stoically, it was apparent he had expected to lose the job.

Every day Joseph expected Westmoreland to stop by to make sure he was complying with his order to fire Tom. Two weeks went by without any sign of the mayor. Guessing his boss was used to being obeyed without question, Joseph finally asked Tom to help him once more with the morning milking, figuring that Westmoreland was unlikely to arrive at the farm in the early hours of the morning. All the same, he was unable to shake off his concern and lived in fear of being discovered. Every creaking board was Westmoreland appearing for an impromptu inspection. Every approaching car had him running outside to check whether the mayor had come. He and Tom even made plans for the event. Tom knew where to hide quickly if Westmoreland were to surprise them.

As the months passed and the bitter cold gave way to the pleasant crispness of late winter, Joseph's vigilance slackened. Added to his already busy day was the imminent birth of a dozen calves. He took to spending nights in the dilapidated old farmhouse so that he would be on hand if a cow needed help. There were nights when he did not go to bed at all. He was weary beyond words.

And so it happened one day that after hours spent working with birthing cows and tiny calves, Joseph was so exhausted that he didn't hear Westmoreland's car pull up outside the barn. A furious bellow alerted him to his employer's arrival, by which time it was too late to warn Tom. Westmoreland bellowed again, so loudly that the cow Joseph was milking bucked, knocking over the pail of milk, while the other cows scattered in fright.

"Get your yellow hide off my property!" Joseph heard Westmoreland yell.

Joseph sat riveted to the stool in dismay, a puddle of milk at his feet. Moments later Westmoreland burst into the milking barn, his face flushed with rage, and fired him on the spot. He also ordered Joseph to move the children and his possessions out of Mrs. Nye's house immediately.

Joseph was walking down the dirt road from the farm when Tom, who had been hiding in the bushes, joined him. They walked silently side by side a few minutes, until Tom finally spoke. "You should not have brought me back to work, Joseph."

Tom knew what had led to this point. He understood that Joseph had lost his job because he had insisted on employing a Chinese man in defiance of his employer's orders. Now he wanted to know why Joseph had done it.

But Joseph had no easy answers for Tom. It was difficult to explain his actions to his friend, when he was unable to explain them fully even to himself. Many would call him a fool for what he had risked and lost, and perhaps they'd have been right.

"What will you do now?" Tom asked.

"Look for work and a place to live," Joseph replied, evenly.

Tom stopped and gazed at Joseph without speaking. Then he walked away.

"Tom," Joseph called. "Aren't you coming with me?"

Tom shook his head. To Joseph, he looked lost and vulnerable; like a child who had just said goodbye to his only friend.

As Joseph walked home alone, he enjoyed a sense of righteousness, as well as pride in his moral behavior. But the euphoria was quickly replaced by his new concerns about food and shelter for his family.

Mrs. Nye greeted Joseph at the door. From her expression it was clear that Westmoreland had already spoken to her. Her eyes were suspiciously red, so that Joseph wondered if she had been crying.

"Winny told me what happened," she said. "I'm so sorry you lost your job."

"I'm sorry too," Joseph said. "I'll get our things together. I won't take long."

Mrs. Nye motioned him to a kitchen chair. "I need to speak with you first. Please, wait."

Puzzled, Joseph stayed where he was, as Mrs. Nye went upstairs to her apartment. She returned a few minutes later with an old shoebox. Unhurriedly, she filled the kettle and put it on the stove. When the water came to a boil, she poured it into the teapot and let the tea steep. When she had poured two cups, she sat down at the table across from Joseph.

"There are things I want you to know," she said, at last. "About Winny, about his father."

Joseph looked at her anxiously. "I should get busy. Your son might come back and if he finds me here—"

"Let me take care of my son." Mrs. Nye drew the box toward her. "Gideon, Winny's father, was very handsome," she began. "Dashing and flirtatious, different from any man I had ever met. He wore diamond rings and nice clothes. He just appeared in town one day. I didn't know anything about him. Where he came from. How he earned a living. But I didn't care. I was in love. After a week we ran off to Saskatoon together."

Mrs. Nye paused a moment and took a deep breath, as if readying herself for a plunge into unpleasant waters. "At first, he was good to me. He brought me flowers every day. Called me his little angel. I was very happy. After a while, though, he began to spend more and more time away from home. He would return drunk and smelling of perfume. He started hitting me, calling me stupid, accusing me of holding him back. I didn't know what he meant. I told myself he was a masterful man and that I deserved what I got. Then Winny was born and things were okay for a while. Not for long, though, because soon Gideon was drinking and getting rough again. He slapped me and pushed me around and did other things, too. This went on for years. I didn't mind so much, just as long as he hit me and not Winny.

"One spring day, when Winny was nine and outside playing, I had a bad headache and lay down in the bedroom with the shades down. I must have fallen asleep because I woke to Winny's screaming. Gideon was beating him. Winny had been at his father's desk and had gotten mud on his ledger. I tried to stop Gideon, but he was too strong for me."

Clenching her hands on the sides of the box, Mrs. Nye looked up at Joseph. "When Gideon went to work that afternoon, I packed a suitcase and took the train back to Philibuster with my son. My parents had passed away a few years earlier and we arrived here with nothing. Some kind-hearted people took us in and we lived off their charity. For the longest time I lived in fear of Gideon. I expected him to come to Philibuster and force us back to Saskatoon. But as time went by, I began to realize he was probably glad we'd gone. Some time later, I found a good man in Edward, God rest his soul. Edward treated Winny and me right."

She handed a photo to Joseph. "My Edward," she said wistfully. Joseph glimpsed tears in her eyes.

He waited in silence until she was ready to speak again. "Winny was 14 when he decided to go looking for his father. He found Gideon in Saskatoon, right where we'd left him. Gideon was running houses of ill repute; had been all along. I begged Winny not to stay with his dad, but he did. He even started working for him. Pretty soon, he stopped writing to me. I was lonesome for my boy, but I was living here with Edward. I couldn't leave Philibuster and I figured that unless Winny came home, the only way for me to be a part of his life was to read the newspapers he might be reading too."

Mrs. Nye took a batch of yellowed newspaper clippings from the battered shoebox. Joseph knew right away what they were, for he remembered seeing piles of the *Saskatoon Star-Phoenix* rotting in the basement.

"One day I came across this." Mrs. Nye handed him a faded clipping.

It was an article, he saw, dated 1922, a story about American prohibition and the bootlegging business taking place across the Canada–U.S. border. According to the writer, any man with the nerve and the smarts to circumvent government restrictions could become wealthy by importing Scotch whisky from overseas into Canada, and then quickly exporting it to the United States. The Bronfmans, a family of brothers, were apparently reaping huge profits—$50,000 every month, by some accounts. But the Bronfmans were not the only people selling illicit liquor successfully. Harry Bronfman, the brains behind the burgeoning family empire, was quoted as saying, "With the exception of two small concerns in Saskatoon, the liquor business in Saskatchewan is controlled by me." Gideon Westmoreland owned and ran one of those two small concerns.

"I read nothing more about Gideon until I came across these," Mrs. Nye said, giving Joseph some articles dating back to the summer of 1926. They referred to an unidentified body that had been discovered along the banks of the South Saskatchewan River in Saskatoon. There was even a grainy picture of a bloated body on a riverbank, surrounded by police. "No name—but I knew the man was Gideon."

Mrs. Nye went on talking as Joseph glanced through the clippings. "Gideon had switched from prostitution to bootlegging. Even though he'd been making bags of money already he wasn't satisfied, and he came up with a scheme to make more. Later Winny told me it was customary for American gangsters to cross the Canadian border with empty vehicles, returning to the States in the dead of night, their cars packed full with cases of whisky. Gideon came up with the idea of selling his whisky to the Americans, waiting till they had paid him and were safely on their way back toward the border, and then notifying the local constabulary. Gideon paid the police to return the booze to him, with the result that he could sell the same load of whisky four or five times. The American gangsters always knew there was a chance they could be caught, and so the first few times they blamed misfortune and bad choice of roads."

"Until they learned the truth?"

"Correct. One of Gideon's customers became suspicious because he was being caught so often after buying whisky from Gideon. He began to mark the cases he purchased with a small red X. After losing another load of whisky to the police, he saw some red X's on his next shipment and realized what Gideon was up to. Gideon was caught and Winny went into hiding. When my boy finally arrived in Philibuster three months later, he was penniless. All he owned was a shiny car and some clothes."

"But he became a success," Joseph said.

Mrs. Nye shook her head. "It wasn't that simple. People saw Winny's car and thought he was rich. Edward's dairy farm made good money, and I gave some of it to Winny so he could keep up appearances. Edward's only son had died in the Great War. When Edward passed away, he left everything to me. I gave Winny the dairy farm and everything else Edward left me, except for the house. Winny always wanted respect, and so did I. I know people talk of me as Dizzy Daisy. I thought if my son was held in high regard, then maybe I would be too. Maybe I was foolish to encourage my boy, but a mother loves what she bore, no matter what."

Joseph heard the sadness in Mrs. Nye's voice as she came to the end of her story. As he put the clippings down on the table and looked into her eyes, he was swept with unexpected compassion.

Mrs. Nye closed the box and looked at Joseph. "These things I've told you ... please keep them secret. I don't have any money to give you, but this is still my house, and you will stay here as long as you wish."

Joseph remained at the table after Mrs. Nye left the kitchen. He felt dazed. The things he'd learned about Westmoreland did not ease his mind. What did it matter if the man was neither a war hero nor the successful businessman he claimed to be? What concerned Joseph was that Westmoreland had spent much of his life in a dangerous world. There was no way of anticipating what he might do next.

CHAPTER 35

Every day Joseph expected the guillotine to fall. He felt certain Westmoreland must be searching for some way, legal or otherwise, of evicting him from Mrs. Nye's home. In Joseph's mind, the man had options: he could hire a gangster to scare Joseph into leaving, or he could try to convince a court that his mother was not in her right mind, and that, as her son, he should take over her affairs before she harmed herself.

Mrs. Nye presented other problems. Clear-headed most of the time—she had been extremely coherent when she had told him her son's story—the glazed look could appear in her eyes at a moment's notice. Joseph worried she might forget her promise and ask him and the children to vacate her home.

Despite his concerns, Joseph remained in the house, although he found a room to rent in case he needed it. There was a fine balance between his fears about Westmoreland and Mrs. Nye's lucidity on the one hand, and his financial situation on the other. He had not been able to save much money, which meant the longer he remained at Mrs. Nye's, the further his money would stretch. If he were to move at this point, without a job, his cash would run out within a month, whereas if he could stay put for a while, he could hold out twice as long.

Tom Wah appeared unexpectedly one day, wanting to speak with Joseph and his family. He began by asking their forgiveness, explaining that he was to blame for Joseph losing his position at the dairy. He said he should have known better than to accept Joseph's job offer, understanding this would eventually cause Joseph problems. It was only because it had been so long since he had felt like a man, with a man's responsibilities and a salary with which to feed his family, that he had accepted.

That was not all Tom spoke about. Addressing himself to the children, he told them of the day their father had stood up to a group of men who had abused him. Any other man, he said, would have ignored the shameful ways in which some men treated others, but not Joseph. He was willing to risk a lot in the cause of noble ideals. Their father was "the most admirable man" he knew and he hoped the children would honour him with love and obedience. Tom's speech—for that was what it amounted to—included words like "esteem," "awe," and "veneration." Listening to him, Joseph felt overwhelmed and embarrassed at Tom's high regard for him. He would have interrupted him, but didn't want to appear ungrateful.

It was because of Joseph, Tom said, that he had decided to "creep out from among the shadows of fear" and take a stand for what was right. He had decided to take on City Hall on behalf of his countrymen, who received only half as much relief money as Philibuster's white citizens. He was going to lead the fight for equal payments. Joseph's courage in risking so much for a Chinese person had inspired Tom to be just as brave.

Joseph listened apprehensively while Tom spoke. Then he urged his friend to abandon his plans. By fighting the authorities he would put himself and his family in danger. By provoking the white population of Philibuster, Tom was courting great jeopardy. Joseph had taken risks, but he had not endangered his life. Tom listened courteously to Joseph's warnings, but would not be dissuaded.

At dinner that evening, while his siblings chattered away, Nolan thought about the things Mr. Wah had said. He had never heard another person, let alone his own father, spoken of with such admiration. "You did a good deed, Dad," he said eventually.

Although Joseph was concentrating on carefully dishing up food for the children from the meager contents of his frying pan, the unaccustomed seriousness of Nolan's tone caught him and he glanced at his son. "Tom made too much of it," he protested.

"That's not true, Dad. Why didn't you tell us?"

"Good deeds are no longer good if you talk about them," Joseph said, uncomfortable with his son's praise.

Nolan said nothing more. His dad was obviously unwilling to discuss Tom Wah's sentiments, but Nolan continued to think about them for some time.

CHAPTER 36

Tom's words had moved Joseph profoundly. He understood the courage it would take for Tom to fight for equal relief payments for the Chinese community. He was, however, more than a little concerned about Tom's safety. Someone could easily use violence to put the "upstart Chink" in his place. All in all, he doubted Tom's fight would be successful.

Tom had also inspired Joseph, showing him he could be brave too. So a day later, when Westmoreland tried to threaten him with talk of lawyers, Joseph threatened him right back. He told the mayor he was aware of his sordid past, the cathouses, the bootlegging and the phony war record. Joseph would not hesitate to expose him if he were threatened again. Westmoreland's eyes narrowed and he walked away without another word. Joseph's boldness—however foolhardy—seemed to have succeeded, at least for a while.

Joseph had more to think about than Winfield Westmoreland. He'd been infatuated with Beth Hoogaboom since the Christmas Dance. He had always considered her attractive, but now he thought her beautiful. Even more than surface beauty, she possessed a femininity which her usual manly attire concealed. Beth's bad reputation—some rumours even had her performing favours for men in the old Maze district—did not matter to him. He did not care that she smoked and used colourful language. Joseph admired Beth for her honesty and straightforwardness. Before long, he could no longer stop thinking about her.

Joseph's fascination with Beth deepened to the point where he started dreaming about her. The dreams were casual, at first, but after a while they became more erotic. Eventually, he would wake up aroused and breathing heavily. His feelings for Beth gave him a new reason to avoid her as much as possible. For one thing, he felt as if he were being unfaithful to Helen. For another, he was concerned that he might say something stupid and betray himself.

For beyond a surprising friendliness, Beth had shown no romantic interest in him—or in any other man for that matter. He didn't want to make a fool of himself with a woman who appeared to be focused only on earning a living.

And then there was his constant concern about money. He had not worked at all since losing his position at the dairy a month earlier. There were no job ads in the newspaper, no Help Wanted signs in store windows, and no interest when Joseph knocked on doors looking for odd chores. Even the company from which he had rented the knife sharpener had gone out of business. Without a whisper of work anywhere in Philibuster, Joseph started looking for work further afield, in nearby towns and villages. Although any available work usually required skills he did not possess, one day he learned of a position at a brickyard in the next town and managed to arrange for an interview. Unfortunately, when Tilda heard about the interview, she had to tell Joseph she would not be able to look after the children that day. It just so happened that she was leaving immediately for Billings, Montana, where her oldest sister was dying.

At his wits' end, Joseph was on the point of cancelling the interview when Beth sent word that she had heard about his predicament, and would gladly mind Clare for the day. Although he knew the arrangement would spark Tilda's anger, Joseph gratefully accepted Beth's offer. With Clare taken care of, he could confidently leave Sarah with Nolan and Cole.

Nolan was determined to take good care of his sister. He gave her toast and jam for breakfast, making sure to wash her face afterward. Later, the children went to the river, where the winter ice was just beginning to melt. They had great fun tossing stones at the ice, tramping along the edge of the river, and kicking at the few small chunks of ice that had drifted onto the banks. They were careful not to walk out onto the ice, because their father had explained why it was dangerous. Had the ever-daring Nolan been alone, he might even have tested the warning, but he had promised his dad to look after Sarah and he would be careful not to disappoint him.

As the afternoon wore on, Nolan got bored. They went back home and made a fort in the basement, but after a while that was boring too. Nolan was running out of ideas for something interesting to do, when he happened to see some empty rifle casings. Now there was an idea! He could make ammunition, just as Nathan McCormick had shown him the previous year. No harm in firing a few shots at the oak ceiling in the kitchen. Why, his dad had often said Mrs. Nye's house was sturdy enough to withstand a German shelling.

Boredom gone, Nolan lit the kitchen stove. Putting Cole to carving wooden plugs, Nolan cut the heads off matches. He stuffed the casings with the match heads, then sealed them with Cole's plugs. Sarah was only allowed to watch the proceedings. Nolan did not want her to get hurt.

Now for the exciting part. Nolan set the first casing on the stove and stood back. Impatiently, the three children waited for the heat of the stove to set off the ammunition. The wooden plug shot upwards and ricocheted harmlessly off the oak ceiling with a noisy bang. The jubilant boys whooped with glee, but Sarah screamed in fright.

"That was too loud!" Sarah objected, when she saw Nolan place a second cartridge on the stove.

Not in the mood for girlish timidity, her brother said, "Scram, if you're scared."

Sarah hurried into the adjoining dining room, where she waited with her hands over her ears. When the next shell did not go off, she returned to the kitchen and stood cautiously in the doorway. Her brothers, waiting expectantly a few feet from the stove, didn't see her. Sarah's nervousness built up to a point where she could no longer bear the tension of waiting. She had to grab the casing before it could go off and make another awful noise. She ran toward the hot stove.

Nolan turned and saw her. "No!" he screamed in horror, when he realized what his sister was about to do. He rushed to her, grabbed her hand and pulled her backwards. At that very moment, Sarah touched the casing and knocked it over. A second later the heat from the stove ignited the matches in the rifle casing. The casing exploded, rocketing a burning wooden bullet at Sarah's face.

Joseph had been a father long enough to know that his children were usually fine as long as he could hear them. Returning to a silent home after an unsuccessful interview at the brickyard, he sensed possible trouble. He did not panic immediately, knowing the children could be playing a trick on him, perhaps a game of hide-and-seek.

Yet he felt uneasy. It was unlike Sarah, who was in the habit of giggling and giving herself away, to remain silent for long. He called her name a few times. Getting no response, he started to search the children's favourite hiding places.

"Okay," he called. "You win, guys. I can't find you. Time to come out."

Still no response.

Anxious now, Joseph walked into the kitchen. Right away, he felt the heat from the stove. Opening it and finding it fully stoked, he realized the kids had to be nearby. Suddenly he spotted a few brown spots on the floor. Blood!

"Christ!" Joseph exclaimed as he had a sudden mental image of the Smith & Wesson. He dashed to his room, tore open his closet door and pulled down the box in which he kept the revolver. The gun and the shells were all there. Joseph smelled the barrel to be sure it hadn't been fired. Thankfully, it had not.

He ran upstairs to Mrs. Nye's apartment, but she was nowhere to be seen. His mind ran wild now, filling with possible scenarios: a robbery gone horribly wrong;, a kidnapping, some kind of stunt by Westmoreland. Joseph felt weak with fear as he ran to Hoogaboom's. The store was empty.

"Beth! Beth!" Joseph shouted.

Seconds later, Beth emerged from the stock room with Sarah in her arms.

"Daddy," Sarah mewed weakly and reached for her father. A piece of bloodstained white cloth covered one ear.

"What happened?" Joseph demanded, taking the little girl from Beth.

"It's okay," Beth said calmly, as Nolan and Cole appeared on the scene. "Everyone is just fine."

Joseph was not reassured. "Where's Clare?"

"Upstairs sleeping," Beth told him.

Joseph turned to Nolan. "What happened?"

"It was an accident, Dad."

Nolan tried to explain, but his father's visible anger made him tongue-tied. Feeling bad for the frightened boy, Beth related what she knew. Joseph listened silently, though inside he was seething. He thanked Beth tersely, then hurried the children back home.

Only when they reached the house did Joseph let his rage erupt. For 20 minutes he yelled at Nolan, listing every small crime his son had committed since the family's arrival in Philibuster. Excessive fatigue and months of too little food, combined with constant fear for his children, caused Joseph to over-react. He followed the trembling boy into his bedroom and raised a fist, ready to strike him. The fear in Nolan's eyes brought him to his senses before he could hurt the boy.

Joseph went to his room and took the Smith & Wesson from his closet. Worried that Nolan might stumble upon the gun and accidentally do something worse than shoot off his sister's earlobe, Joseph hid the revolver and the ammunition inside a steamer trunk in the basement—the one thing in the house with a lock and key.

Left alone in his room, Nolan wept. Had he known how, he would have apologized to his dad for all the foolish things he had done. The last thing he wanted was to disappoint him. Tom Wah's words had inspired Nolan to become as responsible and well

respected as his dad: yet even when he tried his best to be good—
and he really had tried hard today—something always seemed to
go wrong.

Between his sobs, Nolan made himself a promise: *One day, I'll
damn well show you, Dad.*

CHAPTER 37

Tom Wah knew he was endangering himself the moment he
decided to take up the fight for Philibuster's Chinese residents. He
was quite aware of English Canada's attitude toward the Chinese
population: his people were only visiting the country, which made
their stay a temporary situation. He had come across more than
one flyer of the kind that was periodically circulated around the
town. Typically entitled *How To Tell A True Canadian,* it usually
contained the following statements:

A True Canadian?
He is a white man.
He is a Gentile.
He is a Christian.
He is a Protestant.
He abides by the law.
He opposes trash immigration.
He upholds virtuous womanhood.
He believes in one flag and one language.
He believes in freedom of worship and hates nobody.
He believes Black Supremacy is appropriate in Africa.
He believes Yellow Supremacy is appropriate in China
    and Japan.
He believes unequivocally that only White Supremacy
    is appropriate in North America.

Since the Chinese—even those who had lived in the country as long as or longer than people of British descent—were regarded as "guests," Tom realized that English Canadians would see his request for additional relief money for the Chinese as an unnecessary drain on civic coffers. Even when jobs were plentiful and cash flowed freely, people hated to spend money on foreigners. When work was almost non-existent and people were starving, a dollar could be worth killing for. Tom was under no illusions with regard to his fight. This time, he would face far greater threats than gobs of spittle or the occasional shove.

Apart from the threat of violence, Tom was also concerned about deportation. In order to bring attention to the plight of Chinese families and the disproportionate treatment they received, he would need to organize and take part in public protests. Thousands of Chinese had been deported for less subversive behavior. Despite his fake documents, which stated he was a legal immigrant, nothing would stop the authorities from making up anything they wanted to in order to get rid of an agitator.

Tom also had to consider the serious risks to which he was subjecting his family. Betty and the children depended on him for financial support. What would happen to them if he were incarcerated? If he were to be injured and his wife became responsible for meeting all the family's needs? If he were to be deported?

Tom wondered whether his wife would consider him a fool for battling impossible odds. He doubted she could possibly understand the compulsion that drove him to fight. He was astonished to learn that his doubts were unfounded. Betty was the only person in the world who was privy to all the details of his past. She knew he'd been forced to work with the Chinese Labour Corps during the Great War, that he'd escaped from the William Head quarantine station on Vancouver Island and that he'd hidden for years from the law. Tom had always considered himself a coward and a failure. He had no idea, therefore, that Betty understood him far better than he gave her credit for, and that she saw him as a good, kind, brave man.

Left to herself, Betty might not have chosen to marry Tom, for he was very reserved and so much older than she was. But the wedding had been arranged, and she had grown to love him. From the start, Betty had admired Tom's courage and his determination to build a new life in a country that did not want him. She also believed in his medical skills and was distressed that the death of a single patient, which had occurred through no fault of Tom's, had led him to turn his back on his vocation. Betty was a perceptive woman. Years of marriage had given her insight into the passion that Tom kept concealed deep inside him. If only, she had often thought, there was a way in which that inner fire could be kindled.

So Betty encouraged Tom to pursue his ideals. She hoped that by helping his countrymen, he might come to value himself again. In the worst-case scenario—deportation—she would follow him to China and they would live out their lives there. How much better, she insisted, for their boys to see their father as a courageous man doing what was right, than to watch him lead a frightened life. Yet brave as Betty was, even she might have asked her husband to drop his plans had she been able to read the inflammatory statements of some of Philibuster's leading citizens.

At first Tom was uncertain of the best way to begin his campaign. He sensed the importance of shaping the town's Chinese community into a single cohesive voice before bringing attention to their plight. The problem was, how would he go about doing it? He realized he needed a mentor, someone experienced at organizing people and creating awareness. Unable to find a single person with such knowledge amongst the town's Chinese merchants, he knew he'd have to find help outside his own community. The obvious man was Slim Evans.

Evans, of course, was well known by the people of Philibuster for his past activities. Many still remembered him as being partly to blame for the riot a year earlier. Now he was in Philibuster for a few weeks to raise awareness for a movement called the "On-to-Ottawa Trek." The goal of the trek was to draw all the unemployed men languishing in work camps to Ottawa, in an effort to bring their plight to national attention and to force Prime Minister Bennett and his government to improve living conditions in the militarily-run camps.

Tom found Evans addressing a group of out-of-work men at a baseball game. After the speech, Tom button-holed Evans and told him about his plans. Though a busy Evans was, at first, reluctant to help him, Tom was so persuasive that he eventually managed to gain the sympathy of the union man. Tom was delighted when Evans agreed to teach him what he needed to know.

Tom began his battle with gatherings in public places such as parks and street corners. Once the Chinese community started coming together, he ordered them to picket government offices. Sit-down strikes in front of city buses and trains came next. Chief Quentin and his men arrested Tom and the other demonstrators. Each time they examined his documents—although, fortunately, not in meticulous detail—and released him with a warning.

. After the demonstrations, Tom met secretly with Evans in their temporary meeting place, an abandoned barn six miles north of town. Evans instructed Tom on how to proceed with his fight. He coached him on how to conduct himself at newspaper interviews—should he ever be fortunate enough to be asked to give one—and how to respond to questions from interested observers. He gave Tom an understanding of the right time to push his message harder, and told him when it was prudent to back off, lest he alienate the general public. The meetings with Evans often took place late at night, after which Tom walked home in the dark with only the stars to light his path.

The newspapers became involved in the issue soon after the protests began. Neither Tom nor any of his fellow protestors were interviewed. The press simply spewed forth the standard litany: the Chinese were an infectious disease—an inferior race—and, as such, not a civic responsibility. White people were entitled to be looked after first.

Ironically, the *Philibuster Post*'s negative remarks had the opposite effect from that which was intended. Instead of turning the average citizen against the Chinese people, the articles brought the issue to the forefront of their thinking. Unknown to the general populace, over the years many Chinese restaurant owners had helped a number of needy English Canadian families by giving them regular free meals. Overcoming their natural embarrassment, white men and women who had benefited from these acts of compassion came forward with their stories. These stories, in turn, brought about an awareness of other Chinese kindnesses, such as help with clothing and shelter. Before long, white men and women began to join ranks with the Chinese protestors.

One day the *Philibuster Post* printed a vituperative article by Mayor Winfield Westmoreland. Titled "The Chinamen," the article set out to show that although it was true that Chinese people in need received only half as much civic relief as white men, studies had shown the Chinese to have a lower standard of living than people of British descent. The mayor went on to say that the council had had enough of Chinese interference with the running of the city, that the authority of Philibuster had been challenged, and that the matter needed to be dealt with decisively. The final line of the article stated, "The yellow man is overstepping his boundaries and good Canadians should take it upon themselves to send them a message."

That night, several men followed Tom to one of his meetings with Slim Evans in the abandoned barn on the outskirts of town, and back home again.

CHAPTER 38

Apart from Beth, Joseph and his girls, Hoogaboom's was empty. Sarah stared at the candy behind the glass counter, while Clare toddled around the store. The radio was on with the day's news.

"... *Reverend J.T. Gardener, superintendent of the All People's Mission, was quoted as saying that his cupboards are as bare as Mother Hubbard's ever were. Clothing, tools, food and money are urgently needed. Any contributions will be used entirely for relief purposes...*"

Joseph counted out a precious eight cents for ten pounds of potatoes.

"... *Mayor Westmoreland dismissed three officers employed in the department of Children's Aid. When asked about this difficult decision, Mayor Westmoreland ...*"

"How's your ear doing, Sarah?" Beth asked the little girl, whose eyes hadn't left the candy counter.

Sarah looked up. Her ear was healing well. It was not infected, but a tiny piece of the ear lobe was missing. "My Uncle Henri says I have to tilt my head, so I can walk straight."

Beth laughed. "Your uncle is a clever man. Say, Sarah, do you think you and Clare would like a candy each?" And when Sarah's eyes widened in delighted disbelief, Beth offered, "Why don't you just go ahead and choose something?"

"You don't have to do this, but thank you," Joseph said, a little sheepishly.

Beth suppressed a grin. It was easy to see that the accident with the homemade ammunition still embarrassed Joseph. Not for the first time, she wondered why the man weighed himself down with unnecessary pressure. Raising children was not a science. Accidents happened. People dealt with them, then moved on. But not Joseph. Instead of letting go of the past—especially of things that were unforeseen and really quite trivial—he seemed to pile one unfortunate situation on top of another until the resulting burden became unbearable. Since telling him not to worry was unlikely to be effective, she decided to share a personal story with him.

"My girls got into trouble all the time," she said. "It's part of growing up. I remember one time when Ina and Patricia were about twelve and ten. They decided to revenge themselves on a teacher. They claimed she hadn't given them a Hallowe'en treat, so she deserved to have a trick played on her. Of course, the truth is, they simply didn't like the woman."

Joseph leaned on the counter as Beth told her story. The teacher's outhouse had been a big double-holer. The two girls had pulled out all the nails that secured the structure to the base. Then they hid behind the outhouse and waited. When the teacher eventually came to use the privy, she closed the door and sat down to do her business. The girls, in the meantime, crept around the outhouse with a piece of fence wire and knotted it so that she couldn't get out.

"The girls had tried their best to be quiet, but the teacher must have sensed their presence. 'Who's there?' she called, but the girls only giggled. She tried to get out but, of course, she couldn't open the door. 'Whoever is out there, open the door this minute,' she ordered, so strictly that the girls were frightened. They ran off, leaving the unfortunate woman trapped in the outhouse."

Joseph grinned as he listened to the story, its sheer nerve reminding him of the pranks he'd gotten up to when he was young.

Beth grinned too, as she went on. Her daughters had then related the prank to their friends, who thought they should finish the job. The girls, Ina and Patricia among them, returned to the outhouse and heaved it onto its side. Later, a policeman heard someone hollering and investigated. He came upon the teacher, her head poking through the outhouse hole. Unable to straighten it on his own, he got another policeman to help him. Next day, the teacher found a crowbar nearby with the name Hoogaboom scratched into the metal.

The newscast ended and from the radio came Lloyd Huntley's Orchestra playing Beethoven's *Moonlight Sonata*. Beth was still speaking. "People asked if I was raising my kids for the penitentiary. I didn't think it was funny at the time, but looking back ..."

She was laughing as she leaned forwards over the counter, her face only inches from Joseph's. The moment brought a sudden stirring deep inside him, a sensation he had not experienced since Helen's death. At that moment, Joseph and Beth were the only people in the world; even the little girls had ceased to exist. He saw the warmth in her eyes and smelled her sweet cleanliness. He ached to touch her face and feel her skin. He longed to know if she was as soft as she looked. Erotic thoughts filled his mind as he leaned still closer toward her. He wanted to kiss her. She must have understood his intention, for she stopped laughing abruptly and her expression turned serious. Their lips were about to touch when the bell rang over the door. They sprang apart, almost guiltily, as Raven entered the store.

"Have you seen what that snake wrote about me?" Raven demanded, slamming a newspaper down on the counter. In his rage, he was unaware of what he had interrupted.

"What are you babbling about?" Beth asked—without her customary good humour, Joseph noticed.

Raven read aloud: "Mr. William Mullens has once again thrown his hat into the ring as a candidate for the august position of mayor. It was not so long ago that the city's former chief engineer was charged with fraud for his mishandling of civic funds. Though charges were dropped against him—and Mr. Mullens was, therefore, presumed innocent—it cannot be too highly emphasized that even a whiff of impropriety could sully the reputation of our beloved city. Without its excellent reputation, Philibuster would be unable to attract honest businessmen to set up shop here. Civic office requires the highest moral standards. Even if Mr. Mullens was, in fact, innocent—which some people doubt—we must hope that intelligent citizens will remember how much our present mayor has done for us all.'

"And listen to this!" Raven's tone grew even more indignant. "Where is it …? 'It has also come to the attention of this newspaper that charges are pending against Mr. Mullens for incendiary speech as well as for certain actions that may have led directly to the deaths of two civilians and severe injury to three officers of the law during the communist uprising last spring at the Philibuster Dairy. Mr. Mullens could possibly be convicted of treason.' Christ! I wasn't even there!"

Beth shook her head. "People don't believe what they read, Raven," she said, trying to calm him.

"Enough do!" he roared. "Something's got to be done." Whereupon, he read through the entire article again.

Joseph didn't know what to say. Both he and Beth remained silent.

"Hungry," Clare whispered.

Beth smiled at the little girl as Joseph said, "Yes, honey, I know." He picked up the bag of potatoes in one arm and Clare in the other. It was time for him to get home and start supper.

Raven followed him out. They were barely out the door when he started up again. "That bastard Westmoreland! He stops good folks from getting a little relief, and he's hurting those who aren't on relief with his under-the-table deals. Who knows how long Beth can hold on?"

Joseph was taken aback. "Beth?"

"Westmoreland has given a couple of sweetheart deals to big grocery stores he persuaded to set up in Philibuster recently: free land, no taxes for 20 years, all sorts of other concessions. It's getting difficult for Beth to make a dollar. Did you see anyone in the store? People are shopping at the new places. It's killing Beth."

Come to think of it, Hoogaboom's had been pretty quiet the last few times Joseph had been there. Joseph hadn't noticed, perhaps because he had been so busy thinking about Beth rather than her store.

"You know what that man needs?" Raven spoke very quietly now, making sure he could not be overheard. "Lead poisoning. A couple of bullets to the heart—assuming he has one."

Raven went on to tell Joseph about Addison Philibuster, the man who had founded the small city they called home. Addison had cheated people whenever he could, until one day his dishonesty had pushed someone too far. That person had shot Addison in the face, killing him.

"What happened to the man who did it?" Joseph asked.

"He was hanged."

"Your solution isn't any good, in that case—unless you want to hang too."

"Got a better idea, Joseph?"

Joseph was silent as he thought about what he knew of Westmoreland's disreputable past: bordellos and bootlegging. Briefly, he considered sharing his knowledge with Raven, but he thought better of it. Although he liked the idea of disgracing Westmoreland, he had promised Mrs. Nye that he wouldn't pass on what she had told him.

"Humiliate him," he said.

Raven stopped walking. "And how do you propose to do that?"

Joseph had no answer. Besides, his thoughts had returned to Beth Hoogaboom.

CHAPTER 39

Joseph pulled a small roll of baling twine from his pocket and measured out six feet with his hands. As he walked up the hill toward the radio antenna at the south end of town, he pulled off his hat and wiped his head. The hill was much steeper than he had realized and the early morning sun had long since burnt off the cool night air.

When he got to the top he realized he was on a plateau rather than a hill. Surrounding him to the east, south and west, he saw gently rolling hills, many covered with sawn-off wheat stems: like a vista of black earth from which the golden hair had been shorn. There was no movement anywhere on the plateau. Off in the distance, Joseph saw a few one- and two-storey structures: tar-paper shacks with cardboard in place of windows. He wondered whether the houses had been abandoned, whether some farmer had finally given up hope after five years of heat, dust, gophers and grasshoppers.

Joseph began to search for the tell-tale mounds of fresh black soil that indicated gopher holes. Spotting one almost immediately, he used the twine to make a noose about six inches in diameter. Gophers were worthless now, but there was still some meat on their small bones. He wouldn't dare to feed them to the kids but maybe a gopher or two would keep him on his own feet a while longer. Creeping silently up to the hole, he placed the noose around the rim. As he played out the length of twine and sat down to wait, he thought about his aching guts.

After a fruitless hour on the hill, he regretted not having watched his sons a few times. He might have learned a useful trick or two. When he'd wasted yet another hour, a frustrated Joseph kicked at the dirt beside the gopher hole and then walked to the edge of the plateau.

He strolled down the hill toward the river, where he squatted by the edge of the water and rinsed his hands after rubbing them with sand. Then he cupped his hand, brought the cool water to his lips, and splashed his face and neck.

"Mr. Gaston?" someone said from behind him.

As Joseph stood up, he saw a face that looked familiar. It took him a moment to recognize the young boy Tilda and Henri had invited for dinner soon after his own arrival in Philibuster.

"Ethan?" he said.

The young man smiled. "Yes, sir. That's right. Ethan Greene. You remembered."

Joseph had often wondered what had happened to Ethan. "Sure, I do. How've you been making out?"

Ethan was happy to talk about his travels. Soon after the evening at Henri's house, he had hopped a train for Vancouver. After spending some time on the coast, he had headed south into the United States for the winter. He'd been on the road ever since. In fact, he told Joseph, he was waiting for a train to get him back home to Ontario.

Ethan had changed somewhat, Joseph observed. He looked about the same physically, but his manner and speech were different. He no longer ran off at the mouth as he had done two years earlier, and had stopped peppering his talk with hobo lingo. Perhaps he'd gained some wisdom in his time on the road. But his smile was as bright as ever.

"I found some friendly fellows to stay with until my train comes through," Ethan said. "Care to see our place?"

Joseph had nothing better to do, so, why not? He followed Ethan to a flat, dry clearing surrounded by budding trees and willow bushes not far from the river. A group of perhaps thirty men were congregated there, some sitting around a campfire, others on logs or cross-legged on the ground. A few lay on mattresses or threadbare blankets. A bespectacled elderly man sat on a weathered rocking chair beside the fire, stirring a pot suspended from a tripod of branches. Further back, Joseph saw a few shelters haphazardly put together out of cardboard and planks, as well as a couple of canvas tents. This was the hobo jungle: a village of men isolated from the rest of the world by misfortune.

"Hello, fellow traveller," said the elderly man from his rocking chair. "Don't be shy. Plenty of room here."

A few men chuckled.

"This here is Mr. Gaston." Ethan made the introduction with as much pride as if Joseph had been a celebrity.

"Just arrive?" asked the elderly man.

"Arrive?" repeated Joseph.

"In town, son. You just arrive in town?"

"Well, no … Been here a while."

"Mr. Gaston fed me once when I was first on the road," Ethan said.

"That so?" The elderly man looked Joseph up and down. "Hungry?"

"Yes," Joseph blurted out, without thinking.

"Dinner's almost ready. Take a seat."

Joseph and Ethan sat down together beneath a shady tree, its branches covered with budding leaves. At intervals, the man in the rocking chair stirred the pot. When he wasn't stirring, he covered the pot with a bent piece of tin. Joseph's mouth began to water at the aroma coming from the pot. Mulligan stew: its ingredients, he guessed, either begged or stolen.

Ethan asked about Henri, Tilda and the children. Joseph said they were all well. There wasn't much else to talk about and the two men slipped into a comfortable silence.

"How long you staying?" asked the elderly man.

"My money's on lunch," piped up one of the nearby men, to general laughter.

"I'll bet a week," said someone else. Yet others suggested lengths of stay from three nights to three months.

"Well son, how long's it going to be?"

Joseph realized he'd been mistaken for one of their own. A man on the road. A hobo. "Oh, I'm not—"

"Where's your bindle, boy?" the elderly man interrupted. "The bulls get your stuff?"

"Well, no … I live in town …"

"You don't say. Come here to see how the other half lives?"

"Oh, no! I just …"

The man chortled. "Just funnin' you."

Joseph fell silent and listened to the conversations going on around him. Ethan was silent too.

"… So I'm watching this jungle buzzard out the corner of my eye …"

"… More greybacks than you can shake a stick at …"

"… Promised me a gump if I did some honey dipping …"

Joseph couldn't follow most of the talk. It was all hobo speak. He found it interesting how at ease they all seemed.

After a while, the elderly man turned back to him. "Where you from, son?"

"Ontario," said Joseph.

"On the road long?"

"I'm not on the road."

"Right, so you said. Got a job?"

"No …"

"Then you're on the road, son."

Joseph was about to clarify the situation, but thought better of it.

"Shoebox," said the elderly man to someone wearing a battered bowler hat. "Get this here fella a plate and a shovel."

Moments later, Joseph held a pie plate and a homemade tin spoon.

"Time for a man to earn his dinner," cried the man in the rocking chair, as the rest of the men clanged their plates and utensils together. Holding up his hand for silence, he looked at Joseph. "First meal is on us. Second meal costs you a story. After that you put into the pot." His manner suggested a king addressing his court: a hobo king. "Now, I call on young Beach."

Ethan stood up. It appeared the boy had gotten himself a nickname while on the road. He pulled his hat from his curly blonde hair, wiped his face with his hand and left a smear of dirt on his cheeks.

"You must tell a story no one has heard before," the hobo king told him. "An honest tale of the road. Remember, these men have seen it all. Otherwise ..." his voice trailed away as he rubbed his belly, "nothing for you to eat."

"Well, I greatly appreciate you all letting me stay here with you," Ethan said, his green eyes sparkling. "You've treated me right good. Not sure if this's what you all want, but I got a story for you from when I first went on the road."

"Proceed, Beach," the hobo king said kindly.

Ethan stopped and started a few times before getting into the rhythm of his story. Once in his stride, however, he seemed barely to pause for breath. "So. Me and my buddy, we don't want to be a burden to our folks anymore. My pa hadn't worked in I don't know how long and neither had his pa. We figure, what are we going to do—curl up in a ball and starve? So we hit the road. Left Simcoe and headed west. Hopped our first train. Took us all the way to Winnipeg. Met some other fellas who knew the town and told us where the soup kitchen was. Got fed and found a place to sleep. We thought that being on the road wasn't so hard. After two days we smoked out of there and jumped on another train. Got booted off at some small town east of Regina. No soup kitchen. Didn't eat for two days. Couldn't get back on the train. Bulls everywhere. Had a tent. Sold it to buy food. Finally, hopped on a freighter. Continued west to Calgary. It was really nice and warm so we figured we'd stay a while. Found the jungle there and made a shelter. Then a snowstorm blew in. 'It's May,' I say to my buddy, 'what kind of country is this that has a snowstorm in May?' I nearly froze my middle bits off, scavenging, while my buddy sat in the shelter and sulked. When I came back with a plate of cold stew from some nice farm lady, I saw my buddy sitting on a log, crying. 'What are you balling about, you big baby?' I asked. 'I wish I was in my daddy's barn,' he says. 'In your daddy's barn? What for?' I asked. 'If I was in my daddy's barn,' my buddy says, sobbing like a little girl, 'I'd go into the house mighty quick!'"

Everyone laughed, including Joseph. Ethan grinned, happy to have pleased his listeners.

"Well, what do you think?" The hobo king turned to the other men, who laughed and shouted their approval.

"I guess it's up to me then," he said, with the air of a King Solomon about to determine the boy's fate. He waited for silence before giving his verdict. "Your story will do, Beach. You're welcome to stay as long as you like."

Hoots and hollers of welcome.

"Soup's on!" The hobo king shouted.

The men, Joseph and Ethan among them, lined up at the cooking pot as their leader ladled out dinner. Joseph's eyes widened when he received his portion, replete with more meat, potatoes and carrots than those of the other men. As the hobo king winked at him, Joseph sat down with his back against a tree and began to eat hungrily. It felt wonderful to have something warm in his belly. The hobo king sat down beside him with a thinner version of Joseph's food.

"From Ontario, eh?"

Joseph wiped his mouth with his sleeve and nodded, "Yes."

"Got somewhere to stay tonight?"

"In town."

The man nodded. "So you said. I remember my first time on the road. Didn't eat for a week. Thought I was going to die. I was laying on a park bench feeling sorry for myself when this young woman came up to me. Thought she was going to ask me to leave. But she pressed a half dollar into my hand and told me to take care of myself."

Joseph wondered if the man was making a point. He waited for him to continue, but apparently there was nothing more to the story. Joseph finished his food and followed the other men down to the river, where he rinsed his plate and spoon. Afterward, as he sat down again and listened to the talk around him, he wondered why the men—many of them laughing and telling jokes—seemed so relaxed. They were homeless and many did not know when and where they would eat their next meals. It was only a matter of time before Chief Quentin and his force found the camp, busted up the place, and forced them to move on. What reason did they have for happiness?

"You're welcome to stay," the hobo king interrupted his thoughts.

"Thank you, but I've got to be going." Joseph added his plate and spoon to a clean pile. "Appreciate your kindness, I sincerely do. I wish you and your men luck."

The hobo king shook Joseph's hand. "Mind if I give you a piece of advice, son?" He did not wait for Joseph to respond. "Swallow your pride when you got nothing else to eat."

Joseph gave the man a grateful smile, and walked away after saying goodbye to Ethan.

That evening, when the children were sleeping, Joseph looked at himself in the mirror—inspecting himself critically for the first time in a long while. It was as if a stranger stared back at him. His eyes were sunken and surrounded by wrinkles. Deep lines etched his forehead. His cheeks were sharp-angled and hollow, and his hair was thinning. When had he gotten so old, so tired-looking? As he looked at himself, Joseph understood why the hobo king had thought him a man on the road.

He made a deal with himself, then and there. If he saw no jobs advertised in the newspapers, none at all, he would apply for relief. If, however, he saw even one listing, whether or not he was qualified for it, he would continue his struggle. Turning from the mirror, he went to the table, picked up the paper he had borrowed from his brother, and looked for the Help Wanted section.

He was puzzled when he couldn't find what he was looking for. He searched up and down the columns of classified ads. There were listings for public auctions; livestock and houses for sale; but nothing at all under Help Wanted. As Joseph continued to scan the pages, he came across an ad that made him smile: "*2,000 acres, well fenced and watered, good building, corrals, etc.,*" it read. "*Lots of hay land. Outstanding investment. Will sell below cost. If you have no money, I might even be tempted to trade the ranch for something really useful, like a handful of magic beans.*" How, Joseph wondered, did people manage to retain a sense of humour when the world was against them?

CHAPTER 40

It was one thing for Joseph to promise himself he would apply for relief if he could not find an advertised job, another to keep that promise. Four days passed before he finally realized his children would go hungry if he didn't apply for assistance immediately. On the day of the May Day Dance, he decided to face the inevitable humiliation with dignity. That morning, as he always did, he washed his face, combed his hair and shaved. He wiped the dirt off his shoes. Finally, he put on a tie.

"Why are you all gussied up, Daddy?" Cole asked at breakfast.

"Meeting someone important."

"The mayor?"

"No, Cole, not the mayor. This is someone you don't know."

"Well, I sure hope you have a good day, Daddy." Cole thumped Joseph on the back, as if they were pals.

Cole was about to leave, when Joseph clutched him in a tight embrace. "This is why I have to do it," he told himself, as Cole wriggled free and ran off.

After dropping off the girls with Tilda, Joseph walked to the relief office. He hesitated before entering the building, looking around in case he saw someone he recognized. What must pass-ersby think of him? That he was too lazy to work? That he wasn't smart enough to keep a job? Questions that countless men around the country must be agonizing about too. The fact was, other peo-ple's opinions were unimportant. The hobo king's advice had been simple: "Swallow your pride when you have nothing else to eat." Joseph swallowed hard and opened the door.

After filling in the relief application he felt soiled, almost as if he had been branded in some way. He went straight home and didn't leave the house again that day. He did not want to run into anyone he knew, nor did he want to be asked whether he was attending that evening's May Day Dance.

After putting the kids to bed, he pulled out his battered dic-tionary. He began to page through it, but it was extraordinarily difficult to concentrate on impersonal words when he kept looking at the clock and wondering about Beth. Had she gone to the dance? Was she, at that moment, in someone else's arms?

Other questions came to mind. What would Beth think of him if she were to hear he'd applied for relief? It was painful to imagine her looking down on him. Could she possibly understand that he'd run out of options? And could he keep the knowledge from her? Not that it mattered, because, in any event, a capable woman like Beth be would never be interested in a person who could not support his family.

Eventually Joseph closed the dictionary, turned off the light and sat for a while in the dark. As he'd done so often in the past, especially since arriving in Philibuster, he wondered whether he could have made smarter decisions in the course of his life, and whether he faced a future of never-ending worry, toil and loneliness.

Unbeknownst to Joseph, as he sat by the window in his dark room, Beth Hoogaboom had just entered the district of Philibuster known as the Maze. In the past, when men had had money in their pockets and lust in their loins, they had frequented the area.

The women they found there were often desperate. Some needed to be able to pay rent and buy food for their children. Others were saving toward train tickets to better places. Whatever the case, there were so few options for a woman in need of money—other than a poorly paid occupation as a waitress, chambermaid or nanny—that many had been reduced to working in the Maze.

Beth Hoogaboom understood the desperate need for money. More than once she had come close to bankruptcy. The first time had been after the death of her husband, when she had known little about the business of running a corner grocery store. Accounts receivable. Accounts payable. Inventory. Leases. Credit. Debit. Bank deposits. The words had been alien to a woman who had done little more than run errands or work the cash register until then. Raven Mullens had helped her. He had put her books in order and taught her a thing or two about finance. In the years since then, when things had been difficult, Raven had often given her ideas that had enabled her to keep the store open in hard times. Beth had great respect for Raven—educated, well set-up financially, yet never condescending toward people less fortunate than himself—and, in turn, she was willing to agree to his requests for help.

Arriving at a house that had once been a center of Maze activity, and carrying a bottle of whisky, Beth walked quietly to the back door and looked around cautiously. When she was satisfied that the dark house was unoccupied, she slid a key into the lock. The catch released with a soft click, although to a nervous Beth it sounded loud. She opened the door quickly and went inside. Although she'd been in the house before, she was still apprehensive. She took a glass out of the cupboard above the kitchen sink, poured out two fingers of whisky and put down the bottle. She didn't like whisky—wasn't much of a drinker at all, despite the talk of the town's tongue-waggers.

Much of the gossip about Beth was incorrect, but she'd learned to live with the false rumours. Her reputation had never troubled her overmuch. Until quite recently, she'd been content to live her life as she pleased and was glad she could provide for her daughters. Only since Joseph Gaston's arrival in Philibuster had the rumours concerned her. Something had sparked in Beth during the evening Joseph and his sons had spent with her, sheltering from the Black Blizzard. She had felt something for the man, though she had tried her best to deny it to herself. She could not have said why, but Joseph had stirred a desire in her, bringing to the surface sensations she had thought long dead.

"No Joke Joseph," people called him behind his back. So often dour-looking, there was something about him that seemed above mere mortals with their human flaws and desires. He didn't drink or smoke; she had never even heard him swear. He intimidated others with his virtuousness, made them feel inferior and uncom-fortable in his presence. Although people didn't avoid him, they never felt he was one of them. Joseph was admired, but that esteem created a wall around him.

Even though Beth understood the way people felt about Joseph, she saw only a man who was decent and brave. At the same time, she had observed his frequent tension and wished he could be more relaxed. On occasion she had asked Henri and Raven to include Joseph in their pranks, but they were reluctant to consider it. Joseph was above their kind of tomfoolery, they maintained. Beth disagreed. Joseph had been looking so beaten and tired of late; she thought he could do with some laughter and fun.

As she waited in the dark house, Beth tried to put Joseph out of her mind. She needed to concentrate on the task at hand, which was difficult when she kept remembering the kiss that had so nearly happened recently. She knew that Joseph had been about to kiss her when Raven walked into the store. Years ago, after Ambroos's death, she had resolved never to love again. Yet now, as she waited for the arrival of some nameless stranger, she found herself wishing Joseph was coming to visit her instead. She imagined him knock-ing at the door and striding purposefully inside. She pictured him kissing her before carrying her to the room upstairs. She saw their limbs tangled in embrace as they lost themselves in ecstasy.

But Joseph was not the person coming to see her: that man was someone Raven expected to meet at the May Day Dance, a man he had good reason to dislike. Holding her glass tightly, Beth closed her eyes and swallowed the liquor. The whisky burned her throat and her stomach felt warm. She considered another drink, but thought better of it. She needed to have her wits about her in case something dangerous happened. She rinsed the glass and put it back on the shelf with the bottle. Looking at her watch, she knew the stranger would arrive soon. She turned on the outside light and sat down to wait until he came.

CHAPTER 41

As Chief Monty Quentin turned right onto Dairy Road, he thought of how close he'd come to breaking the law for the third time in his life. The mayor had charged him with finding out everything he could about Joseph Gaston. Westmoreland had deprived Joseph of his living and had persuaded his business associates not to hire him. Now he seemed intent on seeing Joseph homeless and broken as well. Monty often wondered what stopped the mayor from simply throwing Joseph out of his mother's house. Obviously he had his reasons, and didn't want Monty to know about them.

Not that the police chief needed much prodding to find dirt on Joseph. He was still angry with the man for making him look like a fool outside Hoogaboom's. He bitterly recalled the anticipation of the people watching when Joseph had challenged him to search the wood in the truck for a deer taken out of season. He had had no option but to back down after that, rather than look like a buffoon if he found nothing illegal.

The mayor was so enraged at Monty's lack of success in finding information he could use against Joseph, that he had threatened to have Monty fired if he did not come up with something soon. A desperate Monty was on the point of inventing something to use against Joseph, when he came across some information he thought the mayor would find interesting.

"What is it?" Westmoreland growled, when the police chief arrived at his office.

Monty came straight to the point. "You wanted something on Joseph Gaston."

Westmoreland looked up greedily.

"He's applied for relief," the police chief told him, and explained his plan.

The news, although welcome, was not enough to improve Westmoreland's mood. His situation infuriated him. He had tried once before to get rid of Joseph Gaston, only to have the man threaten to publicize the facts his mother had told him. The police chief's plans did not impress him, although Quentin insisted Joseph would have no choice but to leave Philibuster. Westmoreland would have been happier to see Joseph dead in a ditch.

Joseph Gaston was, however, the least of his current worries. The Philibuster Dairy was bleeding him dry. Though his step-father's little dairy farm had once been a great cash generator, Westmoreland had wanted it to be even more profitable. He had set up a full service operation without realizing that the town was not big enough to support it. Money grew tight and in an act of despair, Westmoreland burned down one of his own buildings and blamed the Chinese for the fire. Yet even with the insurance money he had been unable to make ends meet. Recently he had fired city relief inspectors and Children's Aid workers. He then added ficti-tious individuals to the city payroll and pocketed their salaries. It still wasn't enough. The only solution left was to embezzle more of the city's money, and that needed careful planning. And how could he off-load the dairy without hurting his reputation as a successful businessman? His reputation was important, because it encouraged people to vote for him.

But now was not the time to make plans. He was too distraught to think clearly. When that happened, there was only one thing to do. Westmoreland gave the police chief time to get back to his office before phoning him. "Set something up," he ordered angrily, disconnecting without waiting for an answer. Chief Quentin called back ten minutes later with the details.

Westmoreland closed his ledger with a bang and left this office, slamming the door before striding down the hall. His secretary did not ask when he expected to return.

Westmoreland slid into his Cadillac, turned the key in the ignition, and peeled out of the dairy parking lot in a cloud of gravel and dirt. He turned the car north and kept his foot hard on the accelerator. He honked his horn every few minutes, tailgating slower vehicles until they pulled over onto the shoulder of the road. He grew angrier with each passing mile. He was tired of having to leave town whenever he wanted a woman. It would take him three hours to reach his destination.

CHAPTER 42

Joseph opened the kitchen cupboards yet again. He gazed despondently at the empty shelves, as if he hoped they might have been magically restocked since the last time he'd looked at them. Pepper, salt and baking powder—that was all there was. What on earth would he tell his hungry children when they woke up next morning?

"Swallow your pride," the hobo king had advised. Joseph had done just that. Not only had he applied for relief, he had also gone to every charity in the city pleading for a handout. He'd once again reached the point where he was prepared to debase himself in whatever manner the charities asked of him, in order to get something—anything—with which to feed his family. Sadly, the charities had nothing left to give. Joseph was not the only man in Philibuster with a hungry family. Either the city was distributing less relief money or times were getting even worse, perhaps both. The best the organizations were able to tell him was to try again at the end of the week.

The situation was so dire now that Joseph had to demean himself still further. He asked his brother and sister-in-law whether they could help him with food for his family. Generous as ever, Henri agreed immediately.

In the kitchen a silent Tilda prepared a substantial breakfast of bacon, eggs and toast. She waited until the children were eating before telling Joseph she wanted to talk to him in the living room. They sat, Tilda on the chesterfield, and Joseph on a chair facing her. Tilda folded her hands in her lap and kept her back straight. She looked so grave that a puzzled Joseph wondered if he was about to hear someone had died.

In fact, Tilda was trying hard to hide her glee. This was the moment she had hoped and planned for—Joseph's admission that he was unable to provide for his family.

"I know you're struggling to care for the children," she said at length.

"It's only temporary," Joseph said quietly.

"Well, maybe it is. But you don't know how things will turn out. And don't think we're not sympathetic, because we are." Tilda smiled at him warmly. "It isn't your fault that times are so tough. So … I've spoken to Henri, and if it's okay with you, we're willing to take the girls."

Joseph stared at Tilda in confusion. It took him a minute to realize exactly what she meant: she was offering to adopt Sarah and Clare. As soon as he understood, he said, firmly, "No."

He did not tell Tilda that he had wondered himself whether it wouldn't be better for the girls to live with their aunt. Yet now that the idea had been verbalized, it was like a shock to his heart.

"Hear me out," Tilda said, her tone serious. "I know it's hard for you to hear this, because you care very much for your children. But think, Joseph. Loving them as I know you do, you must surely consider what is best for them. They love me and Henri, and we can provide a good home for them."

Joseph felt as if Tilda had slapped him. Though he knew that what she said was correct, he could not break up his family. It hurt him just to think of it.

"I'll be getting relief in two weeks time. I only need help until then. After that we'll be okay." Joseph dropped his eyes, wondering if Tilda sensed his lack of conviction.

But all she said was, "Think about it."

Despite the surface finality of his answer, Joseph remained for a while in the living room and thought about Tilda's suggestion. After Helen's death he had decided that no matter what happened, he would keep his children with him. He would not abandon them as he had been abandoned when his own mother had died. Now, for the first time, he wondered whether he was making a mistake. After all, if he were to agree to leave the girls with Tilda it would not be the same as abandoning them. Sarah and Clare would be raised by a woman who obviously loved them and an uncle who adored them.

From the time they first met, Tilda had always been "Aunt Tilda" to the children, but recently both girls had started calling her "Momma." At night, if they woke from pain or a bad dream, they reached out for their father, yet just the other day Sarah had said girls should raise girls, and boys should raise boys. How had she come by that idea? Had Tilda suggested it? Of course, people had said much the same kind of thing when Helen died, but Joseph had dismissed their pronouncements. Was it possible there could have been truth in them? After all, he did not recall ever having met another man who was raising young children—especially little girls—on his own.

Joseph loved his children dearly. They were all he had, and he could not bear to think of life without them. He returned to the kitchen to find Cole still eating while Tilda cleaned up. Henri and the other children were playing outside with Jasper.

"Daddy, what's a lady of the evening?" Cole asked.

Joseph glanced at Tilda, who only shrugged her shoulders as if she didn't know what had precipitated Cole's question.

"Is it a lady who goes out dancing at night?" Cole went on.

"That's right." Joseph was grateful that his son had come up with a harmless answer to his own question.

But Cole went on, "Goes dancing and then has sex for money?"

Joseph caught his breath. "Where did you hear that?"

"From Nolan."

So Nolan was causing trouble again, Joseph thought wearily. He ordered Cole to call Nolan.

"But, Daddy!"

"Now!"

A few minutes later Joseph took Nolan into the living room, where they could talk undisturbed. Joseph came straight to the point. "What have you been telling your brother? Why is he asking about ladies of the evening?"

"He heard Mr. Mullens say it and then he asked me about it. Was I wrong to tell him?"

"Mr. Mullens talked to Cole about ladies of the evening?" Joseph asked disbelievingly.

"No, Dad. Mr. Mullens was talking to Mrs. Hoogaboom. He called her a good lady of the evening."

Joseph's heart skipped a beat.

Nolan continued, "Cole and I were in the back of the store, loading groceries into the wagon. Mr. Mullens and Mrs. Hoogaboom were talking."

"What exactly did they say?" Joseph's mind raced.

"He said she acted a lady of the evening to perfection. Said she should have been an actress in the flicks. Wondered if she'd do it again."

"And what did Beth ... Mrs. Hoogaboom ... say?" Joseph dreaded his son's answer.

"She said she would, even though she didn't really want to anymore."

"You're sure that's what she said, Nolan?"

"Yes, sir."

Joseph felt ill. He must have gone white because Nolan asked, "Dad, what's the matter?"

"Nothing," said his father. "You can go and play outside again."

Joseph waited for Nolan to leave the room before putting his head in his hands. He could not have said how long he'd been sitting there before he became aware of another presence in the room. Instinctively, he lifted his head.

Standing in the doorway, arms crossed, was Tilda. Her satisfied smirk said, quite clearly, "*I told you so.*"

CHAPTER 43

On the same day as Joseph found out Beth Hoogaboom was a prostitute, he heard someone knocking three times on the door of Mrs. Nye's house. There was something menacing about the three pounding knocks. Warily, Joseph opened the door to three authoritarian-looking people, two men and a woman. One of the men was none other than the police chief.

"Afternoon," Joseph said, as steadily as he could.

"Joseph Gaston?" the strange man asked sternly.

Joseph nodded, wondering if Nolan had gotten up to some kind of mischief.

"The Joseph Gaston who recently applied for relief?"

Joseph tried not to let his nervousness show. "Yes."

The man introduced himself as Mr. Wellington, the woman as Mrs. Shaffer; both were from the relief board.

"I take it you know Chief Quentin." A statement rather than a question. "We have come to inspect your residence, Mr. Gaston."

Knowing Nolan was not in trouble made Joseph feel a little easier. He knew the board sent out inspectors to check that relief claimants legitimately needed assistance. Joseph had filled out his application honestly, but the police chief's presence was not reassuring. These people had the power to deny him help.

He led them into the kitchen. Mr. Wellington and Mrs. Shaffer sat down at the table. The woman pulled out forms and a pen. Chief Quentin declined to sit, but stood with his arms crossed.

"Can I offer you some water?" Joseph asked, over his own dry mouth.

On behalf of all three, Mr. Wellington declined the offer. "This is a mere formality, you understand. Must follow the rules."

"Of course," Joseph said. "I have nothing to hide."

"You're claiming for yourself and four children?" Mr. Wellington went on.

"That's right," Joseph said and gave the children's names.

As the woman made notes on a mimeographed sheet, the man continued his questions. "Anyone else living at this residence?"

Joseph mentioned Mrs. Nye and explained his position in her home.

"You've been an inhabitant of Philibuster for 24 months?"

Joseph handed over bills for the rent he'd paid at the rooming house as proof of his residence.

"Mrs. Shaffer will confirm the authenticity of the bills," the relief board man said.

"I can give you the name of the owner of the rooming house," Joseph offered.

"Unnecessary." A dismissive wave of the hand.

The woman passed a sheet of paper to the man. Behind them, Chief Quentin stood silent and motionless.

Mr. Wellington gave the paper to Joseph. "This is a list of extravagances that cannot be in your possession. If you own any of these items, you do not qualify for relief. I take it you've seen the list before. Can I assume you own nothing on it?"

Joseph had, indeed, seen the list. It included such things as automobiles, liquor, radios and telephones, as well as an excess of any kind of worldly possessions. He owned only essentials: a change of clothes for himself and some clothing for the children, a pot, a frying pan, a few pieces of cutlery and a dictionary. He had no need to read the list. "I don't own any of these things," he said.

"Then we'll proceed with the inspection. Let's start at the top and work our way down," Mr. Wellington suggested. He stood up quickly, as if he were suddenly in a hurry. Mrs. Shaffer stood too.

"Mrs. Nye's residence is up there," Joseph protested, as the relief board officers headed toward the staircase.

"We must inspect the entire dwelling," Mr. Wellington insisted.

"But we don't live upstairs. The children and I live on the main floor."

"Nevertheless, the upper storey is part of this residence. Our inventory must also include anything Mrs. Nye owns."

"You don't understand. I'm not applying for Mrs. Nye. I'm only applying for my children and myself."

"Rules are rules, Mr. Gaston. Mrs. Shaffer, follow me, please, and prepare to take notes."

As Joseph tried to follow the relief workers up the stairs, Chief Quentin blocked his way. Helplessly, Joseph stared at him.

"Oh, dear! Oh, my!" he heard Mr. Wellington exclaim. "A telephone *and* a radio. This won't do! This just won't do!" He was like a bad actor, speaking too loudly for the sake of a distant audience. At length, the relief board officers reappeared at the top of the stairs.

Mr. Wellington was grim-faced. "Chief Quentin, I think we are done here."

Joseph could not believe his ears. "But those things, the phone and the radio, they're not mine."

"Nevertheless. Nevertheless. They are in your residence. I can tell you right now, your request for relief will be denied."

"But my children!" Joseph's words were a cry from the heart.

Mr. Wellington's eyes dropped to his feet. Had Joseph been able to think clearly, he might have attributed the man's expression to shame. "Maybe if you lived somewhere else, Mr. Gaston," the man said, as he and his co-worker quickly left the house.

Joseph would have tried to detain them, but he understood there was no point in continuing the discussion. The man's mind was made up and no amount of argument would change it. Feeling numb, he watched the two relief board workers disappear down the tree-lined street.

He turned when Chief Quentin spoke: "He'll never let you get relief. Don't you understand? You should leave while you can." The police chief's face lacked the gloating satisfaction Joseph expected to see there; instead, his eyes were unreadable.

Joseph was puzzled, but he was not thinking about Chief Quentin as the man strode away. He had no money left in his pocket and now, it seemed, there was no longer any chance of obtaining any. He had never felt so helpless.

CHAPTER 44

At two in the morning, Tom Wah stepped out of the barn into the night. He was uncharacteristically excited after the discussion with Slim Evans regarding Tom's efforts on behalf of Philibuster's Chinese community.

As Tom tramped across a farmer's field toward the dirt road, he thought about the new ideas Evans had given him. Some of them might actually work. Both the Sunshine Society, run by Raven Mullens, and the Service To Others Club, run by a local pastor, had recently indicated their support for his cause.

He was gratified by the growing closeness between the Chinese community and Philibuster's more open-minded English citizens. With his confidence growing, he was starting to consider practising medicine again. It was even possible that he might be able to encourage an interest among white doctors in traditional Chinese medicine. How wonderful it would be to introduce something new to English Canadians! His grandfather would have been proud had he lived to see it.

Clouds hung low over the fields. With the promise of rain, there was no light in the sky from moon or stars. Lost in thought, it was a while before Tom noticed the sound of footsteps that were not his own. Evans, who always feared being caught by the authorities, often reminded Tom to make sure nobody was following him.

Tom stopped and listened. The other footsteps stopped too. Was he imagining things? Were his footsteps creating an echo of some kind? He began to walk again, listening intently all the while. At length he heard the other footsteps again—definitely not an echo. He thought about Evans, hoping he had not created a problem for the man who was helping him. Then it came to him that he was being followed back home rather than to a meeting with the labour organizer. Of course, it could well be that the footsteps he was hearing belonged to Evans or one of his men who were also returning to town.

"Hello?" he called tentatively.

No one answered. A shiver of fear ran down Tom's spine. Summoning his courage, he increased his pace. The other footsteps quickened, too.

Tom saw the welcoming streetlights of Philibuster in the distance. He began to run, and saw shadows in front of him. Thinking quickly, he threw himself into the ditch. With nothing to hide behind, he lay on his belly. The footsteps stopped, then began once more. Tom heard breathing, whispering. Suddenly a lantern flamed, then another. As a pool of light surrounded Tom, he counted seven men. They grabbed him roughly by his arms and legs and dragged him from the ditch.

Thinking all they wanted was information about Evans, Tom did not struggle at first. They would take him to the police station where he would be questioned. He would plead ignorance, of course. No way would he rat on Evans. They would check his papers and send him home.

Only when his captors carried him away from town into a small grove of trees, did Tom understand their true intentions. He struggled fiercely as he fought for his life.

But there were too many of them. They tied a noose around his neck, looped the end around a sturdy branch and hoisted him upwards. The noose tightened as Tom's feet lifted from the ground. Instinctively, wildly, he kicked and clawed at the empty air. But he could not escape. The more he struggled, the more the noose tightened, cutting off air to his lungs and his brain. He turned blue and his kicking slowed. Seconds before the end, briefly, a picture of his family appeared in his mind. Tom's last thought was regret that he had not kissed his wife and children goodbye before going out that night.

CHAPTER 45

Joseph was beside himself with rage when he learned about his good friend's murder. He was furious that Tom's life had been taken because of his skin colour, that Westmoreland had been allowed to write an inflammatory newspaper article calling for vigilantes to hunt Tom down, and that no one in authority seemed concerned to discover who was responsible.

As far as Joseph was concerned, Westmoreland was at least partly to blame. Briefly, he considered making public the truth about

Westmoreland's sleazy past in retaliation for Tom's murder. It would be easy enough to tell the men at the Hole what he knew. Gossip would spread quickly and within days all of Philibuster would know their mayor for the bastard he was. But reality soon sank in. For one thing, he'd promised his silence to Mrs. Nye—although he thought she would understand if he went back on his word. More to the point, though, was that Joseph could not prove that what Mrs. Nye had told him was true. To the town's residents, she was just Dizzy Daisy, and who would believe her? If anything, he might be playing into Westmoreland's hands. The mayor would gleefully sue him for slander and have Chief Quentin throw him in jail. With a few well-written newspaper articles, Westmoreland could then shake off the rumours and come out clean on the other side.

As Joseph's dreams of justice faded, guilt replaced his anger. Although he'd tried to stop Tom from taking on the fight for the Chinese, he wished he had done more to discourage him. Maybe he could have convinced Tom that the newspaper articles were dangerous, and that he was risking his life. But it was too late for remorse. And because he hadn't done enough to dissuade Tom from the fight, the man's family would suffer. There was no way Betty and the children could survive on their own.

That night Joseph sat on the back steps of the house, deep in thought. Often on nights like this, when the children were asleep, he would spend half an hour reading the old dictionary, looking for new and meaningful words to learn, but not tonight. For once he could not use the dictionary as a means of escape. Piled one on top of another, his worries and fears had reached the surface.

Sitting in the dark, he knew what he had to do. He had to leave Philibuster. Clearly, he would never find work in the town, nor would he receive help in the form of civic relief or charity. Other than his brother, he had only one reason to stay: the hope that something might develop between him and Beth Hoogaboom.

But now even Beth was lost to him; he couldn't share his life with a prostitute. Not that he despised her. He understood the concept of necessity and the reason a woman might turn to the oldest profession in order to survive. But excusing Beth was one thing. Allowing his children to live with her was another. Having seen the kind of man Westmoreland had become through his association with whores, Joseph realized he could not risk letting his sons be influenced in the same way. And then there was Raven. Even if Beth had managed to keep her activities a secret, Joseph now worried about Raven as well. The man he had respected had proved himself to be a consummate actor. He'd fooled not only Joseph, but also Henri and most of the town, into believing he was an upstanding person. Such a devious man must be avoided.

Joseph's thoughts turned to the children, the girls, in particular. It was torture to think of leaving them with Tilda. He would miss them more than he would miss an arm or a leg torn from his body. But leaving the girls with Tilda was the right thing to do. He had to consider their well-being before his own. Tilda was not perfect, but she was probably more capable than Joseph of keeping Sarah and Clare healthy and safe.

And what about the boys? Should he consider leaving them with Tilda and Henri too? But no, it would be too hard for his relatives to look after four children. The best solution for now would be to leave Nolan and Cole at an orphanage. Joseph had heard good things about the Philibuster orphanage. The care-givers were said to be kind and compassionate, and the boys would have regular meals. And much as Joseph hated the idea of the orphanage as a home for his boys, their stay in the institution would not last long. He would bring his sons home just as soon as he was settled.

Joseph looked up at the stars, as he sometimes did when searching for answers to his problems. The Northern Lights shone above him, a shifting curtain of green. It was rare to see them so clearly this far south and he sat for some time, entranced by the shimmering dance of light.

All at once, his attention was drawn to a plume of smoke in the sky. Puzzled, Joseph wondered why anyone would light a fire on such a warm night. The plume widened rapidly, and he stood to see it more clearly. The smoke was not coming from a chimney, he realized.

Hurrying inside, Joseph woke Nolan. "Something's on fire. I'm going to go check it out. Keep an eye on the others," he said.

"Fire?" Nolan muttered sleepily.

"I think it's the dairy."

Nolan was awake in seconds. "Can I come?"

Joseph shook his head. "Stay here and watch your brother and sisters."

In the days that followed, Joseph realized he should have shouted "Fire!" as he ran. The fact was, he hadn't thought he would be the first to arrive on the scene. He could only think of Copper, possibly unable to escape the burning building. Other people would almost certainly have been drawn to the scene by the billowing smoke, but who knew that Copper worked late at the lab making cheese cultures?

It took Joseph less than a minute to get to the other side of Cree Creek, from where he dashed down the dirt road to the dairy. Smoke was pouring through the upper floor windows. He hurried to the parking lot on the north side of the building. Copper's Napier, with its number painted on the grill, was the only car in the lot. He ran around the building, checking the doors. "Copper! Copper!" he shouted, hoping the man would emerge from the building—or, better still, that he was already outside, waiting for help. There was no response to his shouts and all the doors were locked.

Joseph ran to the front door. Unable to break the lock, he shattered the glass beside the door with a rock and pushed his way through the window frame. As he entered the building to look for Copper, he hoped the fire wagons would arrive soon.

One person saw the smoke at the same time as Joseph, but he didn't intend to do anything about it. He heard Joseph call out, but he stayed well out of sight, in the shadow of the trees, watching him. He had no idea that Copper was inside the building, but even if he had known, it wouldn't have made any difference; he wanted the building to burn.

At first the observer worried that Joseph would notice him. The man's unexpected appearance was annoying. He even wondered whether he should stop him from entering the burning building. Then it occurred to him that this unforeseen intrusion might actually work in his favour. If Joseph were, somehow, able to stop the fire—unlikely as that was at this point—it would be easy to blame the fire on him. His fingerprints would be found all over the place. And if Joseph were to be trapped and die in the fire, so much the better.

At that moment, a fireball erupted with a thunderous bang from the middle of the dairy. People would surely see the fire now. The observer smiled and moved deeper into the shadows, slinking carefully toward the deserted road where his car was parked. Nobody witnessed the Cadillac Fleetwood drive away.

Joseph heard the explosion and felt the building shake. As he hurried through the hot passages, trying to remember the location of the labs, he wondered frantically how much time he had left. Smoke filled the hallways and burned his lungs. He stooped low to avoid the worst of it. Every few seconds he desperately called Copper's name, but got no response. Believing he was close to the labs, Joseph began opening doors. He burned his hand on the hot doorknob of the second door. Biting back a cry of pain, he covered the doorknob with his shirttail and turned it. He pushed the door open to a great "whoosh" of air. In that instant, an explosion threw him against the wall. He rolled rapidly out of the way of the flames licking the doorframe. On his feet again, he staggered away. He wondered if he should escape the dairy while it was still possible, but decided to continue the search for another minute. He was about to give up, when he found the lab. "Copper! Copper!" he yelled, glancing behind the rows of counters stacked with chemistry equipment. The room was empty.

Coughing and gasping for breath, Joseph fled the lab. Fire now blocked the way he had just come. Panicking, he rushed along hallways, turning back every time he encountered fire, until he found a door that led outside. Exhausted, he escaped into the smoky night air and collapsed onto the ground.

Clouds of hot smoke were now pouring from the roof of the cinderblock structure. Fire licked the frames of shattered windows. As Joseph tried to catch his breath, he heard the distant clanging of the fire wagons. When he was able to breathe a little more easily, he got to his feet and staggered to the front of the building, where a small crowd of men and women in various degrees of undress watched the fire from a safe distance. Joseph heard a great roar as the roof collapsed. Another huge ball of flame erupted into the air. The crowd stepped back rapidly. A few people embraced in shock.

Ashen-faced, Joseph emerged from the shadows.

"Joseph!" someone called.

Joseph spun around and saw Copper, scared but unhurt.

"You're okay!" Joseph exclaimed.

"God Almighty! Were you inside?" Copper asked.

Joseph was black with soot. His hair was singed in places and his eyebrows were missing. There were smoking holes in his shirt and his right hand was burned.

"I saw your car. I thought you were inside. You weren't in the lab," Joseph stammered. He was clearly in shock.

Copper took off his jacket and slung it around Joseph's shoulders. "Wear this," he said.

A hose cart, pulled by a two-horse team, rushed into view. Close behind it came two more wagons, another hose cart and an aerial cart stacked with ladders. The horses skidded to a halt. The driver of the first cart shouted orders. Firemen leaped from the wagons and began yanking out the hoses. As the two-and-a-half-inch hoses were hooked up to a nearby hydrant, two more hose carts came barrelling down the street, bells clanking, horses steaming. More hoses were hooked up and aimed at the blaze.

As people noticed Joseph, they gathered around him.

"Christ! Were you inside?"

"What started it?"

"Is there a doctor?"

"Let's sit down," Copper said and led Joseph away from the crowd to a grassy spot.

"What happened?" Joseph asked. His hands shook; adrenaline coursed through his veins.

Copper told Joseph that he had gone in search of the fire after smelling the smoke. Realizing he couldn't fight it, he had run out a side door.

"I'm not feeling too well," Joseph said.

Before Copper could reply, Chief Quentin appeared. A few minutes later, Joseph was wearing handcuffs.

Chief Quentin questioned Joseph at the police station. How had he happened to find himself at the dairy at such an odd hour? Why was he soaking wet? Why did he break into the dairy? What had he done while inside?

Joseph did not render a good account of himself. He felt shaky and faint, and gave short, hesitant answers, as if he lacked a good explanation for his actions. After being questioned, he was taken to an empty cell in the basement of the jail. Dr. Graham arrived to apply ointment to Joseph's burns and bandage his hand. With the waning of adrenaline, Joseph grimaced with pain when the doctor touched him. Then the doctor left and Joseph was on his own.

Some time later he heard footsteps. He looked up to see Winfield Westmoreland, immaculately attired in a blue suit and tie. His hands were in his pockets and he was grinning.

"Hell of a night you've had," Westmoreland said, jauntily.

Joseph immediately experienced a fresh surge of adrenaline. The anger he had felt toward the mayor after Tom's murder came flooding back. He would have liked to reach through the bars and strangle the man.

"Why did you set fire to my dairy?" Westmoreland was still grinning.

"I didn't set fire to anything," Joseph said flatly. Briefly he wondered if he could catch Westmoreland off guard and grab him by the tie before he could take a step back.

"That's not what Quentin thinks and it's not what the rest of Philibuster will think either."

"It's the truth!"

"Nobody cares about the truth, Gaston. Least of all from you."

"They'll care when I tell them about your disgusting past!" Joseph yelled, stepping forward and grabbing hold of the bars.

Joseph expected Westmoreland to get angry. Instead, he laughed.

"I've been thinking about that, Gaston. I don't believe you'll say anything. Most likely you'll be going to prison for arson. In the unlikely chance you get off, you'll fade away quietly."

"Not bloody likely! I will scream everything I know from the rooftops!"

Westmoreland stopped smiling. "Oh no, you won't. You're going to keep your mouth shut, if you know what's good for you."

Joseph was beyond being threatened. "Or what? You'll kill me?"

"No, but something terrible might happen to those brats of yours," Westmoreland said, chillingly.

"You yellow son-of-a-bitch!" Joseph howled. He lunged at Westmoreland, banging his face against the bars as he tried to grab him, but the man was out of his reach. Breathing hard, Joseph gripped the bars so tightly that his knuckles turned white.

"I see I've given you something to think about," Westmoreland taunted.

Joseph did not respond. For a long minute the two men glared at each other in hatred.

"Nothing will happen if you keep your mouth shut and get the hell out of town," Westmoreland said finally. About to walk away from the cell, he turned back. "Stay here the night and think about it."

With Westmoreland gone, Joseph began to pace the floor of his tiny cell. He believed Westmoreland's threat. Would the children be safe until he got out? How much longer would he kept be in jail?

His mind was still whirling with questions when Chief Quentin came down the stairs with a plate of food. "The missus made it," he said, putting a steaming tin pie plate of stew and a cup of water near a hole in the bars on the floor.

Joseph did not acknowledge the man, but continued to pace the cell. Twenty minutes later Chief Quentin called, "Lights out in five minutes." Joseph was still pacing when the cell went dark.

When Chief Quentin checked on his prisoner the next morning, he found him staring impassively at the bars. The stew lay untouched and congealed at his feet.

CHAPTER 46

Henri visited Joseph the morning after his incarceration. He comforted Joseph, telling him the children were at his house, and that he and Tilda would look after them for as long as Joseph was in jail. Joseph thanked his brother and asked him to tell the children he loved them.

Joseph was released late that evening, on the condition that he did not leave town. "You might be wanted for further questioning," Chief Quentin told him.

At a newsstand outside the courthouse, Joseph saw the *Philibuster Post* headline. "DAIRY TORCHED! ARSONIST IN CUSTODY." Glancing at the story, he saw he had been named the alleged culprit.

Joseph was still covered with soot when he returned to Daisy Nye's empty house. He went directly to the basement. The boys' makeshift fort was in the far corner, steamer trunks piled one on top of another like massive blocks. The Smith & Wesson was still inside the locked steamer trunk. As Joseph reached for the revolver, he was surprised to see a bag of groceries: potatoes, carrots, onions, eggs and something that smelled like bacon and was wrapped in butcher's paper. Joseph immediately thought of Nolan and his proclivity for stealing. "Goddammit!" he shouted, slapping the butcher's packet onto the trunk lid.

After his first moments of anger, it dawned on Joseph that stolen food was unlikely to be packed in a grocery bag. Looking inside, he saw a receipt—proof that the food had been paid for. Joseph realized that his children must have been experiencing their own gnawing hunger. The boys had been forced to spend their paltry earnings on food for themselves.

Joseph simply could not imagine feeling worse than he did at that moment. The knowledge that he'd failed his children so completely was another stab to the heart. He could no longer deny that it would be much wiser to leave the girls with Tilda and the boys at the orphanage. They would all be better off without him. But there was one thing he had to do before he left.

As Joseph strode out of the house, he tore the bandage off his right hand and flexed his fingers, ignoring the pain. He took a box from his pocket and counted out six rounds. Then he opened the cylinder of the revolver and filled the chambers. He cocked the hammer back and made sure the gun was ready to fire, before easing the hammer into place. He sighted down the barrel a few times, then stuck the gun in his jacket.

He would not run or hide ever again. He was done with being a coward.

Fists clenching and unclenching, Joseph climbed the hill. As he went, he was aware only of his purpose. He didn't notice the setting sun illuminating the sky with gentle shades of pink and yellow, or the sweet smell of budding trees and spring flowers wafting on the soft breeze, or the sounds of mothers calling their children and men chatting idly about sport and the weather.

Joseph reached the house at the top of the hill and pounded on the door. When there was no response, he pounded again, even more loudly. Then he circled the house and peered through the windows. There was no sign of movement. Glancing through the garage window, he realized Westmoreland's fine vehicle was missing. No matter. He would sit on the front steps and wait. Winfield Westmoreland would have to return home eventually.

Joseph waited an hour before hearing the distinctive sound of the Cadillac Fleetwood. As the car crested the hill, he felt strangely calm. His rage had left him. He was utterly in control of himself.

"Hello, Winny," he called mockingly, as the mayor heaved his bulk out of the car.

In the dark, Westmoreland had not noticed Joseph sitting on the steps by his front door. "What the hell are you doing here?" he demanded.

"Came over for a visit," Joseph answered coolly.

Westmoreland slammed the car door. "Get the hell off my property!"

"That's not very polite, is it? Where's your family, Winny?"

"None of your goddamned business!" Westmoreland yelled, coming toward Joseph.

Joseph remained seated. "Run out on you?" he asked calmly, knowing that the pine trees surrounding the property would make it impossible for any witnesses to see what was happening.

"I told you to get the hell off my property!" Westmoreland yelled again, closing in on Joseph.

"Say, Winny, do your neighbours know about your past? Do they know about your two faces?"

"Watch yourself," Westmoreland growled.

Joseph stood up. The two men stared at each other, eyes dark with hatred. Had they been pugilists in a ring, Westmoreland would have been the easy favourite. He outweighed a sickly looking Joseph by a hundred pounds.

Joseph grinned impudently. "Or what, Winny?"

"Or you'll regret it."

"No more than you will. This is the last day you'll ever see." Joseph said and sprang at his enemy.

Joseph's first punch was intended for Westmoreland's nose. But years had passed since he'd last fought, and the punch went wide, hitting the other man on the cheek. However, he soon regained his skills. The next few blows landed on Westmoreland's jaw. Unprepared for the savage flurry of fists, Westmoreland covered his face with his arms. Then Joseph went to work on the man's body, hitting him in the ribs, the stomach and the kidneys. It was not long before the mayor lay on the ground, with his arms still covering his head. Joseph stood over him, breathing hard. He shoved his hand in his jacket and pulled out the revolver. He cocked back the hammer and pointed the gun at Westmoreland. Westmoreland looked up at that moment, his eyes wide with terror.

Briefly, Joseph was reminded of Nolan the night Sarah had lost part of her earlobe. Joseph had screamed at Nolan, had come so close to striking him. It dawned on him now that Westmoreland had once been a boy, too—Daisy Nye's beloved son. For some reason, Joseph felt an odd pity for Westmoreland and for the child he had once been. He realized he could not kill the man, no matter how evil he was. He pointed the gun into the air and pulled the trigger. As it fired, a loud crack echoed through the still night air, then all was silent once more.

"You threaten my family again, and the next bullet out of this gun will hit you between the eyes," Joseph snarled. Then he walked away.

Westmoreland lay trembling on the ground. After a few minutes he was able to get to his feet. A terrible rage swept him. He ran into the house, overturned furniture, smashed china, broke legs off chairs and stabbed holes in walls. When he had destroyed everything in his path, he phoned the police chief. Yelling hysterically, he complained about being attacked and almost murdered. "I want that man found and killed!" he demanded. As an afterthought, he added, "And if you don't find me a whore within the hour, consider yourself fired!"

When Westmoreland had finished his rant, Chief Quentin calmly hung up the phone, thought for a few moments, and then made a call to Raven Mullens.

CHAPTER 47

The adrenaline that had fuelled Joseph's anger and daring began to ebb as he walked home. He was shaking as he realized how close he had come to killing Westmoreland. The Smith & Wesson was still in his hand. Looking at the revolver, he marvelled at the ease with which one man could take the life of another. It was as simple as putting a finger to a trigger, aiming at a person's heart and firing.

He wondered why he had never thought of killing in quite that way before. He had fired a weapon just like this one during the Great War. But there had been a difference. As a soldier, he had seldom known exactly what he.was shooting at. He had fired at *something*, rather than *somebody*. As a communications runner, Joseph had never seen the faces of the men he'd shot at. He'd observed only the aftermath.

He had been a naïve teenager when he had signed up to fight overseas, persuaded by fervent newspaper articles into believing the worthiness of the cause. It was only after arriving on the battlefield that he realized there was nothing glorious about war. Rather, it was a terrible waste of young lives and valuable resources. Like so many other servicemen, Joseph had returned from Europe wiser and more appreciative of human life. Why was it, then, that having calmed down somewhat after his confrontation with Westmoreland, he felt as if he had learned little from his previous brushes with death? And how terrible to think that if he had, indeed, killed Westmoreland, he would have forfeited his own life to prison or the gallows, as surely as if he had been hit by a German bullet.

Feeling suddenly overcome and unable to walk, Joseph sat down on the curb and thought about the men he'd met in the army, so many of whom had been buried far from their homes and families. He was fingering the revolver, cocking the hammer back and forth, when he realized what he was doing.

As he unloaded the weapon and put it, together with the unused cartridges, back into his jacket pocket, he understood that despite what had just so nearly happened, he had never lost his respect for human life. His recent years of deprivation, struggle and loss had simply made him to forget, for a while, the lessons he had once learned. Grateful that he had remembered, in time, what was important, he was damned if he was going to let what he cared about most slip away. Not only was he going to keep the children, but there was someone else from whom he had no intention of being parted.

Before he knew it, he was running.

The store was warm with the light of incandescent bulbs and the movement of people. Inside, half a dozen customers were doing their shopping. Patricia was at the till.

"Where's your mother?" Joseph asked breathlessly.

The girl was startled when she took in his appearance. "Mr. Gaston, are you okay?"

Joseph realized he had not had a chance to bathe, or even clean up a little, since the fire the previous night. He could only imagine what he looked like, still covered in soot and wearing charred clothing. He found he didn't care, and it felt good not to care.

"Fine. I'm fine. Where's Beth?"

"She left with Mr. Mullens."

"With Raven?" Joseph asked, his imagination running wild all at once. "Where'd they go?"

"I don't know. Mom just said there was an emergency and that she needed me to cover for her until closing time. I have plans to go out later, but I'm looking after things here, until then."

Joseph ran out of the store. Where could Beth be? Where would Raven have taken her? Remembering Raven's conversation with the young stranger at the Christmas Dance, Joseph tried to recall the name of the street he had heard mentioned. What was it? Thompson, Helen's maiden name. Thompson Street, that was it.

Let me get there in time, Joseph prayed, as he ran toward the Maze. Perhaps Beth had seen prostitution as her only solution in the past, after her husband's death, when money was tight and she had no one to help her. He had to make her understand that she didn't have to do the work any longer. They would find a way out of her difficulties together. *Together*. The word made Joseph run harder. He saw the street sign and slowed to a fast walk. Which house was he looking for?

Focused on finding Beth, Joseph didn't hear the footsteps behind him. Suddenly someone grabbed his arm. He turned to find Chief Quentin at his side. Instantly, he thought of the gun he had pointed at the mayor and the beating he had given him. This, Joseph realized, was his third strike. He was on his way to jail. His children would be taken from him and the possibility of a happy ending with Beth was gone.

"Evening, Mr. Gaston," the police chief said, as he guided Joseph roughly through a front yard and into a back alley.

Joseph tried to speak, but Chief Quentin silenced him with a hissed, "Shut it!" Drawing his revolver, he forced Joseph down the alley, across a street, and into the Cree Creek ravine. At the bottom of the ravine they came to a footbridge that crossed the creek. Chief Quentin stopped on the bridge. He seemed to be listening for something.

"Monty?" someone whispered.

"Here," the police chief whispered back.

"Who's with you?"

"Joseph Gaston."

The man came closer. It was Raven. He stopped. "What the hell is *he* doing here?"

"Found him wondering around Lisa's house," Quentin said.

"How'd he find out?" Raven asked.

"I don't know, but we need to get back. He could arrive any minute." Chief Quentin sounded agitated.

"Should we leave him here?" Raven asked.

The two men sounded like conspirators. Joseph was filled with a sudden dread. What were they talking about? Did they mean to shoot him and leave him to rot in the ravine? Raven was obviously even more evil than he'd realized. He felt the cold steel of the Smith & Wesson in his pocket. The gun wasn't loaded, but perhaps he could pistol-whip both men and then run. He was about to pull out the revolver, when the police chief answered Raven. "He'll only screw things up, if we do. The damned do-gooder will end up getting in the way. We'll have to take him with us."

Take him where? thought a totally confused Joseph.

Chief Quentin turned to Joseph "Listen to me, Gaston—you'll say nothing from here on out. Understand? Follow me and keep your trap shut."

"What's going on?" Joseph demanded.

Raven grinned at him. "Come on, Joseph. Just do as the chief says. You're going to want to see this." His tone was oddly reassuring.

Hoping he was not being tricked, Joseph left the Smith & Wesson in his pocket. He could not have said why, but for some reason he still trusted Raven. Silently, he followed the men across the bridge and back up the ravine. At the top of the ravine, Chief Quentin and Raven crouched down behind a row of bushes, motioning to Joseph to do likewise. Joseph could see the length of Thompson Street and the alley behind it. Of the dozen houses on the street, three had their lights on.

"What's going on?" he asked quietly.

The police chief shot him a fierce look. "Squeak or move a muscle without my say-so, and I'll put a bullet in your ear."

"Easy, Monty," Raven said softly. To Joseph, he whispered, "Stay down and be quiet. I'll be able to explain soon."

A young couple came walking toward them. In the silence, Joseph heard them talk about saving for a home. They walked further and all was quiet again. Whenever Joseph looked at Raven, the other man held a finger to his lips.

At length, an astonished Joseph heard the sound of a car engine, one he recognized. The car stopped a block away and a man got out.

The man—no more than a shadow—walked down the alley, stopping at one of the houses that had its lights on. He stood still a few seconds, opened a small gate and entered the back yard. He knocked on the back door and was let in.

"Should we move closer?" the police chief asked Raven.

"No."

"We don't want her hurt."

"She'll be fine."

She? Joseph wondered if they were referring to the mysterious Lisa about whom he had heard Raven talking at the dance. And where was Beth?

Some tense minutes later, Joseph heard the call of a loon. Not a real loon, he realized, but a good imitation nonetheless. Raven responded with a call of his own.

All at once, bursting from the shadows, a large man—his back toward the crouching trio—ran toward the house and barreled in through the back door. "You bastard!" they heard the man yell. "How long have you been sleeping wi …?"

The rest of his sentence was drowned out by a woman's scream and the noise of dishes shattering. A partially clothed man flew out the door, followed closely by the large man, who was still yelling. "She's my wife, dammit, not yours!"

As they raced toward the bushes, the shadowy pursuer waved a gun in the air and screamed, "I know your face! I will kill you, Winfield Westmoreland!"

There was something familiar about the hollering voice, but Joseph had no time to think about it as Raven pulled him to the ground—just in time, as the first shadow, Westmoreland, ran past.

The pursuer fired his gun and Joseph ducked instinctively. He heard Raven stifle a laugh.

"Shut up!" Chief Quentin hissed.

Moments later Joseph heard splashing in the creek, accompanied by more gunshots and more yelling: "I'll get you, Winfield Westmoreland. You'll be sorry you didn't keep away from my wife!"

When all was quiet once more, Chief Quentin said to Raven, "Why don't you take Joseph and check on her?"

Joseph was stunned to see the police chief smile, for the first time ever. Then Chief Grumpy was running in the same direction as Westmoreland and his gun-wielding pursuer.

CHAPTER 48

"Follow me," Raven ordered, "and keep low."

Joseph stayed close to Raven as they left the bushes, went a few hundred feet along the ravine, and then came back up. Staying in the shadows, they made their way quietly through the streets and alleys of the Maze. Houses that had been dark earlier were now lit up, and everywhere people could be heard talking about the mayor. Raven and Joseph did not stop to listen to the gossip as they made their way toward the house from which Westmoreland had been so ignominiously chased. They hopped over the rear gate and entered the house. In the kitchen, a woman was sweeping up broken crockery by the dim light of a lantern. She wore a white dress and her hair fell in glossy curls to her shoulders.

"Okay, Lisa?" Raven asked.

The woman turned.

"Beth?" Joseph exclaimed at the same moment as she said, "Joseph!" They stared at each other in mutual disbelief. Watching them, Raven burst out laughing.

Beth recovered her composure first. "Keep laughing like a hyena and you'll give us away," she admonished Raven.

Joseph was more confused than he had been in a long while. Why had Raven addressed Beth as Lisa? He started to ask the question, but Beth was too busy trying to silence Raven to answer. Impatiently, she told him to go and see to Henri. *Henri?* Something tugged momentarily at the edges of Joseph's mind.

"Now!" Beth said.

Raven was still laughing when she took his arm and ushered him firmly to the door. "Go now," she ordered. "And leave Joseph with me. We need to talk."

"Indeed, you do," chuckled Raven, as he stepped out into the night.

Beth moistened a tea towel. "You're covered in soot," she said, as she began, quite gently, to clean the grime from Joseph's face.

"There was a fire last night…"

"At the dairy. Yes, I know about that."

"Yes, I suppose you do." He stared at her. Then he asked the question uppermost in his mind: "Why did Raven call you Lisa?"

"It's the part I was playing." Finishing up, Beth dropped the towel onto the table and left the kitchen for the front room.

Joseph felt like an actor who had blundered into a play that was already in progress. Having missed the initial acts, he was lost. But he followed Beth and joined her at a dark window. Outside people were gathering, like moths, beneath a streetlight.

"We'd better go before we give ourselves away," Beth said quietly. She threw on a wrap, doused the lantern, opened the back door a crack, and peered outside. Satisfied that it was safe to leave the house, she motioned to Joseph to follow her into the dark alley.

"Pretend we're out for a leisurely walk," she whispered as they were about to emerge from the alley.

"I don't understand …" Joseph began.

Beth cut him off gently. "Shhh," she whispered, as she looped her arm through his. "We'll talk soon."

They had gone a few blocks before Beth was finally ready to speak. "It was a prank," she said.

"A prank?"

"To trap Westmoreland." Beth laughed softly. "Chief Quentin's idea, actually."

Joseph stopped and turned to her. "I don't believe it!"

"I know. I'll explain just as soon as we're well out of this place. Look, let's head to the store. Patricia was planning to go out after the store closed. We'll be able to talk undisturbed."

Joseph knew he had to be patient a while longer. As they approached Hoogaboom's and he pictured himself alone with Beth, his heart quickened. He forced himself to suppress his thoughts.

It had turned chilly by the time they reached the dark store. Beth turned on a few lights and told Joseph to make himself comfortable near the back while she made coffee. She returned with a tray bearing two steaming mugs and a plate with a few cookies. She looked so lovely in the pretty dress and with her hair hanging loose, that Joseph wanted nothing more than to take her in his arms. But there were things he badly needed to know first.

Settling down in the chair opposite his, Beth cupped her cold hands around her mug. She gestured toward the cookies, and when Joseph had taken one, she took a sip of her coffee. When she put down her mug and looked at Joseph, her eyes were sparkling.

It was a prank, she explained, originally thought up by Raven and The Great Henri, that pair of incorrigible comedians. It was their way of teaching certain men a necessary lesson and amusing themselves at the same time. The first time they'd performed it, more than a year ago, they had enlisted her help. Since she could never refuse Raven, who was so often kind to her, she had agreed to take part.

"In case you think us heartless," she said, "I want you to know that we've only done it to a couple of real bastards. You could say we gave them more than they'd wished for."

Joseph was intrigued. "Go on."

Raven, Joseph learned, owned a few houses in the Maze. Two were vacant—the one Joseph had been in that night, and one other. For the purpose of the prank, Beth was Lisa, a woman of easy virtue, not averse to earning a bit of easy cash by entertaining strangers when her husband, a travelling salesman, was out of town. When Raven and Henri came across out-of-town jerks, Raven would offer the man an introduction to Lisa. Lisa would give him dinner; the dessert was left to the fellow's imagination. In fact, the only entertainment he would receive was when Henri burst in on the pair, waving a pistol and pretending to be an outraged husband.

Henri was the outraged husband! No wonder the voice of the shadowy man had sounded so familiar.

"We only did it to men who deserved it," Beth assured Joseph. "Counting tonight, we've done it four times. Last Christmas, the night of the dance, was a bit frightening, though. When Henri fired the gun, our victim was so scared, he ran though town screaming."

Joseph remembered the man he had seen running past the house, shouting for help. Chief Quentin had been close behind him.

He frowned. "Where was the real Lisa when all this happened?"

"You still don't understand, Joseph. There is no Lisa. Never has been. And in case you're wondering, the neighbours haven't been wise to the stunt. Tonight, with more at stake than usual, we used a house we'd never used before."

"Surely Westmoreland would have known if a whore called Lisa lived in the Maze?"

Beth shook her head. "Until today, our illustrious mayor has never frequented local whores. Nobody in Philibuster was supposed to know what a sleaze he is. For the same reason, he never set foot in the Maze. Chief Quentin always set up his "dates" out of town, except for tonight, when he persuaded him to have dinner—and dessert, of course—with Lisa. Westmoreland was in such a state after you'd finished with him today, he was glad not to have to drive out of town."

"You said tonight was Quentin's idea ..."

Beth laughed. "Our police chief set it up with Raven and Henri. I'd told Raven I didn't want to be Lisa again, and that was fine with him. Until Chief Quentin arrived and told us what he wanted."

"Why?"

Beth hesitated. "I'm not certain, although I think I can guess. Why don't you ask your brother and Raven for an explanation?"

"I will."

Silence fell between them. Joseph gazed at Beth and found her eyes on him too. An odd tension filled the air. Joseph longed to kiss Beth. He yearned to hold her, but he didn't know if she would reject him. Besides, after all that had happened in the last few hours, there were things he had to think about.

Slowly, reluctantly, he put down his mug and got to his feet. "I have to go. It's late … And the children …"

"I know," she said softly.

At the door, she reached up and brushed his cheek with her lips. "It's been a lovely evening. Goodnight, Joseph. I hope I'll see you again soon." Giving him no time to respond, she closed the door behind him.

Dazed, Joseph stared at the door. Then he touched his cheek where Beth had kissed him.

CHAPTER 49

"Je-zuz," Raven said, slapping his hand on his knee, "He ran like a bat out of glory."

Joseph, The Great Henri and Raven were sitting at the table in Mrs. Nye's big kitchen. Joseph had just gotten the kids to sleep when Raven and The Great Henri had tapped on the window. Tired as he was, Joseph was glad to see them. Perhaps they would help him make sense of things.

The Great Henri had been telling them about Westmoreland's frantic escape from the vengeful husband. So hilarious was his account that Joseph and Raven laughed until tears streamed down their cheeks. Fearing for his life, Westmoreland had not considered his course, and had inadvertently run a straight line into downtown. Even though it was late in the evening, it was a Friday night and people were roaming the streets, so many citizens witnessed the pursuit of their adulterous mayor.

Most of the town soon knew the story. Some were surprised that their saintly mayor had turned out to be such a disappointment. Others remembered old rumours of deception and indiscretion that had been hushed up at the time. By the following day, city gossip had convicted the mayor of adultery. Tellingly, the *Philibuster Post* made no mention of the incident.

Joseph struck his forehead. "I thought there was something familiar about the big shadow. How come I didn't know it was you?"

"Because, big bro'der, I am a ver' good actor."

"Well, I guess I did have a lot on my mind," Joseph said.

"I brought something special for the occasion," Raven said, and pulled out a bottle of whisky. Joseph took three glasses from the kitchen cupboard and put them on the table.

Raven poured the whisky, and raised his glass in a toast. "A toast to Beth. We couldn't have pulled it off without her."

"To Beth," said the other two.

Raven looked at Joseph. "I gather she told you about the prank."

"She did." The unaccustomed whiskey had relaxed Joseph. "But there's something I still don't understand. Where does Quentin fit in? I thought he was Westmoreland's man."

"Westmoreland thought so, too," Raven told him. "Turns out, our mayor had been blackmailing Monty."

"No!" Joseph exclaimed.

"Yes. For a long time Monty complied with his requests. But recently he saw things that really disgusted him. Westmoreland was inciting hatred against Tom, denying your family relief, blaming the fire on you. Monty knew something had to be done."

Joseph looked at Raven in surprise. "Quentin knows I didn't burn down the dairy?"

"He knows. He also knows that Westmoreland set the whole thing up himself. The dairy was losing him money and the fire was a solution."

"Why did you wait until now to tell me? I could have helped you with the prank."

The Great Henri assumed an expression of mock sorrow. "You said you didn't want to be involved wit' any of my pranks ever again."

"And we didn't think you'd approve," Raven added.

"Why not?" Joseph asked.

"You're so … correct," Raven said. "I've never seen you smoke or even have a drink—until now." He gestured toward the half empty glass in Joseph's hand.

Joseph grinned as he downed rest of the whisky. Raven and The Great Henri followed suit and the three men laughed. Raven refilled their glasses and they began to discuss the events of the previous night. Joseph told them about his encounter with Westmoreland. Chief Quentin had told Raven about it, but The Great Henri's eyes widened with surprise as he listened. The men shared a few more drinks, and were silent for a while.

When Raven spoke again, his expression was grave. "I'm very sorry about Tom. He was a good man. I respected what he was doing. If I get elected mayor, I'll make sure the Chinese get equal relief."

Joseph nodded solemnly. "That's good, but it's too late for the Wahs."

"Betty and her kids will be okay—between the relief and the groceries your two boys are giving them," Raven said.

"Groceries?" Joseph was confused.

"The food your boys have been buying to help Tom's family."

"I have no idea what you're talking about."

"You didn't know?" Raven asked curiously. "Nolan and Cole have been spending their wages on food for the Wahs since you and Tom were fired. Beth said it was a secret, but I thought you'd know about it."

"I didn't," Joseph said slowly, thinking about the bag of groceries he had found in the basement.

"You should be proud," The Great Henri said.

It took a moment for the information to sink in. The night had been full of revelations. "I am!" The words were heartfelt.

"Something else you'll want to know," Raven said. "Quentin has some men in custody, men from the dairy. He believes they were involved in Tom's murder. If they're found guilty we'll make a show of them. I know it won't help poor Tom, but everyone else in this town will know that racism won't be tolerated."

Joseph raised his glass. "To Tom. And to his family."

There was silence again as each man gave in to his own thoughts. A few minutes passed.

The Great Henri was the last to raise his glass: "To Raven Mullens—Philibuster's future mayor." Teasingly, he added, "… if anyone will vote for you, Raven, old friend. Al'dough I guess dey will 'ave to, since nobody else is running who 'asn't been chased tru' duh streets of Philibuster by a cheated 'usband."

Raven would be a good mayor, Joseph thought. He was an honourable man who would put the interests of Philibuster before anything else. The town would be a place worth living in.

Joseph was jerked from his thoughts when Raven addressed him. "When I'm mayor—and I do think I have a good chance—I'll be offering you a job as a firefighter, Joseph. I hope you'll accept it."

Joseph gaped. "Are you serious?"

"Perfectly. How about it, Joseph?"

I'm dreaming, thought Joseph. *I know I'm dreaming.* Grinning, he joined the two men in one last toast.

CHAPTER 50

Joseph felt different when he woke early the next morning—not odd or peculiar or in any way unpleasant, just different from the way he usually felt. He wondered if it was because of the unaccustomed whisky he'd consumed the previous night.

Leaping out of bed with a vigour he'd almost forgotten, he ran to the bathroom. He splashed his face with water and looked in the mirror. With the exception of Helen's death and his time in the trenches, he ranked the last two weeks as amongst the worst of his life. He expected his reflection to show the emaciated, worn-out image he'd grown accustomed to seeing in the mirror, and was surprised to find that his wrinkles looked less deep, the circles beneath his eyes less dark and his skin less sallow. Even his hair seemed a bit thicker—although surely he was imagining this?

In the kitchen, Joseph boiled water and poured it into a cup. He no longer even had any dried barley to add to it. Wondering what to feed the children, he opened the cupboard. He knew he would find nothing there, but he looked inside, anyway. When he saw a bag of rolled oats and a small bag of sugar, he shook his head in surprise. Yesterday there had been nothing but salt, pepper and baking powder. Could he have missed these items? But no, Nolan and Cole must have brought in the provisions, he realized. Normally, he would have felt ashamed that things had come to this. Today it didn't matter. *Things are going to change.*

As Joseph took a pot and began to make porridge for the children, he heard Nolan and Cole banging around in their room. The noise woke the girls. Before long, all four kids were in the kitchen.

Joseph turned from the stove and thanked his sons for the food. They looked at him in bewilderment, and told him they knew nothing about the oats and the sugar. *If not the boys,* thought Joseph, *someone else must have stocked the cupboard—Raven, Henri, Mrs. Nye?*

"I hate porridge," Sarah said, grimacing when she saw what her father was cooking.

"It's all we've got," he told her. *But not for much longer.*

"I want Nolan and Cole's bacon from the basement," Sarah said.

Her brothers froze.

"No," Joseph said quietly, "that's for Mrs. Wah and her boys."

His sons eyed each other accusingly, as if each blamed the other for betraying their secret.

Joseph smiled. "It's okay, boys, I discovered the bacon in the basement, and somebody else told me what it was all about."

No longer restricted by the silence his brother had imposed on him, Cole began to babble about their good deed.

"I'm so proud of you both," Joseph said, and saw Nolan beam.

Joseph felt the beginning of tears. Turning his back to the children, he pretended to stir the porridge. Damn, he really was proud of his boys! But why did he still think of them as boys? His sons were feeding a family who had even less than they did. Despite their age, they had become young men. He marvelled that they had turned out so well.

When he had regained his composure, he joined the children with his own bowl of porridge. For the first time in months, he ate with his family. He even watched indulgently when Sarah sprinkled her porridge liberally with sugar.

After breakfast, Nolan, Cole and Sarah went outside to dig in the back garden. The boys had purchased some seeds and planned to plant peas, carrots, turnip and potatoes. While the three older children worked at making rows in the ground, Clare toddled beside them. She often got in the way of her siblings, but they were learning to be patient with her.

Many years later, when Cole was a grown man—a husband and the father of a young child on whom he doted—he would ask his father whether he remembered the day they had planted the garden behind Mrs. Nye's house. Joseph would be able to say that he remembered that day very clearly.

"I never knew we were poor. I always thought we had it so good. I hope my children have happy memories like mine," Cole would say.

Joseph would be amazed to hear Cole recall his childhood. *If only I had known,* he would later think. *I mightn't have worried quite so much.*

Some time later, Mrs. Nye joined Joseph with two cups of tea. "Nice day," she said cheerfully.

All morning, clouds had been massing in the sky, threatening rain, but for some reason Joseph sensed the promise of sun behind them. "It is nice," he agreed.

"I left something in the cupboard for you. I hope you don't mind," Mrs. Nye said.

"I found the food and was about to thank you. And no, of course, I don't mind. You've been very kind to us. This place has been a wonderful home for the children."

They sat together in silence, until Joseph spoke again. "Mrs. Nye, I have to ask—do you know what happened to Winfield?"

"I do," she said quietly.

"I'm not going to apologize for my own part in it. He had it coming to him. But you've been so good to us and I feel bad for you. You must be very upset."

"Upset?" Westmoreland's mother put down her cup and looked at Joseph, her expression wistful. "Winfield is my son and I love him. I told you that once before. But as you said, he had it coming to him."

"Mrs. Nye—" Joseph said, but she cut him short.

"I feel very sad for my son. He has lost his way in life. He's done some terrible things. I only wish I could do something to make amends."

"You don't have to do anything," Joseph said awkwardly. "He's the one who should be making amends."

"I know. But I want to." To his surprise, Mrs. Nye touched his hand. "I've been thinking about Mrs. Wah. She does such beautiful work with a needle. Do you think she'd mind if I told my friends about her? I know they'd love to have her to do some sewing for them."

"I'm sure she'd be delighted," Joseph said, happily.

The woman seemed to hesitate, as if she were debating within herself whether to go on or not. "What about you?" she asked then. "It's strange to see you here on a Saturday. You're usually out hunting for work."

The time was not yet right to mention the fire department job that Raven had talked about. His friend had to be mayor before the position would be available for Joseph. "I wanted to spend some time with the children today," Joseph said quietly.

"You'd better tell that sister-in-law of yours, in that case. She'll be wondering where this lot is."

"Yes," Joseph agreed, wondering if he'd only imagined the tartness in Mrs. Nye's voice. "I'll go and talk to her. I'll be back soon. Thank you for the tea."

Joseph put down his cup and stood up. He needed to straighten out a few things with Tilda. It wouldn't be pretty, but it had to be done. He would always be grateful to Tilda for her kindness. He'd never have been able to manage all this time without her. Yet despite his gratitude, he had recognized for some time that Tilda was being manipulative and he knew that she wanted his children for herself. She had to be told what kind of woman Beth really was. And she had to learn that the children weren't going anywhere—they were staying with him, where they belonged.

Mrs. Nye said she would be happy to look after the children while Joseph was out. Unlikely though it was that she would have one of her spells, Joseph also asked Nolan to watch his siblings, just in case. "Mrs. Nye is here if you need help," he told his son.

He felt unusually relaxed as he strode along the streets. His mindset had changed since the events of the previous night, allowing him to have a different perspective on his life and his future. Instead of dwelling only on the adversities of his past, he was able, for the first time in a long time, to think of the good times.

He remembered his meeting with the hobo community, cheerful men who had seemed to be without any cares, and the hobo king, who had given him such good advice: "Swallow your pride, when you have nothing else to eat." The hobo king's hangers-on understood the wisdom of those words. Undoubtedly, they would struggle to survive, but they would do so more easily without the shackles of society's expectations.

The good humour of the hobos brought to mind other things: the poor farmer, who had joked that he would sell his ranch for a handful of magic beans; Nolan passing off Jasper as a lion; the jests of his co-workers at the sawmill; Henri's pranks. Joseph was beginning to see that humour went a long way toward softening life's blows. Fretting had only dragged him down, interfering with his ability to function. Humour brightened even the darkest times.

Joseph felt a lightness around his neck and shoulders as he walked, as if a great burden had dropped from them. At the Cree Creek traffic bridge he stopped and looked west. In the distance he saw the ruins of the dairy. The roof was gone and the cinderblock walls had caved into the centre of the structure. *Everyone in town thinks I burned down the dairy*, Joseph thought with amusement. *Won't they be amazed when they find out about my new job!*

He crossed the bridge and passed the library. He would go there some time soon, he promised himself. He'd take out some books about carpentry or plumbing or electricity. He'd bemoaned his lack of education for too long. It was time he learned a trade that would benefit him in the future.

About to turn right, toward his brother's house, he had a sudden impulse to continue down the street. He would speak to Henri and Tilda soon enough, but he had something more important to take care of today.

Rapidly he headed toward the corner grocery store, just a few blocks further on. As he passed beneath the Hoogaboom's sign, the bell rang above the door. Joseph had heard it often, announcing someone's entrance into Beth's store, but this time it seemed to proclaim a different message.

Suddenly he identified the feelings that had been with him all morning. Potential. Promise. Belief that things would get better.

Those feelings could be summed up in a single word, a word he had passed over in his old dictionary so often, thinking he knew what it meant but never having really understood until now. The word was "hope." He had found, at last, what had eluded him in Philibuster until today. The thing he needed above all else. Joseph had found hope.

ABOUT THE AUTHOR

R. L. (Rod) Prendergast was the entrepreneurial kid you saw on your neighbourhood street selling lemonade on a hot summer's day. Recognizing young Rod's preoccupation with money, his mother bribed him to read with an offer of 25 cents per book—and instilled in him a lifelong love of reading. Although he continued down the path of industry—he started and sold his first business before completing his Bachelor of Commerce—he continued to read voraciously. After a number of years working in sales, marketing and management for several companies he spent a year's sabbatical surfing and reading in New Zealand and, free of business pressures, he began to write. Those first words became the backbone of *The Impact of a Single Event*—which was long listed for the Independent Publishers Book Award for literary fiction, and which became a national bestseller in Canada. Spurred on by the success of his first novel, he took another sabbatical and wrote *Dinner with Lisa*. He is currently working on his next book.

ALSO BY R. L. PRENDERGAST

A terrible car accident occurs. Richard and Sonia, a couple with a crumbling marriage, stop to help the critically injured victims. In the process, they find a 140-year-old journal by the side of the road. Six different people have written in the journal. Though the entries span three centuries, the writers share a quest: the search for meaning in their lives. These stories take Richard and Sonia on a personal and historic journey: across Canada to the jungles of India and back to the Canadian Rocky Mountains, where a final mystery awaits.

A NATIONAL BESTSELLER

Available in soft cover or as an ebook

ISBN: 9780978454807